THE *Black* CALLA LILY

BY

ISABEL PIETRI

Isabel Pietri, Saylorsburg, PA

Cover Photo: Robyn MacKenzie

Acknowledgements

Book Cover Design
www.sexybooksblog.net

Editor
Gerald William Shaw

Dedication

This book is dedicated to my husband Juan and sister Jenny for their continuing support, encouragement and never ending love.

Table of Contents

Chapter 1

The black calla lily in Adrian's hand found its way back onto the side table. Adrian took the bottle from me and continued feeding his daughter who had become impatient.

"I suggest you find out how that thing got into our daughter's bedroom," Adrian said in a controlled tone. He disguised his rage well.

"You are aware that there are only a few ways it could have found its way here." He didn't answer, so I left in search of Hilda.

It was late and all had retired to their quarters. Hilda had a suite on the first floor. I knocked on her bedroom door. She opened it wearing a nightgown, ready for bed.

"Millie, is there anything wrong?" The only time Hilda was disturbed at night was when Angelique was born.

"No, Hilda, I just have a question for you that cannot wait until morning."

"Sure, Millie, do you want to come in?"

"No, I hate disturbing you, but I need to know something."

She came out into the hallway, closing the door behind her.

"What is it, Millie?"

"Hilda, has anyone come here today?"

"Yes, a florist delivery for you. The flowers are in the family room. There is a card but I did not open it."

"There are flowers in the family room?"

"Yes. I told the young man to put them there while I brought him a glass of water. He looked awful and asked for some water."

"Did you see the flowers?"

"Yes, I did. They were a big bouquet of white calla lilies. They are there now."

"Hilda, was there a black calla lily in the bouquet?"

"No, only white. Millie, what is wrong? Did I do something wrong?"

"No, Hilda," I said, reaching out to hug her. It was my attempt to set her at ease. "But I would like to continue this conversation in the morning. I'm sorry for disturbing you."

"Not at all, Millie. Are you sure everything is all right?"

"Yes. One last question, Hilda. What time did the delivery come? We all got back at the same time after dinner. The only ones here were Roger and Richard. Where were they?"

"They went out to get something to eat. I offered to cook for them, but they said no. They didn't want to bother me. The delivery came soon after they left. You, Adrian and Angelique were in your bedroom."

"Thanks, Hilda. Have a good night. We can speak tomorrow."

"Sure, Millie, you have a good night also."

Fearing a breach in security, I ran to my office to check the video feeds. Sure enough, a panel truck had requested to come in for a delivery after Roger and Richard left the property. There was one man visible in the truck. He was the driver and delivery person. He was the same person who asked Hilda for water. I was able to get the name of the florist. The film showed a second man leave the back of the panel truck. He entered the house from the front door. The hallway camera on the second floor outside our bedrooms showed the same man entering Angelique's bedroom. The film did not show him leaving her bedroom or the house. Since Adrian had restricted the use of cameras in what he considered private areas, I could not see if he used the terraces to move to other areas of the house to hide.

I immediately called Adrian on his smart phone and told him to stay in Angelique's bedroom because I wanted to run a security check. He knew there was more I wasn't saying. I called Richard and Roger and asked them to do a sweep of the first floor, gym and wine cellar. Then I called Hector and asked him to stand by the front door until I called again.

I went from my office to the bathroom of our suite. Next I went to the dressing room and turned on the lights. There wasn't much opportunity to hide in there. The bedroom lights were already on, so I cautiously went in with my favorite firearm in hand, a Glock, and searched. There was no one hiding. I then went across the hall to the remaining bedrooms to search for anyone who might be hiding. Roger called.

"Mrs. Z, all is fine on the first floor, gym and wine cellar. Where else would you like us to search?"

"Come to the second floor and do a sweep of the right wing. I'm checking the left wing."

"OK, Mrs. Z."

I continued checking the bedrooms and bathrooms. Finally, I entered Angelique's room where Adrian was still holding on to his daughter.

"Adrian," I called, "Hilda wants a word with you about her suite. Can you go there now?"

"Sure thing, baby," Adrian answered as he stood up with Angelique in his arms."

"Angel," I called, "Please call to have the elevator serviced."

"I'll do it first thing in the morning." Adrian had learned to follow my lead on all things dealing with security. 'Angel' was one of our code words that meant just the opposite for everything that followed.

He understood that there was nothing wrong with the elevator and he should ride it to the first floor. He left the bedroom with Angelique in his arms. I heard him ring for the elevator. Once I knew they were on their way safely down to the first floor, I continued my search.

A commotion from the right wing caught my attention. A shot went off and I heard a door slam. I ran towards the stairs where I spotted the second man in the film running towards me. He was unarmed. I quickly slipped the Glock to the waistband at the small of my back. Employing CQD — close quarter defense — technique, I ran towards him, jumping on him and wrapping my legs around his legs, causing him to fall backwards. I then applied pressure on his diaphragm and windpipe. Roger was close behind and assisted me.

"Where is Richard," I asked, observing Roger's red cheeks and obvious limp.

"He needs medical attention. This creep shot him. I was able to wrestle the gun away from him, but he managed to incapacitate me," Roger winced, shifting his weight, "and run."

Roger was too proud to say it, but I knew he had taken a hit in the groin.

"Call for an ambulance and for the police," I ordered, trying not to laugh. Roger tied our intruder's hands and took him down the stairs to wait for the police. I ran to find Richard. He was unconscious on the floor of one of the guest rooms. Not only was he shot, but he also suffered a blow to the head. I took his vitals. His pulse was strong. The gunshot wound was not life-threatening. The blow to the head was of more concern.

There was another commotion on the first floor. It sounded like a scuffle; then there were shots, two shots to be exact. Fearing the worst, I ran down the stairs, this time with the Glock in my hand.

Our intruder had pulled a Houdini act. Releasing himself from the hand ties, he grabbed a concealed firearm from his ankle and shot Roger in the side. Hector reacted immediately and shot Houdini in the chest.

Sirens could be heard as the police and ambulance approached Luna Llena. Hilda opened the gates to let them in. Roger and Richard were immediately taken to the hospital while Houdini waited for the coroner's wagon.

"Milagros, baby, speak to me," came my husband's frantic plea as he emerged from the elevator.

"Adrian, I'm fine," I said as I ran towards him and Angelique. My man had learned our security drills well. He and Angelique had been safely tucked away in the elevator.

We hugged and kissed. Adrian handed Angelique to me and felt my belly. He let out a sigh of relief when he felt the baby kick.

"What happened?"

Adrian listened in disbelief as I gave him a detailed account of what just occurred. Of course the big question was what did Houdini want in our house? What did he hope to accomplish.

"We will have more information tomorrow. The police will identify the intruder and maybe we will have some answers." I paused to stroke his back, then continued, "The driver of the delivery truck, obviously an accomplice, is still at large."

"Milagros, I would like to go to the hospital to check on Roger and Richard." Although Adrian instinctively knew that Roger and Richard had left us vulnerable, he was concerned for their well-being.

"The police are done with Hector. We can all go." Remembering the flowers, I continued, "Give me a moment, Adrian, I want to go see the flower delivery. Hilda said there was a card attached." Sure enough there was a card. Scribbled on the inside was a message that said, "From New York with love."

Hmm, that sounds personal. I didn't need the police to tell me who invaded our home. I had a pretty good idea.

Chapter 2

Richard and Roger were doing fine. The doctor said they would have to stay in the hospital a couple of days.

Angelique was asleep in her crib in our bedroom. We were down two bodyguards for the foreseeable future. Adrian alerted Alfonso and the guys of the need to be more vigilant. Jon Burke was also alerted. Although he did not live on the estate, he offered to come and stay to help out. We accepted his offer and he came immediately.

"Milagros, what did Roger mean when he said you were awesome the way you took that guy down?"

We were coming out of the shower and drying each other.

"I don't know what he meant. I tripped the guy, that's all," I lied.

"There is nothing awesome about tripping someone."

"Ask him next time you see him."

"I'm asking you and I expect a truthful answer."

"Adrian, the guy was unarmed. I put my firearm in my waistband in my back. As he ran towards me, I employed CQD tactics. You know what they are. You and I have practiced them at the firing range."

"Milagros, I won't ask again. I know CQD is very physical. Just how physical did you need to get?"

"As he ran towards me, I ran towards him, jumped in the air wrapping my legs around his, I tripped him backwards. Roger came and assisted."

"Geez, Milagros, you placed yourself and our unborn child in jeopardy. What am I to do with you?"

We were now in the dressing room, walking hand in hand towards our bedroom. I stopped and rounded to face him. I stood close to him, our naked bodies touching front to front.

"I don't know, Adrian. What would you like to do? Do you need satisfaction for my transgression?" He smiled and kissed me on the lips chastely.

"Yes, I think I do," he responded in a low throaty voice. His hot breath was on my face and I inhaled to take him all in.

"Where do you want me? Tell me what to do." I was already panting with anticipation, not knowing what my creative husband had in mind.

"I like this room with the mirrors. I have some new toys. Would you like to try them out?"

"Yes, Adrian, I would like that." My voice, too, was low and breathy.

Adrian put his arms around me, touching my rear.

"Go stand facing the big mirror and place your hands against it high above your head." He stroked my rear cheeks and then continued, "First, I'll get my satisfaction."

The next morning I spoke with a Detective Doran, who was in charge of the investigation. He identified our intruder as Omar Sanz.

That explains the black calla lily and the love from New York. My suspicions were now confirmed.

Detective Doran further informed me that the florist deliveryman had been found by the side of the road unconscious. He told the detective that he stopped to lend a hand to Sanz, whose car was stranded. That is when another man came from behind, knocked him out and took the delivery truck. Sanz had ordered the flowers, paying in cash.

Detective Doran also informed me that Omar was not a resident of California, but of New York and he was originally from Colombia. That didn't surprise me. I knew his brother, Oscar Sanz, from my days with the TARU unit in the NYPD. He had killed my partner and former lover, Danny. I in turn shot and killed Oscar. Danny's murder had never been solved, at least not to my satisfaction. The detectives involved in the investigation had determined that it was a gang-related crime. I always felt there had been more to it.

Oscar and Omar both got what their hand called for. But I could not help feeling a little sad. A mother somewhere had now lost two sons.

My New York troubles found their way to Luna Llena. I needed to alert Adrian.

In the coming weeks, Roger and Richard recuperated nicely, returning back to work. Hector was cleared by the police. They called it a justified shooting of self-defense. Security of the house was intensified by adding two more bodyguards. They would help to relieve Roger and Richard. I chastised them for leaving the premises at the same time. They knew better. Their action compromised the security of the house, leaving us vulnerable. I was furious with Roger for not patting down Omar Sanz. He would have discovered the concealed firearm and the shooting could have been avoided. If it were up to me, I would have fired him, but Adrian and Roger went back many years and I knew Adrian would never approve his firing. I did, however, express my displeasure.

The weather was getting warmer. Adrian and I resumed having our meals out on the patio where we could enjoy the warm gentle breeze. As usual we sat next to each other facing the great lawn and the rose garden to our left.

"Mr. Z, do you ever regret becoming involved with me?"

"Absolutely not, Millie, why do you ask?"

"Our short history together has been laden with abductions, black mailings and violence. And now there still is a threat out there somewhere waiting to appear."

Adrian stopped eating his breakfast. He leaned back in his chair, placing one arm around my shoulders.

"Millie, none of this is your fault. A lot of what has happened had to do with me and not you. I told you this was a dangerous job." He smiled, leaning in for a kiss.

"Not more dangerous than you," I teased, recalling our previous night.

A couple of months passed quickly without any more disturbances from New York. Things returned to normal. I hired a surveillance company of a former colleague to keep an eye on the Sanz family back in New York. They were to report every move Sanz made.

"Milagros, can you please discourage your mother from visiting," Adrian said coming out of the bathroom one morning. "I would never ask you something like this, but I am not up to arguing with her about how our child should be delivered. Quite frankly, I'm not up to much of anything. I just want some down time with you, baby."

Adrian had been stressed since our return home from Argentina. The Pablo Santos ordeal and now the Sanz intrusion were all he could take. Some down time in Tahiti was out of the question now with the birth of our second child due.

My mother had become her opinionated self with Adrian, chiding him about where the baby should be delivered. She had been shocked to learn of Angelique's birth at home and was determined to convince Adrian that I should go to the hospital where I would be surrounded by professionals, not him.

"Not to worry, I have it all under control," I replied.

"How is that possible? Your saintly mother is relentless."

"I told her I was due in August."

"You lied to your mother?" Adrian blurted in disbelief.

"I lie to you on a regular basis, my mother is easy."

Did I just say that out loud?

"So," Adrian said as he stopped walking towards me, "you admit you lie to me?"

"Yes, I admit it."

"Milagros, I demand satisfaction," he said with eyebrows knitted and lips pursed.

"Can you wait for satisfaction?"

It was early Saturday morning. I had been up for hours pacing the floor in the sitting room of our suite. Labor pains had started hours ago, but I had not wanted to wake Adrian. I remembered Angelique's birth and did not want a repeat performance, Adrian being the wonderful but bossy, control freak that he was. I wanted to put off that part as long as possible, but this baby was coming earlier than expected.

"No. I want it now."

"OK, Adrian, but can you call Dr. Johansson first?"

"Sure. But why should I call her first?"

I was silent for a few minutes, giving him time to process.

"Oh, shit, Milagros, why couldn't you just say what was happening?"

"Baby, please call the doctor, I can't wait any longer."

"Milagros, you are very inconsiderate," I did not let him finish.

"Fuck. Adrian, call the fucking doctor. I calculate this baby is coming very, very soon."

Adam, the first boy, made his debut ten minutes later. Adrian, as with Angelique, delivered his son. By the time Dr. Johansson reached Luna Llena, Adrian had cut the umbilical cord, cleaned his child and put his wife back into bed.

"Really, Joanne, what is it I pay you for? I deliver my children, tend to my wife, and so please remind me, what is it you do?"

"Adrian, I put my fucking reputation on the line because of your eccentricities."

"Oh, yes, I remember. Thank you for showing up." He handed her a glass of brandy and they toasted the newborn.

One early morning Adam's crying triggered Angelique to join in. Adrian took Angelique to the kitchen to be fed, announcing that he would keep her with him in the office. I cuddled Adam to breast-feed. The new-found quiet was welcomed and I hoped it would linger beyond the moment. Adam finally fell asleep. I managed a short nap before deciding to shower and dress while the baby still slept.

My smart phone rang and I could see that it was Adrian. It was too early for his summoning me to lunch.

"Hi, Adrian."

"Hi, baby, how is it going for you?"

"Not bad. How about you?"

"Good. Can you come to the office?"

"Sure, give me a few minutes to transport Adam."

"Hurry, please."

Hurry please? I don't like the sound of that.

I dressed quickly, putting on the pale-pink sundress that Adrian was fond of. With not much time for fussing with the hair, I left it loose. A pair of white-canvas flat shoes completed the look.

I dashed down the stairs with Adam in his carrier. As usual, I knocked on the door to Adrian's office and walked in without waiting for a response.

"Adrian, what is the hurry?"

"You have a piece of mail here from a bank in New York." Adrian scanned every piece of mail into his computer that in turn would let him know who the sender was.

"Did you open it?"

"No, I don't open your mail, you know that," Adrian replied indignantly.

"It's OK if you did, you know. We have no secrets."

"Thank you, but I rather you told me about your correspondences. Come, baby, sit on my lap."

I placed Adam in the crib and checked on Angelique. Adrian had sat her in her walker. She had free reign to roam a baby-proof area in the office. So I went and sat on Adrian's lap to open the letter.

It was a letter from the president of a bank in New York. They had been advised that Danny was deceased and were required to reach out to the designated beneficiary of his safe deposit box. Mr. George Allen gave a telephone number where he could be reached.

"Adrian, can I ignore this?"

"You could, but would it be wise?"

"I don't care what is in that safe deposit box."

"I don't care either, but there are some folks out there that care very much. They have left us alone, but I suspect that they are now trying to smoke us out. Someone has been paying the fee for the safe deposit box for the past three years. That same someone has decided to inform the bank of Danny's passing."

"They must have informed the bank of my new name and address."

"That's right."

We sat holding each other in silence for a while, thinking of what to do. Then, as if reading each others thoughts, we blurted out at the same time, "We need to go to New York."

Adrian and I agreed to go to New York, but not before the baby could travel. We would wait until late November. The bad guys would just have to wait.

"Good afternoon, I would like to speak with Mr. George Allen," Adrian said to someone on the other end. "Tell him it is Adrian Zaragosa, attorney for Milagros Zaragosa."

Adrian informed Mr. Allen that I would not be able to travel for another three to four months due to health reasons. The safe deposit box had been paid for until the end of the year, Mr. Allen informed Adrian, so I had time. However, it would be important for me to have the key. If not, matters would be a little more complicated.

"I guess having the key would not have helped whoever it is that is interested in the contents of the box. I'm the only one who can access the box."

"That is right. Milagros, do you think they are watching us?"

"I don't think so. Not here anyway. They will be watching us once we're in New York. We should keep our normal routines. We are safe as long as the contents of the box remain where they are. Adrian, we need to figure out who these people are and what is in that box."

"Where do you start? NYPD detectives never uncovered any useful information."

"That is true. But they never used the talents of TARU either."

"Surely, you can't get that department to help now, could you?"

"No, but I am one of the many talents of that unit."

"But where would you start?"

"Do you really want to know, husband. You do have plausible denial-ability."

"Plausible denial-ability would not work in our case, so tell me."

"Mr. Allen would be the first place to start."

"Mr. Allen, the bank president? Surely you're not thinking of hacking into his computer, are you?" Adrian asked, knitting his eyebrows and pursing his lips.

"No, of course not, Adrian," I lied. "I'll phone him to get information."
What a novel idea.

"I'll check to see if someone has Danny's computer. It could be that they are looking for clues of their own. It's a shot in the dark, but worth following up."

"Sounds like you have a lot of work to do, Mrs. Z. Just don't do anything until we discuss it, understood?"

"Yes, sir, understood."
Gee, what a control freak.

We walked out onto the patio for lunch. Adam was asleep in his stroller and Angelique was in her playpen under the shade of a tree, content playing with a new teddy bear that Daisy and Paula gave her for her first birthday.

"Juan Carlos and Isabel are coming for Adam's baptism," Adrian informed me.

"That's good news. It's strange that I have not heard from Isabel. She has been uncharacteristically quiet. I follow her blog and it hasn't been updated recently."

"If there was anything wrong, Juan Carlos would have told me."

"I'm sure everything is fine. I just find it strange that she hasn't reached out since Adam was born. That is a month already."

"Have you called her?"

"I have called, sent text messages and e-mails, but no reply."

"That is strange. I'll call Juan Carlos and ask him. But we will see them in two weeks. Is your mother coming? Has she gotten over your little lie?"

"Yeah, she's good. Will you send the Gulfstream for them?"

"Juan Carlos and Isabel will be in New York the day after tomorrow, so they can all fly here together in two weeks."

"Good, I'll tell Mom. See, I don't get Isabel," I complained. "You think she would have said something about New York."

"Are you through with lunch?" Adrian asked, ignoring my complaint.
"Yes."

"Good, let's grab a child each and walk to the winery. Harvest will be starting very soon and I need to speak with Jon."

Since we would have to go through the woods, taking the stroller was out of the question. Adrian carried Angelique while holding my hand. I used the carrier for transporting Adam. He was such a good, happy baby.

Jon was happy to see the whole family and made a fuss over the children. He informed Adrian that he would be attending the baptism. Apparently, Adrian had invited everyone he knew, just as he did for Angelique. The party would take place out on the patio. It made no difference to him that I didn't like big functions at the house. This was a security nightmare.

Adrian and Jon spoke of plans for this year's grapes. I had witnessed three years of wine making and its distribution. Adrian and Jon had it down to a science. By now distributors had already placed orders. But this year something was amiss. The two men looked preoccupied, not with the grapes, but sales.

We said good-bye to Jon and continued walking towards the vineyard.

"Adrian, what is wrong? You and Jon didn't have the usual animated conversation about sales. Not to mention that you both look like you swallowed lemons."

"It's nothing, Millie. Business is a little off this year, but I'm on it."

"It's not the wines. You received rave reviews."

"Baby, don't worry about this. You have your own work cut out for you. Besides, it happens from time to time."

"How off are sales?" I asked.

"Our wines are doing fine. It's the blends that are off."

"You received great reviews there, too."

"Millie, please don't worry about this."

"Adrian, please talk to me. Maybe a fresh pair of eyes can see something you and Jon are missing."

"True, but let's do that later. I don't want the guys in the shed to see us worried."

Alfonso and the guys in the shed, just like Jon, were thrilled to see the whole family. And like Jon, they fussed over Angelique and Adam.

Each man had an opportunity to bounce Angelique, who enjoyed the attention, in the air. They were gentler with the newborn.

They all informed Adrian that they couldn't wait for Adam's baptism party. They promised me to behave and not corrupt my husband like they did for our wedding and Angelique's baptism.

Why do men lie? Of course they will corrupt Adrian and get him drunk. Adrian is very entertaining when drunk.

Their wives were wonderful ladies who always brought food or sweets along to share. And, of course, their children were always entertained. Adrian made sure they had games, toys and lots of candy.

Adrian and some of the guys had been playing music together for some time. They vowed to put on a show in honor of Adam.

Oh, goody! As if Adam was going to enjoy it. No doubt he will sleep through the festivities.

Chapter 3

Sunday afternoon, Daisy and Paula came over for an early dinner. Paula had completed her duties with the church in order to baptize Adam. Adrian's first cousin on his father's side would be the godfather. Although I was not happy about all these people in the house or on the property, I was pleased to see Adrian ecstatic. Since our marriage and the birth of the children, he was transformed into a social butterfly. He especially enjoyed having parties for his children. Hilda and Hector, too, enjoyed the festivities along with the preparations.

"Hey, Millie," Daisy called to me while I was serving wine for her and Paula, "Have you spoken to Isabel?"

"No, not since Adam was born."

"That's the last time I spoke to her, too. I did speak to Juan Carlos and the twins. They assure me she is fine, only very busy with her latest book."

"That explains it, then. I feel much better."

"Only one thing," Daisy said conspiratorially.

"What's that, Daisy?" I asked.

"Her blog hasn't been updated with the information of a new book. Don't you find that odd?"

"Why would Juan Carlos, Michael and Gabriel lie?"

"Maybe they are hiding something. Isabel can't lie to us. She would spill the beans immediately."

"Will the two of you stop," Paula blurted out, "They will all be here next week and we will find out whatever is going on with her."

"Don't waste your breath, Paula," Adrian interjected, "These two like conspiracies. They won't stop until they have exhausted themselves."
They laughed. Daisy and I just looked at them in disgust. But that was the end of that subject.

Adrian put on salsa music and took me out to dance. Daisy and Paula joined in. Soon we were exchanging partners. Shortly thereafter, Angelique joined in with each of us taking turns holding her in our arms while dancing. She screeched with delight.

Our New York and wine troubles were momentarily forgotten. There was magic in the air or was it the love of family and friends. I loved my husband, our children, our friends and the life we were building together.

For the third time in three years, our home was slowly turning into a three-ring circus. The Wednesday before the baptism people started trickling in. Adrian's family from L.A. and Spain were housed at a nearby five-star hotel. Adrian had limousines available for their use. At Luna Llena the bedrooms in the right wing were all taken except for one. Adrian wanted it empty in case his mother showed. But he knew she wouldn't come. The empty bedrooms in the left wing, where our bedroom was, remained empty. Adrian did not want anyone sleeping in bedrooms belonging to his children, even though at the present time they were sleeping with us. On this point, he was very strict.

Daisy and Paula were the first to arrive. Daisy had taken some vacation time due her and would stay the week after the baptism. Paula had not worked for some time due to her illness. Next to arrive were Juan Carlos' sons, Michael and Gabriel. They came with their girlfriends. They occupied two bedrooms. Mom and Earl were due on Thursday afternoon along with Juan Carlos and Isabel. I couldn't wait for their arrival. I missed Mom and Earl and my curiosity about Isabel was killing me.

After the incident with Tom, Adrian's former assistant, and Angelique's abduction, some minor changes were made to the house. Adrian had wanted the surveillance cameras, which were housed in my office on the second floor, switched to Tom's old office on the first floor. He had the office redecorated to look like my office upstairs. It was his idea that I use that office instead of the one upstairs. It was a good idea because I was helping him more and more with his own work. He also wanted to keep our living quarters upstairs completely private. On this point, he was again very strict.

The sitting area in my new office was fully equipped with playpen and crib. Hector, Roger and Richard took turns with the surveillance cameras. Having the cameras downstairs made more sense and pleased Adrian. The two new bodyguards, Tony and Frank, filled in protecting Hilda and the children, as well as Adrian and me.

I hired additional security for the week of the baptism. Hector, Roger and Richard would be part of the festivities, but we would all be armed. The new hires would take turns with the surveillance cameras. It was a security nightmare to be sure. Adrian tried to appease me saying our friends in New York were only interested in the contents of the safe deposit box, and we were safe as long as they needed us to get to whatever it was that was in it. I wasn't sure it was that simple. But our friends in New York were only part of the problem.

I was concerned for Adrian and the winery. Although I was still in charge of security for the house and family, Adrian kept many things to himself for fear of worrying me.

That is why I have to constantly hack his computer.

I was also concerned with the Sanz family. They had already made an attempt on my family. It was evident they were not going to let go of losing one son, let alone two. Not knowing the when or where of the next attempt on our family was nerve-wracking. I didn't think Sanz was directly involved with the safe deposit box. Yet, there was a connection between the Sanz family, Danny and his brother, Ed. I just didn't know what it was.

Thursday afternoon, Hector drove up to the house in the Escalade with Mom, Earl, Juan Carlos and Isabel. I was happy to see Mom. We kissed and she carried on about Adam and Angelique. Juan Carlos came equipped with his guitar. Daisy and I fussed over Isabel and chastised her for not returning our calls, texts or e-mails. She apologized saying she had been extremely busy. Finally, she urged us to go to the kitchen where we could have a private moment.

"I didn't want to say anything until I saw you personally and knew my plans for sure."

"Well, girl, what is it?" Daisy asked impatiently.

"I wrote another book and will be traveling the U.S. to promote it. That means I'll be able to see you more often."

The words were barely out of her mouth when the three of us started jumping and screaming. Hearing the commotion Adrian, Juan Carlos and Paula rushed into the kitchen. Adrian came in first calling for me.

"Baby, I'm here."

"What's going on?"

"Isabel wrote a new book and will be spending time in the U.S. promoting it," I answered. "We will be able to see her more often."

Juan Carlos separated the three of us yelling, "It's only for a few months." He hugged his wife protectively. We pushed him to the side and continued hugging her.

"Congratulations, Isabel," Adrian said joining in hugging Isabel.

"Thank you, Adrian." Isabel straightened and announced, "We will be staying in San Francisco when we are not traveling." We started screaming, hugging and squeezing all over again.

"Adrian, please get them to stop. They are upsetting my wife," Juan Carlos protested.

"Give it up, Juan Carlos," Adrian said, "I hear your wife in there also. Come. Let's leave the ladies to their screaming. Help me take care of my two little ones." They left, leaving us alone.

"Isabel, that is great news. I take it Juan Carlos will be traveling with you?" Paula asked.

"Yes, he is. He insists it's only a few months, but in reality it could be up to one year."

"How could he insist that it's only a few months? Doesn't he know it could take up to one year?" I asked.

"He knows, but refuses to accept it."

"How are you going to work around that?" Daisy asked incredulously.

"I figure we can return to Mendoza periodically. That should calm him a little."

"You hope it will," Daisy commented, doubting Isabel's plan would work.

"You both will figure it out," I offered. "I'm glad you're staying in San Francisco so we can see you both more often. When does your tour start?"

"Those details haven't been worked out yet. My publicist is working on a calendar for me."

Adrian called us out to the patio where he had set up glasses and champagne to toast Isabel and her book tour.

That evening we all went to the hotel where we hosted a dinner for our family and friends. It was an intimate affair of about one hundred people. Not everyone in Adrian's family was able to come, otherwise there would have been over two hundred. Adrian had three great aunts in attendance. One great uncle and Adrian's father were deceased. The great aunts and uncles each had five children. These would be Adrian's aunts and uncles, his father's siblings. The aunts and uncles all had no less than three children each. Adrian's father was the only one with one child.

"I thought you more the recluse," I told Adrian when we finally sat to eat our dinner.

"You might say I was. I have always kept in touch with my Father's family. They have visited but under more sedate circumstances." He gazed my way. Leaning back on his chair, he put an arm around my shoulders and then continued, "I have three reasons to celebrate. You have changed my life for the better." We leaned into each other for the sweetest of kisses.

The eleven o'clock Sunday mass was filled to capacity, mostly with our family and friends. The day could not have been more perfect, warm and not a cloud in the sky. A tent had been erected on the lawn beyond the rose garden. A dance floor had been strategically placed in the middle with tables and chairs flanking it on two sides. Dinner would be served under the tent.

Mom and Hilda kept an eye on Angelique and Adam when Adrian and I were called away to tend to our guests. Of course, as proud parents, we paraded the children for all to see. Adam, at six weeks, displayed good humor and a liking for being fussed over.

Although Adrian navigated his home and the property with ease, having this many guests became disorientating for him. I made sure to stay close to him. Hector and Roger also kept a close eye on him. If Adrian and I were separated, they would appear next to him when least expected to engage him in conversation. They were his anchors delicately orientating him. It warmed my heart to observe Juan Carlos and Alfonso also keeping an eye on Adrian, staying close by without seeming obvious.

I had disappeared a few times to check on the security staff. Roger and Richard had accompanied me a few times. A few times I noticed they did the rounds without anyone asking.

The sun was low in the horizon by the time everyone was done with dinner. The waiters and waitresses were making their rounds, distributing dessert and coffee. Adrian, Juan Carlos and Alfonso made their way to the patio where Mom and Hilda helped me move the little ones. Bistro tables with chairs had been placed all along the patio. There was enough seating to accommodate all the guests.

Adrian, Juan Carlos, Alfonso and a few of the guys from the shed appeared moments later on the patio with their instruments. Adrian brought the guitar I gave him for Christmas. He swore it was the finest he owned. Microphones were set up for each of them. They started playing and singing songs in Spanish. They sang "Bamboleo," "Volare," various tango songs and romantic ballads. The lead vocals changed from Adrian to Juan Carlos to Alfonso. Adrian played the lead guitar.

They sounded terrific and were very entertaining until they played "Agua Dulce, Agua Sala." The three men were supposed to sing in unison the beginning, "ay, yai, yai, yai," six times, but Juan Carlos lost his composure, going into a fit of laughter. His face turned beet red. It didn't help his cause that he was slightly inebriated. The men stopped playing. He apologized, clearing his throat, and they started the song again only to have Juan Carlos go into another fit of laughter. Adrian was now getting annoyed, knitted eyebrows and pursed lips. He went on to play the lead guitar solo, trying to buy Juan Carlos time. Juan Carlos inched his way to Adrian, laughing and whispering something into his ear. Now both men were laughing uncontrollably. Adrian's face was flushed. It didn't help his cause either that he was slightly inebriated, also.

Daisy, Paula and I looked at Isabel. She was staring at Juan Carlos with an incredulous look on her face. One might even say it was the look of someone who might kill. They continued playing but no one was singing. Adrian whispered to Alfonso, who then whispered to the next guy until the joke reached them all. Finally Adrian pulled himself together and was able to continue singing until they reached the "ay, yai, yai, yai" part, then they all went into a fit of laughter again. Our guests laughed when they laughed, not knowing exactly what the joke was. Juan Carlos could no longer face our guests. Adrian and the guys rushed to finish the song. Isabel was not amused.

Daisy, being the wise woman that she was, leaned over to Isabel and said, "Remember, don't throw the baby out with the bath water." It was Daisy's way of telling Isabel to forgive Juan Carlos for whatever transgression he was now guilty of. Juan Carlos was always in trouble with Isabel.

It was getting late and our guests had started to leave. I was very tired and had no intention of witnessing a fight between Isabel and Juan Carlos. I said good night to all and went to Adrian, who was putting away his guitar.

"Adrian," I said as I approached him, "I'm going upstairs to put Angelique and Adam to sleep."

"Let me say my good nights and I'll be up shortly. Do you want to wait for me?"

"No, I feel a fight brewing and I don't want to be around."

"I think I know what you mean. I'll be up soon, baby. Give me a kiss." I did and I was off with our children.

Adrian came into the dressing room as I was undressing.

"Mrs. Z, can you help me to undress?"

"It would be my pleasure, Mr. Z." It had been a while since we had been intimate. Dr. Johansson had warned Adrian about having sex too soon after giving birth.

Why she felt the need to do that, I have no idea.

But Adrian took her warning to the extreme and I had been completely cut off.

"Would you like to take a quick shower?"

"With you?"

"No, I meant with the guy next door. Of course with me, silly," Adrian said laughing.

I think my man is a little inebriated.

"Oh, OK."

He soaped me up first, and then I soaped him up. As we rinsed, I couldn't help admiring the fine specimen of a man that was my husband. I fixed my eyes on his broad shoulders and muscled arms. Then I admired his well-defined chest that was lightly covered with silky black hair. The hair trailed down to below his belly button continuing down to the "v" where all pleasure began.

He dried me first. I took my time drying his back and chest with the towel. Next, I moved to his rear squeezing his cheeks, which caused him to laugh. I looked at Adrian's face. He was gazing in my direction, lips parted and smiling. I moved my hands to his front to dry his chest. I gently kissed and licked his nipples one at a time. Taking my time. This met with a groan of approval. I moved to dry in between his legs. He inhaled as I took his now erect penis in my hands. His eyes closed. I continued drying him but slowly went down on my knees. When he was dry, I dropped the towel to the floor taking him in my mouth.

"Baby, what are you doing?"

"I, my dear husband, am going to have my way with you and I am not asking for your permission. It's been too long. I'm not ready for you, but I need our connection. So shut up or I'll have to gag you." He did as he was told. I kissed and licked, and then I put my lips completely around his massive shaft. I went down half way and came up. I kissed and licked some more. I went down on him again a little further. He inhaled sharply. My tongue caressed every inch of him. Each time I went down further until I possessed all of him. His eyes were completely shut. His hand gently stroked my hair and he let out an occasional approving groan. I continued my assault. My mouth worked him over while my hand fondled his testicles.

"Fuck, Millie, I'm going to come," he warned.

I intensified my assault. His hands tried to pull me away but I pushed them away. I continued until he came inside my mouth. I swallowed quickly, milking him dry. He groaned as I licked and kissed him until he couldn't take any more. He pulled me off him, falling to his knees, locking his lips on mine.

"Baby, I love you," he said, kissing me again. My man was very appreciative.

We were embracing each other in bed when I thought to ask him a question.

"Adrian, tell me, what was so funny tonight? What sent Juan Carlos into a fit of laughter?"

Adrian covered his eyes, laughing uncontrollably remembering the evening. He would cover his eyes whenever he wanted to erase an image from his mind. He was laughing so hard he could not speak. I was not letting him off the hook. If it took all night, I would wait. Finally he calmed down. He started several times to tell me but couldn't.

"Adrian, I have all night. Neither one of us is going to get any sleep until you tell me."

"OK, OK," he inhaled deeply trying to gain composure. "You know the song, 'Agua Dulce, Agua Sala,' right?"

"Yeah, I know it."

"You know how it begins, right?"

"Yeah, I know, ay, yai, yai, yai." Adrian went into another fit of laughter.

When he calmed down, he continued, "Juan Carlos whispered in my ear that Isabel yells that when she has an orgasm." I was horrified. He was laughing again uncontrollably.

I sat up in bed.

"Adrian, you know I won't be able to face her in the morning."

He curled his body around mine and laughed harder.

"I'm going to have a heart attack. I can't stop laughing," he cried.

"What the hell do you find so funny about that. Shame on him for sharing something so intimate with you. And how dare you share it with Alfonso, who then shared it with everyone else for the world to witness," I admonished.

Sensing I was not amused, Adrian calmed down a little. He sat up in bed wrapping his arms around me.

"Think about the absurdity of it all. Here we are trying to perform. Everything is going well. Then a song sends a band member into a fit of laughter because it reminds him of his woman in the most intimate manner. That shit is funny." He started laughing again. Now I was laughing because he put it in a general term, not Juan Carlos and Isabel.

"And, my dear wife," he said taking a big breath, "I did not repeat it to Alfonso. I told Alfonso to speed the song up because Juan Carlos had to take a shit." Now we were both laughing hysterically.

"Adrian," I continued once I composed myself, "how did Juan Carlos react to what you told the other guys?"

"Oh, he doesn't know," and we were both hysterical again.

Adrian's family was due to leave Monday afternoon. We would join them for brunch. Adrian had arranged to have a photographer present to take a Zaragosa family photo.

Adrian dressed in a navy blue suit, white linen shirt and striped blue and white tie. Angelique had on a baby blue dress, white lace tights and white patent leather shoes. Adam looked adorable in a cotton baby blue jumper with white shirt, white socks and white booties. I was the last to get dressed.

"Millie, are you dressed yet?"

"No. I forgot about this photograph business."

"You do have something beige, don't you?"

"Yeah, I think I do."

"Do you need help?"

"As much as I would like your help, we will never leave. Take the kids downstairs. I'll join you shortly."

I had curled my hair and it met with my approval. I wore my garter holster to house my Beretta 3032 Tomcat. A beige silk sleeveless dress with a square neckline and a slit over the left leg to accommodate my need to reach the Beretta would have to do. Beige leather pumps completed the look. All I needed was Adrian's approval.

Adrian was in the family room preparing the stroller. Our house guests were all out on the patio finishing breakfast.

"Adrian," I said, announcing myself, "I'm done. Tell me what you think."

He walked over to me and stretched his arms so that his hands could touch my hair. He felt my earlobes.

"Ah, the black pearl earrings." Adrian could tell the difference between the white pair and the black pair by their size.

His hands moved down to my shoulders.

"Um, silk. Beige I hope."

"Yes, it is beige," I replied in a throaty voice.

"Am I turning you on?"

"You know you are."

"Hmm, too bad you're going to have to wait," he said as he brushed his fingers down to my breast. "The dress is sleeveless. It may not meet with the approval of the great aunts, aunts and uncles."

"They will get over it."

His hands traveled down to my hips, to my thighs, finding the slit. He felt for the firearm and smiled.

"You are always on the job, Mrs. Z." He kissed me then continued, "I approve but I don't think the elders in my family will approve of the sleeveless and the slit. But they will get over it."

The hotel did a wonderful job with brunch. Adrian's family enjoyed the food. Soon it was time for the photograph. His great aunts came to kiss and hug Angelique and Adam. They eyed me from head to toe, but kissed me just the same. They promptly went to Adrian's oldest aunt and said something to her. She in turn went to retrieve a lace shawl and headed my way.

"Milagros, you look lovely and the children are just beautiful. I want to thank you and Adrian for a wonderful time. I believe I speak for everyone when I say that we have enjoyed every minute of our visit."

"I'm happy to hear that."

"Would you be so kind to wear this lace shawl? My mother made it for me when I was very young, and it will look beautiful over your dress."

"Yes, of course I will wear it for the photograph."

How can I refuse such a graceful request?

Everyone was dressed in either navy blue or beige. The children were all dressed in baby blue. I learned navy blue was reserved for the Zaragosas, while beige was for the in-laws.

I wonder whose idea that was. Could it possibly be my control freak husband?

The time came for the photographer to pose everyone. Ed, the photographer, knew Adrian. He had taken our wedding photos and photos of us with the children. First, he sat the great aunts. They were flanked by the two oldest aunts and the two oldest uncles. The next row, standing in the center, were the rest of the aunts and uncles, eighteen to be precise. Then on either side was the first wave of cousins. Adrian and I stood next to one of his uncles. In the third row were the rest of the cousins. The in-laws stood with their Zaragosa spouse. All the men with a spouse laid their hands on the hip of their wives. The children sat on the floor at the feet of the great aunts. Angelique and Adam were the youngest, so they sat on the laps of the great aunts.

Ed announced he would be taking two photographs and for everyone to please not move. He snapped the first photograph. Right before he snapped the second, he looked our way. Adrian slipped the shawl off my shoulders, then placed his arms around my waist and rested his head on top of mine. Ed snapped the photo. My man had orchestrated the family photo that we would display in our home.

We collected our children and bid everyone good-bye. Two of Adrian's uncles stopped to talk with us. They were very fond of Adrian and Adrian was very fond of them. As it turned out, they were fond of Juan Carlos also. The uncles assured Adrian that they were available to help him and Juan Carlos should they need it. I found it odd that they would make such a gesture. Did they know something I didn't know?

"Milagros, baby, it's time to go. We have a family meeting to attend back at Luna Llena."

Adrian was vague in discussing the family meeting on our way back to Luna Llena. All he said was some business deals needed our attention and it included Juan Carlos.

I bet it has something to do with sales and the uncles.

"You're going to discuss business in front of Mom, Earl, Daisy and Paula?"

"I bought Judy and Earl a much needed session at the couple's spa. They are there now." Adrian smiled at the thought. "I need Daisy and Paula."

I didn't get it but Adrian was a master planner.

There was a crew at Luna Llena from the tent rental place packing up tables, chairs, the dance floor and tent. The caterer was busy packing up dishes, serving trays, glassware and utensils. The caterer had left dinner that could be heated up later for everyone.

Adrian convened his meeting out on the patio at two in the afternoon. Isabel looked exhausted. Juan Carlos kept her up late into the early morning hours, apologizing and making love under the stars in the rose garden. She vowed to make a rose garden the moment she returned to Mendoza. Daisy and Paula were well rested and relaxed. They fussed over Angelique and Adam non-stop. This was it, the people Adrian and I considered family. Of course, Mom and Earl were family, but this was business that Adrian did not want them involved in.

"I asked everyone here because we have a family matter to discuss." Not being one to mince words, he went straight to it, "The fact is Juan Carlos is facing an invasion in Mendoza that threatens to overtake the independent grape growers as well as independent vintners. In fact, an independent grower has lost his life. The police have not been able to rule it an accident or murder."

Adrian paused. Everyone was stunned both at the news and his delivery. Daisy was the first to speak by asking who the invaders were.

"The Fairchild Group has joined forces with Casa Benedetti. They have been purchasing land in Mendoza, but they have not been able to acquire choice land located at the foothills of the Andes. That is where Juan Carlos and the other growers are located."

"These people," Juan Carlos added, "through their representatives have become aggressive. At one meeting they issued a not so veiled threat by informing us that the market for our wines could dry up. This has some of the smaller growers preoccupied. They could not survive a bad season."

"Luna Llena," Adrian continued, "imports exclusively the Malbec from Bodegas Maria Elena, which is to say Juan Carlos. It is distributed as a Malbec under a subsidiary company of Luna Llena. I also use some of it for one of our most popular blended reds." Again he paused, waiting for comments or questions. Daisy took the bait.

"Adrian, are you and Juan Carlos in trouble."

"Not yet. But sales at Luna Llena are inexplicably down for the Malbec and the blended reds even after receiving rave reviews from the industry. This might be a coincidence but I doubt it."

"So Juan Carlos' business will suffer if you don't move your product," Paula contributed.

"That's correct, Paula."

"So, what can you and Juan Carlos do to fight back?" Isabel asked. Isabel and Juan Carlos were independently wealthy of each other. Juan Carlos was wealthy without the wine business, but it had been in his family for generations and many people depended on the winery for their livelihoods.

"My research has revealed that the newly formed Group of Benedetti and Fairchild is attempting to saturate the market with their Malbec and blends by offering outrageous incentives to distributors." Again he paused, then continued, "I thought of creating another avenue for the Malbec by blending most of our supply and distributing it under a new company, using our own distribution centers."

"Adrian, you don't have distribution centers," I interjected, "you use the traditional distributors."

"I know that is where this plan gets a bit sticky. It will require trusted people in key places, the ability to set up distribution centers quickly and a sales force."

"Are Isabel and Juan Carlos in danger? Adrian, you said someone has already lost their life. Is it wise to challenge these people?" Daisy questioned with a worried look on her face.

"They can't kill everyone. Juan Carlos and Isabel will have to go back to Mendoza to talk to the other grape growers to create unity. They will have to share in the wealth to maintain the loyalty."

"How far are you in this plan?" Again Daisy was asking all the questions.

"The plan is pretty much under way. My uncles offered to invest capital. We have the locations for the distribution centers. We need someone we can trust and who is good in sales to run that whole operation."

"Do you have someone in mind?" I asked.

"I was hoping to find someone." Adrian gazed at the pavers in the patio.

"I can do it, Adrian," Paula said in a small voice. Everyone looked at her. Daisy looked at her in disbelief.

"I can do it, Adrian," she repeated. "I used to be in medical sales until my illness. Then they 'laid me off' due to downsizing. I am cancer free for the moment and would like the challenge."

"No, No, No!" Daisy jumped up yelling. "You are not doing this. You are not going back to that rat race of quotas and pressure. I won't hear of it. Forget it, Adrian. I love you and Juan Carlos, but no, this is my woman you're messing with. Paula, forget it. I'm serious. I'm done with this meeting." She stormed off towards the rose garden and into the wooded area. I had never seen her so upset.

"Adrian, I love Daisy, but I need to do something. I want this."

"All right, the job is yours."

"Adrian, Paula," I was yelling, "what is wrong with the two of you? Daisy's feelings have to be considered."

"That's right," Isabel supported. "Adrian, Paula, you two cannot do this. Daisy has to be considered in this and she won't have it. And for good reason, Paula, she is thinking of you."

Adrian ignored us and continued, "Paula, tomorrow we'll set up your employment. We can work out all the details then. We can tweak your responsibilities to conform to your domestic issues." He gazed in her direction and smiled, "I know a little about those things."

"I'll talk to her, Adrian," Paula said anxiously.

"No, let me talk to her first. I'll see you all later for dinner." He went off in the direction where he heard Daisy take off.

"Adrian, can I help?" I offered, concerned that she might not be on the path he was familiar with.

"No, baby, I have this." And he disappeared. I pulled out my smart phone and turned on the GPS to keep track of my man.

"Millie," Juan Carlos said, "Do you want me to go after him?"

"No, he will be fine."

"Are you sure?"

"Yes. Why don't we go inside and get ready for dinner. I'm going to take care of my children and we can meet back here by seven." I went inside, avoiding any more small talk. Angelique and Adam needed attention. Adrian might need my help and I needed to be ready.

Mercifully, Adrian returned to our suite an hour later.

"Hey, baby," he called out.

"I'm here, Adrian." I was in the dressing room getting ready for a shower. He walked in my direction, stretching his arms until he could touch me.

"Are you getting ready for a shower?"

"Yes."

"Can I talk you into a bath with me? We have a couple of hours before dinner."

Adrian had convinced Daisy that Paula would not be stressed. She could travel as little or as much as she wanted. Initially she would have to travel to set up the sales force in key marketing areas. She would be salaried, so quotas would not be a concern. Paula had lost her health insurance when the company had laid her off, but now she would be covered under the Luna Llena policy. He also made her understand that this was something Paula wanted and needed to do.

Finally everyone was on board and knew exactly what each had to do.

Chapter 4

L una Llena was quiet again. Our house guests had left. Everyone had his or her assignment. Paula went straight to work, setting her calendar of things to do and travel dates. Juan Carlos and Isabel were back in Mendoza. Juan Carlos would need to determine which of his fellow growers was interested in continuing business. Those who were not committed to the business would most likely sell to the European interests, so they would not be included in the plan.

I was busy doing what I did best. George Allen's computer revealed he had been contacted through the mail by an attorney, Ed Gonzalez, notifying him of Danny's death. Notations made by Allen on his computer further revealed that Ed had tried everything he could to gain access to the safe deposit box. One problem; Ed Gonzalez was already deceased himself as of the writing of the letters. There was someone else interested in the contents of the safe deposit box. Maybe it was the same person who killed him.

Over the next few days I contacted some of my friends in the NYPD in order to gather some information about Ed's death. The inventory of Ed's office taken by the NYPD listed all equipment. Not one computer was listed, which was strange. Someone had procured his computer. Maybe the same someone who had written letters using Ed's name. It was possible it was the same someone who had killed him.

So, someone has Ed's computer. May be that someone has Danny's also.

While I never communicated with Ed via computer and did not have an e-mail, I did however have many communications from Danny and was in possession of his e-mail and IP address. But there was another lead. Ed's web page and social network pages gave me his professional as well as personal e-mails. So, I went to work.

Adrian had forbidden me from hacking into personal computer accounts. I knew firsthand that he was capable of hacking into computers, but he chose not to do so. He preferred research to reveal strengths and weaknesses of those with whom he would do business. I was the only one whose computer he hacked. I, however, did not have any reservations about hacking, particularly when justified. Funny thing about justification; I found that every action was justifiable as long as I made it so.

Even though Adrian and I had an agreement not to spy on each other, I hacked him on a regular basis. My justification was security. He would be very upset if he knew I kept tabs on him. He would be equally upset if he knew I continued the practice of hacking into computers. His greatest fear was that I would someday be caught.

He will get over it. I hope.

Both computers were active. Ed had one computer for personal and business use. Some e-mails and documents were intact while others had been erased from both Ed's and Danny's computers. The contact files in both computers were also intact, but I could only assume that they, too, had been tampered with. Too much time had passed for recovery of these files. A thorough search revealed nothing of any use. Whoever was in possession of these computers was keeping them active for some reason, but what? If this person was the same one interested in the safe deposit box, they already knew where I was and they knew I would not be e-mailing Danny or his brother. So why keep these computers active? Who are these people and what is their connection to Danny and his brother? The more I searched the more questions there were and the more complicated this case became. I needed some help.

Dealing with my old colleagues called for finesse and for treading carefully. They redefined the word paranoid. And, since I came from the same culture, I was suspicious of everyone. Who knew if some of them were also involved? So, I called Sarah Jenkins. We had worked together on cases prior to Danny becoming my partner. She and I had been friendly and kept in touch. She was not very popular with the rest of the unit. She was a true wonk, living and breathing tech stuff. Her personal life was nonexistent. Her spare time was spent in the pursuit of all things computer and high-tech surveillance.

"Hi, Sarah, this is Millie."

"Mill, how the hell are you?"

"I'm good. How about you? Did I catch you at a bad time?"

"No, I'm out on the avenue going to get something to eat. How is everything with you?" She asked. "How is the new baby, Adam?"

"I'm great and Adam is just delightful." We both laughed. "How did you hear about the birth of my second child?"

"I ran into your mother in the supermarket." Sarah lived in the same neighborhood as Mom. "She was pissed that you lied about the due date. I thought it was funny, just like you to do something like that. When were you going to tell me?"

"I'm calling now, aren't I?"

"OK, you get a pass on this one. So, tell me what is going on?"

"Sarah, I was wondering if you could help me get the location of two computers."

"That might be a little difficult. The department has cracked down on freelancing, if you know what I mean."

"Yeah, I know." Freelancing was a term she and I used for using department equipment for personal research. "Can you suggest something?"

"Is this important?"

"It is very much important. I wouldn't ask otherwise. My family's safety is at risk, but I don't know exactly who the threat is." I briefly filled her in about the Sanz brothers, Danny and Ed.

"I can suggest something, but two people will be needed and we must use the department equipment."

"Is there anyone you can trust?"

"No, Mill, not really. I trust only you, but you are not here."

"I will be in New York in a couple of weeks. Maybe we can do something then."

"It will be risky. But what the fuck, you and I always walked the edge."

"Yes we did," I said laughing. We had crossed many boundaries, violated numerous regulations but were never caught. The only thing is I had hoped to discover the name of the person or persons interested in the safe deposit box before our trip to N.Y.

"Sarah," I continued, "you and I have a date. I will call you when we schedule the trip. Maybe you can come over to my mom's house when I'm there."

"Sounds like fun. I'll wait for your call. Mill, you take good care."

I did not get the desired result, but Sarah was right about the equipment and the need for two people. Two computers with two people would make the search that much quicker. She was correct not to trust anyone else.

Adrian did not want to stay in a hotel or at Earl's house. He reasoned that since Mom was staying with Earl, we could stay at the house. Part of my security routine at Luna Llena, the penthouse and Adrian's office at the Sentinel was counter surveillance. My mom's house or my former apartment had never been a consideration for surveillance. But things were different now. There was no doubt in my mind that whoever was interested in the contents of the safe deposit box was somehow keeping tabs on us. They would want to know when we arrived in New York and when we would visit the bank. The only way to get that information was surveillance.

I made a shopping list for the trip to New York. Clothing was not the main concern. God bless the internet. In addition to surveillance equipment for our security, I was able to pick up counter surveillance equipment for my mom's house. A bug detector to find hidden cameras, phone taps, GPS trackers, transmitters, you name it, I now owned it. I also purchased a white noise generator to protect our conversations. One gadget in particular was a vibrating pocket-transmitter detector that would alert Adrian or me if we were in the presence of hidden trans-mitters. I also purchased a do-it-yourself alarm for the house. If anyone broke into the house while we were away, I would be alerted via the smart phone. All the equipment was tweaked so that I would be alerted on my smart phone of any irregularities.

Next, I turned my attention to the Sanz brothers. Who were they really? The NYPD file described one brother, the one who shot Danny, Omar Sanz, as a small-time drug dealer with connections to a Colombian drug lord. His brother, Oscar, the one shot at Luna Llena, was also a small-time drug dealer with connections to the same drug lord, but he was also a gang member.

They came from a large family. There were three more brothers and three sisters. The sisters also had files with the NYPD for misdemeanors. There was no other information on them or connections to their broth-ers' crimes. Two of the last three remaining brothers had done time on Rikers Island, New York City's detention facility, on drug charges. The other brother was married and lived in Queens. He had also done time on Rikers for drug and assault convictions. By all accounts they were trying to live life on the straight and narrow working with a cousin in a carpentry shop. But I knew better.

What is the connection to Danny and Ed? What could be in the safe deposit box? It can't be drugs or money. The amount of drugs and money these guys are involved with would never fit in a safe deposit box. Were these brothers going to look for revenge for the lives of their younger brothers? Was one of them the driver of the florist truck?

Then there was Nestor Gardel, an up-and-coming drug lord from Colombia. He was young and ruthless, commanding a small army of thugs in and around the New York area. Gardel ruled from Colombia.

Danny's house had been in foreclosure before his death. Did the need for money cause him to get involved with these guys? Or, was the connection his brother? Ed's computer had been wiped clean of notes or files regarding cases he worked on. The only hope now was the possibility of physical files.

The police had not closed Ed's case. I called the detective in charge of the investigation and learned that Ed's office was still intact. Once the case was closed, his family could empty the office of its contents. I asked the detective, as a courtesy to a former law enforcement officer, if he could give me access to the office when I was in N.Y. He was reluctant at first, but then agreed as long as I didn't make any trouble for him. I assured him all I was interested in was information.

"Milagros, we need to pack a bag for the children. I would like to go to San Francisco and spend a few days. There is work I need to do from there," Adrian announced.

"I can do that this afternoon. Were you thinking of going tomorrow?"

"Yes. I also would like you to assist me in the office there."

"What would you like me to do?"

"I would like you to help me with some research. We should discuss our trip to New York. I want to be back before Thanksgiving. Is that all right with you?"

"Yes, it is. My mother may have another view, but she'll get over it."

"She and Earl can come back with us. We just need to decide when to go. Tomorrow we can make that decision."

Adrian's office at the Sentinel was very busy for a Wednesday. Richard drove us straight there with the children. Just as in Luna Llena, Adrian's office had a baby-proof area where Angelique could roam in her walker and there was a playpen for rest. A crib also adorned the very masculine office. Adam slept a good part of the morning, allowing us productive time.

I sat in Tom's old office, which was a far cry from the closet Adrian had assigned to me when I first came to work for him. I spent the morning researching wine companies with reported increases in sales. Those producing blended red wines were of particular interest.

Adrian telephoned old friends in the distribution business. He was affable and people were willing to give him information. One phone call proved to be revealing.

"Fred, I understand," Adrian said in a conciliatory voice. "Maybe in a few months I'll touch base with you again. But if I can do anything for you, please don't hesitate to call. It was good talking with you, Fred. You keep well."

"What was that all about?" I inquired.

"Fred Brown," Adrian replied, "heads a distribution center back in the East Coast. He informs me that a company, whose name he could not reveal, was offering substantial incentives to distributors who increased purchases of their wines. Even though his inventory of our wines is dwindling, he will not have the space to store any more products once they deliver."

"Could you offer incentives?"

"Not like what they are offering. It doesn't make sense."

"What do you do now?"

"Continue with our plan. The incentives being offered are for the distribution companies, not the retailer. Our new distribution company will offer reasonable incentives directly to the retailer. We will still have to compete to get the Malbec and the red blends into the stores."

"Adrian, won't the distributors you have dealt with for so many years be pissed off at you? Although, why should you care since they are not buying or promoting your wines?"

"I do care, Millie, because they do purchase from us and sell our wines produced in Luna Llena. Besides, they won't know it's me or Luna Llena. The new companies are not tied to us."

"Will Luna Llena be bottling the new wines?"

"No, they will be estate bottled at Bodegas Rodrigo."

"That's Juan Carlos."

"Yes it is. I am selling him the reds for the blends. You know that blend we received rave reviews on?"

"Yes, I know the one you mean, what about it?"

"Juan Carlos will be blending it on his estate also. All those wines will go to the new distribution centers. But, like I said, we still have to compete. These wines won't carry the rave reviews we received."

"Adrian, I don't quite understand. Who else is selling Malbec? Won't the retailers still want the Malbec?"

"I would think so, but the idea being employed here by the Benedetti Fairchild Group is to saturate the distributors and hopefully the retailers with their brand of wines and their Malbec. Their hope is to be successful for this one year, particularly the upcoming holiday season. They are counting this strategy will severely impact the income of the independent growers." Adrian looked pensive, then continued, "It may very well cause some to go under, forcing them to sell."

"I see. What do your uncles have to do with any of this?"

"Besides investing capital, they will be buying and selling Juan Carlos' wines for distribution in Spain. The aim is for Juan Carlos and his neighbors to surpass last year sales. This will give them the will to fight and not sell their land."

"I hope it works, baby."

"I hope it works also. Let's discuss our schedule for New York."

"Can we go to New York in two weeks? That will bring us to the end of September. We can return the last week in October."

"Will we need that much time there?"

"I don't know, but if we finish early, we can return earlier. Besides, going through my dad's things and my things may be time consuming. Mom wants to sell the house as soon as possible. I think she and Earl have some travel plans for February."

"I see your point. That task alone may take a month. What about the safe deposit box? Have you discovered anything important?"

"Everything I was able to uncover leads to a Colombian drug lord. Adrian, this could be very dangerous. This may not only be revenge for a slain brother or two. It may involve money and drugs. A safe deposit box couldn't hold the volume of money or drugs these people deal with." I paused to see if Adrian had any questions, but he was listening intently, so I continued, "I'm not sure the Sanz brothers have anything to do with the safe deposit box, although they do have a relationship to this drug lord, Gardel. The Colombian drug lord may have an interest in it, however."

"It seems there are more questions than answers. Do you have a strategy?"

"Not yet. I may not have one until we are actually in New York."

"I don't like that."

"Neither do I, but I can't get a location on these folks until then."

"Let's go home. Will you cook or do you want to eat out?"

"I would love to cook for my man. As I recall, we do have the fixings for something delicious."

Richard dropped us off at the front of the building. Adrian carried Angelique in his arms while I held Adam in a baby carrier. We looked beautiful. My man was wearing my favorite navy blue suit with white linen shirt and no tie. I was decked out in stiletto heels and a red crepe dress with square neckline and slit over the left thigh for easy access to my Beretta Tom Cat. Angelique had on a light pink dress with a reversed scalloped hem in a darker pink, white leggings and white patent-leather shoes. Adam had the cutest linen navy blue jumper with a white blue striped shirt. He, just like Angelique, was beginning to look more like Adrian, black silky hair, olive complexion and big blue eyes.

The doorman held the door open for us, commenting on how beautiful the children were. Adrian and I stood facing each other, holding hands while we waited for the elevator. Adrian was busy chatting about our next trip to Tahiti. He was lamenting that we would not be able to go until after the Christmas holidays. I was lamenting that we had only been there once this year when I noticed a blonde woman staring at my man. I started to get annoyed when the elevator doors opened. I led the way with Adrian directly behind me and one hand at the small of my back. As Adrian slipped the magnetic card into the slot for the penthouse, the blonde walked hurriedly into the elevator. I had never seen her before.

"Hello, Adrian, it's been a long time," she said, all eyes on him.

I know she sees a fucking kid in his arms.

"Susan," he recognized the voice. Gazing ahead, not in her direction, he continued, "Hello." He was surprised. He shifted his body so that Angelique was between him and her. It was a successful attempt to preempt her kissing him. His neck was flushed and slowly creeping up to his cheeks.

Fuck. This can't be good. She must be the bitch he snuck out to see when I first came to work for him.

I couldn't bear to think of that dark episode in our lives. We came too close to walking away from each other. At the time we were not in a relationship. I only worked for him, but that particular incident caused me to want to leave Luna Llena. Thankfully, Adrian was able to convince me to stay, saving our future relationship.

"How have you been, Adrian? I haven't seen or heard from you in a long time." Now my chest was tightening, I could barely breathe.

"I've been busy as you can see. Susan, this is my wife, Milagros and our two children, Angelique and Adam." He put his arm around my waist like a drowning man trying to hang on to a lifeline.

We exchanged hellos, but I made no attempt to shake hands. I kept both hands on the baby carrier. She eyed me from head to toe, then reverted to staring at Adrian. I don't know if Adrian felt her stare or my tension but he tightened his grip on my waist.

"How cute is that, Adrian, Angelique and Adam. All start with an 'A.' Did you plan that?"

"Yes, as a matter of fact we did," I interjected, getting her to look back at me. "Adrian and I plan everything. By the way, did you press for your floor?"

"Oh, I forgot." She turned and pressed the button for the twentieth floor. Seconds later we arrived on her floor.

"Adrian, give me a call some time," she said as she got out of the elevator.

No she didn't!

"Oh, do you have children and want a play date?" I asked.

"No, I don't," she replied, looking annoyed in my direction.

"Then why the fuck would my husband call you?" I asked with much attitude. You might say the New York in me came out. She gasped and the doors closed.

"Did you have to say that?" Adrian asked, knitted eyebrows and pursed lips.

"She was disrespectful and you didn't say a word."

"You didn't give me a chance." My poor husband was turning purple. I could only hope it was because of me.

The doors opened onto the foyer of the penthouse.

"Is she the reason you sneaked out of here when I first came to work for you?"

"Yes." He proceeded to our bedroom with Angelique in his arms. I followed in silence with Adam, who was beginning to become irritable.

Sometimes I wish he would lie.

"Adrian, can you please watch Adam while I go to the kitchen to take something out of the freezer for our dinner?"

"Sure, give him to me."

When I returned to the bedroom, Adrian had changed his clothes, Angelique's and Adam's. The three were on our bed. They were quite a sight. Adrian had changed to lounge pants and wasn't wearing a shirt. He held Adam to his bare chest. Angelique sat by his side chewing on a teddy. I couldn't resist, so I snapped a photo.

I announced myself asking him to help unzip my dress. With my dress lowered and bra removed, I took Adam from Adrian so he could be breast fed.

Adrian brushed his fingers down my chest until he felt the baby's mouth, then said, "Lucky baby." We both laughed. Adrian re-positioned himself behind me so I could lean on him. He stroked my bare back lightly with his fingertips. The sounds coming from Adam and Angelique entertained us. We sat there in silence listening to our children.

"Adam fell asleep. We should hurry and feed Angelique."

"Why don't you change and get comfortable? I'll start her dinner," Adrian offered.

A quick dinner of shrimp scampi with linguine was on its way to completion. Adrian set the table. He poured one of his white Albariño wines to complement our dinner. We worked together in silence, listening to relaxing guitar instrumentals by a jazz ensemble. Finally we sat down to eat. Adrian was the first to address the elephant in the room.

"Baby, thanks for not making a big deal about Susan," he said cautiously.

"You are welcome. I'm trying to learn to pick my battles. But, Adrian, I will not tolerate being disrespected."

"I know you won't, nor should you have to." He grabbed my hand and kissed it, then continued, "I hope there isn't a next time, but if there is, please give me an opportunity to handle it. Do I have to sell this building or should we move?"

"Neither."

"We may have to move eventually."

"Why?"

"The side of the penthouse where our bedroom is doesn't have spare bedrooms to accommodate three children." Adrian was obsessed that bedrooms for the children should be close to our own. I couldn't blame him. Angelique's abduction was still fresh on our minds.

"Well, we are not there yet," I reasoned.

"We will have to take some action sooner or later."

"We have enough on our plate right now, don't you think?" I sensed that Adrian's solution to one of his paramours being discovered in the same building where we lived was to move or sell the building. I added, "As long as Ms. Hot-to-Trot on the twentieth floor keeps her distance from you, me and the children, you and I will be fine."

Another kiss on the hand, "Thank you."

That's right, baby, no fights for now. I have other plans for us tonight.

Chapter 5

We arrived in New York on Saturday afternoon. The limousine Adrian arranged picked us up at the airport and pulled up in front of Mom's house, just as she and Earl parked in front of the house. They helped with the luggage and the children. I was delighted to see my Subaru Outback parked in the driveway.

Another car pulled up in front of the house across the street with two women inside. Both women wore slacks, high-heeled boots and tan trench coats. They walked through the gate and joined us at the door.

"Mrs. Zaragosa," the taller one called. I walked forward to greet her and her partner.

"Mrs. Zaragosa," she repeated, "My name is Jackie Reid and this is Vanessa Diaz. I believe you are expecting us."

"Yes, I am. It's good to meet you," I said as we shook hands.

I introduced them to Adrian and then asked, "Where are Roger and Richard?"

"They are positioned outside at opposite ends of the street observing the house."

"Please come in. Let's talk inside." Once inside I asked Mom and Earl to settle Angelique and Adam in one of the bedrooms. Earl understood we wanted some privacy with Jackie and Vanessa. He ushered Mom upstairs with the children and one piece of luggage.

"What would you like us to do?" Vanessa asked.

"I would like for you two to accompany us in a couple of hours when we go out to dinner. When we return your assignment will be to watch the entrances from the inside of the house. You will relieve Richard and Roger for a few hours so they can take a break.

"Your assignment will change throughout our stay. Did you bring luggage?" I asked.

"Yes, we both did. They are out in the car."

"Did you bring wigs like I asked?"

"Yes, Mrs. Zaragosa," Jackie answered. "That was an unusual request."

"I'll explain later. Why don't you bring in your bags? I'll show you which bedroom is yours. My husband and I are going upstairs to settle in and get ready for dinner."

Adrian and I took Mom's old bedroom. It was the largest bedroom. But with two cribs it suddenly shrank in size. Richard and Roger would share one bedroom, and Jackie and Vanessa would share my old bedroom. Each bedroom had a daybed with a trundle bed underneath. I apologized for the tight quarters but, like good bodyguards, they were not concerned with their comfort.

Mom and Earl took Angelique to the kitchen to feed her, while I took care of Adam. I was glad to finally be alone with Adrian. He lay on the bed looking overwhelmed.

"What's wrong, Adrian?"

"Nothing, I was just thinking how small this house suddenly became. Do we need all this security?"

"The ladies are here only for this week. Hopefully we can find out who is interested in the contents of the safe deposit box and devise a plan to put all this to an end." Without another word he rolled to his left side and fell asleep.

I sat at the foot of the bed to stare at my husband. Something didn't feel right to me. Was Adrian overwhelmed because of this business with the safe deposit box? Was he worried about the new business with Juan Carlos? Was he feeling claustrophobic in this house? Did he fear for all our safety? Or was it all of the above? I realized that I had not considered Adrian or his needs in the planning of this trip. Adrian was out of his comfort zone. Although he was familiar with the house, he was not as familiar with the outdoors as he was at Luna Llena. He was used to roaming the grounds at Luna Llena at will and alone. In this environment, feeling like a caged bird was understandable. He was too much a gentleman to complain. The two additional bodyguards undoubtedly added to his stress. I decided to fix what was ailing him.

Mom and Earl left early, sensing we were tired. I asked Jackie and Vanessa to leave, citing a change in plans. They would be paid regardless. Richard and Roger came in the house. They could protect from within. Adrian was accustomed to having them around.

I used the counter surveillance equipment to make sure the house was not bugged. Richard and Roger quietly and quickly set up surveillance cameras outside. Once the house was secure, I focused on getting dinner ready.

I decided to minimize Adrian's exposure to the upcoming events with the safe deposit box. That would be difficult.

Adrian looked much better after his nap. After dinner, the four of us settled in the living room to listen to music. Richard and Roger made themselves at home in the family room. They could watch television and the surveillance cameras from there.

We listened to our favorite guitar instrumental music. I poured wine for Adrian. Prior to our visit, I had a premium liquor store on Arthur

Avenue in the little Italy section of the Bronx deliver a selection of wines I knew Adrian would love.

Adrian closed his eyes and smiled with the first sip of the Barolo wine.

"Wow," he finally said approvingly. "Baby, where did you get this? This is a Pio Cesare, right?"

"Very good, yes it is. A premium liquor store not far from here delivered a selection of wines to the house last week. I gather you like it."

"I love it. Thanks, baby."

"I'm glad you like the wine."

"I mean thanks for everything, letting me nap, the home made food, and the serenity of the house," he said, referring to my dismissing the additional bodyguards, and then he continued, "and, yes, the wine." My man was appreciative.

"Anything for you."

Sunday was a low-key day. Our only visitor was Sarah. She played with the babies. Adrian and I both enjoyed her visit. She and I managed to spend a small amount of time with our laptops to coordinate our mission. I also managed to engage her in the wine industry.

"What time will you be at the offices of TARU," Sarah asked.

"I'll be there around eleven-thirty, just before lunch. What do you think?" I asked.

"Perfect."

"What do you mean, you?" Adrian asked.

"Mom wants you and the kids to go visit her and Earl. I think she has a trip for you. I don't know exactly what she has planned, but she will tell you. Anyway, Adrian, if you don't want to go on a field trip with her, let her know," I informed him.

"I thought the children and I were going with you." He sounded disappointed.

"I changed the plans, Adrian. Sarah and I need time with TARU equipment. Lunchtime is perfect for doing what we need to do. I thought you and the children could be a good distraction, but as it turns out, it won't be necessary. Besides, Mom wants to fuss over you and the kids. Is that OK with you?"

"I guess, but please don't do anything without letting me know. Can I trust you?"

"Always, baby," I lied.

It was settled. I would meet Sarah at the TARU offices the next day, alone. Adrian and the kids would be with Mom and Earl. Mom had strict instructions from me not to stress Adrian. No arguing. No opinions on child rearing. If he wanted to rest she was to allow it. Adrian's comfort was a concern for me, but I needed to accomplish my mission, or at least part of it.

The next morning I was fixing breakfast when Adrian strolled into the kitchen wearing a sweatshirt, sweat pants, sweat socks with slippers.

"Surely, you are not going to visit my mother and Earl dressed like that."

"Millie, I decided not to go."

He argued that he wanted to do some work and welcomed the peace and quiet.

"Angelique and Adam are not a bother," he offered, "I am perfectly capable of taking care of them. Roger can stay with me while Richard accompanies you."

I wasn't totally comfortable with this arrangement, but I had to give in so that I could take care of my business.

Richard rented a black SUV so that Roger could have use of the Subaru should Adrian and he need it. I had Richard drop me off at the train station. He argued with me, but I reasoned with him that I needed him to meet me somewhere else downtown and separating was necessary in order to thwart any attempts of someone following me.

On the way to Sarah's office, I picked up lunch for the both of us.

At precisely eleven-thirty I called on the offices of TARU. My old colleagues were happy to see me. I went equipped with plenty of photos of Angelique, Adam and Adrian. The ladies did not disappoint, foaming at the mouth over Adrian. They were entirely too disappointed that he did not accompany me.

I joined Sarah in her office where we sat to eat our lunch. Slowly people started to leave to get something to eat while others stayed behind. The office we needed was empty now, but it wouldn't be for long. Sarah and I moved quickly. We took out our personal laptops to route our way to IP addresses in two other continents and eventually we would hide in the NYPD network. My favorite was the African prince who was always surfing the net looking for gullible people to help him claim a fortune, but first they must demonstrate good faith and deposit money in his account. This elaborate labyrinth would finally lead us to the computers at TARU that would triangulate the position of Danny and Ed's computer. Waiting was torture. I could only hope that the computers were still online, otherwise this would not work. After a while I saw the elevator doors open to let out the team whose computers we were using remotely.

"Shit, Mill," Sarah groaned, "We're not going to be able to finish."

"We're close, Sarah. Stay connected. Give me your cup of coffee. I'll see if I can distract them."

I walked out to intercept them. "Hi, Jay, hi, Sam. How have you guys been? I didn't see you when I first arrived."

"Hi, Mill, it's been awhile."

"Yeah, Mill, how have you been?"

"Not bad, loving the West Coast. I've been keeping busy with two babies."

"Wow, two babies. I never figured you for the family type," Sam snickered.

"Me neither. But here I am, the mother of two little ones."

The small talk seemed to never end. Mercifully, Sarah popped her head from her office, "Hey, Millie, your telephone is ringing. I think it's your hubby."

"It was great chatting with you guys."

I hurried back to Sarah's office, closing the door behind me.

"Quick, Mill, log off your computer and shut it down. Your African prince is hot on your tail. We have what we need." She too was powering down her computer.

"Shit, I can't use him again," I complained.

"He didn't get as far as your computer. However," Sarah gloated, "he won't be surfing the web for victims for a while."

"Oh, is he coming down with a virus?"

"You might say that, but it's a mild case; nothing that can spread." We both laughed, enjoying the mischief. It had been a long time since she and I collaborated.

We put our laptops away in their cases out of sight and resumed eating our lunch.

"What did we get, Sarah?"

"Both computers are located in Sunnyside, Queens. Here is the address. But guess what?"

"What, Sarah?"

"Both computers have web cams and guess what?"

"For heaven's sake, Sarah, spill it already," I said impatiently.

"The idiots have the web cams facing the center of the room where naked women are cutting cocaine."

"No shit! That is rich," I exclaimed with excitement.

"Are you going to use that?"

"Oh, yeah, you bet. Are you ready for phase two of this operation?"

"Yeah, you leave first. I will be twenty minutes behind you."

I left and took the "D" train to midtown to meet up with Richard.

The SUV was parked down the block on the corner opposite from the bank where the safe deposit box was located. I sat in the back seat and opened my laptop. Using another series of IP addresses and another elaborate labyrinth, I uploaded the images from the two computers directly to the computer of a detective I knew in the narcotics squad. This guy was a real media hound. He would act quickly on this. In the past he had acted on information that had not been confirmed, so this was good bait he was sure to snatch.

"Richard, you remember my friend from yesterday?"

"Yes, Sarah, right?"

"That's right. She is walking down the block across the street now wearing a blond wig. Do you see her?"

"Yes I do."

"She is going into the bank. I want you to stand in front of the bank and wait for her to come out. Then escort her back here to the car and sit her up front with you."

"Yes, Mrs. Z."

Richard left to wait in front of the bank. I scanned the area. The counter surveillance equipment I brought along picked up a signal nearby. Someone was using an audio transmitter. I looked up and down both streets. There were pedestrians everywhere moving to and fro, but no one was loitering. I checked the cars in front of me and they appeared to be empty. Across the street the parked cars were empty with the exception of one. It was a black Dodge Charger. There was one man inside. I could not get a very good look at him, but I could see that he appeared to be talking to someone. I looked in the entrance of the bank. A tall dark man was standing near the glass wall looking at the guy in the car.

Bingo!

He was also looking at Richard. I sent Richard a text alerting him to the two men. He casually took a pack of cigarettes out of his pocket. He lit one, turning around and spotting the guy in the car. He took a few puffs from the cigarette and turned to face the bank once again. I could see Sarah approaching the revolving doors of the bank. She recognized Richard, who had already started to walk towards her. Richard threw the cigarette on the ground and before she could speak, he bent down and kissed her on the lips long and hard.

Hmm, I wonder if Richard is enjoying this assignment. I bet Sarah is. I didn't know Richard smoked.

They finished the public display of affection with Richard putting his arm around her waist, leading her back towards the SUV. Richard opened the door for Sarah and then walked around to the driver's side and got in.

"Hurry, Richard, let's get out of here. Those two guys did not make either one of you. Clearly they were looking out for me."

Richard pulled out gently, not attracting attention. We drove past the bank and both men were exactly as they were before.

"Here, Mill." Sarah handed me the fake ID with her picture and my name. She handed me a purse that was empty but for the contents of the safe deposit box. "Mill, I don't like this. These people will not have a sense of humor once they know the contents are gone."

"They won't know. You paid for the next year, right?"

"Oh, yeah, the bank manager was delighted to take your check. I signed new cards in your name and you have a new box with a new key. It's all in there in the purse."

"Thanks, Sarah, for all your help. Sorry you were subjected to that appalling public display of affection." Richard looked in Sarah's direction with a sly smile. She looked at him, returning the same sly smile.

"Oh, it wasn't that bad. Anything for the cause, you know," she purred.

Hmm, *I may have started something here. There is a definite charge of electricity in the air.*

The office of Ed Gonzalez was our last stop. The detective in charge of the case was already waiting when we arrived.

"Make it quick, please," Detective Burns said after the introductions. He protested Sarah and Richard's participation, but I explained that they would make the process go much quicker.

We went to work looking through Ed's files. Richard concentrated on files that began the date of Danny's shooting, working forward. Sarah concentrated on the year after his shooting. I worked backwards, starting with the day before his shooting.

Detective Burns watched carefully that we did not remove any material from the files. We did take notes of documents containing certain buzz-words, certain names, and we paid special attention to files dealing with criminal drug cases. Ed had plenty of those. That raised my curiosity since Ed was not by any means a top-notch litigator. We found that those cases had two attorneys assigned to them, Ed and a Mr. Abe Nussbaum.

Mr. Nussbaum will require further investigating.

Another oddity was there was not much communication between Ed and Nussbaum regarding their clients. The files that they worked on together did not reveal much in the way of Ed providing a defense for his clients. What services did Ed provide?

"Detective Burns, can you tell me what happened to Ed's apartment?" I asked.

"It has been processed."

"Do you know if bank statements were processed?" I pressed Burns for information.

"I think so. What is your interest in this case, Ms. Angeles?" Now Burns was pressing me for information.

"You can say it's a loose end for me. Someone I cared for very much, a fellow officer, my partner, was killed and I don't know why. His case was never solved. I was hoping there might be a link to this case." Detective Burns had a sympathetic look on his face, so I decided to stretch the envelope.

"Detective Burns, do you think I or my associates could have a look at the evidence the department has from Ed's apartment?"

"I think we can arrange something. Maybe you can help me, too," Detective Burns offered.

"How can I help you?" I asked.

"You can let me know if you find something that can help me solve this case."

"It would be my pleasure. Do you suspect Ed's murder had to do with drugs?"

"More like money laundering gone awry."

"That's interesting. Why do you think that?"

"Mr. Gonzalez was living way above his means. His business bank records, which are here, don't support his lifestyle. The income just isn't there. He was getting funds in the form of cash. His personal bank records show regular large deposits. They were all under ten-thousand dollars so to stay under the radar." Detective Burns paused as if in thought, then continued, "Someone was paying for a service and maybe Mr. Gonzalez failed to deliver."

"That makes sense. But who was his benefactor?"

"That," Detective Burns said smiling for the first time, "is the sixty-four-thousand-dollar question."

It was already getting late, so we dropped Sarah sans blond wig back at work. Richard drove to the car rental office to return the SUV. The agent drove us back to the house.

Roger was sitting in the living room.

"Hi, Roger," I greeted, "where is Mr. Z?"

"He is upstairs in the bedroom with the children. He said they were all going to take a nap."

"How was his day?"

"Good, I think. He worked on his computer, made a few phone calls, fed the children and played with them. They only went upstairs about a half hour ago."

"Thanks, Roger. I think we can head back home tonight. Mr. Z is tired and a bit out of sorts here. I'll suggest it to him and see what he says."

"I think he might take you up on that." We both laughed knowing Adrian very well.

"Richard won't be happy if we leave tonight," I said teasingly.

Roger looked at Richard who couldn't contain his smile. I left them to check on Adrian.

He was rolled on his side with his back towards me, snoring lightly. Angelique and Adam were fast asleep. I crawled into bed spooning him. He stirred waking.

"Hey, baby," Adrian greeted, rolling on his back and stretching his arm out for me to snuggle in. "How did your day go?"

"Good. How was your day? Did the children behave?"

"You know they did. They are the best. I totally enjoyed the peace and quiet."

"Adrian, would you like to go home tonight?"

"What about your mission at the bank? What about going through your things and your father's? What about those people who are interested in the contents of the safe deposit box? We still don't know who they are. Or do we?"

"We can go home, Adrian, if you would like. They, whoever they are, can wait to collect the contents. I arranged to pay for another year. Since we don't know who they are, we need to let them make the first move."

"What about those two brothers connected with the drug lord?"

"I don't think they have an interest in the safe deposit box. Besides, we can defend our family better in Luna Llena."

"Fuck it, baby, let's go home."

Richard drove us to Earl's house so we could say goodbye to Mom and Earl. I explained that Adrian was exhausted and this trip had proved too much for him. Mom was disappointed that we didn't have a chance to visit, but she understood. We agreed they would come to Luna Llena for Thanksgiving. Then we were off to LaGuardia Airport. Richard drove the Outback where the Gulfstream was waiting.

"Richard, you're not going back with us?"

"No, Mrs. Z. I asked Mr. Z for some time off. I'll be back at Luna Llena in one week. Mr. Z said I could stay at your house, if that's OK with you."

"It's fine with me, Richard."

"It seems Richard wants to explore a love interest," Adrian teased.

Richard looked at me with a half-cocked smile and I stared back inquisitively.

"Are we done here? Are the two of you done staring? Why don't you just ask what you want to know?" Mr. Multiple Question was back. Not waiting for an answer, Adrian continued, "Apparently, Richard has a thing for your friend Sarah. As it turns out, she has a thing for him. She slipped him her number."

My man is a wealth of information. He should consider employment with the tabloids.

"I hope you don't mind, Mrs. Z."

"Why should I mind? Have a good time, Richard, and take good care of my friend. See you next week."

"Sure thing, Mrs. Z, I'll take good care of Sarah, if she lets me. And thanks for the use of your home."

"It's my mother's home," I corrected.

63

"Milagros, please let's go," Adrian pleaded.

We boarded and soon were on our way.

It had been a few weeks since our return from New York. Two days after we left, the local news in New York reported on a big drug bust in Sunnyside, Queens. Along with millions of dollars in street value of cocaine, illegal firearms were confiscated. Detective Delatorre gave an account of how a sting operation led to the arrest of Edgar Sanz, the leader of a local drug ring. The picture of Edgar did not match the picture of the man who had delivered the calla lilies. Arrested with him were five others. Neither of his two brothers was among the ones arrested. That left Tito and Sam Sanz at large.

My research revealed that Tito was the one who delivered the flowers. The research also revealed that he was currently back east with his brother Sam. Were they busy for the moment trying to take care of Edgar's drug empire? I would have to continue to keep tabs on them.

I decided not to have Richard and Sarah go through the evidence the NYPD had stored from Ed's apartment. Detective Burns had answered my question regarding Ed's bank accounts. I was not sure whether the Sanz brothers were involved in Ed's murder and the safe deposit box, but I was sure they had revenge in their hearts. I had mentioned the Sanz brothers as possible suspects for Ed's murder to Detective Burns. The fact that one of the brothers had also killed Danny, a cop in the line of duty, intrigued the detective. He was grateful for that piece of information and promised to let me know if anything materialized. He informed me that his department was spread thin, but he would try placing surveillance on these two characters. My story about Danny caught his attention. As it turned out early on in his career, Detective Burns had also lost a partner in a shoot-out that was drug related.

Adrian was feeling better once we returned to Luna Llena. His new business with Juan Carlos had taken off nicely. Through Paula's efforts, a new clientele was developed in China. That was unexpected but welcomed. Then the first of many phone calls came.

"Fred, how are you?" Adrian greeted the distributor, placing the call on the speaker so he could play with Angelique who was on his lap. They spoke for thirty minutes about business and wines before getting to the heart of the phone call.

"Adrian, I am short on stock due to a supplier who failed to deliver," Mr. Brown informed. "The supplier blamed a computer glitch, but I don't believe him."

"Why would the supplier lie?" Adrian asked.

"I am convinced the supplier's main objective was to destroy the relationship with Luna Llena," Fred replied, adding quickly, "and to dominate the Malbec business."

"Fred, I can send you some stock," Adrian paused before continuing, "but due to our previous conversation, we found other avenues for the Malbec. There isn't much left. We also had to make some adjustments to the business, causing a price increase, Fred."

"I will be happy to get what I can and I accept and understand the price increase."

More importantly, Fred Brown promised not to allow himself to be lured in the future to exclusivity. Adrian informed him that the weather had been extremely favorable for the crop picked this year and next year's wine promised to be exceptional. Mr. Brown offered to sign a contract with Adrian for future purchases.

"Fred, that won't be necessary. You and I go back many years and your word is gold with me." Adrian had people skills.

Other distributors called Adrian with the same problem. He promised to send them small quantities since there wasn't much to go around. They all accepted the price increases.

My man was in a particularly good mood.

Later that evening over dinner, Adrian asked, "Milagros, did you have anything to do with the computer glitch at Benedetti Fairchild?"

"Of course not, Adrian, that is tricky business as you can well imagine," I said, trying to convince us both.

"Sarah would be an able accomplice."

"Adrian, no I did not have anything to do with that glitch, but it couldn't have happened to more deserving people."

"I agree but you know how I feel about hacking into computers. You could get caught someday."

"Yes, yes, I know how you feel but I didn't do it. Are you done with dinner?"

"Yes, thank you." We both cleared the dishes and cleaned the kitchen.

"Angelique and Adam are asleep. Would you like to take them upstairs?"

"Can I talk you into a bubble bath?" Adrian asked with that mischievous smile that always made me tingle down there.

"Yes, you can. You run the bath and I will put the little ones to bed."

Neither Adrian nor I had gotten over Angelique's abduction, so now there were two cribs in our bedroom.

Adrian was already submerged in the tub drinking a glass of his Albariño wine. He knew it was one of my favorites.

"Hey, baby, is there room for me?"

"Always, baby, always," he said, putting down his glass. He straightened, spreading his legs so that I could sit in between. Stretching out his arms, his hands felt for my body, settling on my hips, guiding them where he had made room.

"Ah, Mrs. Z, this is wonderful. You make me so very happy."

"Hmm, Mr. Z, I aim to please."

"I never thanked you for cutting the New York trip short."

"I could tell you were out of sorts. You know, Adrian, when you don't care to do something, you should say so."

"I will next time. Here, baby, have a glass of Albariño. I know it's your favorite."

"Hmm, yes it is. Thank you."

I snuggled into his chest. He wrapped an arm around my shoulders and his legs around mine. We sat there sipping our wine contently, listening to the occasional lapping of the water against the porcelain tub.

Chapter 6

We were in the swing of having the house decorated and making plans for the holidays. Mom and Earl divided the holidays between his son in Georgia and us. They decided to spend Thanksgiving with his son and visit us for Christmas. I felt guilty after our abrupt departure from New York, but Mom understood. I promised to get back there soon to go through my things and my father's. She assured me there was no hurry, that I could take my time.

"Mom, I thought you needed the money from the sale of the house for your trip with Earl in February?"

"Don't worry about that, I have the money. The sale of the house can wait."

I was glad Mom was in no hurry to sell the house. It made me a little sad to think of not having the house where I was raised. Not to mention that going through all my things and my father's would be a daunting task.

Daisy and Paula also confirmed their stay for the holidays. Isabel and Juan Carlos were meeting the twins for their traditional ski trip, but promised to visit us the week before Christmas. Isabel was due to start her book tour by mid-January. Adrian, the children and I were scheduled to go to Tahiti after the holidays.

Adrian and I were into our routine of working from Luna Llena and at times from the office in San Francisco, taking our babies everywhere with us. The wine business was doing better than expected. Paula was enjoying her employment, performing beyond her own expectations. I kept busy assisting Adrian in the office and keeping tabs on the two Sanz brothers.

Hilda and Hector had developed their own little routine. They would take off on Friday evening and return Monday morning. Roger, Richard, Frank and Tony alternated taking weekends off. Richard made frequent trips to New York. According to Sarah, they were in love.

"Baby," Adrian crooned into my ear while placing his arms around me from behind, "how about a date night?"

"That sounds like fun. What did you have in mind and when?"

"How about we go out to dinner tonight? We can try that new restaurant you read about."

"That's fine with me. What time did you want to go so I can have the children dressed?"

"This is date night. No children," he blurted. "I asked Hilda to babysit. Do you mind?"

"Leaving them behind will be a first," I commented.

"I know," Adrian agreed, kissing my hair and inhaling my scent. "But I think you and I need some time alone. It will be for only a few hours. I made reservations for seven. What do you think?"

I turned around to look at my husband. He was gazing in my direction with glistening eyes, smiling with lips slightly parted. Placing my arms around his neck I answered, "I'm all yours, baby."

Delicieux was a new trendy French restaurant that had received rave reviews. I was amazed that Adrian was able to get reservations with short notice. We arrived promptly at seven. My man looked gorgeous in a navy blue suit, white linen shirt and blue-striped tie. His outfit coupled with olive complexion brought out the blue in his eyes. I wore a sleeveless red-orange, tight-fitting shift with a low V-neck that showed just the right amount of cleavage. The back also formed a V-neck to the zipper. The waist was adorned with a narrow attached matching belt that had a tiny heart-shaped rhinestone buckle. Since the night was chilly, I wore a red trench coat that was tailored but for the skirt that was adorned in layers of ruffles. Red stiletto heels and clutch bag that concealed my Glock completed the outfit. The Lady in Red had nothing on me.

"Mr. Zaragosa, Mrs. Zaragosa," exclaimed the Maître D. "It is a pleasure to have you here with us this evening."

"Thank you, Franco," Adrian replied.

Franco showed us to our table.

"Do you know this man?" I asked.

"Yes, he worked at another restaurant nearby. I was surprised to hear that he had made the move to this one."

"Why would that surprise you?"

"He had been at the other place for a long time. Usually, long-time relationships like that are accompanied by loyalty on both parts."

Adrian was big on loyalty. He expected loyalty and he gave the same. He tolerated nothing less from associates, friends or family.

"Why do you think he left his former employer," I asked.

"I don't know, but I won't be surprised if we find out before the evening is through. Tell me, Mrs. Z," he said, changing the subject, "what's good on the wine list?"

I had already been looking through the wine list so I answered quickly, "Nothing."

Adrian's eyes opened wide and he laughed repeating, "Nothing?"

"No, Adrian, there is nothing good on this list. Not one of your wines is listed here," I informed him indignantly.

"You see," he started while gazing lovingly in my direction, "that is one of the many reasons why I love you. Your loyalty sometimes clouds your judgment." He leaned into me for a kiss, and then continued, "I'm sure there are plenty of fine wines on that list."

"Still, they should patronize the local growers. For God's sake, they are in the middle of wine country here," I continued my protest.

"Good evening, Mr. Zaragosa, Mrs. Zaragosa," came the greeting from our waiter. "It is a pleasure to see you here this evening. My name is André and I will be your server. Would you like to start with a cocktail or some wine?"

"André, my wife and I would like to start with two vodka martinis with two olives, please. May we also have a sampler of your seafood appetizers?"

André flashed a great big smile and said, "Of course, Mr. Zaragosa. I'll be right back with your drinks."

"Adrian, isn't that a lot of food for an appetizer? And how did you know I wanted a martini?"

Sometimes I get offended when he doesn't ask what I want. He just assumes that he knows what I want.

"I'm sorry, baby. I should have asked you first." He looked contrite but continued, "The truth is I like it when you have a martini."

"Oh, and why is that?"

"You become very agreeable. Tonight I want you agreeable."

How can a few words make me tingle all over, especially down there?

"Mr. Z, you sure do know how to disarm a woman."

"Hmm, baby, I like disarming you."

"What else do you like?"

"Mrs. Z, I like sitting here with you, taking in your scent and imagining all the wicked things I will be doing to you later tonight. Nothing brings me greater pleasure."

"You are wicked, Mr. Z."

"You're not so bad yourself."

Our waiter came back with two huge martinis and our appetizers.

"Here's to you, my lovely," Adrian toasted.

"To us," I answered, clicking glasses.

The appetizer dish was artfully displayed. There were fried calamari, cocktail sized shrimp, clams casino and oysters.

Continuing his seduction, Adrian felt his way around the platter and picked an oyster.

"All right, Mrs. Z, open wide." I did as I was told. I never quite believed in the myth of oysters being an aphrodisiac, but my husband feeding it to me certainly was.

With one hand he held my jaw. This helped guide the other hand to my lips. His middle finger brushed my lips. He gently placed the oyster shell on my lower lip and slid its contents down. I swallowed enjoying my husband's seduction.

"All right, Mr. Z, open wide," I mimicked. He complied. After quickly swallowing, Adrian leaned into me locking his lips on mine for a deep passionate kiss. My man was not bashful with public displays of affection.

"That's enough for now, Mrs. Z, let's eat so we can hurry and get home." Adrian gave me a mischievous smile and then said, "All this seduction has made me horny. If we continue, I'll not be able to stand up."

"Ay, yai, yai," I exclaimed and we both laughed, relishing our private joke.

It was a lovely dinner. The restaurant was beautifully detailed down to the napkins and tablecloths. Noise was down to a minimum with only the background music of a string quartet that played in a corner.

Adrian entertained me with his stories. He shared dreams that he had for us as a couple and dreams he had for his children. I couldn't help thinking what a lucky woman I was to have such a wonderful husband. We talked about the upcoming holidays. Adrian loved the preparations. I think he was trying to make up for the holidays he missed out on by not having his mother present.

"Adrian, this weekend can we go shopping for Christmas ornaments for the children?" We had agreed to start a tradition of purchasing ornaments specifically for each child. Angelique was about to receive her second and Adam his first.

"Yes, baby, we can do that. We can make a day of it. What do you say," he replied enthusiastically.

"That would be great. Maybe we can do some Christmas shopping."

"Yes, we can do that," Adrian agreed. "Do you remember where we bought Angelique's ornament last year?"

"Yes, I remember. Funny thing, this year we will be purchasing two."

"Yeah," Adrian said with a smile on his face.

"Next year it will be three."

Adrian was about to take a sip of his coffee when he stopped in mid-air. He placed the cup back on its saucer and covered his mouth with the linen napkin. He was trying to hide a smile. He gazed up directly in front of him. After what seemed to be a long while, he put down the napkin and gazed in my direction. Smiling, he leaned close to me and whispered, "I need to hear you say it."

I placed both arms around his neck, leaned in close to his ear and whispered back, "By this time next year you will have your third child. We are pregnant again." We held this pose for another long while before he leaned into me for another deep passionate kiss.

He was about to say something else when a gentleman suddenly appeared at our table.

"Mr. Zaragosa," came the greeting from a tall portly man. "My name is Justin Fairchild."

Still gazing in my direction, he gave me a chaste kiss on the lips. Adrian then stood, adjusting his belt, a 'tell' sign I recognized as his changing gears to alert status. He stretched his hand to shake hands with Mr. Fairchild.

"Mr. Fairchild, from Fairchild Group," Adrian stated rather than asked.

"Yes, that's right, Mr. Zaragosa. I'm flattered that you knew."

"Who isn't familiar with your wines?"

"Again, you flatter me."

"Mr. Fairchild, this is my wife, Milagros Zaragosa." We shook hands.

"Good to meet you, Mrs. Zaragosa. I don't mean to interrupt your dinner, but I couldn't pass up the opportunity to meet Mr. Adrian Zaragosa in person."

"Now it is you who flatters me," Adrian replied, yet he didn't look flattered.

"It's not every day one gets to meet the mastermind behind Bodegas Rodrigo."

"Well, then I will have to disappoint you," Adrian said smiling. "The mastermind is a friend of mine. I have nothing to do with Bodegas Rodrigo." Adrian's eyes were open wide, eyebrows arched upwards and his smile was slanted to one side.

That's an unfamiliar look for my man. That's his lying face!

"You are modest, Mr. Zaragosa. Ours is a tight industry. Not much goes on that eventually isn't discovered."

"That is true," Adrian agreed. While his facial expression did not change, his neck was visibly starting to redden. "I'm sorry, Mr. Fairchild, but I will have to leave you to your intrigue. My wife and I are trying to enjoy a rare night out without the children. I'm sure you understand."

"Yes, of course, I didn't mean to intrude. Perhaps I can call on you in the next few weeks when Mr. Rodriguez is in town."

"Please call my office in San Francisco to set up an appointment. I'm sure you know the number," Adrian said without changing facial expression.

"Yes I do. I look forward to speaking with you again."

Adrian sat again, gazing now in my direction, he placed one arm around my chair. Without a word, he leaned into me for another deep passionate kiss.

"Well, that was interesting," I commented.

"That asshole interrupted a beautiful moment between us. To use one of your phrases, I need to reset the clock."

I had used that expression a long time ago when I first worked for Adrian. He had sneaked out of the penthouse apartment to visit Ms. Hot-to-Trot, compromising his security. Fearing I could not perform my duties as director of security, I resigned my position. Adrian convinced me to stay but I told him I would first have to reset the clock. That meant I mentally had to go back in time before the offending event. When I explained the concept to Adrian, he liked it immediately. Now he adopted it for his own.

Since Adrian was busy trying to reset the clock, I was afraid to bring up the subject of Mr. Fairchild. Clearly Adrian did not want to speak of him, but I felt this man was threatening. He made no attempt to disguise the fact that he knew Adrian was the mastermind behind the newly formed Bodegas Rodrigo or that he knew Juan Carlos would be in town in just a couple of weeks. This man was bold, but my man was not up to discussing it. So I went with the flow and reset my clock for the time being. 'After all,' to quote my favorite literary character, Scarlet O'Hara, 'Tomorrow is another day.'

I grabbed Adrian's face with both hands and went for another deep passionate kiss.

"Congratulations, Mr. Z. It seems you are to be a father for the third time. What do you say to that?"

"Mrs. Z, I can only say one thing. You make me extremely happy. Now let's go home. I had a sensual evening planned but I will have to tweak it a bit," he said smiling again.

"Oh, baby, why tweak?" I purred, pursing my lips and kissing him on the cheek while cradling his face in my hands. He liked when I did that.

"Well, my original plan did not include a pregnant wife," he replied, gazing in my direction, smiling with lips parted.

"Pregnant wives don't break, you know."

"Hmm, well then, let us away from here so we can find out."

I drove the Corvette home. As far as I could tell, there was no one following us. I didn't think there would be, but I kept the Glock on my lap at the ready.

Back at Luna Llena, I parked the car inside the garage. I checked the premises for intruders. Roger was standing outside by the kitchen door waiting for us.

"Welcome back, Mr. Z, Mrs. Z," he greeted. "How was your evening?"

"It was very nice, Roger," Adrian answered.

"How was everything here, Roger?" I asked.

"Quiet, Mrs. Z, just as I like it." We both laughed.

"Roger, is Hilda still up?" Adrian asked.

"Yes, I believe she is. I saw her in the kitchen heating a bottle for Adam not too long ago."

"Millie, let's drop by her suite and pick up the children. I want them to wake with us."

"Sure, let's go." Adrian was protective of his children. He wanted for us to be with them during their waking moments as much as possible.

"Millie," Adrian said as he placed Angelique in her crib, "I need you to send one of your cryptic messages to Juan Carlos."

"What do you want to say?"

"I want to warn him that our adversaries are onto us and he should be careful. Tell him that they are aware of his pending trip to the U.S."

"I'll get on it right away."

I booted up my laptop, thinking of how to best approach the matter. I decided to Skype Daisy. She and Paula were both home.

"Hey, girl," Daisy greeted me. She and Paula were dressed for bed.

"Hi, Daisy, hi, Paula," I greeted back. "Sorry for the lateness of the hour. Hope I wasn't disturbing anything."

"No, we were just watching a movie," Paula contributed. "How are you, Adrian and the children?"

"We are just fine. How are you two?"

"Can't complain," Daisy said. Paula stood behind Daisy with her arms around her neck. They looked peaceful and happy.

"That's great. I can't wait to see you," I offered. "I was thinking of our mutual friend, Isabel. Angel, I don't wish to communicate with her, her husband is such an ass. Angel, he is reckless. Angel, he does not need to be concerned about his friends because they are not on to him."

"I see," Daisy replied. She thought for a moment, then continued, "But surely we can forgive him for her sake." Daisy had a serious expression on her face indicating she understood. "Angel, I wouldn't ask them to communicate. What would be the point?"

"Precisely my sentiment also, Angel, so don't bother. It is not important. Have you spoken to Sarah?" I asked, now changing the subject.

"Yes, I did. She is hot for her new guy. It's Richard, right? It seems he travels to see her as often as he can."

"Yes, it is Richard. I wonder how that will play out. This is the first serious relationship she has had."

"Well, she is a geek. But he seems really interested in her. He's a good looker."

"That he is. He is also very nice. I hope something comes of it."

"Well, ladies, I'm off to bed," Paula interjected. "Millie, give my love to all."

"Will do, Paula, you have a good night. Daisy, I'll be saying good night also. See you soon."

"Give big hugs and kisses to the babies," Daisy said, blowing me a kiss. We terminated the call. I was certain she would immediately reach out to Isabel and Juan Carlos. He would be told not to communicate but to be careful. The message of his friend, Isabel would understand their enemies. A message from the U.S. meant something happened here. They are not onto him meant they were.

"All done, Adrian," I said as I powered down my laptop. "Now, how about that sensual evening you promised me?"

My man was coming out of the dressing room naked. "I filled the tub, let's start there."

"Milagros," Adrian called out.

"Yes, Adrian, I'm right here," I responded as I entered his office.

"I need to go to San Francisco tomorrow."

"Oh? I thought you would work from home until after the New Year?"

"I thought so, too, but Fairchild called to set up an appointment. Tomorrow is the best day for both of us. Benedetti will be joining him."

"Does he know that Juan Carlos isn't coming?" Once Isabel and Juan Carlos received my cryptic message from Daisy, they canceled their trip to the U.S. Juan Carlos immediately ordered his sons to return to Argentina.

"I don't know. I didn't mention Juan Carlos and neither did he."

"I'll pack bags for us this afternoon."

"I don't want you to come, Millie. Stay here with the children."

"Surely you don't plan on meeting with those two men by yourself?"

"No, I'll take Richard and Roger. Hector can drive us."

"Adrian, I don't like this. I don't like being left out. These men are dangerous. I want to go," I asserted raising my voice.

"Milagros, I will be fine. These two jokers wouldn't try anything in my office. I won't be alone. Besides, you have plenty to do here. Your mom and Earl will arrive in two days and so will Daisy and Paula."

"I don't like this, Adrian."

"Pack a bag for me please. Be a good girl, will you?" he purred in my ear.

Remembering our fight of last year behind his request for 'space,' I backed off. Roger, Richard and Hector would be with him. The truth was I did have plenty to do.

"All right, I'll pack your bag after lunch. But I still don't like it."

"It'll be fine," he said hugging me. "I'll see you for lunch. I have some work to do now." I was effectively dismissed.

I was looking forward to Mom, Daisy and Paula visiting. I invited Sarah to visit. She and Richard could spend some quality time together. We arranged for her to fly out with Mom and Earl.

I put Adrian and his San Francisco visit out of my mind and busied myself with pending investigations.

Mr. Nussbaum was an attorney employed by Nestor Gardel to represent his drug dealers who from time to time were arrested. My research revealed that Gardel paid Nussbaum with checks. Their dealings were legitimate. Nussbaum, in turn, gave Ed checks for services rendered on the cases they worked together. However, there were some cash transactions between Nussbaum and Ed. Nussbaum withdrew large sums of money from his business account at regular intervals. The withdrawal dates coincided with deposits Ed Gonzalez made to his personal account. The amounts did not match.

Were those large amounts meant to include Danny? Was this part of the money laundering? This couldn't have anything to do with Gardel. The money Gardel dealt in was greater than the money between Ed and Nussbaum.

It was almost time for me to meet Adrian for lunch when I received a phone call from an investigator I had hired in New York.

"Mrs. Zaragosa, its Ralph White." Ralph White was the investigator I had tailing the Sanz brothers.

"Hi, Ralph. What's going on?"

"Tito is on the move. He left today for California, L.A. to be exact. Sam is still in New York."

"Thanks for the heads up, Ralph. Is there anything else?"

"Yes, their drug operations are up and running. They set up in a warehouse in Brooklyn. As far as I can tell, there are no uniformed agencies onto them."

"We won't do anything with that information just yet. Ralph, can we get cameras in there?"

"That is going to be hard. This is a twenty-four-hour operation, seven days a week."

"All right, I'll give that some thought. Tito is of more interest right now. Thanks again, Ralph. Please keep me posted. By the way, did you receive your Christmas gift?"

"Yes!" he exclaimed with delight. "You were much too generous and the wine was appreciated by me and the Mrs."

"I'm glad. Ralph, have a good Christmas. Let me know if anything else happens."

"Sure thing, Mrs. Z"

Now more than ever I felt uncomfortable with Adrian's solo trip.

"Mr. Z," I called as I entered Adrian's office, holding Angelique by the hand, helping her to walk and holding Adam in my arm, bracing him on my hip.

Gee, I barely recognize myself.

"Mrs. Z, are you ready for lunch?" Adrian asked, barely looking up from his computer.

"Your daughter is walking towards you."

"Is she walking unassisted?" he asked, delighted, turning to where he thought she would be approaching.

"Well, I helped her a little but she is walking directly towards you alone. So be ready to catch her."

To our delight, she reached her father without incident and unassisted. Adrian swept her up into his arms, kissing and hugging her.

"Ah, my family is here. Milagros, where shall we eat?"

"I thought we could sit in the family room. The children ate. I fixed us a nice lunch."

"You, not Hilda?" he asked surprised. Hilda did all the cooking during the week.

"I can cook, you know."

"I know you can. You're a damn good cook, too."

"Nice recovery, Mr. Z."

He kissed me and Adam. We walked hand in hand to the family room where I had set two covered plates, a bottle of white wine with a glass, and a glass of water for me. The iPod was in its dock playing jazz that Adrian had downloaded from my music collection.

"I love the music, baby."

"I hope you like what I cooked."

Adrian placed Angelique in her playpen. I placed Adam in his swing. He was sure to fall asleep.

"Um, this smells wonderful," Adrian commented as he lifted the cover off his plate.

"It is shrimp cooked in a red and yellow cherry tomato sauce with penne pasta."

"It is delicious," Adrian said, wiping his mouth with a cloth napkin. "Give me a kiss." I did as I was told.

I sat on the floor next to him and we ate in silence, listening to the music. Adrian was the first to finish. Again he reached out to me for another kiss.

"I am a very lucky man. Two kids, another on the way, a beautiful wife that lets me have my way with her and she can cook. Life does not get any better than this." Adrian was sporting that broad smile that melted my heart.

"Adrian, I don't want you to go to San Francisco," I blurted out.

"Millie, please let's not do this. We already discussed it. Don't ruin this wonderful lunch."

I crawled in between his legs, kneeling on the floor.

"I spoke to Ralph White this morning. He called me. Tito Sanz left New York this morning headed for L.A.," I said holding his face in my hands. "I'm afraid his destination is not L.A."

"Millie, we should then worry about you here in Luna Llena."

"This place is a fortress. It is also easier to defend."

"Mr. Sanz will have no idea that I am in San Francisco. I should leave Richard with you."

Why doesn't he suggest that the children and I go with him?

"Adrian, why don't we all go together?"

"Millie, you said it yourself, you are safer here. Now, I am going back to work. This was a lovely lunch, thank you." This time I received a chaste kiss on my forehead and he was gone. I was dismissed.

Am I becoming a nag? Is he tiring of me?

I cleared the dishes, collected my children and headed for our bedroom. I did not feel like working in the office next to Adrian, so I sent him a text that I was upstairs.

A nap was in order.

The next morning I woke up alone. Angelique and Adam were gone. I figured Adrian took them with him to breakfast. He had been distant since our lunch together. My man was being difficult.

"Good morning, Richard," I greeted as I walked into my office next to Adrian's.

"Good morning, Mrs. Z."

"Where is Mr. Z?"

"He left hours ago with Roger and Hector. He brought Angelique and Adam to Hilda. They are in the kitchen." He paused, looking away from the surveillance feeds. "Mr. Z asked me to advise Jon at the winery and the guys at the shed to beef up security around here."

"Yes, I received news yesterday that Tito Sanz was headed to the West Coast."

"Isn't there anything else we can do?"

"Funny you should ask, I'm working out a plan in my head right now."

"Mrs. Z, are we going to have an adventure?"

"Yes, Richard, I believe we are."

"Mr. Z won't like that."

"Screw him," I said, walking towards the kitchen.

Hilda and the children were there listening to music and having breakfast. Angelique was in her high chair and Adam was in his carrier.

"There they are! My little angels," I greeted my children, kissing and hugging them. "Good morning, Hilda. How are you?"

"I'm fine, Millie. It's good to see you in such a good mood."

Have I been in a bitchy mood?

"I'm feeling particularly good today."

"What would you like for breakfast?"

"Sit Hilda, please. I will serve myself some green tea."

"What will you eat?"

"I'm not hungry right now."

"Millie, you must eat something. Adrian will be very upset if he knew you didn't have breakfast."

"Then don't tell him," I said curtly. "Hilda, can you watch the kids this morning?"

"Sure, Millie. May I ask why?"

Yeah, so you can report to Adrian.

"I need to finish some work in my office. Afterwards I will take Richard with me shopping. I want to buy Adrian's Christmas gift," I lied. I already had Adrian's gift. I was going shopping but not for Christmas.

"So, can you take care of them?" I asked again with a little more attitude than called for.

I guess I am a little bitchy.

"Of course, Millie, I'll look after them."

"Thanks, Hilda," I said a little softer. "I'll be in my office. I will let you know when we are ready to leave."

Back in my office I used a network I had developed while at TARU to trace the movements of Tito Sanz. It took some time, but I did get a hit on a credit card in his name that was used to check into a motel, not far from Luna Llena.

So, the vendetta continues.

I looked at my smart phone and there were no messages from Adrian. I was now furious at him. He left without saying good-bye and he hadn't called. Richard had left to talk to Jon and the guys at the shed. I walked into Adrian's office and sat in his chair. For a moment I felt sad. The familiar connection was missing. Was it me? Was I chasing my husband away? Was this pregnancy making me bitchy?

I touched everything on his desk, trying to feel his presence. I touched his Braille keyboard and his earphones. I sat back in his chair, feeling the supple leather. I then touched his desk. The wood was beautifully finished. Adrian made sure that all the wood furniture in the house was professionally maintained at least once a year. I opened the drawers. They were in immaculate condition, just like everything else in his life. There was one file drawer locked.

Locked? Really, he has got to be kidding.

I easily picked the lock. There were a few files that meant nothing to me except one. It was a file on the sale of my apartment in New York. I had asked Adrian to handle it for me. I knew it fetched a good price but I never asked him about it. The money was donated to my favorite charity, a hospital for children. I opened the file out of curiosity. There was a letter from a law firm specializing in real estate. It simply said, "Dear Adrian, the property in New York has been sold for five-hundred thousand. The proceeds have been sent to the charity you requested in your wife's name. Attached is a copy of the canceled check." It was informally signed SM. I put the file back and locked the drawer.

I then went to the locked file cabinet that had once made Adrian uncomfortable, knowing that his former personal assistant had been prowling around it. I picked that lock also. Inside there were manila folders.

The first one shocked me. The label read "Angeles, M." I opened it and inside was a single photo of Adrian and me dancing many years ago at a party in his house outside of Cambridge. I was sorry I opened that file. All of a sudden I was overwhelmed with sadness. I put the file back. The other manila folders were similarly labeled. I recognized another name, "Winston, R." I lacked the courage to open it. I quickly closed the drawer and locked it. I felt sad, but mostly I felt shame for going through his things.

He went through my things in the apartment in New York.

I still felt shame. Adrian openly admitted going through the things in my apartment. What I did was wrong because I was doing it behind his back and I had no intentions of telling him. I needed to get out of the house.

I did the unthinkable in the Zaragosa household and changed into a pair of flat shoes and jeans. Richard was back by the time I returned to my office.

"Mrs. Z, you changed. I have never seen you wear jeans," Richard said amused.

"I needed to get comfortable. We're going shopping. Let's go, Richard. We're taking the Corvette."

"Can I drive?" Richard asked, elated at the prospect of driving the impressive sports car.

"Sure," I responded, giving him the keys.

Blue skies and warm temperature were the perfect mix for riding with the top down. The V-8 engine let out a throaty roar the instant the key turned the ignition. Richard eased out of the garage, taking his time to the gate. It was obvious he was savoring every minute.

"Richard, when you get to the main road, make a left turn."

"Sure thing, Mrs. Z."

I checked my smart phone and still no message from Adrian. It wasn't like him to be out of touch for so long. I turned on the GPS to track the signal from his bracelet. It showed he was in his office.

That's not spying. He can track me with my matching bracelet.

"Mrs. Z," Richard interrupted my brooding, "what are we shopping for?"

"Oh, there's a place I know of where we can cop some drugs."

"What!" he yelled, "You're kidding, right?"

"No, Richard, I'm as serious as a heart attack."

"I know you have a good reason for doing this," Richard reasoned, "but Mr. Z will be furious. Anyway, why are we coping drugs?"

"I need someone to be arrested for his own good."

"Not Mr. Z, right?" he asked cautiously.

"No, silly, not Mr. Z. Can you imagine him in jail?" and we both laughed.

"If Mr. Z finds out, it could cost me my job."

"I won't tell him if you don't."

Daisy had given me a tip on a local drug dealer who, for reasons she could not say, was off the DEA watch list. But he was a person on the FBI list. I gathered it was her case. She informed me that he had what I was looking for and that, also for reasons she could not tell me, he was desperate to unload.

We drove forty-five minutes to Oakland. Richard parked the Corvette on the street in front of a fenced-in lot. Inside the lot were junked cars. To the extreme left in the back was a small one-story building that looked like a garage. I asked Richard to stand by the Corvette in case I had trouble.

I went through the gate into the lot. The door to the garage was open. I could see a tall red-headed man working on a car's engine. He was tall and burly-looking with a full beard. As I got closer I could see he had more facial piercings than I could count.

"Hey, dude," I yelled from a safe distance, "are you like the head dude in charge?" I tried my best valley girl imitation.

"Who wants to know?"

"Me, duh?"

"Funny girl. What do you want?"

"A friend told me I could get some party stuff here."

"Who told you that?"

"Pablo Escobar, dude, what difference does it make?"

"Go home, little girl." He returned his attention to the car engine.

"C'mon, dude, I was sent to get some goodies for a party tonight. Don't make me look bad."

"Are you a cop?" he said, looking over my shoulder at Richard. Thankfully, Richard was in jeans and Converses.

"No, that's my boyfriend."

"He lets the little lady take care of business, does he?"

"You can say I'm the brains of the outfit," I quickly replied, laughing. "C'mon, big dude, help us out here."

Richard and I were dressed down but clean. Driving a Corvette that I am sure he assumed belonged to a daddy somewhere. It said we had money.

"OK, little lady, what would you like?"

"Some weed and blow," I said with all the authority of someone who is in the know of these things.

"How much you want?"

"It's a big party, big dude. Can I see what you got?"

"I don't work like that. Tell me how much you want, then I'll fetch it for you and you pay me. Got it?"

"Yeah, yeah, I got it. I want fifty Gs worth. More blow than weed. Got it?" I back talked him.

"Holy shit, little lady, that's some party. Can I come?"

"No. Can I get my shit, yes or no?"

"Yeah, but show me the money."

"Stand your distance and don't make the mistake of thinking you're going to rip me off. Got it?"

"Yeah, yeah, let me see. I need to know you're for real."

I opened the top buttons to my blouse exposing cleavage and there was a small velvet pouch.

"That doesn't look like fifty Gs."

"There are fifty grand worth of diamonds. Get the shit and I will let you examine the goods."

"Baby doll, I don't deal in diamonds. They have laser etched serial numbers."

"These don't. No one is missing them. You can sell them for cash without raising questions or red flags."

With not another word, he disappeared to the back of the garage. He was gone for a while. I started to get nervous. Richard was now standing at the ready looking my way. I could swear Richard was growing gray hairs.

"OK, little lady," the voice of my burly friend came from the back. He was carrying a duffle bag. He threw it on the floor and opened it so I could see what was inside. Truthfully, I had no idea what fifty grand of cocaine and marijuana looked like, but what was in the duffle bag was enough to get someone arrested for a very, very long time. Burly dude pulled out a loop to examine the diamonds while I examined my goods. We were both satisfied and concluded our meeting.

"Mrs. Z, you have balls," Richard blurted out as we pulled away from the curb.

"Richard, head back to Napa." I called Detective Doran.

"Hi, Detective Doran, this is Milagros Zaragosa."

"Hello, Mrs. Zaragosa. To what do I owe the pleasure?" Detective Doran and I had developed a professional relationship. He appreciated that I was former law enforcement.

"A friend of mine back in the NYPD has notified me that Tito Sanz, that is the driver of the flower delivery truck, is in California. The fact is he is at the Napa Motor Lodge. He checked in this morning."

"Milagros, may I call you Milagros?"

"Please do, Detective Doran."

"Please call me Phil. Milagros, I can't arrest the man. We have nothing on him. The delivery man from the florist could not identify his assailants."

"Phil, I know you can't. I was hoping that maybe you could pay him a visit. I can defend my family from him. But, Phil, I can't defend my family if he has a high-powered rifle. His last attempt with his brother was to invade our home. But now he is alone. My instincts tell me he will attack from a distance."

Phil was quiet for a while. He felt my fear.

"OK, Milagros. I'll pay him a visit. If he acts stupid, then we can go into his room and search; otherwise we can't."

"I understand, Phil. I appreciate it very much. By the way, call me Millie. All my friends do."

I developed some people skills, too.

"I'll call you as soon as I've paid him the visit. That should be within the hour. Millie, talk to you soon."

Richard drove me to a local department store where I purchased a knapsack. Using latex gloves, we transferred the drugs to the knapsack and threw out Burly Dude's duffle bag. Then we drove to the Napa Motor Lodge and parked down the block across the street. I spotted a rental car that must have belonged to Tito. There were no other cars parked in the courtyard of the motel. I called the motel and asked to be connected with Mr. Tito Sanz. The manager was very nice and complied.

"Hello," Tito answered.

"Mr. Sanz," I said, "Can you please come to the front desk? It seems your credit card has been rejected."

"That's crazy. I'll be right down."

"Thank you, Mr. Sanz."

I jumped out of the car with the knapsack and ran towards the courtyard of the motel. Tito came out of his room and walked down the stairs closest to him. I ran up the stairs on the opposite side. He never glanced my way. Once I reached his room, I picked the lock and let myself in. I dropped the knapsack in the closet where his suitcase was stored. Next to his suitcase was a long, slender object wrapped in brown paper.

As I reached the bottom landing of the stairs, I saw Tito leave the manager's office and head back to his room. I walked quickly back to the Corvette to wait.

Ten minutes later Detective Doran arrived with his partner. They knocked on Tito's door. Tito did not disappoint. When Doran identified himself, he acted like the asshole that he was. A very pissed Doran knocked him to the floor, cuffing him. They went inside his room and soon after two squad cars arrived, sirens and all.

"OK, Richard, let's head back home."

My smart phone rang. My heart stopped, hoping it was Adrian.

"Hi, Millie, it's Phil. I told you I would call you back to give you an update."

"Hi, Phil," I responded as the sadness returned.

"I just wanted to let you know that I paid a visit to Mr. Sanz. He, as expected, acted the fool. We went into his room and struck the mother lode of evidence against him."

"Really!" I sounded genuinely surprised. "Tell me what did you find?"

"Millie, he had a knapsack full of drugs. It's enough to charge with intent to sell. That should put him away for a long, long time. Then we found a Smith and Wesson thirty-eight, which I suspect is the firearm he used to kill Mr. Ed Gonzalez back in New York. We will have to wait for forensics.

"I did a little snooping," he continued, "with my comrades in New York and Mr. Gonzalez was shot with a thirty-eight. But Millie, I also found a high-powered rifle. Your fears were well founded.

"You can rest a little easier now," he said sympathetically.

"Phil, you are amazing. My husband and I will be forever grateful. Will you let me know what forensics tells you?"

"Sure, you can count on it."

"Thanks, Phil."

Richard and I arrived back at Luna Llena by two in the afternoon. Hilda and the children were in the family room. I felt more at ease knowing Tito Sanz was in custody.

"Hi, Hilda," I announced myself.

"Hi, Millie," she replied. "How was your shopping?"

"It was a success, I'm glad to report. My darling husband will be very pleased, at least I hope so." Hilda looked away, avoiding me, as I finished speaking. "How did the little ones behave," I continued, trying to engage her in conversation.

"Oh, Millie, they were perfect. They are a joy and entertaining."

"Entertaining is a good word, Hilda," I said as I sat next to her. "I hope this little one in here," I said patting my belly, "is just as entertaining. We should find out the sex soon."

"Whatever sex, the baby will be wonderful, I know," she quickly said as she stood. "Can I get you a tea and something to eat?" she offered.

I realized I had not eaten all day and I was starving.

"Tea would be nice. Maybe a small sandwich to go with it," I requested.

"I'll get you something nice. I'll be right back."

"Thank you, Hilda," I yelled after her.

Lady, what is eating at you?

There were no messages from Adrian. I was starting to worry so I called him.

"Hello, Milagros," Adrian answered the phone.

"Hi, Adrian," I responded. "I was worried baby. I haven't heard from you all day. How have you been?" My anger had subsided. All I wanted to know was that he was safe.

"I'm good. Sorry I didn't get to talk to you earlier. I've been busy."

"How did your meeting with Benedetti and Fairchild go?"

"Fine, I'll tell you all about it when I get home tomorrow night. How was your day?"

"What do you mean tomorrow night?"

"I'll be home tomorrow. I'm tired and don't feel like traveling back to Luna Llena. How was your day?"

"Traveling back to Luna Llena? Adrian, it's five o'clock. You will be home by six or six-thirty if you left now. And, it's not like you're driving."

"Milagros, I'm tired. I asked you twice, how was your day?"

"My day was fucking great!" I blurted out and hung up on him.

Well, that went well.

Chapter 7

The next day it was after eight PM when I heard Adrian enter the house through the kitchen. He was sure to speak to Hilda first. She would fill him in on all the activities of the household. I was waiting for him in the family room listening to my favorite guitar music. The children were asleep upstairs in Angelique's bedroom.

"Milagros," finally came the voice from my husband.

"I'm in the family room." I did not get up to greet him. I was seething.

"Where are the children?"

"They are sleeping upstairs."

"Why did you move them from our bedroom?"

"It's good to see you, too. How are you?" I said sarcastically.

"I asked you a question."

"Doesn't Hilda know why?"

"No, she doesn't," Adrian replied irritated. "You know, forget I asked anything. I'll be upstairs."

"Surely, you are not going to shower again," I blurted out. Adrian smelled freshly bathed and looked well groomed for someone who had worked all day.

"Good night, Milagros."

Go to hell.

It was two in the morning when I turned off the music and headed upstairs. I grabbed a blanket from the linen closet, entered Angelique's bedroom and made myself comfortable on the sofa. Sleep eluded me so I stared at my two angels, who slept peacefully unaware of my heartache.

This was the longest night of my life. At five I decided to bathe and dress before Angelique and Adam woke. After I dressed, I decided to check in on Adrian. The bed was empty. I walked to the sitting room. He was asleep on the sofa. My heart was breaking. I had no idea what was happening to us. Somehow, I had lost the ability to talk to my husband. Not that he made it easy. He had become unapproachable. But I loved him and did not want to lose him.

I went back to Angelique's room. She was wide awake and Adam was beginning to stir. As I picked her up, the door opened and Hilda walked in.

"Good morning, Millie," she declared. "I came to get Angelique to feed her breakfast."

"Good morning, Hilda," I replied. "That won't be necessary. I will take care of them."

"Are you angry with me?"

"No, Hilda," I lied. "I want to take care of them today. We will be downstairs shortly."

"Should I start their breakfast and yours?"

"No, Hilda, thank you. I'll do it." She left without another word.

The children were bathed, dressed and ready for breakfast. I briefly checked in on Adrian. He was awake and in the shower.

I prepared Angelique's breakfast and while Adam nursed, I fed her. Hilda prepared Adrian's breakfast without a word. Hector was surprised to see me with the children and a little embarrassed to see me nursing Adam, although I covered us with a baby blanket. Richard and Roger also paraded through. The household was waking and everyone was getting breakfast before heading to his work assignments. Frank and Tony made a quick appearance. Hilda always prepared a buffet for all of them.

Adrian was the last to appear. He was refreshed, dressed casually in slacks and a pullover shirt. Everyone announced himself to him. I was the last. He too was surprised to find me in the kitchen. Adrian stood behind me, placing his hands on my shoulders. He felt the baby blanket that was draped over Adam and me. He knew what that meant. Angelique screeched for her father's attention. His broad smile came back as he lifted his daughter to hug and kiss her. He returned her to her high chair and then turned back in my direction, slipping his hand under the blanket and feeling Adam until he felt his lips on my nipple and said, "Lucky baby." As if on cue, everyone exited the kitchen leaving us alone. Hilda was the last to leave, placing Adrian's breakfast on the counter. Adrian pulled out the stool next to mine and sat.

"Have you had your breakfast?" he asked.

"Not yet, I'll get something when I finish here."

"Milagros, we need to talk."

"When would you like to have this talk?"

"After you finish your breakfast, I would like to go to our bedroom. I'll wait here with you to help with the children."

"OK."

Adrian placed Angelique on the carpeted area of our bedroom that had been sectioned off and child proofed. I placed Adam in the playpen where a teddy bear and a clown rattle caught his attention.

"Milagros," Adrian started, "I don't want to argue with you and I don't want us apart." I started to say something, but he interrupted by continuing, "Let me finish. I love you and our children. I want peace between us. Can we have peace?"

"I love you, Adrian, and I want peace between us. But I need to know what is bothering you. Have I done something?"

"Yes, you have. I asked you if you had something to do with the computers at Benedetti and Fairchild and you said, 'no.' Fairchild believes that it was either you or me. They researched you and know what you did for the NYPD. They don't have any proof, but they are convinced."

"Adrian, I had nothing to do with their computers."

"So, that's how you're going to play this."

"I'm not 'playing' anything. I had more important things to do if you remember."

"All right, I believe you. I thought you did, so I needed some time to cool off. That is why I stayed away. Baby, I need you, but please, don't push me."

"Adrian, I need you and I want to be with you. But you need to clarify for me what 'don't push me' means."

"I don't want you lying to me. I don't want you hacking into computers. I don't want you taking matters into your own hands. I want you to discuss matters with me before acting on impulse."

The heat from my neck was slowly reaching my ears where the thumping from my heart echoed. Impulse? Was he fucking kidding me? I desperately tried to restrain the anger that was rising inside.

"I don't act on impulse," I said indignantly. "I analyze every situation carefully. I have been trained by the best to do that. I am not accustomed, in the area of security and or self-defense, to ask for permission on how to react. My doing as you ask might cost one of us, if not both, our lives. Adrian, I don't know how to be anything other than what I am.

"For these reasons, I have a hard time telling you the truth. If I consulted every plan of action with you, what would you expect me to do if you disagreed with the plan? Please tell me.

"I'll tell you," I continued, not letting him speak. "You would have me stand down. That might endanger us all. Adrian, I trust your judgment in your area of expertise. You need to trust my judgment in my area of expertise."

He held me by the shoulders close to him and exhaled. His hot breath felt good. I was suddenly afraid we would reach an impasse.

"What about the hacking?" he asked.

"You do your research and I do mine. I don't know how to be something other than what I am," I repeated. "You knew what I did for a living. Besides, I don't do it for fun or with malicious intent, well not always. Information is all I seek most of the time."

"You frighten me."

"I don't see why. When have I ever not had your back? When have you never been number one?"

"I worry for you."

"Again, you need to have some faith in me. I am not reckless. But I told you a long time ago, I will do anything to keep you and our children safe."

"You spy on me," he accused.

"If I spied on you, I would know exactly what you were doing these last two days. You don't spy but you have others do it for you." He knew exactly what I meant.

He removed his pullover shirt, exposing the silky black chest hair I was so fond of.

"Can we go to bed?"

"Yes," I replied in a throaty voice. Then I added, "If you accept me as I am."

"Will you keep me informed of the things you do once you have done them?"

"Starting today?" I asked.

"OK, starting today."

I'm like putty in his hands.

"Very well then, just so that you know I will be busy this morning trying to keep my husband happy."

With that we went to the bed to do what we did best together.

We spent the rest of the day avoiding any further conversation that would spoil the mood.

"Good morning, sleepy head," Adrian greeted. "It's time for you to get up and feed your children and husband."

"Umm, baby, it will be my pleasure. A certain brute has adequately taken care of my needs. It's only appropriate that I take care of his family."

"I love you, baby," Adrian responded, pulling back the covers and climbing all over me. Geez, he felt good.

Shit! It's five o'clock in the fucking morning. Is he nuts?

We did what we did best together, and then I was off to the kitchen with my children to take care of them and the hubby. I don't know if it was the sex or the knowledge that my husband still loved me, but the early hour and lack of sleep did not bother me.

Hilda was still sporting a sour puss. My presence in the kitchen in the early hours of the morning was not welcomed. My preparing breakfast for the children and Adrian was not welcomed either.

I assumed my position on the stool, feeding Angelique while Adam nursed. Adrian enjoyed the change in the early morning kitchen activity with his wife and children. We talked, laughed and planned the activities of the day together.

My man is back.

Our guests for Christmas added to our new-found bliss. Mom and Earl, Daisy and Paula were just delightful. Sarah and Richard were a welcomed treat, although they made their presence scarce during the day. At seventeen months, Angelique wanted to walk everywhere. Adam was as engaging as Angelique. They commanded attention and they received it from all within range.

Christmas eve the adults exchanged their Christmas gifts. Adrian gave me another deed. This one was to the house where I grew up. My mother had managed to keep a secret from me. She and Adrian had reached an agreement about the sale months before. I loved my gift and told him so. I never thought of purchasing my childhood home. Adrian was very thoughtful.

"OK, now it's my turn," I exclaimed enthusiastically as I gave Adrian his laptop. "Now, put on your earphones," I commanded. He did as he was told. I entered a flash drive onto his laptop that I had prepared. He was able to hear that his present was a twenty-four-foot catamaran. He heard its description and that it was berthed in Tahiti.

"How much did this set you back?" he asked, gazing in my direction.

"Not much. As you know, I came into a little bit of money." That was my way of letting him know I used my personal account.

"You can try it out in a couple of weeks when we go to Tahiti," I told him excitedly.

His look was less than enthusiastic. He forced a smile for our guests. Then finally, he leaned into me for a kiss.

"We can discuss our trip later, yes?" he asked.

"Of course, baby," I replied with a sinking heart. This was not the reaction I was expecting.

"Adrian," I called out to him in our bedroom.

"Yes, Millie, what is it? I'm in the dressing room."

"Oh, you showered already?"

"Yes, I'm very tired. It's been a long day."

So, you are not interested in sex tonight.

"I wanted to discuss Tahiti."

"Millie, please not tonight. Can we discuss it tomorrow or after everyone leaves?"

"Yes, Adrian, it can wait. I'm going to my office for a while. You go on to bed. The children are fast asleep."

"Thanks, Millie. See you in the morning."

Thanks, my ass! Now what is going on?

I sat at my desk contemplating the events of the evening. I looked out onto the patio and there were Sarah and Richard making good use of a beautiful chilly night. I thought of hacking some computers, namely my husband's. For some strange reason, I lacked the interest.

I marched myself to the bedroom where Adrian was already asleep. Angelique and Adam's cribs were back in our bedroom, so I sat in the sitting area on the sofa to watch them.

By the time our guests woke, Angelique and Adam were dressed and fed. An impressive buffet table was exquisitely laid out in the dining room, all cooked by me. Mom and Earl, Daisy and Paula, Sarah and Richard were impressed. Everyone waited for Adrian, who was the last to join us. He too was amazed by the selection of food.

After breakfast we all went to the family room, which was lit up with a Christmas tree for the children. It was their turn to open gifts. Of course, Adam was too young to open gifts but he did enjoy mouthing them. Angelique still preferred the wrappings and bows. Many photos were taken of them so that someday they could appreciate the fuss that was made over them.

By mid-week all our guests were gone. Richard had decided to follow Sarah back to New York until the New Year. Except for Frank, Tony and Roger, who took turns with the surveillance of the property, we were once again alone to enjoy the quiet.

"Milagros," Adrian began, "I never told you how impressed I was at breakfast Christmas morning. You put on quite a spread and the way you handled so many people was really impressive."

"Thank you, baby. It's nice to hear you enjoyed the day."

"I more than enjoyed it. Baby, I love you."

Oh my, that's music to my ears. I think I'll cry.

"I love you, too, Adrian. What would you like to do today?"

"I thought maybe we could just lay back and take it easy. You have worked very hard entertaining. There is food left over, so you don't have to cook, right?"

"We have enough food to take us into the next year."

"Millie, what would you like to do for the New Year?"

"I would like to have an early dinner, put the children to sleep, lay in front of the fireplace with my favorite man making wild passionate love."

"I think we can make that happen."

Things are great between Adrian and me. I won't bring up Tahiti until after the New Year. Hopefully, he'll broach the subject first.

It was the beginning of the second week into the New Year and Luna Llena was back to normal. Hilda was still upset at my early morning presence in the kitchen. Hector performed his duties as usual and helped with the surveillance without too much interaction with me. Apparently, whatever ailed Hilda was affecting him.

Roger, Richard, Frank and Tony were developing their own bond. They constantly teased Richard about his long distance relationship with Sarah. Richard displayed his good nature at the teasing. In fact, one might say that he even enjoyed it.

Adrian divided his time between Luna Llena and San Francisco without the children and me. This I did not like. His excuse was that I had my hands full with my own work and the children. He also argued that the older the children became, the more he wanted them grounded at Luna Llena. That meant me as well. This, too, I did not like. Ms. Hot-to-Trot was also in the back of my mind and was rapidly becoming a loose end for me. Above all else, this I did not like.

Mom and Earl were eagerly planning a month-long trip to Australia and New Zealand. Earl, at Mom's urging, retired from teaching, but would continue teaching art in a studio when he returned to New York. It was nice to see them make long-term plans.

Isabel and Juan Carlos were doing fine. The twins were back at Berkeley resuming their studies. They convinced their father to let them return. Isabel on the other hand was having trouble convincing him to let her go on her book tour. He did not want to leave his estate at harvest time. His friends and neighbors were all looking to him for leadership. They believed in him. Juan Carlos was concerned that their resolve to continue in the wine business might waver if he left. So, Isabel agreed to postpone her book tour for a few months when it was winter in Argentina.

Daisy was basking in her own success at the FBI. Her career was progressing to her satisfaction.

Paula reveled in her employment. It was what she needed to recover from her ordeal with Pablo Santos. Her selection of sales staff coupled with her motivational skills quickly launched Casa Imperially Wine Distributors to the forefront of the industry. She was featured in a trade magazine as a pioneer for opening up the China market to U.S. wines. This did not sit well with Benedetti/Fairchild.

Adrian never told me of his meeting with Benedetti and Fairchild. So, I never updated him on Tito Sanz. Now we each kept secrets. Adrian, I knew, would not discuss Benedetti and Fairchild until it served a purpose for him to make a point or get something in return. I, on the other hand, didn't update him on Tito Sanz because he did not ask. Were we keeping secrets or drifting apart? This I did not like. Worse yet, it made me sad.

It was close to lunchtime and Adrian had not summoned me as he usually did, so I took the initiative, grabbing each child to seek him out. He was in the sitting area of his office playing "Samba Pa Ti" by Carlos Santana on his guitar.

"Adrian," I announced myself, "I'm here with the children."

He stopped playing and gazed my way with that big broad smile that melted my heart every time.

"Hi, baby," he responded. "What is my family up to?"

"We came to take you to lunch."

Angelique ran to her father. Adrian set aside the guitar so that he could smother her with kisses. He then stood to kiss and hug me and Adam.

"Put Adam down in the playpen for a minute, Milagros. I'll get a toy to entertain Angelique." I did as I was told.

"OK, Adrian, now what?" I asked.

"Pick up your guitar and accompany me with this tune. It needs another guitar."

"No it doesn't," I protested. I knew how to play but not nearly as well as Adrian. "You sound terrific."

"C'mon, baby, please. Do it for me," he pleaded.

"Adrian, I can't play as well as you. I find it hard to keep up."

"Nonsense, please, baby, for me," he pleaded again.

"OK," I replied reluctantly.

We played the Carlos Santana tune together. For the first time I felt I did keep up with him. We sounded pretty good. Adam stood in his playpen quietly listening. Angelique sat on the floor to look and listen.

"That was great," Adrian exclaimed when we finished. "Let's play the classical version of 'Perfidia.' I'll take the lead and half way through you'll take the lead, all right?" Without waiting for an answer, Adrian began. At first I struggled to keep up, but I hung in there. Then it was my turn to lead. The soulful tune made my heart ache.

We finished the tune but now I made a request, "Let's do that one over. This time the jazz version. You lead on the guitar, but let's both take turns singing."

We began the song. The meaning was not lost on him. It is a love song of treachery and betrayal. He gazed my way and I felt his sadness. I wondered if he sensed mine. Towards the end of the song, we both joined in perfect harmony.

"Millie, that was great. Thank you for indulging me. You and I not only make beautiful babies, but we make beautiful music together." We put away our guitars in silence.

"Give me a kiss," he said with stretched out arms. I walked into them so he could lean down. Together, we locked lips for a much needed passionate kiss. We parted for a moment and then went for another.

"Mrs. Z, I do love you."

Do you, Adrian?

"I love you, too, Adrian," I replied, not being able to shake my sadness.

"I'm hungry, woman. Are you going to feed me?"

"Yes," I said, handing him Angelique's hand. She now wanted to walk everywhere. I braced Adam against my hip and together, holding hands, we walked into the kitchen.

After lunch I gained the courage to ask him about Tahiti.

"When can we go, Adrian? If we wait any longer, we won't be able to go because I won't be able to travel."

"Why don't you invite your friends? You can have a girl outing."

That was like a stab to my heart.

"Why don't you want to go?"

"I have a business to run, Milagros," he responded, agitated.

"That has never stopped you before," I countered just as agitated.

"Things are more delicate now."

"How delicate are things now? What could possibly change if you were to go with me and our children to Tahiti?"

"Milagros, I don't like the catamaran," he exclaimed. "I won't get in it. I don't like boats. I feel too vulnerable in them. Another thing, it didn't set you back one-hundred grand. What did you use fifty grand on?"

This was a game he was good at. He would put me on the defensive in order to deflect from him and win the argument. Adrian knew about the money way before Christmas, but held on to the knowledge until it could serve him.

Well not today, buddy. I've learned from the master himself.

"What did you, Benedetti and Fairchild discuss during lunch?" I challenged him.

"I asked first," he barked, knitting his eyebrows and pursing his lips.

"I don't care who asked first," I asserted myself. "I am the director of security for this outfit and you continually violate our agreement."

The best defense is a good offense.

"You violate agreements all the time." He was now red in the neck.

"Don't change the subject."

"You changed the subject first," he argued.

"What are we in first grade?" I protested. "Can we please have an adult conversation?"

"Behave like one and then, yes, we can have an adult conversation." He tried to bait me.

It's not going to work, mister.

"Adrian," I said, softening the tone of my voice and inching closer to him so that he could feel me, "please, baby, take me and the children to Tahiti. They need their father and I need my husband. I'll sell the catamaran. In hindsight it was inconsiderate of me. You already have sailing skills. I thought we could both learn together how to handle her. I secured someone who would teach us." I was sufficiently contrite that the redness in his neck disappeared and his facial expression softened.

"Baby," I continued, "will you please take us to Tahiti? Adam has not been there with you."

He pulled me onto his lap, feeling my belly. His gaze was on the belly. Adrian was silent for a moment, deep in thought.

"All right," he finally said. "Don't sell the catamaran. If I die at your hands, so be it."

"You used to sail. You have sailing skills," I repeated. "Adrian, you have well developed sensory skills for tracking and localization. We have proved it on and off the firing range, as you may recall. This boat," I continued excitedly, "is a twenty-four-foot trailer able cat that has a tiller, not a wheel, so you'll have a better feel for the helm. One person alone can sail it. Plus you already have a talking GPS and I purchased auditory sonar. I can serve as a guide. We can arrange to visit the Bay Area Association of Disabled Sailors so you can become acquainted with the equipment."

"As usual, Mrs. Z, you gave this a great deal of thought."

"Yes, I did," I said proudly. Silently, I prayed this trip would ignite the spark that had gone missing.

"What about the money? Are you going to tell me?"

"Yes, I'll tell you. Will you tell me about Benedetti and Fairchild?"

"Yes, I'll tell you."

In order to demonstrate good faith and that I was the adult in the room, I spoke first. I told him Tito Sanz had checked into a motel not far from our home. I also told him of my fear that he would try to pick us off with a high-powered rifle. He listened intently as I described the purchase of drugs. His neck started to redden again, but I continued. Since he asked, I was committed to the whole truth. I left nothing out. The recounting of the telephone conversation with Detective Doran, the placing of the drugs in Tito's room, and the subsequent arrest captivated his attention. As I told my story, I re-positioned myself on my knees between his legs, placing my hands on his thighs.

"Wow," Adrian exclaimed when I finished my story. "Tell me, Milagros, why did you feel the need to go through such an elaborate and dangerous mission?"

"I felt sorry for his mother. She shouldn't have to lose another son."

"I've been with you too long. I understand your logic."

"There is something else, Adrian."

"I don't know if I can take any more. Mrs. Z, you should confess on a more regular basis so you don't overwhelm your father confessor."

"Well, father confessor, the money issue is another matter. The catamaran is worth a lot more than fifty Gs. She is hooked up nicely, baby."

"Where did the money for the drugs come from," Adrian asked, alarmed.

"It was courtesy of Ed Gonzalez."

"Oh, no, the safe deposit box," Adrian shouted, the redness creeping to his face.

"Yes, that's right, Adrian," I agreed quickly.

Fuck it. He doesn't need all the details now. He admitted he was overwhelmed.

"Milagros, is this following us here to Luna Llena?"

"No. But, Adrian, that's a whole other story. I want to hear your story."

"Not so fast, Mrs. Z. What role did Richard play in this drama?"

Oh, oh!

"He did as I ordered him to do. Adrian, please don't take your anger out on him," I pleaded.

"I'm not angry, baby," he said in a soft tone. "I won't retaliate against Richard. I value his loyalty towards you. You know the kind of loyalty that Hilda has towards me."

Ah, yes, Hilda.

"What about Hilda, Adrian? I know she is loyal to you."

"She feels you are retaliating against her because she fills me in on everything having to do with this house."

"I'm not retaliating against her. I enjoy cooking for my husband and children. Quite frankly, Adrian," I said with some indignation, "I think it's my duty to be present at breakfast when my children are being fed. And since I'm up, I might as well fix their breakfast. Feeding you has always been a pleasure for me. I am your wife."

"I know you're my wife." Again he spoke softly. "Baby, I love you and appreciate your efforts in the kitchen. I especially enjoy our interactions in the morning with the children. You are a good mother and wife. This isn't about me. It's about Hilda and her feelings."

"I already told you I am not retaliating against her. What is it that I'm doing to offend her?"

"I believe you, baby. I'll handle Hilda. Will you do me one favor?" he asked again in a soft, loving voice.

"Sure, Adrian, what is it?"

"Don't stop your ritual in the mornings with me and the children. I couldn't bear it now if you stopped." I looked into his glassy eyes and my heart melted.

"I will never stop," I said, cradling his face in my hands. We kissed chastely. I inhaled him in as we did.

"Mrs. Z," Adrian spoke in the same soft voice, "Benedetti and Fairchild are intent on proving you or I hacked their computers. They are intent on destroying Casa Imperially, Bodegas Rodrigo and Luna Llena. If it takes a lifetime, they vowed."

"Oh, no," I blurted out. There would never be peace for us. "Do you think this is my fault?"

"No, not entirely, it's mostly my fault." His voice was almost a whisper now. "I brought this upon us. My loyalty for Juan Carlos has put many people in jeopardy."

"How so, Adrian," I asked.

"Now, Paula is also involved. They have their sights on her as well. God knows, she has been through enough."

"But why would they retaliate against her?"

"They know Casa Imperially is connected to us and Juan Carlos. They were able to link you, Isabel and Daisy by doing background checks."

"What can we do, Adrian?"

"They asked me not to help Juan Carlos any longer or they will continue their search for proof against you or me and seek our destruction."

"They will find no proof, because there is none," I offered. Adrian knew Sarah and I caused the glitch that prevented Benedetti/Fairchild from making deliveries to distribution centers. He also knew that we had covered our tracks through an inexhaustible labyrinth of networks. Ultimately, my African prince would be accused, but not held accountable since he too was savvy in his ways.

"Can you set up protection for all our computers, including Juan Carlos'?"

"You know I can, baby," I said excitedly.

Finally something I can sink my teeth into. Sharpen my geek skills.

"Then do so," Adrian ordered. "Milagros, I can't turn my back on Juan Carlos. He is like a brother to me. He helped me in my darkest hours when I first became blind. I just can't do it. The time Benedetti and Fairchild are expecting me to turn on Juan Carlos is rapidly approaching. Baby, I just can't do it."

"I don't expect you to turn your back on him. We can do this together. If I may suggest something," I added cautiously.

"What?"

"Go public. Announce to the world the birth of your wine conglomeration. Officially merge the companies and announce it to the world."

"That is an interesting concept," Adrian said, pondering the idea. "Millie, that could provoke them further."

"Assume the offensive position. The message you'll be sending is you're ready for war. Here we are united and strong. They will have to make the first move, risk being caught and exposed for the bullies that they are."

"Again, baby, we've been together too long. I can understand your logic. Let me give it some more thought, but I like it."

"Do you want to take the children upstairs for their nap?"

"That sounds like a good idea," he said too willingly. "I feel I want to have my way with you."

"That sounds delicious, Mr. Z."

"But, Milagros," he said, taking my face in his hands and bringing it close to his own, "I'm going to want satisfaction first. You have been extremely bad."

"But, Adrian," I pleaded, "I'm pregnant."

"You're the one who said, 'Pregnant wives don't break.'"

Shit! I have a big mouth and he has a memory like a steel trap. But it's all good.

Adrian placed the sleeping Angelique in her playpen. Adam too had dosed off and I placed him in his crib. Adrian reached out for me and I walked into his embrace.

He whispered in my ear, "Are you ready?"

"Would it help my cause if I said no?"

"Not really. So are you ready?"

"Yes," I replied in a small voice.

Taking me by the hand, he led me to the dressing room, stopping at the dressing table. He backed me into the counter top, placing his arms on top of the counter effectively fencing me in.

"Now, Mrs. Z, I want you to remove your clothes."

"Step back, Adrian. Give me a little room."

"No."

"Then, help me with the zipper."

"No, we've been down this road before, Milagros. You're not getting away with your tricks again. Understood?" he said while gazing down in my direction. I could feel his hot breath on me. I was already turned on, but what the heck, I was willing to play.

Let's see how much you can tolerate, Mr. Z.

"OK, Adrian," I said in a small voice.

Since I was trapped with very little room to move, I gingerly brought my arms up and behind to grab the zipper of my dress. I stretched and as I did my elbow caught Adrian in the chin.

"Oops, I'm sorry," I apologized, looking up at him. His lips were parted slightly smiling.

I pulled down the zipper all the while looking at Adrian. No doubt I was amusing him. Instead of pulling the dress down from my shoulders, I opted to lift it from the hem to above and over my head. Doing so this time caused me to brush against Adrian's chin with my little fist. I looked at him and he was sporting a half-cocked smile. He briefly bit his lower lip. Now I was amused.

He inched closer, tightening the space around me. Leaning down he whispered in my ear, "Hurry, before I lose my patience."

I could feel his hot breath on my neck. It felt divine. Not heeding his warning, I slowly brought my arms around to the back of the bra. I leaned forward to better grip and unfasten the hooks. In doing so I bumped my head against Adrian's chin.

"Bump my chin one more time and you won't be able to sit for a week," he warned. I looked but his facial expression had not changed. His lips were still parted in a halfcocked smile. His tongue came out to moisten his lips. Gee, he was sexy. I couldn't help myself, so I stood on the tips of my toes to give him a love bite on his jaw.

"Stop that," he growled in a throaty voice, "you'll receive no mercy from me."

Again I looked into his face. He was still amused.

"Hurry I said," he growled in the same husky voice. "Take off your bra and panties before I rip them off."

If he was trying to frighten me, it wasn't working. Now all I wanted was for him to rip them off, hurl me onto the bed and give me a good thrashing about. Holding my bra to my chest, I slowly slipped one strap off my shoulder, then the other. I was prepared to give him a show. He would not be able to see, but I knew he was able to sense and mentally picture my every move.

Adrian suddenly straightened. Placing one hand in his pocket, he brought out his pocketknife. I gasped in horror. He felt for my panties, cut one side, then the other. He slipped his hand in between my legs, grabbing the crotch of the panties and discarding them onto the floor. I gasped again. Now he reached to my chest. With one hand he grabbed my hand and with the other hand he clutched the bra and tossed it to the floor. He placed the pocketknife away again in his pocket. Adrian bent over, flinging me over his shoulder. I protested to no avail; the man was on his way to the bedroom.

He tossed my naked body onto the bed ordering, "Don't move and keep your eyes opened. Do you understand?"

"Yes," I panted.

His facial expression had changed from amused to more pensive as if giving thought to what he was going to do next. I was wet with anticipation. Adrian was very creative.

My man began to take off his own clothes. His moves were slow and deliberate. It was he who was now putting on a show for me. He unfastened one button at a time while gazing in my direction. Off came his shirt. It was tossed with much attitude onto the floor. His tee shirt came off and it too was tossed onto the floor. Slowly he undid the belt buckle and slower yet removed it from the loops of his slacks. Once removed, he folded the belt and with precision tossed it on the bed next to me. I swallowed hard.

"Hold on to the belt, Milagros. Do you understand?"

"Yes, I understand, but why, Adrian?"

"Just do it, don't ask questions," he barked.

I was done with this game. I was hot and bothered and wanted him badly.

"Baby, I want you badly," I begged. "Touch me, I'm ready for you."

"I don't have to touch you to know you're ready for me," he said in a sultry voice. "Don't speak again, Milagros."

What can I do to get even?

Adrian was fully naked. Adonis had nothing on him. He approached the bed where he had tossed me crosswise. One hand gently caressed my inner thigh, then the other joined caressing the other inner thigh. His fingers found their way to the apex of my sex. The gentle stroking intensified my arousal and my body responded.

"Don't move," he barked again as he slapped the side of my hip with one hand. "Are you still holding the belt?"

"Yes, I am," I responded in a throaty voice. He smiled.

"Don't lie to me, Milagros."

"I'm not, I promise it's right here in my hand." I lifted it to show him. He smiled again. Of course he couldn't see.

"Open your legs for me, baby, expose yourself."

How can a few words excite me like this?

I did as I was told.

He placed one knee on the bed in between my legs. His hands again felt for me.

"Baby, open wider," came the soft command from my man.

I did as I was told. My heart was beating at a rapid pace, my chest heaving. I could barely breathe. The blood rushed to the inner walls of my sex, causing swelling and a pulsating sensation.

Adrian leaned down to kiss my inner thighs, working his way to my sex. The assault began slow and gentle. He slipped two fingers inside to stroke that very special place he had become very familiar with. His tongue became more aggressive as did his stroking. It didn't take long. I felt the wave of convulsions take over as I climaxed.

"Oh, Adrian," I exclaimed as I tried to close my legs to stop the assault. He kept them parted.

"Don't you want me inside, baby?"

"Yes, I do."

He proceeded to kiss, lick and nip lightly at my skin as he journeyed up, paying close attention to the breasts. Finally, he eased his massive erection into me. It filled all of me, bringing pleasure and anxiety all at once. Without breaking our connection, he lifted me onto his lap as he sat back on his heels. He continued thrusting inside me. I answered each thrust with my own. The friction against that special sweet spot caused my insides to swell and contract again.

"Adrian, I can't hold on," I warned.

"Come for me, baby, let me feel you."

The pulsating turned into the familiar wave of convulsion as I climaxed once again. Adrian gently placed me back on the bed and he went for his own relief. We lay in each others embrace until our breathing returned to normal. A nap was in order.

When I awoke I found myself still in Adrian's arms. My stirring woke him. He hugged me tight, kissing the top of my head and discovered I was still clutching the belt in my hand. He took it from me and tossed it onto the floor.

"Silly girl," he said, laughing.

Chapter 8

Cryptic messages were sent back and forth between Juan Carlos, Paula and Adrian. Everyone agreed with going public. Casa Imperially would officially be bought by Adrian and kept as a subsidiary company, running independently under the leadership of Paula. Domestically, Casa Imperially would distribute to its old distribution friends rather than directly to retailers. Paula would continue handling sales between Argentina, the U. S., Europe and China.

Bodega Rodrigo became a subsidiary of Viñas Rodriguez, which also owned Bodega Elena. Bodega Rodrigo and Bodega Elena, at the appropriate time, would announce it would sell exclusively through Casa Imperially. All the companies became a neatly tied package without excluding independent distributors. This was sure not to sit well with Benedetti/Fairchild.

I went to work protecting all of our computers. This is to say, I supplemented the protection that was already there. Everyone who worked for Adrian and used a computer received an instructional e-mail on daily routines they should perform for safety. One hour before the end of the day, I checked all computers remotely, removing all suspicious attachments, cookies, etc. All computers were powered down when not in use. Communications between Luna Llena, her subsidiary companies and business associates were constant. So I wrote a special program that would alert me of any new contacts. It wasn't unusual to receive solicitations from various vendors offering a myriad of products or from organizations making some sort of request, but from now on those communications would be routed to me where I alone would screen them.

Adrian was specific in his request that only new contacts be screened. Clearly he did not want his privacy invaded by me. I did, however, add Benedetti and Fairchild to my list. Juan Carlos, on the other hand, did not care and gave me free reign.

Who communicates with Adrian that he doesn't want me to know?

"Hi, Adrian."

"How are my wife and children?"

"We are fine, missing you very much."

"I should be home by seven. Will you wait for me to have dinner?"

"Of course, I will wait for you. But why will you be home by seven?"

"I need to make a quick stop. I also made arrangements for us to leave for Tahiti this Friday. When I get home we need to discuss some logistics. I have to go now," Adrian said, effectively dismissing me and avoiding any follow-up questions.

"I love you. See you when you get home." With that I sent him a kiss and hung up. There was no use pursuing the question. If he felt like it, he would tell me and if he didn't he wouldn't. But I was happy about Tahiti.

I went into the kitchen carrying Adam and holding Angelique by the hand.

"Ilda," Angelique screeched for Hilda's attention, leaving the 'H' out. Hilda promptly stopped what she was doing by the stove, ran to

Angelique, scooping her up in her arms. She then turned her attention to Adam, slobbering kisses all over him.

"Hmm, something smells good," I commented.

"I hope you don't mind, Millie. I made a lamb stew, enough for everyone."

"Why should I mind, Hilda? I love your lamb stew." Since my talk with Adrian, I was trying to be nicer and more understanding. I still didn't care for her reporting on my every move, but I was learning to cope.

"Adrian will be home by seven," I continued. "I want to feed the children so that I can bathe them before Adrian gets home."

"Would you like some help feeding them?"

"If you're not busy with the stew, I could use the help."

We sat each child in their high chairs, making small talk as they ate.

By the time Adrian reached home, everyone except me had dinner. Adrian and I sat in the kitchen. On the other side of the kitchen and the island was a long, antique oak table with matching chairs. This is where we had our informal dinners when the weather was too cool for dining out on the patio. As usual we sat next to each other, rather than across or adjacent. Adrian draped his left arm around the back of my chair while we ate. Once in a while, if the spirit moved him, he would tenderly stroke my hair if it was loose or the nape of my neck if I wore it up. Tonight Adrian made small talk wanting to discuss the upcoming baseball season. He predicted my team would again be disappointing. I called him an ass.

"Would you like coffee?" I asked.

"Yes, thank you, I would. Are the children asleep, I can't hear them?"

"Yes, they are asleep."

"While you prepare the coffee, I'll take them upstairs and put them to bed."

I served the coffee in the family room where our favorite guitar music of Paco de Lucia and Al DiMeola filled the room.

"The coffee smells delicious," Adrian said, giving one of his broad sexy smiles.

"Thank you," I responded. "I served us chocolate cake I made earlier. There is whipped cream on top with sliced strawberries."

"Hmm, baby, this is delicious," Adrian crooned. Chocolate was his favorite. Adding fruit made it all that much more delectable for him.

"I'm happy you like it."

"Millie, I want to discuss our trip." He jumped right into business.

I'd rather discuss your quick stop.

"I'm excited, Adrian," I blurted. Truth is I couldn't wait to get away.

"There is a logistical problem for me."

"Really?" I asked, "Like what?"

"I don't feel comfortable taking a maiden voyage on the catamaran with the children. They are much too young and if something were to happen, I am afraid I would be of no use in rescuing them. The thought terrifies me." I could see the terror on his face.

My heart sank, thinking this was his way of canceling our trip.

"What can we do, Adrian?" I asked, afraid of what he might say.

"I know I have made it a point in the past that no one would stay with us while we were in Tahiti," he began, "but we could use the help with the children." He paused but I did not comment.

"Would you mind," he continued, "if I asked Hilda to join us? She can sit on the beach with the children while you and I take the cat out for the first time." I was so relieved I could have cried.

"No, Adrian, I don't mind," I exclaimed joyously. "That is a great suggestion." We faced each other for a while before Adrian lifted me off my knees onto his lap. The assault that followed made me forget his quick stop.

The weather in Tahiti was warm during the day with temperatures dipping into the low seventies at night. It was the rainy season, so we had brief showers most days.

The first order of business was to pick up 'Betty Boop,' Adrian's name for his cat, from the marina and sail her to the private beach where our house was located. We stayed docked at the marina while Adrian acquainted himself with the boat. He turned on the audible sonar, taking his time to familiarize himself with it. The salesman went over a few things with both of us and offered to take us out for a trial run, but Adrian thanked him, telling him we would be fine.

My man is ready to take the helm. His broad smile tells me he is ready and eager to take her out.

Adrian sat at the helm and started the eight-horsepower engine. With my guidance, he set the controls on reverse and the cat eased out of its slip. I informed him when we were clear of the slip. He slowly turned the tiller so the boat now faced the open water. Adrian set the controls to move forward. Once we cleared the marina and were out in open water, he cut off the engine and lifted it from the water. Single handed he hoisted the sail and we were off. 'Betty Boop' sailed gracefully over the calm waters. Her sail filled with the propelling wind. The sun caressed our faces while the warm sea breeze embraced us. Adrian positioned me between his legs where I could lean back against his chest. He leaned into me to kiss my hair. Neither one of us uttered a word until the approach to our beach.

"Adrian, I can see our house," I exclaimed excitedly. "Hilda and the children are on the beach. It is to your left," I informed him, expecting our journey to end.

"Baby, let's go a little further. I'm getting the feel for the controls."

"OK, but not too far, it's getting late. Would you like to take Hilda and the kids for a ride?"

"I'll go ten minutes further out, and then we can turn back." He was all smiles. "I would love to take them out for a ride."

That is exactly what we did. We sailed for another ten minutes before heading back to the house. Adrian eased the cat by the shore where I let down the anchor.

We boarded Hilda and the children and we were off again. Hilda loved the ride, warm breeze and scenery. She praised Adrian's skillful handling of the cat. I, too, joined in the accolade of my husband. I sat in between his legs. It was simply perfect. Overwhelmed with love and gratitude for this moment, I turned towards Adrian, placing my arms around his neck to kiss him. He laughed out loud and returned the kiss.

"Stop that, Millie," he whispered. "You're making me hard. Our family is on board. I can't concentrate."

"Oh, all right," I replied, resuming my original position of leaning against him and I could feel his dilemma.

The salty air rendered Angelique and Adam sleepy. It was time to head back.

Adrian sailed 'Betty Boop' up to the beach in front of a boathouse adjacent to the house. Adrian and I helped Hilda take the children onto the beach before turning our attention to 'Betty Boop.' Adrian used an outside hose to wash away the salt water. With a remote control, the two hulls came together under the boat and, with the help of a winch, we guided 'Betty Boop' onto a trailer and secured her. The mast came down so she could fit into the boathouse. Again using a winch, she was tucked away.

Closing the doors to the boathouse, Adrian commented, "When I bought this property for you, I never imagined we would be using the boathouse."

"There is enough room to store the jet skis, flotation devices and other toys we might acquire," I added.

"Knowing you, I'm sure there will be other toys. Thank you, Millie. I had a great time today." We kissed, and then he continued, "Would you like to go for a swim?" He was sporting that big broad smile I could not resist.

We walked back into the water and swam to one of the timbers under the house.

"Are we alone?" he asked.

"Yes, we are," I answered. "Hilda and the children are on the beach on the other side of the house. And it looks like the three are napping."

"That's good, Mrs. Z, because I want to take you hear and now." I felt his erection as we kissed. Adrian removed my bikini and his bathing suit, tying them together with the biking top. He grabbed on to the ropes that were tied to the timber pinning me against the log.

"Wrap your legs around me," he ordered, "and hold on tight. I am taking you for a ride."

Much to my delight, Adrian extended our stay in Tahiti by another week. We spent our days languishing on the beachfront property, riding the jet skis, sailing 'Betty Boop' and sightseeing with Hilda and the children. Eventually, Adrian became more comfortable having Hilda, Angelique and Adam on 'Betty Boop.' He was a skilled sailor, requiring very little of my guidance.

One evening after dinner a storm rolled in. Hilda nervously asked Adrian if it was safe to stay in the house.

"I think so, Vieja," he responded affectionately. "Besides, if anything happens you won't know, you'll be asleep."

"Very funny," she retorted, pulling out her rosary beads before continuing. "If you don't care for me, your wife or yourself, you should think of your children."

"Think of it, Vieja," he teased. "We will be in heaven together."

"Adrian, stop it," I admonished. "Can't you see she is upset? Hilda, don't listen to him. We are perfectly safe here."

"OK, OK, Millie, let's entertain the family." Adrian gave me my guitar and sat next to me with his. We played our favorite tunes, which helped to ease Hilda's anxiety that had been brought on by the thunder and lightning. The children fell asleep and Hilda soon started to doze off. She bid us a good night and went to her bedroom. The night was humid, but the breeze coming in from the open windows cooled the temperature inside the house. Adrian and I bundled Angelique and Adam to keep them warm. We, however, slept as usual, naked. The storm outside started to subside with only an occasional clap of thunder. Adrian and I were asleep when I thought I heard a crackling noise outside by the tree-lined area of the beach. I sat up with a jolt, waking Adrian.

"What's wrong, baby?" he asked sleepily.

"I thought I heard someone outside."

"It was probably a branch breaking and falling to the ground."

"No, I don't think so," I asserted, fumbling for my firearm.

"Shh, baby," Adrian ordered. "Let's listen," he continued while wrapping his arms around me. "You secured this house like a fortress."

We listened in silence for a few minutes. Another clap of thunder sounded in the distance. More silence. Then I heard it again. This time the cracking sound was accompanied by a rustling in the wooded area. I jumped out of bed in the darkness, Glock in hand, and went to the open window, concealing myself behind the curtain. A few yards away, on the other side of the wooded area by the road, an engine roared and I saw the taillights of a car go on as it rolled away towards the main road.

"What is it, Millie? Was that the engine of a car? Is someone here?" Adrian whispered as he came up to the window behind me.

"There was someone here. I saw the taillights of a car. I wonder why they didn't come up to the house?"

"Here," Adrian said, handing me a flashlight.

"Oh, I see why they didn't come up."

"What do you see, baby?"

"The water has risen to the back of the beach, almost to the wooded area. The ramp to the house is hidden by the water. Adrian, it's like the house was surrounded by a moat." We both laughed.

"It's a good thing Hilda is asleep." Adrian laughed some more.

"Adrian, seriously, who could that have been?"

"I don't know. Maybe we will find out tomorrow."

"It's well past midnight. I don't think I want to be around to find out who was calling on us at this hour." My mind jolted to my New York concerns and Adrian's wine adversaries.

The peace and tranquility was nice while it lasted.

"Would you like to go home tomorrow?"

"Maybe we should go home. We have many loose ends that need tending to," I offered.

"I'll make the arrangements," Adrian said as he walked to the dresser to retrieve his telephone.

"Adrian, why have you kept your cell phone off all the time we've been here?"

"I didn't want to be bothered. I told my staff to email me if they needed anything or if something important came up. I check my emails daily."

"Good thinking, Mr. Z."

Chapter 9

We drove directly to Luna Llena from the airport. Usually after a long trip we would spend a night or two at the penthouse in San Francisco, so that Adrian could catch up with work at the office. Adrian said he was anxious to be home and work could wait. That was a bit out of the ordinary for him, but I was glad to go home.

We all went to bed early. It had been a long day. After three hours of sleep, I woke. Adrian and the children were sleeping soundly. The thought of the previous night visitor was bothering me. Who knew we were in Tahiti? Who would care to follow us there? And what was their intent? Then again, maybe it was nothing.

I put on my robe and went to my office. There was no particular reason for going to the office, but since I couldn't sleep I might as well do some work. As I descended the stairs towards the office, I heard a ping on my smart phone. It was alerting me of new activities. All new contacts trying to communicate with anyone associated with Luna Llena and its subsidiaries were routed to my computer. It was the only computer active 24/7.

There was one email for Adrian from an Abe Nussbaum, requesting a meeting for the purpose of discussing real estate investments. He stated in his email that a prospectus was in the mail. Attached to his email was an impressive list of clients. Also attached was a list of prominent investors endorsing Mr. Nussbaum's product. Adrian would know what to do with this.

The email had a time stamp of seven-thirty in the morning, which was odd since it was only five in the morning in New York. Mr. Nussbaum is savvy trying to disguise an ulterior motive. I immediately searched the backdoor to my computer. A backdoor is a computer programmer's way to access files without going through normal channels. Mr. Nussbaum was at my backdoor trying to access files. There was no doubt that he thought this was Adrian's computer. Since this was not my personal computer, it was loaded with viruses for anyone trying to access the computer through the backdoor. One virus in particular could fry Mr. Nussbaum's computer.

"Millie, where are you?" Adrian asked as he entered the office wearing a matching robe.

"I'm at my desk, baby. What are you doing up?"

"I woke and you weren't beside me. I wanted some comforting."

"Hmm, Mr. Z, you are insatiable."

"What are you doing up?" he repeated.

"I received an alert on my smart phone that a new contact was trying to communicate."

"Oh," he exclaimed walking around my desk. "What do they want at this hour?"

"It's an attorney associated with Ed Gonzalez back in New York, Mr. Abe Nussbaum. He sent you an email requesting a meeting to discuss real estate investments. He also says he sent you a prospectus. Anyway, you can listen in a minute," I informed Adrian. "In the meantime, I noticed the email had a time stamp of seven-thirty in the morning, so I went to work and found that Mr. Nussbaum was trying to access my computer through the backdoor."

"What surprises do you have there?"

My man knows me well.

"This computer is loaded with nasty stuff if the backdoor is violated," I said as I looked at Adrian. His eyebrows were knitted and lips pursed. "His computer should be toast about now," I continued. "If it isn't, Mr. Nussbaum will be busy until the wee hours of the morning. He won't be trying this again."

Adrian smiled at that thought.

"Well done, Mrs. Z," Adrian said with stretched out arms. I stood to walk into his waiting arms. "Mrs. Z, you have some explaining to do about how it is that you know Mr. Nussbaum. I have not heard that name before."

"It's the other half of that other story I was telling you, remember?" I asked, looking up at him feigning innocence.

"Ah, yes, I do remember. The story you never finished telling," he breathed, kissing my hair. "Right now I would like to explore a backdoor. Will you join me in our dressing room?"

I knew exactly what that meant.

"I would love to."

Mr. Nussbaum was either a very clever computer geek or employed one. Either way, I had to be careful. Hacking him was not an option. Surveillance and research would have to suffice. I called Ralph White.

"Hi, Ralph, it's Millie Zaragosa," I said.

"Mrs. Zaragosa, how are you."

"Ralph, please call me Millie. I wanted to know how my friend Sam was doing."

"His girlfriend just had a baby. He has been laying low keeping busy with his girlfriend, new baby and the warehouse."

"Has he had any visitors or visited anyone?"

"His visitors are the same friends and family, no change there. He did pay a visit to an attorney named Nussbaum. It was probably in connection with his brothers who are behind bars, one in upstate New York and the other in your neck of the woods."

"When did he visit this attorney?"

"The visit was last week. It lasted thirty minutes."

"Sam didn't leave the country, did he?"

"No, I would have notified you. Millie, is there a problem?"

"No, Ralph, there isn't, I was just curious. Can you keep an eye on Mr. Nussbaum as well?"

"I can put one of my guys on him immediately if you want."

"I would like that very much, Ralph. Tell your man I want to know his every move."

"You got it, Millie."

"One other thing, Ralph, have your guy investigate who works in his office."

"You'll have that information soon," Ralph assured me.

Adrian busied himself with work. The deadline with Benedetti and Fairchild was in a few weeks. News releases were prepared to go out simultaneously for all the companies. Communications between the companies remained on the cryptic level until the news releases made public their relationship.

My investigations on our night visitors in Tahiti lead me nowhere. Everyone on my watch list was accounted for on the night in question. Of course someone not known to me could have been hired to pay us a visit. So, I tightened security once again. Adrian resisted but finally gave in without too much of a fuss.

We resumed training at the firing range. All the bodyguards took turns at the firing range under my supervision. I convinced Adrian to have his personal trainer, who was an accomplished martial arts teacher, train everyone in self-defense. Richard, Frank and Tony were not too much of a concern because they were physically fit and had self-defense training. They welcomed the new challenge. My main concern was Roger. He was Adrian's personal bodyguard. He was loyal and fierce like a pit bull, but he was a little flabby around the middle and had little to no experience in martial arts. He resisted attending the training exercises.

Hector was the only person excused from this particular training, much to his relief.

I had set up the first training session to take place in the gym at seven in the morning.

"Millie," Adrian called, "can you help me look for my sweat pants?"

"They are on the dressing table. I put them there for you."

"Thanks, baby. I'll meet you in the kitchen for breakfast after our training."

"I thought I would join you for the training. Not that I need training, but I could use the workout."

"No, Milagros, you will not be joining us."

"Why can't I join you, Adrian?" I asked indignantly.

"For one thing, you are pregnant. Second, I don't want men getting physical with you, and the third reason is you have a family to take care of."

"But Adrian," I protested, but he didn't let me finish.

"No, I said, no," he barked loudly, startling me.

"Fine," I replied in a small voice.

I was hurt and feeling dejected. It reminded me of our first fights when I came to work for him at Luna Llena. I had fought him tooth and nail to establish myself as a capable director of security regardless of my gender. Eventually I learned that his motives in hiring me were personal, but I refused to let that get in the way of performing my duties. Adrian made great strides towards listening to my direction when it came to his safety and that of our children, but apparently not enough. I would not be joining in on the training.

At eight, the children and I were in the kitchen. Hilda and I were busy feeding the children and talking when Adrian made his presence felt. Hilda could tell I was upset with him.

"Millie, can I take the children out on the patio for some fresh air?" she asked.

"That sounds like a good idea, Hilda. Thank you." I stood to get Adrian his coffee.

"Adrian, what would you like for breakfast?"

"I'll have whatever you are having."

"I haven't had anything yet. I was waiting for you."

He turned in his chair to face me and stretched out his arms. I walked into his embrace.

"Sit on my lap," he ordered.

I did as I was told.

"Don't be angry. I love you and I am concerned about your condition. But the fact still remains," he said while rubbing my belly, "I don't like the idea of men, not even the ones we know, putting their hands on you. Call me old fashioned but I can't help how I feel.

"Baby, I know you can take care of yourself. You could kick everyone's ass that was there this morning. At the appropriate time, after you give birth, I promise you'll get back in the gym."

"OK," I said in a soft voice.

"Do you still love me?"

"Yes, Adrian, I still love you. What would you like for breakfast? You're going to be late for work and I wouldn't want you to get in trouble with your boss."

"Funny lady." Adrian laughed. "Give me a kiss."

I did as I was told.

"Can you make oatmeal with the mascarpone cheese and strawberries for breakfast?"

"Sure thing. Coming right up, Mr. Z."

Chapter 10

The weather was getting warmer and once again the time had come to resume our meals out on the patio. Adrian and I both looked forward to eating outside. The scenery was spectacular. The grounds at Luna Llena were my favorite things about living here. The flowers had started to bloom in the rose garden. The lawns were lush green. Mother Nature was doing her best work. Adrian, of course, could not see but did remember how it looked. For many years since the loss of his eyesight, the landscaper and gardeners went through great pains to maintain the grounds to his specification. Just the way he remembered them. Hilda and Hector made sure they complied.

Adrian was in San Francisco for the day and I had done as much work as I could by noon. I decided to go to the supermarket to find ingredients for dinner. Our first dinner of the season out on the patio would be cooked by me.

"Hilda, can you watch the children for a couple of hours after lunch," I asked.

"Sure, Millie," she replied, not asking why or where I was going. I was grateful she was respecting my space. Besides, she couldn't report to Adrian what she didn't know.

"I want to cook for Adrian tonight," I volunteered.

"I'm sure he will love that," she offered.

"I hope so. Richard will accompany me to the supermarket for a few things. Would you like me to pick up something for you?"

"No, Millie, thank you. What are you making for dinner?"

"I was thinking of paella."

"I know Adrian is going to love it. It will be a nice surprise."

That was her way of telling me she was not going to inform Adrian. I was so overwhelmed by her gesture, I hugged and kissed her.

Richard drove us in the Corvette to the supermarket. As I shopped, he followed a few feet behind to keep an eye on me and on our surroundings.

"Richard," I called.

"Yes, Mrs. Z," he responded coming nearer.

"Can you help me look for some of these ingredients?"

"What would you like me to look for?"

"Sometimes the supermarkets place fresh chorizo in the meat department and sometimes in the deli department. Other times, they will place the dry chorizo in the international aisle. Can you ask at the courtesy desk where the fresh ones might be?"

"I'll be right back."

He was gone for a few minutes when a geeky-looking young man approached my shopping cart and nudged it into my belly. Startled, I looked at him.

"Well, well, if it isn't Ms. Milagros Angeles Zaragosa," he spat out.

"Do I know you?" I asked.

ISABEL PIETRI

"No, but I know you," he answered, walking around the shopping cart. He made the mistake of extending his hand towards me and the intention was not to shake my hand. I reacted faster than I could think. Using his hand as leverage, I simply pushed it back against itself. He landed on his stomach while I held his arm straight up behind him. My black, patent-leather, stiletto-heeled left foot was on his neck.

"Don't move, dip-shit," I warned as I bent to search his back pockets, "or I'll break your arm." Richard was already racing down the aisle towards me.

"Are you all right?" he asked with a horrified look on his face.

"I'm fine. This idiot bumped my stomach with the cart and then presumed to know me. I didn't take kindly to that." Richard snickered in that way he did when he approved of something. I pulled out dip-shit's wallet from the back pocket.

"Mrs. Z, please let me take over," Richard pleaded.

I slowly straightened up, holding the wallet with my free hand.

"Richard," I spoke softly, beckoning him closer. I whispered in his ear, "Go outside and call Mr. Z. Tell him to power down all computers, including Luna Llena, Juan Carlos and Paula. I'll take care of this dirtbag until you get back."

Richard looked conflicted as to what to do, but he did as I asked. I lifted my foot off the neck of dip-shit and let go of his arm. I took a few steps away from him to create distance.

"Stand up," I demanded. He did as he was told.

"Empty out your pockets," I ordered. There was some loose change and car keys.

"Keep the loose change and toss the car keys on the floor by my feet."

"Hey, you can't do that," dip-shit protested.

"I can do anything I want. I seem to have the upper hand here, not you. If you do something stupid, I'll have you back on the floor," I informed him as I went through his wallet. I pulled out his driver's license.

THE BLACK CALLA LILY

"Your name is Richard Simmons?" I blurted out. "You have got to be shitting me." My Richard was back again and snickered.

"People call me Dick," he volunteered a little more humbly.

"I can see why," I responded. My Richard laughed outright this time.

"So, Mr. Richard Simmons, what is it you want with me?"

"I wanted to offer my services to you."

"Really? That was a strange way of introducing yourself."

"It's not every day one meets a master hacker."

My Richard looked at me surprised.

I wonder, what does he think Sarah does?

"What services are you looking to offer, Mr. Richard Simmons?"

"Information," he declared.

"What kind of information, Mr. Richard Simmons?"

"I've been asked to hack into you and your husband's computers."

"Who asked you to do that?"

"Mr. Benedetti."

"Why does he want you to hack our computers?"

"He wants to prove one of you hacked into his business."

"And what have you come up with?"

"Nothing, yet," he offered.

"Where did you go to school, Mr. Richard Simmons?"

"Berkeley."

"Ha, a BQS," I retorted. BQS stands for Berkeley Quality System, which is a sarcastic reference to college programmers.

"Mrs. Zaragosa, I don't care for this Benedetti guy," Mr. Richard Simmons responded, ignoring my comment. "I would like to work for you and your husband."

"Would you now," I said thoughtfully before continuing, "Here is the thing, Mr. Richard Simmons. You are being disloyal. I suggest you go back to Mr. Benedetti and do the best possible job you can. Maybe someday, if you redeem yourself, I'll consider you and your talents."

"Give me back my wallet and car keys," he barked, obviously upset that I didn't bite.

"No, Mr. Richard Simmons. I will mail them to you. You better go now. It's a long way back to San Francisco and I don't want you hitchhiking at night. It's not safe. Richard, can you escort Mr. Richard Simmons out the door and make sure he doesn't remove anything from his vehicle." Richard escorted Richard Simmons out of the supermarket.

Richard and I ransacked Richard Simmons' car. In the back seat was an active laptop. Richard Simmons was running a program soliciting through email. He was running another program searching for back doors.

Mr. Richard Simmons had hoped to keep me busy while his computer did the dirty work. I terminated all the programs he was running, not because they were dangerous; clearly this was amateur stuff, but because I wanted to search his computer.

There was a wealth of information. Mr. Richard Simmons was kind enough to supply a flash drive. I copied all the files of interest to the flash drive and then ran a program to my computer, attempting to go through the backdoor and bingo, his computer was toast.

I felt sorry for Mr. Richard Simmons. Hitchhiking was dangerous and the poor soul was without money or identification. Richard followed me as I drove Mr. Richard Simmons' car in search of him. He was not too far down the road trying to thumb a ride. He was glad to have his vehicle back as well as his wallet. The computer, he knew instinctively, was a lost cause. What he didn't know was that his vehicle would take him only a short distance before all four tires went flat.

I need time to get back home and do some work before he can get to a computer and cause more mischief.

By the time Adrian returned home, the children were fed; the computers to all the companies associated with Luna Llena were protected and cleared for business for the next day. I had showered and changed into a sexy silk shift that was designed by Grace DaSilva, who was my go-to designer for all my maternity needs. Dinner was almost done, waiting for the final touches.

Adrian entered through the kitchen and instead of Hilda, I greeted him.

"Hi, Baby. Where is Hilda?" he asked.

"She is in her suite relaxing."

"Oh?"

"Yes, she is relaxing. I cooked and your children are waiting for you to hug and kiss them," I said as I handed Angelique first over to him. Then it was Adam's turn.

"Now, my big girl," Adrian turned to me with outstretched arms.

I walked into his arms, where we exchanged a long passionate kiss.

I could have been angry that he expected Hilda and that he seemed disappointed, but the kiss made up for his transgression.

Dinner was a gustatory delight, according to Adrian. The shrimp, lobster, mussels and clams were cooked to perfection. The wine, an Albariño from Adrian's estate, was the finishing touch. Dessert was one of Adrian's favorites, a homemade vanilla flan topped with a dollop of whipped cream adorned with strawberries and blueberries.

Whoever said that the way to a man's heart was through his stomach wasn't kidding.

Adrian did not mention my anxious call to power down computers until after dinner.

"Mrs. Z, that dinner was definitely one of your finest."

"Thank you, Mr. Z," I said coyly, "I'm glad it met with your approval."

"Now, will you tell me about the events of this afternoon that caused all our operations to come to an early end?"

I recounted my afternoon. The monotonous details of shopping did not interest Adrian, but my encounter with Mr. Richard Simmons did pique his interest.

"Do I need to ask Richard for the actual details?"

"Why would you ask Richard? I just told you what transpired," I said indignantly.

"I'm sorry, baby. It's just that sometimes you leave out details."

"If I do, it's because they are not important," I said assertively.

"OK, I accept that. Well, Mrs. Z," he stretched out his arms, "are we secure?"

"Yes," I responded as I walked into his waiting arms. "It's business as usual tomorrow. He was an amateur."

"Hmm, Mrs. Z," he said, holding me tight and snuggling his nose in that tender spot between my shoulder and neck before lowering his tone, "put the children to bed and meet me in my office."

I did as I was told.

I announced myself as I entered Adrian's office. He had soft music playing in the background.

"Hi, baby. Come here, sit by my side," he said softly, patting the seat next to him on the diamond-tufted Chesterfield sofa.

I did as I was told. Just then Richard walked into Adrian's office, announcing himself, as was the custom of all the staff.

"Hello, Richard," Adrian greeted him. "Mrs. Z just told me all about your experience this afternoon with Mr. Richard Simmons." Adrian gazed in his direction snickering at the mention of Mr. Richard Simmons. I did not look at Richard.

This in retrospect might have been a mistake.

"It was funny," Richard snickered back. "Mrs. Z had that sucker flat on his stomach with one arm twisted behind him. I swear it was the funniest thing I had ever witnessed."

Richard is a good guy but his enjoyment of funny things can be a liability.

"I know," Adrian agreed, clearly baiting Richard into more conversation. "This guy was a real amateur."

"He didn't stand a chance," Richard asserted. "Mrs. Z not only had him on his belly, but she took his wallet, car keys, and whatever dignity he had left."

"That's my girl," Adrian agreed, squeezing my shoulders with his arm.

Shit! I'm so screwed, thanks to my loyal bodyguard, Richard.

"Mr. Z, was there something else you wanted?" my poor Richard innocently asked.

"No, Richard, thank you," Adrian said before dismissing him at once.

"Good night, Mrs. Z."

"Good night, Richard."

Adrian waited a few minutes to make sure we were alone.

"Baby," he finally said, "would you like to go upstairs?"

"Sure," I responded, fully aware that there would be hell to pay. "Did you have something in mind?"

"I would like something special tonight. Do you think it would be possible?"

"You know I like pleasing you."

"Good, then let's take this party upstairs to the dressing room."

Adrian's favorite room was the dressing room. Mirrors were strategically placed so that I could see myself from various angles. I could also watch as Adrian and I played our games. He was not able to see, but knowing that I was watching turned him on.

"Milagros," Adrian spoke softly, "I need satisfaction before I have my way with you."

"Why, Adrian?" I asked, trying to sound innocent.

"You know why," he said, embracing me from behind. "You weren't exactly truthful this evening, were you?" he asked in that deep throaty voice while one hand caressed my breasts and the other invaded my privates. I might have been concerned except that it was all very exciting and inviting.

"Adrian," I pleaded weakly and unconvincingly, "I was truthful."

"Hmm," he let out while kissing and nipping at my neck and shoulder. "You left out the part that you had Mr. Richard Simmons on his belly, that you took his wallet and car keys."

"What does all that matter," I asked, reaching back with one arm to caress the back of his head and bring his face closer so I could plant a long, passionate kiss on his lips.

"Mrs. Z, you drive me crazy. It matters," he said trying to catch his breath. "You know how I feel about your getting physical. Then there is this child you are carrying."

"I know, Adrian," I said sufficiently contrite, "but neither I nor the baby was in danger. I promise you."

"So, I shouldn't have satisfaction?" he asked, still assaulting me on all fronts.

"Do with me as you please," I let out softly melting in his arms, chest heaving. Adrian knew how to get me in the mood for his special kind of sex.

"I think I will," he asserted. "I need to teach you a lesson."

He stopped his assault. I looked back and up at him. He was gazing in my direction with lips parted in that half-cocked smile of his. He knew he had my attention.

"Baby, turn around," he said while straightening up." Go to my side of the dresser and in the bottom drawer there is a wooden oblong box, condom, lubrication tube and switch. Bring those items here to me," he ordered.

"Switch?" I questioned.

"You'll know when you see it. Don't fail me," he warned.

I went to the bottom drawer on his side of the dressing room. There was a wooden oblong box, condom, lubrication tube, just as he said. The only other article was a thin pliable whip.

Surely, he is not going to use this on me.

I brought all the items to him.

"Give me the switch and place all the other items on the floor by my right foot where I can access them easily," he ordered sternly.

I did as I was told.

"Now, turn around and face the mirror. Place your hands on the mirror above your head," he ordered again.

I did as I was told.

The switch was in his left hand held tightly. He resumed kissing my neck and shoulder while his right hand fondled my body. He pressed the switch against my left leg, brushing it upwards to my hip. Then he slid it down my leg. Once it reached my calf, he positioned it on the inside of my leg in one fluid move without losing the connection. Again pressing the switch against my skin, he moved it up the inside until reaching the apex of my sex. I gasped as he pressed the switch lingering in my inner most private part. He pulled the switch away and then tapped it against my privates gently, but firmly. I was now panting at the raw assault.

Suddenly, he stopped the fondling and kissing.

"Close your eyes," he whispered, "I don't want you to see this."

My heart sank. Would this be the one time he would carry out his threat? I knew I could stop him. He would never do anything to me that I didn't allow. Yet, this was all part of our game. Cat and mouse. Dominant and submissive. He would never hurt me. On the contrary, my reward was multiple orgasms.

I closed my eyes and rested my head against the mirror to wait.

He straightened, separating his body from mine. I could no longer feel him or his breath. I braced myself to wait for the assault, which was sure to come. Not a full minute passed that I felt his spread hand against my bottom. It was forceful and it stung, but I was grateful that it wasn't the switch. I opened my eyes and saw the switch where Adrian had thrown it on top of the pile of our clothes.

There is something impersonal about a switch.

After each smack, Adrian would gently rub and squeeze the offended cheek. He continued kissing and nipping the neck and shoulder areas.

His other hand continued fondling my breasts. Each cheek received three smacks apiece.

"Don't move," he ordered. He knelt reaching for the oblong box. He removed the top. Placing a hand between my legs, he ordered, "Spread your legs."

I did as I was told.

"You never disappoint," he declared. "You're already wet. I have a toy for you. Would you like to play?"

"Yes," I replied, panting with anticipation.

He removed a rabbit-type vibrator from the box and inserted it gently, saying, "This comes with a remote for your enjoyment, baby."

He lubricated me and placed the condom on his already erect penis. He then stood to fondle my breasts, rolling the nipples between his index finger and thumb. In the other hand he held two clamps. Each clamp had a chain attached with a black feather dangling at the end. Adrian brushed the feathers lightly against my jaw, moving ever so slowly down my neck, across the chest and finally the nipple. He placed a clamp on each nipple. My back was arched and chest heaving.

"Oh, baby," he crooned. "You're so delicious. Are you watching?"

"Yes," I answered in a deep voice.

He turned on the vibrator to a low setting.

"Hold this for me, but don't touch the controls. Only I do that, understand?"

"Yes," I replied in the same throaty voice. My husband's sensual touch and loving kisses up and down my neck and shoulders caused my whole body to throb. Heat radiated from my skin. My heart was pounding against my chest as blood raced through my veins. I was ready. Ready to enter that special place where only the most intimate lovers go.

Adrian eased his massive erection into me. He increased the pulsating of the vibrator. The rabbit ears massaged my clitoris while the vibrator massaged that sweet spot. With his free hand he pulled on one chain, then the next, causing a sensation that traveled from my nipples to my sex. I threw back my head against his chest and closed my eyes. The sensory overload quickly lead the way for the familiar wave of contractions.

"Adrian," I panted, "I can't hold on."

"Go for it, baby."

The contractions turned into full body convulsions. Adrian quickly removed the clamps, the vibrator and gently eased out of me. With his front to my back, he held my face seeking out my mouth. We locked lips for a deep passionate kiss. I was spent, leaning against his body. He pulled away from my lips and bent down to scoop me up into his arms. Adrian carried me to the bedroom. He tended to us both before slipping into bed beside me.

"How do you feel?"

"Good," I purred, "I experienced nirvana."

"Wow, lucky you," he whispered. "Are you ready for round two?"

He didn't wait for an answer. Another orgasm later, we were both sound asleep, wrapped in each others arms.

Chapter 11

A few weeks had passed since my encounter with Mr. Richard Simmons. Adrian chose to ignore Mr. Nussbaum's request for a meeting. Sam Sanz was still in New York taking care of the "family business" as well as his girlfriend and new baby. My universe was at peace.

"Adrian," I called to him from the dressing room.

"Yes, baby," he answered, walking out of the bathroom with a towel drying himself.

"I want to go with you today to the office."

"Why?"

That's interesting. I expected a flat out 'no.'

"I want to go to lunch with Daisy and Paula," I lied.

"Well," he said, throwing the towel on the floor as he walked naked to where I was. His lips were pursed and eyebrows knitted. Adrian stretched out his arms to locate me. I walked closer. He placed his hands on my shoulders, standing so close that I could feel his hot breath on my face.

Shit! This can't be good.

"Having lunch with them *today*," he stated more than asked. "That might be difficult," he added, tightening his grip.

"Oh, why is that?" I asked in a small voice.

"Daisy is in Los Angeles attending a seminar and Paula is with her," he replied exhaling deeply.

"How do you know that?" I asked indignantly. How could he have information about my friends that I didn't have?

"Paula works for me. Did you forget?" He exhaled deeply again.

Shit! This is not going well. What to do?

"I guess I should have called them first."

Good recovery, Mrs. Z!

"Yes, you should have," he agreed as he exhaled deeply once more. He did not move, but continued gazing down at me with a serious expression on his face.

I stood on my toes and gave him a chaste kiss on the lips, trying to draw out that broad beautiful smile that melted my insides.

"That is not going to work, Milagros."

Oh, Milagros is it. Shit!

"What is not going to work?" I responded innocently. "Can't a wife kiss her husband?" I tried to back away from him but he was too quick. He placed his hands on my shoulder keeping me close.

"A wife, you, can do whatever she wants with her husband, me," he let out in staccato fashion. He looked as if he wanted to say more but was restraining himself.

He exhaled deeply again. His hot breath bathed my face. I knew something was eating him, but Adrian was hot and I couldn't help being turned on. His naked body in front of me didn't help matters. But experience had taught me that this was not going well for me.

"Well, can I go with you anyway? I can do some shopping."

"No," he replied without hesitation.

I tried to back up away from him, but he held me firmly in place.

"Why can't I go with you?" I demanded.

"Because," he spoke low and slowly dragging out each word, "I said no."

Who the fuck does he think he is? Well, I can't have this macho behavior.

"Fine, Adrian," I said coolly. "I can have Richard drive me."

"No you won't," he said lowering his voice, bringing me closer to his body so that we were now touching.

"Adrian, what the hell is wrong with you?"

Maybe I should have asked a different question.

"You is what is wrong with me. There is no need for you to go to San Francisco. I canceled your appointment."

I gasped as I realized that he knew all along where I was going. Then fury hit at the thought that he would cancel an appointment that I had made without consulting with me first. I tried to push away, but he wouldn't let go of me.

"Let me go, Adrian," I spat.

"No." He held me closer so that not even air could get through.

"How dare you cancel an appointment I made without consulting me?" I hissed.

"How dare you lie to me?" he whispered. "Why did you make an appointment to meet with Lorenzo Benedetti without telling me? What business do you have with him?"

"Let me go and I'll tell you my business with him," I replied in a softer voice.

He loosened his grip on my shoulders, saying, "No, I want you close."

"Let me go, Adrian, I need room to breathe fresh air."

He exhaled deeply again, bathing me in his heat. He did remove his hands from my shoulders.

"Thank you," I said, taking a step back. "I didn't want to bother you with this Benedetti matter. The Pablo Santos incident quite frankly was too much to bear. It was a nasty affair that took a toll on all of us."

Adrian had been very supportive and loving during that whole mess, but it had affected him. How could it not? The violence, the heinous acts of a deviant sexual predator were enough to break the strongest of decent, law-abiding people.

"What has that got to do with Benedetti?" Adrian asked as he gave me more breathing room.

"Do you remember the files I copied from Mr. Richard Simmons' computer to a flash drive?"

"Yes, I remember."

"I discovered an encrypted folder that contained material on Benedetti's granddaughter, Sofia Benedetti."

"Help me dress, but keep talking."

"Sofia Benedetti is sixteen years old, Adrian. There is a video of her with Fairchild's grandson, who is twenty. There are other men." Adrian stopped dressing and gazed in my direction. The color had gone from his face.

"Please, Millie, tell me it's not what I'm thinking," he pleaded with a sad look on his face.

"Sorry, baby, it is exactly what you are thinking. It is worse. Sofia was not a willing participant. The video shows Fairchild's grandson drugging her at one point. He boasted how he would doctor up the video to compromise the young lady by showing her as having been willing."

"Why would old man Fairchild have this on his computer?" Adrian asked as he finished dressing.

"I don't exactly know. But one could guess that he was holding onto it as leverage against Lorenzo Benedetti should their business relationship go sour."

"Why would Mr. Richard Simmons not tell his boss?"

"I don't know, Adrian. Maybe he wanted leverage should he need it or want it."

"So, Benedetti has no knowledge of this video," Adrian stated.

"No."

"Do I want to know how you know this?"

"No."

"What did you hope to accomplish by giving Benedetti this video?"

"I researched Sofia. She is a lovely young lady. Up to recently, she was outgoing. She played on her school's softball team, she was on the swimming team, she did charitable work for the church and the community, and she was a straight-A student."

"You're talking in the past tense," Adrian commented as we continued dressing.

"That's right. Since the video was made, young Sofia has dropped out of all sports activity, she stopped all church and community activities and her grades are a solid D."

"Oh, my God!" Adrian exclaimed in anguish.

"Her family has no idea of what is the matter with her. Adrian, if I could speak with Benedetti, maybe I could make him understand that his granddaughter needs help. She deserves to be helped."

Adrian turned to me and held me tenderly in his arms.

"I didn't cancel your appointment," he confessed. "Benedetti called me. He said he received a request from you for a meeting and he asked what I wanted to discuss with him."

"What did you tell him?"

"I told him to accept your request and he would find out."

"Oh, Adrian," I said, burying my face in his chest. "I love you."

"I love you, too, but I wish you wouldn't exclude me from your plans or lie to me."

"I try very hard to protect you."

"I, just like pregnant wives, do not break."

"Point well-made and taken." We kissed, then I continued, "Adrian, would you like to join us for the lunch meeting."

"I thought you would never ask," he said smiling.

Hector drove us, along with Richard and Roger, to Adrian's office at the Sentinel. Hilda watched Angelique and Adam. Adrian and I arrived at the restaurant at exactly one o'clock. At ten minutes after, Benedetti had still not arrived. I was getting upset at his poor manners.

"Adrian, Benedetti is ten minutes late. What if he doesn't show?"

Adrian inspected his Braille watch.

"If he doesn't come in the next five minutes, you and I will order our lunch, eat and go home to our children."

Just as he finished speaking, I saw a tall gray-haired man walking towards us. He was well dressed in a pin-striped suit. He kept his hair short and sported a well-trimmed full beard. I had never met Mr. Benedetti, but I guessed this might be him. I discreetly alerted Adrian.

"Mr. Zaragosa, Mrs. Zaragosa, forgive my tardiness but the traffic was incredible." Adrian stood extending his hand for Mr. Benedetti to shake.

Once both men were seated, the waiter came to take our drink order. I had water while they both had wine. Benedetti asked the waiter to also take the lunch order since he was pressed for time.

"Well, Mr. Zaragosa, here I am. What is this meeting about?"

"Baby," Adrian said turning to me while placing his arm around the back of my chair, "would you like to start?"

"Sure," I replied, feeling uncomfortable. Mr. Benedetti was a brusque man and he didn't look pleased to have me as part of the conversation.

"Mr. Benedetti," I started as I placed a disk from my purse on the table, "this conversation has to do with your family."

"Are you threatening my family," he interrupted, slamming his hand on the table, causing the other patrons to stop what they were doing to look in our direction. I was about to become Hannibal Lechter at this display of poor manners.

"Mr. Benedetti," Adrian said abruptly, straightening in his chair, "I am going to ask you to lower your voice and show some good manners. Neither my wife nor I invited you here to threaten you. Not that you don't deserve it." My man's throat had begun to redden and I was beginning to have second thoughts about this meeting.

"Mr. Benedetti," I said quickly, trying to diffuse the situation. "This meeting is not about threats or about the wine business. But it is about a personal matter. Personal to you. I also want to caution that it is a delicate matter." He leaned back in his chair and stared at me.

So, now I have your attention.

"I have a DVD," I continued, gesturing towards the disk I had placed on the table, "that shows a young lady in a most unfavorable way."

I paused, half-waiting for him to react and half-searching for the right words.

"This young lady is in the company of several men older than herself," I continued.

"Why are you telling me this, Mrs. Zaragosa? Are you trying to injure me?" Benedetti interrupted. Instinctively, he knew.

"No. I am not trying to injure you. I am here as a mother. I have a young daughter, Mr. Benedetti. I am telling you because the young lady in question is in need of help. She deserves to be helped so that she can get her life back on track," I pronounced with a little more passion than I had intended.

"The young lady in question," I continued, "was not a willing participant. She is the victim of a cruel and devious plot."

"How did you come to possess this disk?"

"I have many friends in law enforcement. The owner of this disk tried to sell it over the internet. My friend on vice was able to prevent the sale and, recognizing the name of the owner, decided to show it to me," I lied.

"Are there copies of this disk?" he asked with great concern on his face.

"I have no way of knowing that. I can only assume that the owner must have it saved on a hard drive."

"Mrs. Zaragosa, may I have the disk?"

"Yes, but I warn you it is difficult to watch. I also want to say that I am the only one who has seen its contents. My husband has no idea what is on it."

"Thank you, Mrs. Zaragosa, for your discretion," he said a little more humbly. "What do I do now? She won't speak to anyone. She has shut herself off completely. Her parents are at their wits end."

"If it were me," I said softly, "I would let her know that I knew what happened. I would also assure her that it was not her fault. I would insist that she speak to a professional who has had experience dealing in these matters. And above all else, I would reassure her that I loved her." I felt my eyes pool with tears and I tried blinking them away. I pushed the disk towards Benedetti. He took it and placed it in his jacket pocket. Adrian placed his arm around my shoulder and leaned in to kiss my hair.

The waiter brought our food and we ate in silence. I silently prayed that I had done the right thing and I prayed that Sofia receive help. I also silently prayed that the scumbags got their just desserts.

Our life was back to normal. Adrian was going off to San Francisco without me. I stayed home taking care of the little ones and keeping tabs on all our loose ends.

Sam Sanz was still doing what he did best in New York. His two brothers were still in jail and would be for a long time. Adrian had official-ly given notice to Benedetti and Fairchild that he was going to continue helping Juan Carlos. That in turn generated a new threat from Fairchild.

Abe Nussbaum sent Adrian another request to meet. This time Adrian thanked him in a letter and at the same time informed him that he was not interested in his offering. I was getting bigger and could no longer get in and out of the Corvette.

The urgent need to pee woke me up early one morning. I made my way to the bathroom without waking Adrian. On my way to the bathroom, I noticed his smart phone on his night table. It was turned off.

I know he didn't want to be bothered in Tahiti, but powering his phone at home is unusual for him.

After breakfast, I walked Adrian to the waiting Escalade with Adam in one arm while holding Angelique by the hand. He kissed us and as he entered the Escalade, Angelique began to scream for her father. Thankfully, Hilda appeared sweeping the crying toddler into her arms, taking her into the house, leaving me and a bewildered Adam alone in the front of the house.

It was a beautiful July morning, so I decided to walk the grounds with Adam. I took a side path between the garage and the house to the back. I strolled through the rose garden, stopping to admire the blooms. I told Adam the name of each rose and then I held a bloom to smell it, offering Adam the opportunity to do the same. He, however, was not interested. He just looked at me. I then strolled beyond the rose garden to the great lawn. I decided to go to the winery, so I headed towards the woods.

"Mrs. Z, Mrs. Z," Richard called as he ran towards me.

"What is it, Richard?"

"Nothing, I just wanted you to wait until I could catch up to you."

"This isn't necessary, Richard. I can walk by myself on the grounds without a bodyguard."

"I know you can, Mrs. Z. But Mr. Z gave me strict orders to accompany you everywhere. Especially now that your delivery time is getting close."

"I see," I said. "Well, it's a good thing I enjoy having you around."

Richard snickered as a demonstration of his own approval.

We didn't return to the house until lunchtime. Hilda looked a bit annoyed, but I didn't ask what was bothering her. I was too tired. After lunch, I took Angelique and Adam to my office. They settled in for a nap.

I sat at my desk to listen to voice mails and quickly checked the emails that were being routed to my computer. The emails were time consuming. Adrian received an extraordinary amount of solicitations from vendors or organizations that wanted his participation in one function or another. There was one particularly interesting email. This was not a solicitation. It was from S. Mathews at a Gmail account. The subject read, "Our Venture Together." So, as was my duty, I read it.

My Dearest Adrian,

I wanted to thank you for investing in my real estate project. Hopefully it will make us both a great deal of money. I also wanted to thank you for a wonderful afternoon yesterday and I look forward to our meeting later this evening.

Yours always and whenever,
Susan

I could barely breathe. My head was reeling and my ears pounding as the veins in my neck throbbed. I thought to forward the email to Adrian but decided not to. I didn't know why. I guess I lacked the courage to confront him. Perhaps I didn't want to confirm my worst suspicions of him. I decided to do nothing. My head was about to explode. I needed some air.

"Hilda," I called as I entered the kitchen, "the children are napping in my office. Could you keep an eye on them?"

"Sure, Millie, but why?" she asked with a concerned look on her face.

"I need some fresh air and exercise."

"It's none of my business, Millie, but you were out this morning for a long time."

You're damn right it's not your business!

She looked as if she were going to say something else, but I did not let her go on.

"I'm fine, Hilda," I barked.

"Shouldn't you be resting for the baby's sake?" she continued.

"I'm fine," I repeated as I walked out through the kitchen door to the back of the house.

I was in no mood for Hilda's inquisition. My head was reeling with thoughts of Hot-to-Trot and Adrian. He entered into a real estate project with her after I had told him she needed to keep her distance. It was more than I could bear. Then there were the unanswered questions. What were they doing yesterday afternoon that she was so thankful for and why was she expecting to meet with him again this evening? Adrian didn't mention he would be late. Maybe this would be another one of his 'quick stops.'

How long has this been going on? He has made 'quick stops' before.

Now my brain was racing. I quickened my pace as I headed out to the rose garden. My chest became tighter. It was beginning to hurt. I thought to head towards the firing range to blow off some steam. Literally.

"Mrs. Z, Mrs. Z," Richard yelled as he ran after me. "Please wait."

I didn't. I used one hand to support my belly while the other clutched my chest. My pace had quickened to a jog as I cleared the rose garden into the woods.

Poor Richard. He has done nothing but chase me all day.

"Mrs. Z, please stop," came his plea as he closed in on me.

Go away, Richard! I would speak if I could.

Then I felt his hand grab the back of my dress and he pulled me into his chest, bringing us both to an abrupt stop. I should have been angry. I should have been outraged that he would do such a thing. Instead I slumped into his arms and cried. He gently eased us both down onto the ground as he maintained a firm hold around me.

"Go ahead and cry," he whispered as he rocked both of us. "Let it all out."

I did just that. He never asked what the matter was. He just let me cry. I don't know how long it was before I was all cried out. There was another long period of sitting in silence.

"I'm sorry, Richard," I finally uttered in a small voice.

"You have nothing to be sorry about."

"Yes I do," I replied, pulling away from his grip. "Twice today you had to chase after me. Then this pitiful display of tears."

"You are entitled to have a mini breakdown," he replied with that familiar snicker of his. "We should get back," he continued. "Can you walk?"

"Yeah, I think I need a nap."

Chapter 12

I was sitting in my office at nine o'clock staring at my computer when I heard Adrian arrive at Luna Llena. As expected he entered the house through the kitchen where Hilda was sure to fill him in on all the activities of the day. He was freshly showered and rested, not at all looking like someone who had been hard at work. I, on the other hand, looked like hell.

"Millie?" he called out from the hallway.

"I'm in my office."

Adrian entered my office and waited for another cue.

"I'm at my computer," I said. I did not stand to greet him in the usual fashion where we would kiss and embrace.

"Where are the children?"

"In Angelique's room sleeping."

"Why haven't you had dinner?"

So. Hilda filled him in as expected.

"I was waiting for you."

"Didn't you get my text message that I had a dinner appointment?"

"No. Why is it, Adrian, that sometimes you call me and other times you send impersonal texts?"

"What are you doing at your computer at this hour?" he asked, ignoring my question.

"I was reading an email for the hundredth time today."

"What is so important about that email that you've read it so many times?"

"Can I share it with you?"

"Yes, I would love to hear it."

"This is a new email contact that has been routed to my computer. You requested that only new contacts be routed to me," I reminded him.

"It is addressed to you," I continued. "The sender is S dot Mathews at gmail dot com." His face reddened as he instantly recognized the name and as he realized that this was a new email address, otherwise it would not have been routed to my computer.

"The message reads," I continued in a low voice, "'My Dearest Adrian, I wanted to thank you for investing in my real estate project. Hopefully it will make us both a great deal of money. I also wanted to thank you for a wonderful afternoon yesterday and I look forward to our meeting later this evening. Yours always and whenever, Susan.'" I stood and walked around my desk to where he was standing.

"So, Adrian, what am I to make of this?" I asked.

"Millie, I can explain."

"I sincerely doubt it," I said, walking away from him.

"Where are you going?"

"Upstairs to sleep."

"You should eat something first."

"I'll take something with me, Adrian," I said, pausing at the threshold of my office. "Angelique's youth bed was delivered today. I had Tony and Frank move the cribs into the nursery. I want the children to stay there. Please do not contradict me again on this matter.

"I will be sleeping on the sofa in the nursery room," I concluded.

"Millie," Adrian walked towards me, "please, baby, don't do this. I can explain."

"There is nothing to explain. I told you Hot-to-Trot needed to keep her distance from us. 'Us' meant you, too. Not only has she not kept her distance, but I find out that you are involved in a business project with her. Quite frankly, Adrian, I don't want to know about your afternoon or evenings with her. I want to be alone. Do not come near me."

I walked into the kitchen to make some tea and fix a light snack. As I walked towards the stairs, I could see Adrian still standing where I had left him.

Early the next morning I bathed and dressed Angelique and Adam. I did not change from my nightgown, but opted to throw a robe that didn't wrap around my belly to take the children to Hilda. She was in the kitchen cooking for everyone.

"Good morning, Millie," she greeted. Hilda could not disguise the look on her face. I was a total mess and her face said it all. But I didn't care.

"Good morning, Hilda," I replied in a small exhausted voice. "I'm a little under the weather today. Could you look after Angelique and Adam?"

"It will be my pleasure. Can I get you something to eat?"

"No, thank you. I'll come back down later to eat."

"Is Adrian aware that you don't feel well? Is it the baby?"

"Yes, Adrian knows and no, it is not the baby."

"Millie where are you?" Adrian called out. "What are you doing? What is wrong with you?"

Mr. Multiple Questions is back. I might find him endearing if I weren't so pissed off.

"I am in the bedroom, Adrian. I am crawling into bed. And you know what is wrong with me."

"Millie, we need to talk," he said, approaching the bed.

"Yes, we do but it is not going to happen now," I barked. "I want to rest and you are the last person I want to see right now. So, go off to do whatever it is you do these days." I effectively dismissed him.

There was a light knock at the door. I looked at my smart phone and saw it was eleven in the morning.

"Mrs. Z," Richard called from behind my bedroom door.

"Yes, Richard, what is it?"

"May I come in?"

"No."

"Mrs. Z, you haven't had anything to eat. Can I bring you something?"

"No, thank you. I just want to rest."

The phone rang. It was Daisy. I let it go to voice mail. There was another knock on the door.

"Millie," Hilda called, "may I come in?"

"Hilda, please, I am trying to rest."

"Millie, can I bring you something to eat?"

"No, Hilda. Thank you. I promise I'll go to the kitchen in a while and get something. Please, I need some rest," I pleaded.

She left and my phone rang again. This time it was Isabel. I let it go to voice mail. The phone rang again before I could put it down. This time it was Richard. I decided to power off the telephone.

My thoughts turned to Adrian and I wept. I crawled out of bed and sat in the sitting area of our bedroom. My heartache wasn't enough, so I placed the iPod on the docking station and played all our favorite tunes. I locked all the doors to our suite. I was determined to wallow in my misery.

It was days after that Richard recounted to me the drama that had unfolded in the kitchen between him and Hilda. I was sorry that I had caused them so much anguish.

When Richard could not reach me on the telephone after a few tries, he called Adrian to notify him. Adrian told him not to worry, that all I wanted was to be alone and rest. That didn't sit well with poor Richard. He then went into the kitchen and began working on Hilda's nerves.

"All she wants is to rest, Richard," she repeated Adrian's words.

"But you do agree that she should not be alone?" he asked her.

"It's what she wants, Richard. What can we do?"

"Maybe Mr. Z should come home."

"I already called him, Richard. He is busy at the office."

"His wife is close to her due date, Hilda. He should be here with her."

"It is none of our business, Richard," Hilda responded, exasperated.

"I know it's not, but it's not like her to leave the children alone for such a long time."

"There is always a first time," Hilda reasoned.

"It's not like her to spend the day in bed. And now she is up there playing sad songs."

"How do you know that?"

"I heard it from the patio below their bedroom."

"Richard, that doesn't mean anything. It is a good sign that she is playing music. It helps her to relax," Hilda reasoned again.

"Why does she need to relax? Maybe she's in labor."

"She would tell us."

"Would she? Can you be sure? She has been behaving strangely. I had to chase after her twice yesterday."

"Richard, please stop it. You are making me nervous."

"I'm just saying, Hilda, she should not be alone. Mr. Z should be here with his wife."

"Oh, for God's sake, Richard!" She picked up the house phone and called Adrian who was about to leave the office to go to a lunch meeting.

"Adrian," she said anxiously, "you need to come home immediately."

"Why, Vieja, what is wrong?"

"Millie has locked the doors to the suite. She won't answer her phone. She hasn't eaten. She hasn't checked on the children. She is not herself."

"All she wants is some peace and quiet, Vieja," Adrian barked at her. "Obviously, neither you nor Richard are letting her rest."

"What if she's in labor, Adrian?" she asked, getting irritated with him.

"The baby is not due for another two weeks," he barked.

"Did you forget Adam was two weeks early?" she barked back.

"Oh, for God's sake, I'll be home as soon as I can."

"No! You come home now, Adrian. It's your duty. Your wife needs you."

"My wife doesn't want to see me right now."

"I don't care, Adrian Zaragosa, you come home right now," she ordered and hung up the telephone.

Richard swears Adrian was home forty minutes after that conversation. And it wasn't a minute too soon. I had already called Dr. Johansson and asked her to meet me at the hospital. I was not interested in having Adrian deliver this baby.

Fortunately, for all concerned, Adrian felt differently.

"Millie," Adrian called out as he unlocked and opened the door.

"I'm in the dressing room."

"What are you doing?" he asked as he followed my voice to the dressing room.

"I'm trying to get dressed."

"Trying?" he asked as he slowly inched his way towards me. "Are you all right?"

"My water broke and I'm having labor pains. I want to get dressed so I can have Richard drive me to the hospital. Dr. Johansson is going to meet me there."

"Millie, why are you doing this?"

"I can't bear to have you near, Adrian," I sobbed.

"Don't do this, baby. She asked me to do her a favor and help her out on a short-term basis with a real estate project. There is nothing between me and Susan," he said in a soft voice.

I looked up at him. He was gazing in my direction, eyebrows knitted and lips pursed. I wanted to believe him.

"You are right though," he continued, "I should never have entered into a business deal with her. It's a stupid business deal, but more importantly it violated the understanding you and I had. Please, baby, I am begging for your forgiveness."

He was contrite and I needed to hear him say that I was right and he was wrong.

"Don't shut me out from the baby's birth. Please, Millie," he pleaded.

I was too weak to argue and I wanted to believe him.

"OK," I said softly slumping into his arms.

Adrian did what Adrian did best. He took charge of everything, but this time Dr. Johansson arrived before the baby. As usual, they argued, made up and toasted the newborn, little Adrian, with a glass of brandy.

Later Adrian confessed the reason he powered off his smart phone was not to receive Hot-to-Trot's constant calls begging him to meet with her for a business meeting. He also confessed that he had met with her for an hour one evening to deliver a contract between them that spelled out the terms of their agreement. He told me that she was insisting that he become a partner in her real estate venture. His only interest was to help her on a short-term basis and that is exactly what the agreement stated. She eventually accepted and signed. He further told me that he had no intentions of meeting her for lunch that following day. He had another appointment and he had told her so. What could I do? I believed him and I forgave him.

We were back to our routines. Adrian worked from home more and when he needed to go to San Francisco, he would ask that the children and I accompany him.

"Millie," Adrian called for me as he entered my office from his, "you will never guess who I just got off the phone with."

"Who?" I asked, turning away from my computer to look at him.

"Benedetti."

"Really? What did he want?"

"He asked if you could do him a favor."

"Me?" I asked incredulously. "What kind of a favor?"

"The kind that only you can do."

"Mr. Z, please spit it out."

"Come, baby, let's sit in the family room."

We settled little Adrian in the crib, Adam in the playpen and Angelique free to roam her baby-proof area.

"Tell me, Mr. Z," I started as we sat down on the sofa, "what favor does Mr. Benedetti want?"

"He informed me that he has a young man working for him who is supposed to be a computer whiz. He asked him to remove the video of his granddaughter from the computer of Fairchild's grandson, but he has not been able to do so."

"So, he wants me to hack someone's computer?"

"He didn't ask in so many words."

"I can't do that. My husband has prohibited me from doing things like that."

"I told him that was a favor neither of us could do for him."

"He must have been disappointed."

"Yes, he was."

"We can't do it, Adrian. He would know for sure that we had something to do with hacking his own computer and disturbing his deliveries last year."

"Well, Mrs. Z, 'we' didn't hack his computer, you did."

"Adrian, you know what I mean."

"Benedetti is a wise old man."

"Why do you say that?"

"He said that he knew that a caring and gentle woman such as yourself would never do such a thing. And he acknowledged that I am an honorable man who would not engage in matters of that sort. But he said he would be grateful if we could recommend someone."

"We can't do that. First, I wouldn't want another person viewing that video. Second, nobody we know would be willing to expose themselves as a hacker."

"I told him that. So he asked if one of us could arrange it on his behalf."

"That we could do."

"I agree."

"Consider it done."

"It's lunchtime," Adrian said, touching his Braille watch.

"Before we go, I have a piece of information for you."

"Oh, what is it?"

"An architect from New York sent you an email requesting a meeting. He offers a choice of three dates and he is willing to travel here. He further states that he has looked at the property." I paused to look at Adrian's reaction. His hands were on his belt, eyebrows raised and he was sporting a mischievous smile. He looked guilty.

"He has made some drafts and," I continued, "he is excited to work on the project. Your purchase of the two adjacent lots has made the project more exciting. He believes you will like one of the two options available.

"Well, Adrian, tell me what the hell is this man referring to? Are you involved in another project that I am going to be pissed at?"

"Maybe you'll be pissed," he said gazing my way. "But I can explain over lunch, baby. Please, let's go eat."

I waited patiently for his explanation. First we fed the children, then we sat down at the kitchen table.

"I'm waiting, Adrian."

"Oh, I thought we would finish our lunch first."

"You're stalling, Mr. Z."

Hilda made a quick exit and didn't bother to ask if she could take the children with her, which she usually did if she felt Adrian and I needed some privacy. She probably figured we wouldn't fight in front of them.

"Well, Mrs. Z, I haven't engaged in any project without consulting you," Adrian offered as he placed one arm around the back of my chair.

"Millie, I like your house in New York very much. But, as you know, our family has grown. You are also aware that I get claustrophobic when we are there and there are a lot of people around. I thought that given our security needs we would have to travel with all our bodyguards in the future.

"That is why I bought the two adjacent properties to the house. I propose making the house a little larger. Large enough to accommodate our family and security detail."

"Adrian, neither property was for sale."

"You would be surprised the things that are for sale given the price is right."

"I can't believe you did this. Pushing people out of their homes. Adrian, I knew those people." I was furious with him.

"Baby, I didn't push anyone out. They named their price and I paid it. That is fair. I did it for us. I want to be able to feel comfortable there. I know you try very hard to make that happen, but I can't help myself. Now there are more of us. Don't be upset. Tell me you understand," he concluded, palming my face tenderly.

"I guess I understand, but why didn't you tell me how you felt?"

"I was afraid of offending you."

"I wouldn't be offended. I understand our family is larger now. Our need for additional security is a fact. I would have understood, Adrian."

"Can we proceed?"

"Yes, we can proceed. But I can't travel to New York to pack my things and my father's."

"Don't worry about that. I will have a moving company professionally pack everything. Email Mr. Ayers back and give him a date. The Gulfstream can fly him here and back."

Adrian looked pleased with himself. I couldn't argue with him. I knew he was uncomfortable and there was no denying we had grown as a family and that we needed more security.

"There is something else, Adrian."

"Is it about the house?"

"No, it is about Benedetti."

"Were you able to find someone to do the deed?"

Oh, so he doesn't want to know that it's me.

"Yes, I found someone to do the 'deed,'" I mimicked. "As I understand, the 'deed' was quite easy. Three computers, Fairchild's, his grandson's, and Benedetti's whiz kid were alleviated of the video in question. Said video has been destroyed. Unfortunately, the computers had to be rendered useless to avoid the possibility of a recovery. The video had also been stored in a cloud account by the younger Fairchild. That was also alleviated of said video. The cloud account had to be completely invaded in order to disguise the true target."

"Wow, a cloud account," Adrian exclaimed in awe. "I have never thought about those things. I wouldn't store anything of value in them. But still, the idea that they can be had is intriguing."

"It is not very difficult. Security is tight in their infrastructure, but that is where it ends. Will you let Benedetti know? I wouldn't email that information and I would be very careful how I communicated it."

"I don't think it wise for us to engage in that conversation with Benedetti. I still don't like the idea of people thinking that you or I are capable of such things."

"Did you ever assure him that we would arrange to have someone do this?"

"No."

"Hopefully that young lady is not going to be bothered with that video. There is no way of knowing if a hard copy exists. I suppose an anonymous message could be sent to Benedetti informing him of all this. The kind that can't be traced."

"I like that."

"Consider it done."

"Mrs. Z, is there anything else? Because if there isn't, I would like to take a walk with you and the children. Harvest time is upon us."

Chapter 13

Mr. Benedetti turned out to be someone not to be trifled with. He was as passionate about his family as Adrian and I were about ours. Perhaps more so.

The newspapers reported that young Mr. Fairchild's apartment had been trashed by burglars. Young Fairchild's body was found in his car, which was parked under an overpass in San Francisco. Drug paraphernalia was found both in his apartment and in his car. The police determined that his death and burglary were drug-related. Soon after that the newspapers reported that the Benedetti/Fairchild partnership had been dissolved because of philosophical differences.

My research revealed that Mr. Benedetti had dismissed Mr. Richard Simmons from his employ. Mr. Benedetti no longer had use of him. He was also disappointed in his non-performance.

Adrian and I met with Mr. Ayers to discuss the plans for renovating my parent's old home. He did a good job in satisfying Adrian's need for space while addressing my concerns for keeping it in line with the neighborhood and understated. He promised the project would be completed before Thanksgiving and Adrian vowed that we would visit once the renovations were completed.

"Millie," Adrian called as he walked into our bedroom.

"I'm in the dressing room," I called back.

"We have been invited to a wine tasting at the home of one of the local vintners this Friday night. Would you like to go?"

"I don't care for that sort of thing, Adrian. I don't have a sophisticated palate like you and your friends," I teased.

"OK, I'll let them know we will be delighted to attend." He laughed, grabbing me by the waist. "Wear something red and sexy."

"Why something red and sexy?" I asked.

"While we are there, I want to fantasize about undressing you."

"You are fresh, Mr. Z."

"Are you ready for our workout?"

"Yes, I am."

I had returned to the gym to work out. Once a week Adrian's personal trainer came to the house to work out with Adrian and me. He would return on another day to work with the staff. Richard, Frank and Tony enjoyed the opportunity to work with a martial arts expert. Roger was more resistant. He missed more sessions than the ones he attended, making up all kinds of excuses. He was exhausting my patience. I wanted everyone on our security staff to be fit and able to engage in hand combat. But since Adrian was fiercely loyal to him, I did not make an issue of it.

Friday night I wore a red cocktail dress that bared one shoulder. It was adorned with ruffles from the one shoulder strap to the hem. Since there was no way to conceal my firearm on my body, a matching red clutch bag would have to suffice. The red stiletto heels met with Adrian's approval. I wore my hair in a high bun and the diamond earrings Adrian gave me for our first Christmas.

Hector drove us in the Escalade to the Wagner's home. Richard rode shotgun.

Carl Wagner and his wife Evelyn were an elderly couple who had been in the wine business their whole adult lives. They were very fond of Adrian and had been good friends with Adrian's father.

There were three other couples in attendance. They, too, were in the wine business with estates nearby. There was a middle-aged single woman named Estelle Lewis. She was a friend of Evelyn's and had nothing to do with wine besides drinking it. Then there was Mr. Justin Fairchild.

"Justin Fairchild is at your ten o'clock," I whispered to Adrian.

Adrian's only reaction was knitted eyebrows and pursed lips.

We greeted everyone we knew. Mr. and Mrs. Wagner introduced us to Estelle Lewis. Then they introduced us to Mr. Fairchild.

"We have already met," Adrian informed our host. "How are you, Fairchild? I was sorry to hear about your grandson."

"Thank you," he replied, looking displeased at the mention of his grandson. "It's good to see you and Mrs. Zaragosa. I hear congratulations are in order on the birth of your third child."

"Thank you," Adrian said. "Yes, we recently had our second son."

Adrian and Fairchild made polite small talk before moving on to mingle with the others. I personally did not like his mentioning our children.

"Adrian," Mr. Wagner said as he approached. "I want to apologize."

"Apologize?" Adrian asked.

"Yes, Adrian," Mr. Wagner whispered. "Fairchild insisted I Invite him. Damn near threatened me."

"Really," Adrian returned the whisper, "how so?"

"Well, it was a veiled threat. He said it would be in my interest to have him as a friend."

"Carl, there is no need to apologize. I don't have a problem with his being here."

"Well, I know he has not been kind to you. You can say I heard it through the grapevine." They both laughed.

It was a lovely evening. The wine tasting was held in their cellar, which was nicely decorated. The room was kept at a constant temperature of sixty degrees. I was thankful I brought a pashmina along. The floor, walls and wine racks were all done in the same oak wood. A center island of oak was topped with a dark-green granite counter top. On the counter were various cheeses, crackers and fruit.

Mr. Wagner called for everyone's attention, beckoning all to gather along a table that had been set up for the wine tasting. We all participated in the tasting of the wine, but mercifully for me, only Adrian and his counterparts commented on the wines.

"All right, now here we have a bottle that has been covered so that no one but me knows what it is," Wagner teased. He poured a glass for Adrian and one for Fairchild. "Everyone will have a taste, but first a game. A challenge to the finest palate I know, Adrian Zaragosa, and to our special guest, Mr. Justin Fairchild."

Carl Wagner likes to stir the pot, I see.

"To be fair," he continued, "I will give you a hint."

"Nonsense," Justin Fairchild blurted out. "We don't need any hints, do we Zaragosa?"

"If you say so," Adrian returned. Everyone laughed.

Carl slid a glass across the table towards each man.

Adrian felt for his glass. All eyes were on him. My eyes were on Fairchild. He smirked at Adrian and abruptly grabbed his glass. He twirled the glass in the air, inhaled its aroma and sipped quickly. He held it in his mouth for a second and then swallowed. He continued to hold the glass to his nose.

Adrian kept his glass on the table. He placed the fingers of his right hand on the base of the crystal wine glass and gently swirled its contents. He had that half-cocked smile on his lips. He lifted the glass to his nose, inhaling deeply, then placed the glass to his lips, taking a small sip of the wine. He closed his eyes and held the wine in his mouth for a second or two before swallowing. He then returned the glass to the table.

"Well, gentlemen, what do you have to say about this wine?" Carl Wagner asked.

Adrian was about to speak when Fairchild uttered he would go first. Sporting his half-cocked smile, Adrian acquiesced.

"This is an elegant style with red berry, cherry, floral and wild herb aromas and flavors. It has a lingering aftertaste of fruit, spice and mineral. I would guess it is a 2007 Biondi-Santi Brunello de Montalcino Tenuta Greppo Riserva."

"Adrian," Carl said, turning to him, "what do you think it is?"

"I taste truffle, macerated cherry, leather and spice aromas and flavors," he responded thoughtfully. "It is sweet and balanced with fruit, spice and savory elements in its aftertaste. It is a youthful wine that should peak in another year or two. I guess it is a 2004 Guiseppe Mascarello & Figlio Barolo Monprivato Ca` d'Morissio Riserva."

"Youthful?" Fairchild scoffed at Adrian's guess. "Besides there were only two hundred cases made of that wine. To my knowledge none made it to the U.S."

"Well, ladies and gentlemen, let us see," Carl teased as he slowly removed the velvet bag that served to cover the bottle. Onlookers clapped and congratulated Adrian as they saw that it was the Barolo and not a Brunello.

"Fortunately," Carl Wagner continued, "we have enough for everyone to sample." He glanced at Fairchild and continued, "I was fortunate to buy a case while in Italy."

I quickly glanced at Fairchild. He looked like he had swallowed a lemon. He begrudgingly congratulated Adrian. As mingling continued, Adrian engaged in conversation with Carl and the other gentlemen. I found my way back to the island to fix a plate of fruit, cheese and crackers.

"Mrs. Zaragosa," came Justin Fairchild's voice from behind. "That is quite a husband you have there."

"Yes, he is special," I answered, not turning around.

"Keep a keen eye on him."

"I always do," I replied again without looking back.

I did not like his tone or his remark. I didn't know if it was my dislike for the man or my usual paranoia, but I took his words as a threat.

Chapter 14

"Millie," Adrian called from his office.

"Yes, Adrian, I am right here," I said as I walked into his office from mine.

"This Nussbaum is relentless," he blurted. "He is getting downright aggressive."

"Did he send another email," I asked.

"Yes, he did," Adrian said. "Come look."

Sure enough, Mr. Nussbaum had become more aggressive in his solicitation for business and for a meeting with Adrian. This time he assured Adrian that this meeting would be beneficial and should not be ignored. He suggested meeting Adrian at his office in San Francisco.

"Agree to meet him in New York, Adrian," I offered.

"Why?" Adrian asked, exasperated.

"Obviously, he has something to do with my troubles in New York," I contributed. "I think we need to bring this chapter to an end, don't you?"

"I'm not so sure, baby."

"I am."

"Stall him and make an appointment to coincide with our visit to New York to see the remodeled home in November."

"Sure, Adrian," I answered.

My email to Nussbaum simply stated scheduling conflicts, but I suggested a meeting date for the Monday before Thanksgiving Day. It was only a month and half away.

I sent another email to Mr. Ayers, setting fire to his heels by insisting the house renovation be finished by the first of November. I wasn't interested in having him drag his feet and my being disappointed because he couldn't finish my house by Thanksgiving Day. I was delighted when he emailed me instead of Adrian, assuring me that the renovations would be completed by the first. He would add another construction team to work on the east wing of the house.

Adrian could not help himself in the renovation of the house. In fact, it was more of a new construction than a renovation. He had designed a miniature Luna Llena, complete with east and west wing. In between the two wings was my mom and dad's old house. This was the only renovation.

"Adrian," I announced myself as I walked into his office, "Mr. Ayers says that the renovation will cost a little more."

"Oh, why is that?"

"He had to add another team on the project in order to beat the inclement weather. I think that is a good idea, don't you?" Before he could answer, I continued, "I'm anxious to see the finished product. I hope he doesn't disappoint me."

I eased my way onto his lap. Adrian gazed in my direction and smiled.

"I think it is a good idea. I don't want him disappointing my big girl."
We kissed.

I knew he would agree.

We visited Mendoza in early October. The weather was beautiful. In the evenings the temperature dipped to the low fifties and during the day it reached the low seventies. We stayed in an old villa that had been turned into a resort. Adrian, as he had done for Juan Carlos and Isabel's wedding, rented the entire resort for us. He was a little familiar with the facility, but he relied mostly on my guiding him around. He particularly enjoyed listening to my description of the view from the patio outside our bedroom. The snow-capped Andes provided a beautiful contrast to the arid landscape that is Mendoza.

This was a business trip for Adrian, who insisted that Daisy and Paula come along with us. Our visit was an impromptu one. Juan Carlos wanted Adrian's opinion on his new blend as well as other business matters. Both men also wanted to discuss marketing strategies with Paula. While they met, Isabel, Daisy and I and the children spent quality time together. We shopped, visited some museums and went to see the famous Martin Park in Mendoza City.

We also spent time touring their property. Juan Carlos had built Isabel a barn. The barn was divided into an office for her to write, a small eating area with kitchenette, a bath with a shower, and at the end a storage area for her gardening and chicken supply.

We would all reunite in the evenings at Isabel and Juan Carlos' home for dinners.

One evening, Isabel prepared whole chickens and cooked them on a rotisserie in their outdoor grill. It was a rare occasion that Isabel cooked and not Juan Carlos. We had a typical Argentinian 'asado' except with chicken.

"Thank God," Adrian blurted out, "finally, Juan Carlos, something other than beef." Adrian loved teasing his old friend.

"Thank Esabel," Juan Carlos said, pronouncing the 'I' like an 'E,' "she owns the chickens."

"I needed a break from the beef," Isabel chimed in, "so Juan Carlos bought me baby chicks. I wanted them mainly for the eggs, but one of the chicks turned out to be a rooster. Now we can have eggs and chicken."

We all laughed. I could hardly recognize my friend. The city girl that I knew as a teenager in the Bronx and now published author looked very much at home, living in a farmhouse on a ranch/winery estate at the foothills of the Andes Mountains, married to a rambunctious, macho, controlling husband. Then again, I could hardly recognize myself from that carefree, ass kicking, computer geek who called New York home to the dress-wearing, stiletto-heeled mother of three and wife to a less rambunctious, macho control freak of a husband, living in a mansion in Northern California.

Daisy, of the three of us, was the only one who had not changed. She remained true to who she was. She lived the life she had always imagined for herself, working in law enforcement and sharing her life with a woman who loved her as much as she loved her. Daisy and Paula shared a home overlooking the Bay area of San Francisco.

Daisy did not like the idea of Paula working in sales because of its fast pace and quota pressures, but the association with Adrian and Juan Carlos proved to be good for Paula. They applied no pressure and were fiercely loyal to her. Paula was self-motivated. She created her own schedule that included the time zone for China. She tried to limit her travels because of Daisy, who constantly worried about her health, but Paula did manage two trips to China to solidify her relationship with a major distributor. It was good to see she had recovered from the brutal beating and humiliation she suffered at the hands of Pablo Santos. All of us had not been together since that awful day and it was not an accident that not one of us mentioned the incident. Paula, however, was the first to address the proverbial gorilla in the room.

"The trip to China was grueling, but thanks to all of you and my darling Daisy, who has taken good care of me, I am stronger than ever and up to any challenge." She paused and looked around at each of us as if waiting for a remark. When none came she continued, "It will take a lot more than that asshole, Santos, to keep me down."

"I don't even like the mention of that scumbag's name," Juan Carlos blurted.

"I take pleasure in knowing he got what his hand called for," Isabel contributed.

"Thankfully, we had Millie, who knew how to track us," Daisy offered, looking my way with glassy eyes.

"That's what we do, isn't it? Take care of each other," I said, trying not to get too sentimental.

"Paula, please don't push yourself. You have done a wonderful job with distribution for all the companies. Juan Carlos and I want you to hire an assistant," Adrian offered.

"I don't need an assistant," Paula protested.

"Oh, but you will," Juan Carlos insisted.

"Paula," Adrian interjected, "some of the vintners here, who are friends of Juan Carlos, would like to be represented by Casa Imperially. That will be a substantial amount of additional work for you."

"How many more companies are you talking about?" Paula asked.

"At the very least, ten," Juan Carlos answered.

"Wow," she exclaimed, "that is a lot."

"Paula," Adrian continued, "I am assigning you a driver and a personal bodyguard."

"Now, Adrian, that is not necessary," she protested.

"It is, Paula," Juan Carlos said. "Taking on these additional companies will make Fairchild very angry. He has not been able to purchase the wineries he was interested in. When the partnership with Benedetti dissolved, he became more aggressive. Recently, when I ran into him at a function in Buenos Aires, he issued a veiled threat to me.

"I don't care about his threats," he continued, straightening his posture, "Esabel and I are well protected."

"So are we," I chimed in. "And just recently at a wine tasting event, he approached me and issued a not so veiled threat against Adrian."

"Paula, it sounds like a good idea," Daisy contributed. "I wouldn't worry so much about you if I knew someone was with you. I can take care of myself, but, baby, you refuse to carry a firearm. Please," she pleaded, "don't argue with them about this. It is for your own safety."

"Geez, all right. First an assistant and now a bodyguard and driver."

We all breathed a sigh of relief when she didn't put up a fight. Paula could be quite feisty.

While we visited our friends in Mendoza, Adrian managed to convince Juan Carlos to buy a jet for personal and business use. Juan Carlos had never seen the need to own a jet, but Isabel liked the idea.

Hector drove us from the airport to the penthouse. Adrian wanted to go to his office the following day to catch up on business. He held Adam in one arm and with the other he held onto Angelique's little hand. I held her other hand. Together we would lift her in the air to hear her giggles. I carried little Adrian in a baby carrier. The elevator took an unusually long time to reach the main lobby.

"Adrian," I spoke, "Paula is going to be pissed when she finds out she has two bodyguards."

"I know," he said, laughing. "She will get over it."

"These two guys are well recommended," I offered.

"Good," he said, gazing in my direction. "I feel better knowing she has protection. This elevator is taking an awfully long time."

Finally, one of the elevators came. As we walked in, Hot-to-Trot rushed in behind us.

"Hi, Adrian."

"Hi," Adrian responded, closing his eyes briefly as if in exasperation. "I thought you were leaving the country?"

How the hell would you know that, dear husband?

"The trip was postponed."

I let go of Angelique's hand to enter the card key for the penthouse and I punched the button for her floor, not that she noticed. My chest was starting to tighten, but I decided to give Adrian the benefit of the doubt.

"I was wondering, would you like a tour of our real estate project," she asked, eyeing me daringly.

"It is your project, Susan," Adrian barked. "I am not interested in a tour. I am interested in your upholding your end of the agreement. That is all."

"Sure, Adrian."

Mercifully, the elevator reached her floor and the doors opened.

"Good night," she said as she stepped out of the elevator. Then quickly as the doors were closing, she added, "I sent you photos of our project and our evening together."

Adrian's neck and face were beet red. I could barely breathe, so we rode to our floor in silence. I was surprised to see Hilda waiting for us in the foyer. She greeted us joyfully, hugging and kissing each child with the warmth of a grandmother.

"How was your trip?" she asked.

"It was wonderful," I answered before Adrian. "Juan Carlos and Isabel asked for you and Hector. You would have enjoyed this trip, Hilda."

"I know, but I needed the time to visit my family in Mexico. My aunt is very old and frail. I hope you tell me all about it."

"I will and I took lots of photos."

She helped settle the children in one of the bedrooms across from our bedroom. It had been turned into a nursery to house the three little ones.

Adrian and I excused ourselves to go to our bedroom to bathe and change.

"Millie," Adrian called with stretched out arms.

I walked into his arms and buried my face in his chest.

"Baby, I swear there is nothing between Susan and me. She is trying to antagonize us both."

I looked up into his eyes. He was gazing in my direction with eyebrows knitted and lips pursed. He wasn't lying.

"Adrian, how did you know she was supposed to be out of the country?"

"She had told me."

"When did she do that?"

"Millie, please, do we have to do this?"

"Yes, we do, Adrian. When?"

"The week before we left for Argentina, she telephoned me."

"Why would she do that, Adrian? Is she in the habit of reporting her whereabouts to you?"

"No, Millie. Please let's not do this."

"I need to know, Adrian. Again, I ask, why would she feel the need to tell you where and when she is going?"

"I don't know the answer, Millie. Please," he pleaded, embracing me tighter, "don't let her get to you."

"She doesn't. It's you that gets to me, Adrian. I'm trying to understand what is going on here. I don't want to wake up one morning to the realization that I have been played by you and feeling like a complete fool."

"That is not going to happen. I would never play you, baby. I love you. You need to trust me."

"Fine, Adrian. You don't know why she reports her whereabouts to you. You didn't think it odd at the time," I stated more than asked.

"Fine, Adrian," I repeated. "I am exhausted. Why don't you shower and I'll take care of the children. I'll shower after we have dinner."

"Kiss?"

"Sure." I gave him a chaste kiss on the lips. He knew I wasn't over this incident.

"Oh, by the way," I said before leaving the bedroom, "I want to see those photos she sent you. It will be nice if you volunteer them." He threw his shirt on the side chair and slammed the door to the bathroom.

What is he so upset about? He knows I can access his computer any time I want. Isn't it better that he volunteer them?

Hilda and I were sitting on the sofa when Adrian appeared bathed and dressed in lounge pants, T-shirt and slippers.

"Millie," he called.

"I'm on the sofa with Hilda."

"Where are the children?"

"Little Adrian is asleep in his crib. Angelique and Adam have been fed and are waiting to say good night to you."

"Give them to me. I'll put them to bed."

I walked Angelique to her father, who grabbed her hand. I then placed Adam in Adrian's free arm. Hilda and I watched as he carefully walked to the nursery.

"He is a good father," Hilda proclaimed.

"Yes, he is," I agreed. "Was his father as hands-on with Adrian as Adrian is with his children?"

"No. Adrian is very involved with his children. He loves bathing, changing and feeding them. His father was not good at those things. He was involved in Adrian's schooling and sports activities. His father enjoyed him better as he grew older."

"Millie," Adrian called again as he entered the living room.

"I'm here on the sofa with Hilda. I was showing her the photos of our trip."

"Oh."

"Millie has them on her computer," Hilda volunteered. "I love the photos of Isabel's chickens."

"She takes good care of them," Adrian said, walking around the sofa to sit. "What else does Millie have on the computer?"

"Oh, Adrian," Hilda gushed with pride, "photos of you and the children in Argentina and of our trip to Tahiti. Now we have to go back and take little Adrian. Come, let me serve you both dinner. It's getting late."

After dinner, Adrian and I retired to our bedroom with a bottle of wine and two glasses. Adrian served us each a glass. I took a sip.

"I'm going to take a shower," I announced.

"OK, I'll be here."

The wine bottle was half empty by the time I returned. My computer was neatly placed on Adrian's night table and I noticed it was turned on. Adrian was lying on the bed naked, sipping his wine. He had one arm over his head, holding on to one of the spindles of the headboard.

Now that is an inviting pose. The things I could do to him.

I announced myself.

"Hey, baby," he crooned, obviously a little tipsy.

"Hey, yourself. What have you been up to besides drinking half a bottle of wine?"

"I booted up your computer."

"What for?"

"I want you to do something for me." He sipped more of his wine.

"What would you like me to do?" I asked as I sat on the edge of the bed in front of the computer.

"Please go into my emails."

"OK." I did as I was told. I immediately could tell that he had not accessed his email account since yesterday morning. I also immediately saw that Hot–to-Trot had sent him an e-mail shortly after running into her in the elevator.

"I'm in your email account. Now what, Adrian?"

"Is there an email from Susan?"

"Yes."

"Open it, please." I did as I was told.

"I suppose you want me to read it to you."

"Before you do, tell me if there is an attachment."

"Yes, there is."

"OK, please read the email." He sipped some more of his wine.

"My Dearest Adrian, Attached are the photos as promised. I hope I didn't get you into hot water with the wife. Anyway, our project is coming along nicely. I know you will reconsider my request to modify the agreement. Love and kisses and more, yours always and whenever, Susan."

I was already seething. Love and kisses and more. Yours always and whenever. Really?

What is wrong with this bitch?

"I don't know why she would send me photos. She knows I can't see. Please open the attachment," he said as he sipped some more of his wine. I did as I was told.

"Adrian, don't be so dense. She sent them after she saw us. She sent them after saying she had sent them. These photos are not for you. They are for my benefit."

"Well, what do you see?" he asked, sipping some more of his wine and ignoring my comment.

"Photos of what looks like an upscale housing complex called Sunny Gardens. There is a total of five photos of the complex. Then there are another three photos." I paused to look at Adrian. He sipped some more of his wine. His glass was almost empty. I poured him more wine.

"Well, Millie, tell me. What are the other three photos?"

"They are of you and Hot-to-Trot outside this building in the evening," I said in a small voice. "One picture is of you and her by the Escalade and you're kissing."

"I swear, she kissed me on the cheek," he quickly said, sitting up on the bed.

"The photo shows the back of her head. One can easily mistake it for a kiss on the lips. But I know better, Adrian."

"Thank God, Millie. You can see I was not receptive."

"Yes, I can make that out, but only because I know you. Adrian, what is troubling to me is why you have allowed yourself to be manipulated by this woman. She had someone photographing the two of you. First, it was the emails that she knew I would see; second, this real estate project; and now these photos. What is it going to take for you to realize that she won't stop until she gets you in a worse compromising situation?" I asked incredulously.

"I understand that now. I had no idea how devious she could be. Millie, I promise you, I will extricate myself from that agreement as soon as I can. I promise never to be anywhere near her again."

I could tell he was sincere. I knew she was setting him up. But I couldn't help being angry with him for being so naive.

"Baby, are we good?"

"Yes, Adrian, we are good."

"May I have my way with you," he asked, leaning back on the head-board and resuming his pose as before.

"Here, baby, drink some more," I purred as I poured him more wine. He did as he was told.

I powered down the computer and put it away. I then went to the bottom drawer in Adrian's dresser where I found the handcuffs and an-kle cuffs he had used on me. I brought them to the bed. I fastened each cuff to each corner of the bed as quietly as I could.

"Well, baby, what do you say? May I have my way with you?"

"I was thinking about mixing things up a bit," I almost whispered.

"Oh?" he asked, sipping his wine with a wild look in his eyes. "I can hear the swishing of a nightgown. Why are you wearing a nightgown? Take it off." He was slightly slurring his words.

Oh, this is going to be fun.

"I will eventually, but first I want your permission to have my way with *you.*"

"That is mixing things up a bit." He laughed and sipped more wine. "What exactly did you have in mind?"

I glanced at his penis and it was already showing interest.

"I want to have my way with you," I repeated, this time palming his face with both hands and planting little kisses around his eye, nose and lips. He was putty in my hands whenever I did this. He swallowed hard.

"Before I give permission, I want to know what you have in mind."

"I never ask you before I give permission," I answered as I worked my lips down to his neck. "Don't you trust me?"

"Yes, I do, but you are inexperienced. I ..." I didn't let him finish, planting a passionate kiss on his lips. My tongue invaded his mouth, searching out his tongue and drinking all of him in. Adrian was quick to respond, taking his free arm to pull me closer. I pulled away to leave him wanting more. I took off my nightgown and lay on top of him. He sipped more wine and used his free hand to touch my body.

His hand slowly ascended up my right arm, fingering the inside of my elbow. Using his fingertips only, he continued to my upper arm and paused to finger my shoulder, then my neck and throat. His facial expression became serious as he concentrated. He moistened his lips, parting them slightly. I let his hand journey down my chest. He fondled one breast, then the next. I was getting hot.

"OK, Mr. Z, you have had enough wine." I removed the glass from his hand and placed it on the night table. "I don't want you falling asleep."

"That is not likely to happen, Mrs. Z," he panted. "I am intrigued."

Adrian was now sporting that big wide smile that melted my inside, and his big blue eyes were gazing dreamily in my direction.

"Tell me, baby. What is it you have in mind?"

"I want to tie you up," I responded, rubbing my body on his.

"How about I tie you up?"

"No. I want to tie you up. I want to do things to you."

"I don't think so." He laughed nervously.

"You do it to me."

"That's different."

"Why is it different? I trust you to do it. Why can't you trust me to do it to you?"

He started to sit up, lifting himself with one arm while he attempted to hold me with the other. I knew this move well. Eventually, I would end up on my back underneath him. But I was too quick. I slapped his arm away from under him, pinning him down with my hand on his wrist. At the same time, my other hand caught his free hand that was in midair in route towards me.

He yelled and laughed out loud all at once.

"Fuck, Millie! That was a good move. Although not fair since you got me drunk." He laughed again nervously.

"C'mon, baby," I crooned in his ear, darting my tongue in and out. "Let me do this."

"I don't think I'm going to like it. You know I like the control."

"I know. But now you get to surrender." I straddled him, bringing my breasts up and against his face. He promptly sought out a nipple and sucked wildly at it. I gently pulled away and he sought the other, sucking and kissing it.

"Let my arms go, baby. I want to touch you."

"No. No touching."

"That's torture for me."

"I know. Let me torture and pleasure you all at once. It truly is exhilarating. You should try it. Give your permission," I purred.

"I don't think I'll like it," he repeated in a small voice.

"Try it. You might like it," I purred again.

"OK," he responded in a lower voice yet.

Before he could change his mind, I quickly cuffed his right hand.

"Millie," he started to complain, but I quickly cuffed the other hand.

"Baby, I don't know." I didn't let him finish. I cuffed his right ankle.

"Fuck, Mill, the legs, too?"

I didn't answer, quickly cuffing the other ankle.

Now you are mine, Mr. Z. And what a delicious dish you are!

While I was south of the border, I caressed and kissed the skin on the inside of his legs, slowly working my way up to his knees.

"Fuck, Mill, this is torture," he complained and he said a few other things I chose to ignore.

"Keep quiet or I'll have to gag you."

"You wouldn't dare," he exclaimed.

"You are in no position to dare me." He laughed, recognizing his own words to me. Then he began to wriggle around.

"Stop moving," I warned as I slapped his left thigh, "or I'll have to spank you."

He roared with laughter. He finally got it. I was using all his techniques. The student learned well from the master. His right leg twitched nervously. He inhaled deeply and stilled his leg. He settled his head on the pillow and closed his eyes. I could see his lips form that half-cocked smile of his. He was surrendering to me. He was trusting me.

I began my assault up to his inner thighs, kissing, licking and gently nipping at his skin. I blew air on his balls, causing him to giggle. I glanced up to see his broad smile with lips parted. His eyes were now open, gazing straight ahead, visualizing everything that I was doing to him and perhaps anticipating what was to come.

I continued my kissing-and-licking assault, journeying up his now erect shaft where a bead of semen topped the crown. That too was licked and kissed tenderly before being taken into my mouth. My man groaned with pleasure. My hands massaged their way to his nipples. I gently rubbed them with the tips of my fingers. Once they were hard, I rubbed them with the palms of my hands.

Adrian's body was responding to my touch. He inhaled deeply as I worked his fully erect penis with my mouth. I stole a glance up at him and he had shut his eyes, but he was all smiles. I went down on him, tightening my grip on him slightly and he inhaled sharply through his parted lips.

I stopped playing with his nipples and withdrew my mouth from his penis.

"Not yet, baby," I ordered. "Don't move."

I kissed, licked and nipped my way up to his belly button. I rubbed my breasts against his erection. Adrian groaned with delight. He lay still, waiting for my next move. I straddled him and, bending over, I kissed and gently sucked on his nipples.

"Baby, please," he begged, "I need you."

I eased myself down onto his erection. My rhythmic thrusts were met by his. I searched for that sweet spot inside of me and found it. It didn't take long before I climaxed over him.

"Baby, can I touch you?" Adrian asked sweetly.

"Yes," I whispered, releasing him from his shackles.

He sat up and wrapped his arms around me, snuggling his face in that tender spot between my shoulder and neck. We both picked up the pace. I felt another wave of convulsions and we climaxed within seconds of each other. We exchanged a passionate kiss without changing our pose or breaking the connection.

"You are something, Mrs. Z," Adrian finally said, stroking my back with both hands. "You are full of surprises."

Chapter 15

"Millie, where are you?" Adrian called out from our bedroom.

"I'm in the nursery with Hilda," I warned him since he had a habit of walking around naked.

"Good morning, Vieja," he greeted Hilda with a towel wrapped around his waist. He held his arms out for a hug from her, which she immediately gave.

"What are you two up to in here?"

"Well, the children are fed, bathed and now dressed. I was waiting to have breakfast with you. So go get dressed," I ordered.

"Gee, you're bossy this morning," he said, laughing as he exited the room. "I'd better hurry before I get spanked."

Hilda looked at me startled.

"He is just kidding."

The three of us had breakfast together. Adrian asked Hilda about her visit with her aunt. He was genuinely interested in her family.

"You know, Adrian, my Tía Carmen always asks for you. She would love to meet Millie and the children. She feels terrible that her health did not allow her to come to your wedding."

"Maybe we can go visit after the Christmas holidays," he suggested. "Millie, we can visit Tía Carmen before going to Tahiti. You will love her. It has been a long time since I've been there."

"That sounds like a great idea. Where does she live?" I asked.

"She lives in a small quiet town forty minutes south of Cabo San Lucas. Will you ask Hector to come along?" Adrian asked Hilda.

"No. I think he should stay at Luna Llena."

"Are you two fighting?"

Hilda looked very uncomfortable speaking about Hector to Adrian. It was no secret that they were sweet on each other, but for some reason she didn't like discussing him with Adrian. When we took her to Tahiti, she refused to ask him along. I was beginning to believe she didn't feel comfortable with Hector when Adrian was around. I couldn't understand why. Adrian was completely at ease with Hector and sometimes treated him like a pseudo father.

"Millie, my father used to take us there on vacation. Do you remember, Hilda?"

For a moment I thought Adrian meant him and his biological mother.

"I remember," she answered softly, not looking at either of us.

"My father would send me and Hilda down first. He would wrap up his business, then join us a week later," Adrian recollected. "My father always did that. He never traveled with us. He would join us a week later. I could never figure that out."

Hilda looked uncomfortable with the subject matter, so I tried to steer the conversation in another direction.

"I bet there is great scuba diving there."

"There is," Adrian offered. "We are not going scuba diving."

"Why not?" I asked indignantly. "I am certified."

"So am I, but I do not want to go scuba diving, Milagros. This is an argument you are not going to win."

Mission accomplished. We are off the subject of Adrian's father.

"Will you and the children accompany me to the office?"

"No. Not unless you wanted me to help you with something in particular. I thought Hilda, the children and I could go to the zoo, have lunch out and maybe do some shopping. I want to buy some clothes for the children."

"Then I will pick you up at five and we can head back to Luna Llena together."

I knew why he asked if I was going to the office with him. He figured after yesterday I would want to keep an eye on him. But I was going to demonstrate to him that I trusted him. Besides, I had bigger fish to fry.

An hour after Adrian left for the office, we were all ready to head out to the zoo. Angelique and Adam were still too young to enjoy the experience, but I could take photos of them and it was a day out. I also wanted to spend some quality time with Hilda. Before little Adrian's birth, I had behaved like a beast on more than one occasion. There was also a mission I had to go on and the trip to the zoo would serve as cover.

"Mrs. Z," Richard called out, "Hilda and the children are on their way to the lobby. The Escalade is parked and waiting in front of the building."

"Thank you, Richard," I said as I entered the foyer. "Go ahead to the zoo with Hilda and the children. I'll take a cab and catch up with all of you."

"Mr. Z is not going to like that."

"I won't tell him, so make sure you don't," I warned.

"I would never say anything. That is, of course, unless he asks."

"Of course. Don't worry, Richard. He won't ask."

"Hilda is sure to tell him," Richard said conspiratorially.

"I don't think she will. Richard, please go. I am thirty minutes behind you and no more."

"OK." He glanced at my feet. I was wearing a pair of canvas flats that did not go with the rest of my outfit. He smiled knowingly, then asked, "What should I tell Hilda?"

"Tell her I have been held up by a telephone call."

I waited for Richard to ride the elevator down before I started the twelve-flight descent to the twentieth floor. Through the building security cameras, I was able to see that Hot-to-Trot had left the building just fifteen minutes before. She hailed a cab so it was safe to say that she would be gone for a while. At least long enough for me to do what I needed to do.

I picked the lock and was not disappointed to discover there was no alarm or secondary security. The apartment was a two-bedroom with a balcony. It had a nice sized kitchen with separate dining area. It was nicely furnished. The color scheme was a monochromatic white. Too sterile for my taste, but nice. The apartment was clean and neat. Too neat.

What is your game, lady? And it isn't real estate. What is your hold on my husband?

At the far end of a long hallway was one bedroom. Her bedroom. This room was also done in monochromatic white. It too was clean and very neat. I went to her dresser and instinctively opened the bottom drawer. Just as I suspected, there were sex toys. My chest began to tighten.

You didn't think you were the only one he played games with, did you?

The other drawers were neat and orderly, so I did my best not to disturb anything. The lingerie drawer was the last I investigated. Beneath the clothes was a data disk labeled "insurance." I removed it.

Geez, this bitch is predictable.

The closet revealed nothing of interest. The other bedroom had been turned into an office and it, too, was nicely furnished in the same color scheme.

Geez, lady, put some color in your life.

On top of the desk was a laptop computer. This had to be her personal computer. I booted it up and entered the disk. I noticed the computer had a web cam. My heart sank.

If I am to protect my husband, my marriage and my children, I have to be strong.

I opened the file. It was a sex tape taken in her bedroom. I did not have the time to view all of it nor did I have the courage. There was three hours' worth of material. I decided to take it with me since my husband was the star of the video. I searched her computer and cloud accounts. She stored similar videos in her computer but not in the cloud accounts. I searched the office and there were no other disks. There was an external hard drive neatly tucked away in the credenza behind the desk. I opened those files also. There were more similar videos. I looked around the office. There were no pictures of her, family or pets. Time was starting to get away from me. One more thing I need to look at. I went through the desk drawers. I went through the closet. Nothing. Nowhere in this apartment was there anything that said this person had a personal life. There were no musical discs. No movies. No magazines. No books. A sterile life.

I don't think so. Hot-to-Trot does not live here. She hailed a cab. Surely, she has to drive. If she lived here she would park in the garage like all the other tenants.

Lady, you just became a loose end.

"Millie," Hilda called as soon as she spotted me. "We just got here."

"Hi, Hilda. How is that possible? You left before me." I was careful not to mention the time.

"Richard ran into some traffic. I told him what route to take, but he didn't listen." We both laughed at poor Richard's expense.

He purposely took the longest route. Richard is a treasure.

I took plenty of pictures of Hilda with the three children. Richard took some of all of us together. It was noon. I decided I had had enough of the zoo and suggested we go for lunch. We had just been seated when Richard gave me his smart phone.

"Mrs. Z, Mr. Z would like to speak with you."

"Hello, Adrian."

"Hello, Milagros. Where are you?"

"We are not far from the zoo. We just sat down for lunch. Did you want to join us?"

"No."

"Why are you calling me on Richard's phone?"

"I called you on your phone but you didn't pick up."

"Let me check the phone." I panicked. Did I leave the phone in Hot-to-Trot's apartment! I frantically searched for my smart phone. It was at the bottom of my purse. I let out a sigh of relief. I checked for calls and sure enough, Adrian had called twice. "Baby, I'm sorry. The phone was at the bottom of my purse."

"That's all right," he said with a laugh. "I was calling to find out how your day was going."

"It's going great. We took a lot of photographs. After lunch we are going shopping."

"That is great. I'm glad you are all having a good time. Millie, I also wanted to ask you to look into the security cameras at the penthouse and the entire building."

"Why? Is there a problem?"

"Security at the building called me to tell me the cameras are down."

"I don't have my computer with me, Adrian. You can tell them to call Abbott Security. They can check out the hardware. Let me know what they tell them. If it is a software problem, I can take care of it as soon as I get back to the penthouse."

"I'll do that. Thanks, baby. Well, I will leave you to your lunch."

We hung up and I remembered to remove my wedding bracelet from the baby carriage where I had hidden it and placed it back on my wrist. Luckily, Hilda never noticed. I had a suspicion that Adrian would track me. We had matching bracelets with tracking devices that would aid either one of us to find the other should the need arise. That was my brilliant idea. The children had similar devices in their baby bracelets. Also my brilliant idea.

Richard opted not to eat with us but sit at the counter. He wanted to phone Sarah. No doubt he wanted to confirm his next visit. Hilda was relaxed, enjoying the outing with the children. She doted over them like a grandmother. I suppose in a way she was.

"I'm looking forward to our trip to Baja California, Hilda. I don't know very much about the area."

"Oh, Millie, it is beautiful. Take plenty of beachwear. The children will love it."

"Did Adrian's father take many vacations with Adrian?"

"Yes, of course. But mostly it was to Baja. He was very fond of the weather and it was not too far to travel to. Every other year he would take Adrian to Spain to spend time with his family."

"Why did Adrian say his father never traveled with him?"

"I don't know. He doesn't remember, I guess."

"Did you accompany Adrian to Spain?"

"Yes, of course. His father was not very good with him as a child. You know, the daily routines. I took care of those things."

"Well, I am looking forward to this trip and meeting your family."

The thought of the trip made her smile.

"My family wants to see Adrian. It has been a long time since he has visited."

"Adrian is a very lucky man to have two wonderful families and people that love him. He is especially lucky to have you in his life."

"Millie," her eyes swelled with tears, "it's nice to hear you say that."

"Hilda, we are all lucky to have you." I leaned over and planted a kiss on her cheek. A tear escaped and rolled down her cheek.

"We'll have none of that," I said as I dried her tear. "What do you say we head back to Luna Llena? Adrian can follow us when he finishes with his work."

"I don't mind heading back. What about our shopping?"

"We can do some shopping. It's early yet."

On our way back to Luna Llena, I sent a text message to Ralph White asking if he could help me with a West Coast matter. He was more than happy to oblige. The surveillance cameras in front of the building captured the license plate of the cab that picked up Hot-to-Trot. She was taken to another residential building across town. I gave Ralph the address of the other building, her place of employment and name. I was also able to send him a photo of her from the security cameras at our building. He promised to get right to it.

I booted up my computer and fixed the software problem at the building.

"You are always working, Millie," Hilda commented.

"Your son is a twenty-four-seven job."

"My son?" she repeated.

"Hilda, you are the only mother he has known. He doesn't speak of his biological mother. She certainly doesn't come around. She has never met Adam or little Adrian. She saw Angelique once. As a matter of fact, I have only seen her once.

"Trust me," I continued, "he loves you like a mother."

She turned away and not another word was spoken until we reached Luna Llena.

"I love him very much, Millie. I'm glad you are his wife. You protect him better than all these bodyguards put together."

"Hilda," I called as I gently grabbed her by the arm, "invite Hector to come with us to Baja California. Adrian is fine with it. You deserve happiness, Hilda."

"Thank you, Millie. Maybe I will invite him."

The children were bathed and fed by the time Adrian came home. I had cooked him my signature dish of rice with chicken. It was too cold to eat out on the patio and so I decided we would eat in the family room in front of the television. I placed my iPod in the docking station and played our favorite guitar instrumental music.

"This smells delicious, baby. Where are the children?"

"Hilda is upstairs with them. I wanted us to be alone. Do you mind?"

"Not at all."

Adrian sat on the sofa while I assumed my usual place on the floor by his side. We ate making small talk. He told me about his afternoon. Paula was doing an outstanding job. He confessed that she might be doing too good a job and he might not be able to keep up with the business she was generating. We both agreed that was a happy problem.

"Would you like dessert? I made a chocolate cake."

"No, thank you. I am full. I do, however, feel like an after-dinner drink. Will you join me?"

"Sure. Let me clear the dishes. I'll be right back."

Adrian served us a Spanish brandy. It was smooth and warm going down. We sat close together. His arm was around me and I was snug against his body. But I knew this bliss could not last. He needed to know what I knew. Eventually, the proverbial shit would hit the fan. I waited for him to finish his drink.

"Adrian, I need to speak to you about something."

"Sure, Millie, what is it?" he queried, knitting his eyebrows and pursing his lips. "Have you been a bad girl?"

"Sort of."

"Ah." He let out a sigh. "Tell me what you have been up to. Will I be needing satisfaction?"

"Maybe. Actually, Adrian, this is not pleasant."

"Oh," he said straightening.

"This situation with Hot-to-Trot has been eating at me."

"Baby, please, I already told you she means nothing to me."

"I believe you, but your behavior and hers for that matter say something else."

"Millie, please, I don't want to rehash this," he barked.

"You have accused me in the past of withholding information and you have been correct. Now I have information and find I can't keep it from you."

"Millie, what are you trying to say? What does this have to do with Susan? What is going on?"

"Adrian, I needed to know why you entered into a business transaction with her after I asked you to keep your distance."

"Millie, for God's sake, what have you done?"

"It's not what I have done, Adrian. It's what Hot-to-Trot has done. It's what she has on you."

Instinctively, he knew I knew.

"Fuck, Millie," he yelled, getting up abruptly from where we were seated. Leaning against the fireplace with his back towards me, he continued, "What the fuck have you done?"

"Did you think acquiescing to her demands would keep her quiet? How far are you willing to go? How much are you willing to give?"

"I would give everything to erase her from my life."

"Your actions are having the opposite effect, but you can consider her erased."

"What?" He turned from the fireplace to gaze in my direction.

"Adrian, consider her erased," I repeated. "There might be some fallout, but it is nothing we can't handle."

"You had no right involving yourself in my business," he yelled.

"I have every right. I am your wife."

"You have no right," he roared, smashing the crystal brandy glass on the floor. He stormed into his office, slamming the door behind him.

I was stunned. I could not believe what I had just witnessed. I might have cried had I not been so angry. I went to my office to where I had hid the disk and took it with me into Adrian's office. I did not knock or announce myself. He gazed up at me with fire in his icy blue eyes.

"Here," I said, throwing the disk on his desk. "I know you can't see but you will recognize the voices. The conversations and events should bring back pleasant memories.

"You know, Adrian," I continued as I stopped at the side entrance to his office, "you are guilty of only two things, being naive and stupid." And I walked out.

Angelique and Adam were asleep. Hilda had just finished giving little Adrian a bottle and was rocking him to sleep.

"Hi, Hilda," I said, announcing myself.

"Millie, hi," she greeted, looking back at me. "Little Adrian just fell asleep."

I looked at him and all of a sudden I wanted to cry, but I didn't.

"He looks like an angel," I commented.

"Yes he does. They all do. They are such good babies," she said lovingly.

"Thank you, Hilda, for looking after them tonight."

"It was my pleasure, Millie. Are you all right?"

"Yes, everything is just fine," I lied.

"Well good night then, Millie. I will be in my suite if you need me."

"Thanks, Hilda."

I had started to run a bath when the house alarm went off. I flew out of the bathroom with my Glock in hand and raced down the stairs. The alarm suddenly stopped. I could hear all three children screaming upstairs.

"Mrs. Z," Richard called out to me as he ran towards me, "I turned off the alarm."

"Why did it go off in the first place?" I demanded.

"Mr. Z and Roger left for San Francisco. They forgot about the alarm."

Just then I heard the Escalade speed out of the garage and down the driveway.

"Millie, what is wrong," cried Hilda, wrapping a robe around her.

"Nothing, Hilda. It was Adrian and Roger. They had to head back to the office."

"Is there something wrong?"

"No, Hilda. Adrian forgot something he needs for a meeting in the morning. So he decided to stay." I lied, but there was no sense upsetting her.

"Well then, good night again," she replied chuckling and went back to her suite.

"Good night, Richard. I have three screaming babies upstairs."

"Mrs. Z, are you all right?"

"Yes, Richard. Thank you for asking. I'll see you in the morning."

I stopped by the wine refrigerator and took one of Adrian's premium wines upstairs with me. The children were finally back asleep. I finished running the bath and got in with a glass of some fine wine. I thought I should be crying. I thought I should be thinking of Adrian. I should be trying to make heads or tale of his reaction this evening. But the truth was that I was exhausted. The wine and the bath were doing the trick. I was relaxing. Adrian, Hot-to-Trot, scandalous videos, diamonds worth a fortune, psychotic drug dealers and unethical lawyers were a distant memory. I was re-setting my clock. Tonight would be a good peaceful night.

Chapter 16

Hilda came to the nursery to help me with the children. We bathed and dressed them.

"Oh, Hilda," I exclaimed.

"What is it, Millie?"

"One of the outfits I bought for Angelique is the wrong size. I hate to have to drive back to San Francisco just to exchange this."

"Can I go with you?" she asked. "I left a package back at the apartment."

"Sure thing. Richard can drive us to the store first. I'll make sure Adrian is at the office so we can make a quick stop at the apartment. Then we can escape back to Luna Llena."

"Are you two fighting?"

"No," I replied, exaggerating the word.

Richard drove us to the store where I exchanged Angelique's outfit. We then all stopped to have lunch. I checked the tracking device on

Adrian's bracelet. He was at the office. The coast was clear at the apartment. Richard waited in the car while Hilda, the children and I went upstairs. I might have left them in the car, but two of them needed a diaper change. I was beginning to hate that apartment.

Hilda picked up her package and helped me change the two little ones. We didn't take long and I was anxious to leave. The elevator slowed its descent and came to a complete stop on the twentieth floor. My stomach tightened. The doors opened and there stood Hot-to-Trot with Adrian.

"Dada," screeched Angelique.

She tried to run to him, but Hilda restrained her. Angelique's voice startled Adrian. Without thinking, I took off my bracelet with my left hand and threw it at him. Despite being a left-handed throw, I clocked him nice and hard on the forehead.

The elevator doors were closing when I heard him say, "What the fuck," as he caught my bracelet in his hands.

Poor Hilda had a horrified look on her face. We rode to the lobby in silence. There was nothing either one of us could say. Not a word was uttered in the car ride back to Luna Llena.

Hector was waiting for us by the garage door. He helped us unload the children and take them inside. We were in the kitchen when Hilda finally spoke.

"Millie, let me make some tea for us. Let's sit the children in their highchairs."

"Thanks, Hilda. I could use a cup of tea." We were busy with the children when my phone rang.

"Richard, could you please see who it is?"

"Mrs. Z, it's Roger."

"Put him on the speaker. Hi, Roger, my hands are busy right now, that is why Richard put you on the speaker. What can I do for you?"

"Mrs. Z, I don't know what to do." He sounded upset.

"What is the problem, Roger?"

"Mrs. Z, I tried to protect him."

I finished what I was doing and gave my full attention to Roger, taking him off speakerphone.

"Roger, tell me what is going on. Where is Mr. Z?"

"We were ambushed outside. They took Mr. Z. I don't know where he is. They knocked me unconscious. Ms. Mathews is still unconscious."

My head began to reel to think that they had still been together. I tried to compose myself.

"Roger, call nine-one-one and request an ambulance for you and the bitch. I can track Mr. Z."

"Mrs. Z, he left his bracelet at the office."

"That is not a problem. Roger, get medical attention and let me know what hospital they take you to. Once I recover Mr. Z, I'll go to you."

"Mrs. Z, I am very sorry. There were three of them."

"Don't worry, Roger. Get medical attention, please."

By now everyone was in the kitchen. Hilda was crying on Hector's shoulder. Tony and Frank were blaming each other for not being in San Francisco with Adrian. Richard was the only calm person there besides me.

"OK, guys, listen to me. Stop the blame game. Frank, I want you and Hector here to protect Hilda and my little ones. Tony, you come with me and Richard."

"Mrs. Z, he doesn't have his bracelet. How are you going to track him?" Richard asked.

"I gave him my bracelet earlier. Let me check if he still has it with him."

I put the GPS on my smart phone and instead of calling for Adrian, I called my name. The tracking device was working. I had a location. Besides, if that failed I had a backup plan. I could always use his smart phone to track him.

"Let's go, guys."

Richard was driving like a mad man.

"Slow down, Richard," I yelled from the back. "Don't get us killed."

The sun was already low on the horizon and the temperature had dropped, chilling the night air. The GPS took us to an old two-story home on a dirt road just outside of San Francisco. There were no other houses nearby.

"Richard!" I called. "Turn off the headlights and the engine. Let the car roll past the driveway. There is a spot to your right where we can hide the Escalade. Do you see it?"

"Yes, I see it." He did as he was told.

We exited the car, closing the doors quietly.

"Mrs. Z, can you walk in those shoes?" Tony asked.

"Yeah. Take your firearms out and rack the slide. We can assume the three men who attacked them are inside. There are three of us. If Mr. Z is OK, they stand a chance of living. If he is not OK, they are dead men. Do you understand?"

"Yes, ma'am," they both responded.

"Does anyone have a problem with that?" I asked.

"No, ma'am," they both responded.

"Let's rock'n'roll."

Tony went to the front door. I crept towards the back entrance. Richard walked the perimeter to check for any other entrances to the house and to look inside through the windows. The back windows were dirty and had old curtains hanging. There was one window where the curtains were slightly parted. I could see a light. It was the kitchen. There were no sounds coming from that part of the house. I tried the doorknob, but it was locked. Richard made his way towards me.

"Is the front door locked?"

"No. Tony tried it. He can get in when you give the go."

"Did you see anyone in the front part of the house?"

"No and there are no lights on upstairs either."

"OK. I'm going to let myself in through here. You and Tony go in quietly through the front. Our first mission is to secure Mr. Z. Go."

Richard left and I picked the lock to let myself in. I took off my heels and quietly checked the back rooms. There was a half bath and a family room off the kitchen. I then walked down the hallway towards the front. Richard and Tony were headed my way. They, too, had taken off their shoes as a precaution. It was an old house and I had no doubt that our movements could be heard. I motioned for Tony to check the upstairs. Richard and I located the cellar door. We listened but could hear no sounds. I opened the door slightly. There was a light on at the bottom. I backed up.

"Was there a cellar door outside?" I whispered in Richard's ear.

He nodded yes. I motioned for him to go and enter from the outside. Richard knew how to pick a lock if necessary. I had taught him. I waited to hear that he was on the outside before continuing through the door. Two steps down I crouched, but I still could not see anything. I could hear Tony's footsteps coming down from the second floor. That was my cue. This is where my husband had to be. I walked a little further down. This time I could see Adrian tied up to a chair and badly bruised. His face was a mess. He was gagged. My instincts told me he was not alone. The old, creaking floorboards alerted them and they were waiting for us.

I decided to make my move. I knew Tony was minutes behind me and Richard should be close to making an entrance. I walked leisurely down the steps. There was nowhere to hide to the right of the stairs. The left side was totally dark. I hid my firearm by my right side and walked towards Adrian.

"Baby, are you OK?"

He looked up and shook his head no. I removed the gag from his mouth with my left hand and cradled his head against my chest while scanning the rest of the room. One corner was very dark. I could not see into it.

"Millie," Adrian whispered. "They are here waiting for you."

"I know. Let's draw them out," I whispered back.

I bent down to untie his hands when I heard a noise from the dark area. I waited a few seconds before I continued untying his hands. I heard a noise again. This time I didn't stop. Instead I gave whoever it was my back.

"Stop right there, bitch. Turn around slowly or your husband dies."

I didn't stop. That was a stupid threat. My body was shielding Adrian. I finished untying his hands and I whispered to Adrian, "Don't move."

"Bitch, I said stop or he gets it."

The voice was coming from the dark area of the basement.

What the hell was taking Richard so long?

I placed the Glock between Adrian's back and the chair. I then bent down to untie his feet.

"Millie, one of them has a broken arm," Adrian whispered.

"Did you do that?" I asked.

"Yes," he whispered.

"Cool," I said with a chuckle. "Don't move. Are they all here? Do you know?"

"I can't say for sure. Maybe not all. I think I heard one take off in the car. Millie, why did you come? Our children need you. They are going to kill us both."

"Not today they're not."

"That's it, bitch, lover boy is dead," came the voice from the back accompanied with movement.

This time I had to believe the threat. All at once I straightened, pulled the Glock from its resting place between Adrian and the chair, and yelled, "Henry." Adrian hit the floor. I turned and took the first shot into the dark immediately changing my position. Tony ran down the stairs and took a shot at the single light bulb. Two shots came back in our direction. Richard finally popped open the cellar door. The shooter was now exposed. He turned and aimed at Richard. Tony and I blasted two bullets into him.

A second guy came running, spraying the room with bullets. We crouched to return fire just as we had trained. He dropped like the sack of shit that he was.

We heard a car drive to the front of the house. This had to be the third guy.

"Richard, Tony, go out the cellar door. I want you to come behind them. Let them get here first."

They did as they were told.

"Millie, don't send them away. You might need them," Adrian spoke in a small voice. I was worried that he was badly hurt.

"Lay still, Adrian. Your injuries might be worse than you think."

I checked him out to make sure he had not been caught by a bullet. None of the bullets shot in our direction hit us.

I tipped over a round table to shield Adrian and positioned myself away from him by the steps to wait. Upstairs I could hear the front door open. Two men entered laughing. They were celebrating prematurely.

The door Tony and I used to get to the cellar was ajar and where there had been light, there now was darkness.

"Wait, Mr. Fairchild," called out one voice. "Something is wrong. That door should be closed. Let me go first."

The first man slowly descended the stairs with a firearm in his hand. The second man, Mr. Fairchild, was close behind. I couldn't resist causing some mischief. There was an old broom near where I was crouching. I slid it silently and quickly through the spindles of the stairs, causing the first man to stumble and fall. Fairchild, who was close behind, became tangled in the first man's feet and fell. Immediately, I jumped from where I was crouching and spotted the firearm in the first man's hand.

"Don't move, asshole," I said as I put all my weight on his hand. "I have a nasty Glock pointed at your miserable head."

Tony and Richard reached the stairs that were now littered with two bodies. Tony grabbed Fairchild by the scruff of the neck and stood him up. Richard passed them on the stairs. He relieved the firearm from the first man and stood him up as well. They secured both men, checking for concealed firearms and tying their hands behind their backs.

"What the hell do you think you're doing!" Fairchild spat out.

"Shut the fuck up," Richard spat back. And for good measure he slapped the top of his head.

"Take Fairchild upstairs, Richard. And don't leave him alone. Tony, bring that dip-shit over here and sit him down," I ordered.

I helped Adrian to his feet and onto a chair.

"Adrian, stay still. I'm calling for the police and an ambulance." He did not protest.

I called my new best friend, Detective Phil Doran, and explained our situation. He responded before the police and took charge. I was confident that his investigation would lead to a solid arrest of the third man and Fairchild.

The emergency medical team examined Adrian and determined that he needed to go to the hospital.

"I'll meet you at the hospital, Adrian. I have to follow up with Detective Doran."

"OK," he said weakly.

Roger, Hot-to-Trot and Adrian were all in the same hospital. Roger was being kept overnight for observation. Hot-to-Trot suffered a concussion and would be kept longer, but she was expected to recover. Adrian had a couple of cracked ribs, bruises, a busted lip and a fractured pinky. His private physician informed me that Adrian needed to stay for a few days for observation.

I went to the suite in the hospital where Adrian was resting. It was time for a showdown of a different kind.

"Hi, Adrian," I announced myself.

"Millie," he said, trying to sit up.

"Don't move, Adrian, you have a couple of cracked ribs. The doctor ordered some pain meds for you. They should be here shortly."

"Tell me," he began, holding my hand, "what is going on? How is everyone? What is happening to Fairchild?"

"Detective Doran is confident he has enough evidence against Fairchild for kidnapping and conspiracy to commit murder. The third guy, too, will serve time. Our shootings will be ruled justified in self-defense.

"Roger will be released from here tomorrow. They are keeping him for observation. Your girlfriend is on the sixth floor. She is expected to recover from a concussion."

"She is not my girlfriend," he said, letting go of my hand and turning his face away.

"She is something. The question is what," I spat out.

"Your behavior of last night is unacceptable. Adrian, I can't go on like this."

"You should not have involved yourself," he began, but I didn't let him finish.

"No, this is not about me. Don't turn this on me, Adrian. Your behavior was offensive to me regardless of what you thought I had done. Which by the way, all I did was to free you from that bitch.

"It has occurred to me," I continued, "that maybe you didn't want to be freed."

"Milagros, you ..." again I didn't let him finish. I was gaining courage by the second to do what I needed to do for me.

"Milagros, nothing. I'm done here, Adrian. I need a favor from you."

"What?"

"I want you to call your flight crew and ready the Gulfstream for tomorrow."

"You said I had to be here for a few days."

"You do. I'm leaving tomorrow with the children."

"I am not going to call the flight crew. You are not going anywhere and neither are *my* children," he growled.

"I am leaving and I am leaving with our children. You will call the flight crew and ready a flight for us," I ordered. "If I stay, Adrian, I will end up hating you. Is that what you want?"

I placed my smart phone in his hand and he made the phone call.

"Your flight leaves at ten in the morning," he said coldly.

"Thank you," I said, taking my phone back from him. "Good night, Adrian."

"Wait," he ordered, "please come near me."

I did as I was told. He placed the bracelet I had thrown at him on my right wrist.

"This is for your own safety. It works. Please don't take it off."

And that is how we parted.

Chapter 17

I continued monitoring emails that were sent to Adrian and running software to protect the computers associated with Luna Llena Winery, Zaragosa Enterprises, Juan Carlos' businesses and Casa Imperially.

Adrian and I had not spoken since the night I left him in the hospital. We sent text messages back and forth to briefly discuss his businesses and the children. I sent him a box of Godiva chocolates for his birthday from the children. An invitation was extended to him, Hilda and Hector to visit for Christmas. He had not responded. I was not softening my attitude towards Adrian. I could not forgive his behavior our last night together at Luna Llena nor would I tolerate it. But I knew we needed to be civil for the sake of our young children.

Hilda did reach out a few times. I extended the invitation to her directly. She told me she would love to visit but it all depended on Adrian. She would not leave him.

Richard had taken the flight to New York with the children and me. He informed Adrian he was resigning from his employment, stating that he wanted to work in New York to be close to Sarah. Adrian offered to continue paying him if he would stay on as my personal bodyguard for as long as I was in New York. He accepted Adrian's offer. Richard spent his days babysitting me. He would sleep at Sarah's home. They had started making long-term plans and he was actively searching for employment in law enforcement.

My parents' home was finished. It turned out beautifully. It was spacious and updated. I put the finishing touches with alarms and surveillance cameras everywhere.

My mother was glad to have me near, although she confessed she missed Adrian. She was not happy that we were apart.

"What is going on with the two of you," she asked one afternoon we spent together shopping.

"I don't know. We are in limbo."

"Do you think you will reconcile?"

"I don't know, Mom. I wish I could say something encouraging, but the truth is I don't know. He is a stubborn man."

"You're no peach either," she chided.

"Yeah, well, and there lies the problem. Two headstrong people who refuse to give in."

"I don't understand why you are upset with him. You left him. He should be angry."

I couldn't tell my mother about Hot-to-Trot. That was a private matter between Adrian and me. I preferred she think I was the villain in all of this.

I had other matters keeping me busy. I kept tabs on Mr. Sam Sanz, who for the moment was quiet. Ralph White was also following Mr. Sanz's every move. Ralph's reports were always the same. He reported that the drug business was doing well and keeping Sanz busy. He continued to operate under the radar of the local authorities. He did make frequent visits to Nussbaum. I asked Ralph to find out what those meetings were about. Ralph assured me he would get on that right away.

If I were Ralph I would plant surveillance equipment in Nussbaum's office. But that's me.

The appointment with Mr. Nussbaum was rapidly approaching. Adrian must have forgotten because he never mentioned it. I intercepted Nussbaum's email to Adrian confirming the date. I gave him the time and place. I had rented a meeting room at the Hilton Hotel in mid-town Manhattan. Richard would accompany me.

Richard and I reached the Hilton at nine-thirty the morning of the meeting. The meeting with Nussbaum was scheduled for ten. The meeting room was small with a long, oblong boardroom-style table and black-leather swivel chairs surrounding it. There were two pitchers with iced water placed on either end of the table. Outside in the hallway was a long table that the hotel had set up with a coffee urn, a thermos of hot water for tea, a selection of pastries and muffins, and a platter with a nice variety of fruit. Richard was already serving himself when I saw the elevator doors open.

Adrian emerged like a bat out of hell. His trench coat was wide open and flapping in the air as he walked briskly towards me. His smart phone was in his hand and he was wearing the ear buds. He was tracking me. Frank and Tony were close behind him. Richard glanced worriedly in my direction. I just smiled.

It's show time with Mr. Z.

"Adrian," I called to orient him.

"Why didn't you notify me of this meeting?" he barked.

"It's nice to see you, too, Adrian," I said sarcastically.

"Why didn't you notify me?" he repeated, ignoring my sarcasm.

"This has nothing to do with you."

"The hell it doesn't," he spat out with eyebrows knitted and lips pursed.

"Would you like some coffee?"

"Yes, thank you. Are you going to answer me?" Again he barked.

"There are pastries, muffins, and a selection of fruit. What would you like?" I asked, ignoring his question. I knew how to push those buttons.

"I'll have whatever you're having," he replied. "Millie, don't ignore me. Answer me. Why didn't you tell me about this meeting?"

"How did you find out about the meeting?"

"Never mind how I found out. Millie, for Christ's sake, answer me."

"You hacked my computer, didn't you?"

"You left the back door open," he said smiling. "That was very careless of you. Or were you sending me an invitation?"

"Funny guy. Here," I handed him a cup of coffee, "I'll carry my cup and a plate of muffins and fruit. You and I can share. Let's go into the meeting room and sit."

He put his free arm around my shoulders, allowing me to guide the way to the table and chairs. I set down my cup and plate. Then I took his cup and set it down.

"Let me have your coat, Adrian."

He took off his coat and I placed it on a hanger next to my own. It felt familiar to me. I missed our routine. I missed him. He looked and smelled delicious.

"Millie," he whispered, "tell me why you didn't notify me."

"Adrian, this isn't your fight. I have what this man wants. I need answers before I give him anything."

"Baby, this is my fight too. You're my wife. You are my business."

"Is that a two-way street?"

He looked away for a moment. He took a sip of his coffee and a bite from the muffin.

"It's a two-way street," he said in a small voice.

Mr. Nussbaum strolled into the meeting room, ending any further conversation between us.

"Mrs. Zaragosa, Mr. Zaragosa, I am Abe Nussbaum," he greeted.

We shook hands and everyone took a seat. Mr. Nussbaum was probably a few years older than Adrian. He was as tall as Adrian and very good-looking with brown, wavy hair, hazel eyes and great physique.

"Well, Mr. Nussbaum, you asked for this meeting. What is on your mind?" Adrian asked with authority. My man was in his element. Taking charge. This is what he did best.

"It appears that Mrs. Zaragosa has something that belongs to me."

"Mrs. Zaragosa is in the room. Don't speak as if she weren't here." Adrian issued the first smack down.

"I didn't mean any disrespect, Mrs. Zaragosa."

"Mr. Nussbaum," Adrian continued, "my wife is not giving you anything until she gets what she wants."

"Ah," he sighed, "you want answers."

He looked at me with a smirk on his face.

"That's right," I retorted.

"I can tell you why your boyfriend Danny got shot. I can tell you why his brother met with the same fate. I can tell you why you and your family had been targeted for assassination, but what good would it do? What could you hope to accomplish? Two of the Sanz brothers are in jail, two are dead, and Sam is too busy to give you a second thought."

"Be that as it may, Mr. Nussbaum, I still want answers. I need closure. I'm sure you can understand."

"No, I can't understand. That is all now in the past. You have moved on. You're married with three children. Do you really want to open up that can of worms that might turn into a dangerous situation for you and your family?"

Adrian had been sitting quietly, running his fingers along the grain of the wood table. That last remark caught his attention.

"Are you threatening my wife and our family, Mr. Nussbaum?"

"No, I'm warning you both. The Sanz and Gardel family are ruthless. Right now, all they want are their diamonds."

Gardel was a young drug lord that operated out of Colombia. The Sanz brothers worked for him.

"You said I had something that belongs to you."

"In a matter of speaking you do. I get a finder's fee for returning the gems to their rightful owners."

"What were they doing in Danny's safe deposit box? Why wait till now to claim them?" I pressed.

He leaned back in his chair and let out another exasperated sigh. Richard, Tony and Frank were strategically positioned. Tony was at one door, Frank at the other door while Richard stood behind Mr. Nussbaum. Mr. Nussbaum was not the least bit intimidated.

"Mrs. Zaragosa, your boyfriend was involved in laundering drug money. So was his brother. The diamonds belong to Gardel. The Sanz brothers were charged with delivering the diamonds to Gardel but failed. Mr. Gardel has been very patient trying all means to get to his property. I am the final straw for him."

"Danny's house was being foreclosed on. If he were involved in laundering money, certainly he would have had the funds to keep his home," I pressed some more.

"Maybe he didn't know how to manage his money. What can I tell you? He loved the hookers. Maybe that is where his money went." He looked straight at me, trying to gauge my reaction. I had none. He was lying about Danny.

"Who murdered his brother?" I pressed again.

"I said I could tell you the why. I don't know who murdered Ed." He turned his eyes down to the wood table. He was lying. He knew.

"Baby, let's step outside," Adrian suggested.

"Mr. Zaragosa," Mr. Nussbaum called, "I hope you and your wife understand this is a serious matter. Gardel wants his diamonds. He is not about to write off three-million dollars."

"Excuse us," Adrian replied.

We stepped out into the hallway and closed the doors behind us.

"Three-million fucking dollars. Millie, are you kidding me? Where are these diamonds? I know what you did with fifty-thousand dollars, but where are the rest?"

"Adrian, what does it matter now? I have them. That is not the issue. I need to know why Danny was murdered. What were those diamonds doing in his safe deposit box? And Ed. What was his role in all this?"

Adrian put his arms around me, drawing me close to his body, and held me there in a warm, loving embrace.

"Baby, sometimes the simplest answers are the correct ones. You don't want to believe the worst about Danny. But let's examine the facts," he said softly.

"Danny had a safe deposit box. It could be that his brother gave him a package and asked that he keep it in a safe place like the safe deposit box. It is inconceivable to me that Danny would not look into the package that he was supposed to safeguard. The other option is Danny knew what was in the package, making him a participant in the money-laundering scheme.

"The house in foreclosure," he continued, "could have been a ruse to confound anyone that might someday investigate him. His brother, Ed, lived way above his means. Danny was portraying someone who was financially broke.

"Danny and Ed were murdered for those diamonds or for failing to perform. You know who murdered Danny. There's a better-than-good chance that Ed was murdered by one of the Sanz brothers. Nussbaum is never going to tell you who did it. That would make him complicit. Besides, Gardel pays him handsomely for protecting his thugs.

"Baby, you've made perpetual enemies of the Sanz brothers. Don't do the same with Gardel. Give him what he wants."

"OK. Adrian, can you do me a favor?"

"Sure, baby, what is it?"

I pulled away from his embrace to look up at him.

"Buy me some time."

"Time? Time for what?" he asked incredulously.

"The diamonds are in California. I don't want to go back until after Christmas." That was true. At least the part about going back to California. I also didn't like the idea of dealing with Nussbaum. It didn't feel right.

"I see," he said sadly. He loosened his embrace, inhaled my hair and then let go of me.

"Let's go back in. I'll see what I can do."

Adrian placed his hand on my shoulder and let me lead us back to our seats.

"Mr. Nussbaum, we are satisfied with your answers. However, we do have a small inconvenience."

"Oh," he said straightening, "what would that be?"

"The parcel you seek is in safe keeping. We will not be able to re-trieve it until after the holidays. That is just slightly over a month away."

"That is unfortunate," Mr. Nussbaum replied. "Gardel is not going to like this."

"Tell him his gems are safe. Surely, a man with a thriving business such as his isn't hard up for three-million dollars. He has waited three years. Give Gardel the assurances he needs," Adrian ordered with the most authoritative tone I had ever heard him use.

"I know him. He will not like this delay."

"Tell him," Adrian commanded again. "We are not hiding, we are not going anywhere. Perhaps Mr. Gardel would like to speak with us directly. Let me know, Nussbaum. We have another appointment to get to now." Adrian effectively dismissed him and ended our meeting.

Mr. Nussbaum left without another word.

"That went well," I commented.

"Hopefully, it buys the time you need."

"When did you get in?" I asked, changing the subject.

"This morning. I came here straight from LaGuardia Airport."

"Shall we go to the house now?" I asked, hopeful that he would join me.

"No. I want to go to my suite first and freshen up."

My heart sank.

"Your suite?" I asked.

"Yes. I have a reservation here at the Hilton," he answered as a matter of fact.

"I thought you would stay at the house."

"No, Millie. You and I have things to sort out, together and separately. I will call Hilda and ask her to reach out to you so that you can make plans for Christmas. I know you asked her to come."

"Will you spend Christmas here, too?" I asked again, hopeful that he would.

"You know I won't be separated from my children for the holidays," he spat out as he stood to leave.

Of course, the children. But Adrian, what about me?

"I would like to visit with the children today. When can I come?"

"Anytime. Come early so you can enjoy them. Will you stay for dinner?"

"Do you want me to stay?"

"Yes," I replied in a small voice.

"Then, yes. I will be delighted to stay for dinner. Millie, are you having Nussbaum followed?" He, too, was good at changing the subject.

"Yes," I replied.

"Good. Until later then."

Tony fetched his coat and led him to the elevators.

"Mrs. Z," Richard said, bringing me out of a melancholy trance, "are you OK?"

"Yes, Richard, thank you. Let's go home."

Adrian rang the doorbell at precisely three in the afternoon. He had changed clothes. He was wearing gray slacks and a burgundy, cashmere-pullover V-neck that showed his black silky chest hair. He looked scrumptious.

"Hi, Adrian," I greeted. "Please come in."

"Thank you. Where are the children?" he asked immediately.

"In their playroom. The one you designed for them."

He gazed straight ahead with that big broad smile that melted my insides. He was obviously pleased with himself.

"May I go to them?"

"Sure. Would you like the nickel tour of the house first?"

"No, thank you. I prefer to be with the children, if you don't mind."

"Of course not. Come this way."

I lead him to the playroom. Little Adrian was in his playpen. Adam was trying to crawl while Angelique tried to make him stand. My mother was enjoying the show instead of supervising.

"Adrian," Mother blurted.

"Dada," screeched Angelique at the sight of her father.

Adrian knelt on the floor with open arms and waited for his daughter to come to him. He smothered her with kisses. My mother brought Adam to him. He too was smothered in kisses. Next was little Adrian's turn. Adrian cradled him in his arms, inhaled his scent and smothered him also in kisses. Then it was my mother's turn. She and Adrian kissed and hugged.

"It is so good to see you, Adrian," Mother greeted with a little too much enthusiasm.

"Thank you, Judy. It's kind of you to say."

"I'll be leaving now, but will I see you tomorrow?"

"I don't know, Judy. I hope to spend time with the children tomorrow, but it depends on Millie and her schedule."

"I'm sure she has nothing to do," my mother volunteered.

"Goodbye, Mom," I said, annoyed with her. "I'll see you tomorrow."

She finally left. Adrian, the children and I were alone. Richard, Tony, and Frank were in an office that had been set up for security purposes.

"Would you like me to acquaint you with the room?" I offered.

"Yes, please."

I had kept it similar to the nursery at Luna Llena. The position of the furniture, toy chests, changing table, and night stand with rocking chair was placed identically to the arrangement at Luna Llena. Adrian walked around the room, still cradling the baby in his arms with a broad smile on his face.

"Wow," he exclaimed, "this is great. It is identical to Luna Llena."

"This house is a miniature Luna Llena," I commented.

"Miniature?"

"Yeah. Luna Llena is a mansion. This is a smaller version."

"Do you miss Luna Llena," he asked softly.

"Yes, I do," I answered in a small voice.

I miss you more, Adrian.

He inhaled little Adrian. Angelique was looking up at her father, tugging on his pants leg. Adam was trying to stand while holding onto his father's other leg. I stepped away to snap a photo with my smart phone.

"What are you doing?"

"I snapped a photo of you and the children. Trust me, this one is priceless."

He laughed loudly.

"Adrian, would you like something to drink or eat."

"No, thank you. I just want to enjoy the children."

"Please make yourself comfortable. I'll be in the kitchen, if you need me."

I busied myself in the kitchen, preparing dinner for all of us while sneaking away periodically to the playroom to observe my family. Adrian had taken off his shoes and was lying on the area rug, wrestling with Angelique and Adam. Little Adrian was safely tucked away in the play-pen. I quietly snapped another photo.

The kitchen was smelling delicious. A chocolate cake was in the oven baking. A second oven was baking a three-chocolate cookie. I made a spice rub for a rib-eye roast and placed it on the rotisserie in the outdoor grill. Garlic mashed potatoes, a cold salad of string beans with beets and red onions smothered in a simple olive oil dressing would accompany the roast. I wanted dinner to be perfect. I would let Adrian select the wine.

Another trip to the playroom. This time Adrian was lying on his back on the floor with a pillow at his head, snoring lightly. Angelique and Adam flanked their father on each side and they too were asleep. Little Adrian was napping on his father's chest. Adrian held his three children in a loving embrace.

What I would give to be in that picture.

I snapped another photo.

Ralph White sent me a text informing me that after the morning meeting, Nussbaum headed back to his office. Ralph's surveillance inside of Nussbaum's office revealed nothing new, only that Nussbaum did call Gardel. Which was weird, since my own surveillance indicated he had not. At least not from his office. It was possible that he telephoned from his car. But how would Ralph know that?

Adrian helped to bathe and feed the children. Finally, we were ready for our dinner.

"Adrian, will you please select a wine?"

"What are the choices?"

I recited a list of wines that were chilling in the wine refrigerator. He picked a Pio Cesare.

"Where would you like to eat?" I asked.

"What are the choices?"

"The dining room, kitchen or family room. It is much too cold to eat out on the patio."

He shivered at the thought. My man did not like the cold weather and made no bones about it. He was frank to the point of being rude.

"The family room sounds like a good idea." He smiled, gazing in my direction.

I was happy with his choice. It was familiar and it gave me hope.

We assumed our usual positions. He on the sofa with me sitting on my heels on the floor next to him. Adrian had requested music. I played my iPod with our favorite guitar music.

"Will you ever outgrow sitting on the floor?" he asked.

"Am I being childish," I asked indignantly.

"No," he quickly responded. "I didn't mean to imply you were childish. It was a poor choice of words. I meant will you ever sit next to me?"

"Maybe, when I'm old and can no longer kneel."

"In my mind you will be forever young," he said softly and stroked my hair. "Thank you for wearing a dress."

"Old habits you know."

We laughed and continued with our dinner. Adrian made small talk about sports. He knocked all my favorite teams while lauding his own. We bantered back and forth.

"Dinner, as usual, Mrs. Z, was a gustatory delight."

"I'm glad you enjoyed it. I made dessert. Would you like coffee with it?"

"I would love some coffee and dessert. Let me help you with the dishes."

"First help me put the children to bed. They fell asleep."

I made coffee for everyone. Tony and Frank went back to their office with cake, cookies and coffee. Adrian had a big piece of the chocolate cake. He tried the cookies and declared they were the best he had ever eaten. It was the first time I baked the three-chocolate cookie. And my man was definitely a chocoholic.

"Can I get you more coffee?"

"Sure. Where is the iPod docking station?"

I guided him to the docking station and then disappeared into the kitchen. When I came back he had replaced my iPod with his. He was playing a new play list of ballads he had compiled.

"Adrian," I announced myself, "here is your coffee."

"May I have this dance, Mrs. Z?" he asked with his arms stretched out waiting for me.

I walked into his arms and we started to dance. His embrace was warm and inviting. I buried my face in his chest, inhaling his scent. His scent was divine. I wanted to desperately kiss his chest hairs but didn't dare. Instead, I settled for resting my face on them.

Adrian must have been feeling the same way because he stopped dancing. He tightened his grip around my waist, drawing me closer to his body. With his other hand, he stroked my hair.

"I love when you wear your hair loose. Did I ever tell you that?"

"No."

"Well, I do and you should know it." He gently pulled my hair, tilting my head back. He bent down and kissed me passionately, his tongue swirling around exploring. Our cheeks hollowed, drinking each other in. He palmed my behind, pressing me against his hardening cock. I wrapped my arms under his arms and around his back, holding him tight to my chest. My chest was heaving with desire. I was aching to have this man.

He slowed his kiss, then pulled away. I could feel his hot breath on my face.

"Baby, I need you. I need you now," he whispered.

"Adrian, I need you too," I whispered back.

He kissed my cheek, then worked his kisses down my neck to that tender spot between my neck and shoulder. I wanted his lips and kisses all over my body. He returned to my lips for another passionate kiss.

"Oh, baby," he crooned, pulling away from my lips. "I have to leave."

"Don't leave," I begged.

"I have to. It's getting late."

"Don't go," I pleaded again. "This is your home."

"Thank you for saying that," he said, inching away. "I want you, but it would be a mistake now. We have too many unresolved issues. I want to take it slow. That is if you still want me."

"I do," I said.

"Tony, Frank, let's go," he ordered. "Millie, can you send the children to me at the hotel tomorrow?"

"Don't you want to come here?"

"No. I need space to think."

"Fine, my mother will take them to you, but she will have to stay to bring them back."

"That's fine with me. I hope she doesn't mind."

"I'm sure she won't mind."

He left without another embrace or kiss. I went to bed and cried. He was right. We had many unresolved issues. I wanted my husband back. But I wanted him free of Hot-to-Trot. I had freed him from her and he had reacted violently. That was another issue. I could not accept that behavior. The breaking of a crystal glass and leaving our home in the middle of the night because of an argument was unacceptable. I needed an apology. I needed assurances that Hot-to-Trot once and for all was history. I needed to know that he wanted to be free of her. I cried because in my heart I believed I was not going to get what I wanted.

Chapter 18

I did not see Adrian for the next two weeks. The children were delivered to him every day by one in the afternoon and they were back with me by five. We communicated by text message only when necessary. I was losing hope of having a meaningful conversation with Adrian. He had acknowledged the need for us to address our issues, but he made no efforts on that front.

"Millie," my mother started her conversation one morning before taking the children to Adrian, "Earl and I had made plans months ago to spend Thanksgiving with his son and family in Atlanta. But if you and the children are going to be alone, I will stay here with you. Earl will understand."

"Don't do that, Mom. I will have a quiet evening with my children. Please go with Earl. I'll be fine. Quite frankly, the notion of having a full house for Christmas has me stressed already."

"Is Hilda coming?"

"Hilda and Hector are coming. Daisy and Paula will be here also. Then, of course, Adrian and his security detail. Sarah and Richard will be here for Christmas dinner. Trust me, I will welcome a quiet evening."

"Why don't you invite Adrian? I bet he's waiting for an invitation."

"I doubt that. He is deliberately keeping his distance. That was his decision, not mine."

"I don't understand you two. How can two individuals be so in love and yet remain apart? It is a mystery to me."

"Me, too, Mom. Me, too."

"Millie," she continued, "don't let this situation drag on. These things have a way of taking on a life of their own. You don't want that to happen. You don't want to reach a point of no return."

I didn't answer. What would be the point? I couldn't tell her everything. So I used the children to get her off the subject.

The Tuesday before Thanksgiving Day, I went food shopping while the children were with Adrian. I decided to buy a turkey and some yams just in case Adrian made a gesture to spend the day together. Mom and Earl had already left for Atlanta.

The phone rang just as Richard was returning with the children. It was Adrian.

"Hi, Millie," he greeted.

"Hi, Adrian," I replied enthusiastically.

"I wanted to tell you not to send the children tomorrow. I am flying to California in the morning."

I almost fell to the floor. I sat on one of the stools by the kitchen island.

"I thought you were staying for Christmas."

"I have to get back to work. I'll return before Christmas. Millie," he paused before continuing, "I have had a lot of time to think things out and analyze our situation. I would like to set a day aside to spend with you. A day we can devote to talking."

"Sure, Adrian. Let me know," I said in a small voice as I tried to fight back my tears. "Have a safe trip back. Goodbye, Adrian." I didn't wait for his goodbye.

I fought back the tears, greeting my children with a happy face.

"Mrs. Z, Sarah and I would like to have you and the children over for Thanksgiving dinner," Richard announced.

"That is so sweet of you both and I appreciate it. But I have a fun filled day planned for myself and the children. With Adrian out of my hair, I thought of taking them to the Macy's Thanksgiving Day Parade."

"Mr. Z won't like that," Richard chuckled.

"Too bad for Mr. Z." That made Richard laugh. In the past I would have dropped an 'f' bomb. But that was in the past. I had to watch my language. I was now a mother of three.

"Well, if you change your mind, the offer still stands. I'll see you in the morning."

"Richard, take tomorrow off. I know Sarah is home tomorrow. Stay with her."

"I can't do that, Mrs. Z."

"Yes, you can. I order you to stay home."

"What if something happens?"

"You're not here in the evenings. Anything can happen any time of the day. So, I insist you stay home tomorrow. I'm going to tell you what I told my mother. I am looking forward to spending time alone with my little ones."

"I'll stay home only if you promise to reach out if you need me for any reason whatsoever."

I choked a little. Richard was very kind and protective of the children and me.

"I promise."

Wednesday morning I noticed the black Escalade parked in the driveway next to the Outback. I had purchased the SUV so that Richard could commute back and forth from Sarah's house to mine. He sent me a text advising me that he and Sarah had dropped the SUV very early that morning. He explained that he wanted anyone watching the house to believe there were other people inside with the children and me. Again I choked up.

Children bathed. Check. Mother bathed. Check. Everyone dressed. Check. Children fed. Check. Mother fed. Check. Turkey seasoned for next day cooking. Check. Adrian arrived safely in San Francisco. Check. Now I was free to play with the little ones. I blasted oldies music and danced with Angelique. Adam had his turn when I held him by the hands and helped him along. Little Adrian got his chance, too. I held him in my arms and twirled us both around the family room. We danced to the point of my exhaustion. It was time for lunch.

I had three text messages from Adrian. The first was advising me that, according to Nussbaum, Gardel had accepted waiting until after the holidays.

That is odd since Nussbaum has not spoken with Gardel.

The second was to inform me that Hilda and Hector would be arriving on the twenty-third of December.

Spoiler alert. I already knew. Hilda and I had communicated with each other.

The third was to ask if I still wanted to go to Baja California with him. I didn't know how to respond to that question, so I left it alone. As a matter of fact, I didn't respond to any of his text messages.

There was a text from Ralph White asking me to call him at my convenience.

"Hello, Millie. How are you?" Ralph greeted.

"I'm doing fine. What about you?"

"No complaints. Millie, I wanted to talk to you personally about Ms. Mathews."

Oh shit. This can't be good. Why does he need to talk to me personally? People only do that when there is bad news.

"It sound serious, Ralph. What's up with Ms. Mathews?" I asked as I sat on one of the stools in the kitchen.

"Well, for one thing," he started, "she is a real estate attorney, not a real estate agent like you said."

She still is a piece of shit.

"She has an apartment at the address you gave me on Chauncey Street and an apartment in your building."

"I know that, Ralph. What else do you have?"

"The lease for the apartment in your building is in your husband's name."

"The lease is for our penthouse," I offered.

"No. This lease is for an apartment on the twentieth floor. But that is not all."

"What else is there, Ralph?"

"Your husband owns the penthouse suite in the Chauncey Street building."

"It must be rental property. Adrian has lots of real estate."

"Well, this one is not rented. My investigator gained access to the suite."

"What did he find?" I asked, trying to keep my emotions under control.

"It is furnished much like the other penthouse. It is well lived in. Millie, your husband has been staying there since you left for New York."

My chest tightened. I could barely breathe. I managed to continue our conversation. I felt as if I were having an outer body experience.

"What about Ms. Mathews?"

"Millie, they both are staying there. She in her apartment, he in his. I think. They have been observed in each others company."

"Fuck, Ralph. What does that mean? Do they go out to dinner? Are they having an affair?" I barked.

"I can't say for sure. They are careful not to touch in public. But, Millie, they are spending most evenings together."

"I see," I said expressionlessly. "What else?"

"She is into memorializing her sex acts."

"What?" I asked incredulously. "What the fuck does that mean? How do you know this?"

"My investigator gained access to her apartment. He noticed a laptop computer with a web cam strategically placed on a desk facing her bed."

"Did he gain access to the computer? Does he know what is on it? Spare me the details, Ralph. Just tell me if Adrian is in those tapes."

"No, he is not."

I let out a huge sigh of relief. Adrian has not been with her recently. Then it occurred to me to ask another question.

"Ralph, when you say they spend most evenings together, what exactly do you mean."

"Millie, those are the words of my investigator. He said since you have been gone, they have met at least twice a week at a restaurant near the Sentinel building."

"Has your guy observed them inside? Are they alone or are there other people with them?

"He did not go in."

"Do they leave the restaurant together?"

"No. She hails a cab and, as you know, he has a driver."

"Shit, Ralph. You know none of this really means anything.

"Concentrate on Nussbaum and Sanz," I continued. "Don't bother with Ms. Mathews anymore. Is there anything new to report on Sanz? Are his brothers still tucked away in jail?"

"No," he replied. "No changes there."

Of course not. You ask to speak to me to give me bullshit news about my husband, but nothing is ever new with Nussbaum or the Sanz brothers.

"Millie, I'm sorry if I upset you before."

"Don't worry about that. Have a happy Thanksgiving with your family."

"Thanks, Millie. You, too."

"OK, kiddies," I said, turning to my brood, "Mommy is emotionally and physically tired. How about a nap?"

Thanksgiving Day the temperature went below the freezing mark. I bundled the children in warm clothing and we headed for the Macy's Thanksgiving Day Parade. I didn't want them out in the street for too long, so we caught the last hour. Angelique loved the big balloons flying overhead. The highlight was seeing Santa Claus make his appearance. I snapped photos of the parade and of the children. I posed them in the stroller in front of Rockefeller Center. I then strolled with them to St. Patrick's Cathedral. I asked a nice elderly couple if they would snap a photo of me with the children in front of the cathedral.

"Why certainly," the man said. "Where is your husband? Doesn't he want to be in the photo?"

"He is not with us. He had to work."

"That is awful," exclaimed the woman. "We live in such a fast paced world, young people don't have the opportunity to enjoy family life."

"That is true," I agreed.

The nice man snapped our photo. Together they fussed over the children, then bid us goodbye, wishing us a happy Thanksgiving.

"You see, children," I addressed my brood, "this is how normal people live. No paranoia. No firearms. No threats. No hand combat. Just ordinary folk outdoors enjoying the day. Now, we will head home to cook our turkey and watch some football. And, if mommy is a good girl, I'll fix her a cocktail."

There were several text and voice messages from Adrian. Daisy and Isabel also left messages. Mom and Earl had called to wish us a happy Thanksgiving. I made a mental note to call them later in the evening.

After dinner, I made that cocktail I promised myself. I dimmed the lights to the family room, lit the gas fireplace and sat on the sofa in front of the television with Angelique and Adam by my side. Little Adrian was asleep in his crib. I opted not to watch the football game. Instead,

I popped in a DVD of *March of the Wooden Soldiers* starring Laurel and Hardy. The video was more for me than them. It brought pleasant memories of my own childhood and I was glad to share them with my little ones, although they were oblivious to the proceedings. Adam was the first to fall asleep, then Angelique followed. I reveled in the peaceful evening and silently gave thanks for my children.

My smart phone buzzed. It was Adrian. The second martini was doing its job. I decided to take his call.

"Where the fuck have you been all day?" he barked.

"Hi, Adrian," I said sweetly.

Definitely the vodka martini talking.

"Happy Thanksgiving to you too. The children and I went to the Macy's Thanksgiving Day Parade, St. Patrick's Cathedral and Rockefeller Center. We took lots of photos. You know, like normal people. Then we came home to cook a turkey, smashed yams, veggies. It was very good. A gustatory delight. We even had some apple pie that I baked. Angelique and Adam helped. Not really. So," I stopped to breathe, "how was your day?"

"Apparently, not as good as yours. Have you been drinking?"

"Yes. Sorry about your day though. I am on my second vodka martini. It has been a long time since I have had one. I'm enjoying the shit out of it."

Surprisingly, he laughed.

"I'll call you tomorrow when you are more coherent."

"Don't hang up, Adrian," I pleaded. "I have an idea."

"What idea do you have?" He sounded amused.

"How about we engage in some phone sex? It's been a long time. It's harmless fun. It won't violate this thing between us."

"What thing is that, Millie?"

"You know, this thing between us that now has a life of its own. *It* is now the puppeteer and you and I are the puppets."

"Hey, baby," he crooned, "what are you wearing?"

"I'm wearing a nightie and panties."

"Leave the nightie on," he ordered softly, "but take off those nasty panties."

And so the game began.

Chapter 19

*T*he room was dark. A hand invaded my private parts. Stroking my sex while lips kissed and sucked on my nipples. I felt pleasure and anxiety all at once. Then my body bowed in ecstasy.

The cries of little Adrian woke me. Angelique and Adam were still sound asleep. I removed him from the crib, changed his diaper and took him to bed with me where he nursed. It was six o'clock in the morning. I decided to give his father a call.

"Hello, Mrs. Z," greeted a sleepy Adrian

"Hello, Mr. Z."

"Why are you up so early?"

"I'm being tormented by two Adrians. One on the West Coast, one on the East Coast."

"What is the Adrian in the East Coast guilty of? I already know what West Coast Adrian is guilty of."

"East Coast Adrian was crying."

"So what did you do?"

"I put a nipple in his mouth and he shut up."

"Lucky, baby. I wish I were there."

"Do you, Adrian?"

"Yes, baby, I do with all my heart."

"I wish you were here, too."

"Soon."

"When, baby?" I whispered.

"Sooner than you think."

"I'll be waiting."

"Millie," he said softly.

"Yes, Adrian."

"I want a date with you. Will you go out with me?"

"You know I will."

"I'm going to send you a package this week. I will be in New York Friday morning. I will be at your front door at seven in the evening to take you out."

"Why not come straight here from the airport?"

"I want to court you."

"Adrian, we are married," I reminded him.

"I know. This is something I want to do. I never courted you properly. We can talk about our issues after I court you or whenever. I promise I will make things right between us. Have faith in me.

"Baby," Adrian continued, "I'm glad you had a good day yesterday with the children. You said something very important last night. Albeit under the influence of alcohol."

"What did I say?"

"You described your day with the children and then said, 'You know, like normal people.' I got it. I understand your fondness for spending the holidays in New York."

"You did?" I asked.

"It's about your experience as a child. I got it. You want to share that side with our children. I have been selfish wanting to spend every Christmas holiday at Luna Llena. Millie, we can do both. We can give our children both experiences.

"The phone sex was good, too," he added.

"Adrian," I whispered, "I love you."

"Baby," he crooned, "I love you, too. You are my life. Go back to sleep. Look out for that package."

Late Tuesday afternoon a package arrived via UPS. There was a card attached. It was from Adrian. It read, 'To my lovely bride, Milagros, you are the light of my life. I hope you like the gift. I will be with you on Friday. Love always, Adrian.'

The box was from a very popular designer in San Francisco named Marcela. I opened the box. Inside was the most beautiful dress I had ever seen. It was white and knee length. The body of the dress was done in a satin-finished silk tight fitting to below the hips. The skirt below the hips was of three tiers of ruffled tulle. The neckline to the bust line was a see-through nylon.

"It reminds me of your wedding dress," Mom observed.

It fit beautifully.

"Millie, there are two more boxes. One looks like a shoe box."

I opened the box to find a pair of Manolo Blahnik pumps in white silk. They too were a perfect fit.

"Here," Mom said, shoving a box towards me, "open this one."

I felt like a kid at Christmas time. I tore the wrapping. Inside was a sexy white bustier, white-lace thong panties, and nude-colored, lace-top stockings.

"Here," Mom said, this time shoving a note towards me.

The note was from Adrian. It read, 'I will dream of removing these from your beautiful body soon, very soon.'

"That Adrian, he's so fresh," Mom commented as she read the note over my shoulder.

"Mother!" I reprimanded her, then added, "You have no idea how fresh."

We both laughed.

"I thought you said he wanted to court you?" Mom asked.

"That's what he said."

"It looks and sounds like he's going straight for the honeymoon."

We laughed again.

"Do you think he wants me to wear this on Friday?" I asked.

"Maybe he doesn't expect you to, but it would be nice if you did."

"I don't know where he is taking me."

"What difference does it make where you go? He bought that outfit for you. Wherever he takes you, I'm sure it will be appropriate."

"I guess I should call him to let him know I received his package."

Adrian answered the call on the first ring.

"Hi, baby," he said hurriedly.

"Hi. Did I catch you at a bad time?"

"I'm on my way to a meeting but we can talk."

"I won't keep you. I wanted to let you know that I received your package."

"Good. Did you like your gift?"

"Yes. Very much. Everything is beautiful. I can't wait to wear it for you."

"I can't wait to take it off you," he whispered and chuckled at once.

"I can't wait either. Thank you, Adrian. I won't keep you."

"I love you, Millie."

"I love you, too, Adrian."

Adrian was not out of the doghouse with me. He had some explaining to do and I still wanted an apology. The hurt of my last night at Luna Llena was still fresh in my mind and heart. Hot-to-Trot was still a thorn in my side. I knew there was nothing between them, but she needed to go. That, I also knew, was a job for Adrian to do, not me.

I was willing to wait. He said he would make things right between us. I believed him. I had a renewed faith that he would.

Friday couldn't get here fast enough. Mom and Earl came to the house for an early dinner. They agreed to baby sit. Adrian was on time. My heart started to pump vigorously when I heard the doorbell. I heard Mom tell him that I was still getting ready.

Angelique and Adam were downstairs in their playroom. Little Adrian was with me. I wore my hair loose and curly for that wild look that Adrian liked. I wore the diamond stud earrings he gave me for our first Christmas. Finally, I was ready.

"Judy, how did we get to this point," I heard Adrian lament to my mother as I exited my bedroom.

He was at the foot of the stairs, leaning with one hand on the banister and one foot resting on the second step.

"I have faith the two of you will work this out," Mom reassured him. She patted his arm lovingly.

"I hope so, Judy. I hope so," he responded.

He gazed my way when he heard my heels approaching the stairs. He looked gorgeous. His jet-black silky hair was slightly in disarray. The way I liked it. His blue eyes outlined by jet-black eyelashes shimmered. He sported a perfectly groomed goatee, broad smile with slightly parted lips. He wore a black suit, black shirt and a black tie as the finishing touch. My man was looking good.

I walked down the stairs slowly with little Adrian in my arms. Adrian did not move as I approached the bottom steps.

"Hi, Adrian," I greeted softly.

"Hi, baby."

"Here is your son," I said as I handed the baby to him.

Adrian took him into his arms, closing his eyes while inhaling his scent. He smothered him in kisses and hugged him.

"I'll take him, Adrian," my mother offered.

Adrian handed him over reluctantly. I took another step down, walking into his stance directly in front of him.

We kissed chastely. He then leaned in again for another more passionate kiss. His arms were around my waist when he pulled away.

"May I see you?" he asked.

Having become blind in his twenties, Adrian knew what things looked like. Now he relied on his touch so he could mentally visualize how things looked.

"Yes."

He proceeded to run his fingers through my hair.

"Ah, the wild look. I like that."

His fingers caressed my earlobes. He smiled.

"The diamond studs I gave you our first Christmas."

His hands descended downward feeling along my back and chest. His fingers lingered on the breasts, lightly outlining their contour before continuing their journey. He squeezed my rear and gazed in my direction with that big broad smile of his that made me tingle down there. Adrian rested his hands on my hips.

"The hips are wider now," he commented, still smiling and squeezing.

"I have you to thank for that," I said, softly wrapping one arm around his neck.

"Are you sorry?"

"No," I whispered.

His hands traveled to the ruffled tulle-layered skirt. I swallowed hard anticipating his next move. Still gazing in my direction, he slipped his hands under the skirt to my thighs. He felt the lace top of the stockings.

"Nice," he said in a throaty voice.

Both hands slid their way to my backside. He felt my exposed cheeks with the tips of his fingers.

"Ah, you wore them."

"That's why you bought them, right? So that I could wear them for you."

"Yes," he exhaled. "That is why I bought them. I will be fantasizing all night about removing them."

I was ready to forego an evening out and head back upstairs to the bedroom. He must have been feeling the same way.

"Mrs. Z, we better go now before I change my mind and take you right here on these steps." He pulled away, holding out his hand for me to take.

"Where are we going?"

"A new supper club. A friend of mine from college just opened it. We can have dinner and dance."

"It sounds like fun."

"I hope you don't mind but I invited Richard and Sarah. Tony and Frank will be hanging around us as well."

"I am delighted and surprised to hear that you are taking security seriously." I couldn't help taking a jab at him. I slipped my Glock 19 to the back of Adrian's waist were I could get to it quickly.

"I deserve that, but can we call a truce for tonight? I have thought of nothing else since last week when I planned the evening. I promise, tomorrow, I will make everything right between us."

The club had an elegant retro look. The band played salsa music, some tango and house music. Sarah and Richard were waiting for us at a table. Next to our table Tony and Frank sat with two women they picked up from the dance floor.

Who knew these guys could dance? Who knew Sarah and Richard could dance?

Adrian was an excellent dancer and we had a particular way of dancing. We never let go of each other. When our bodies separated, our hands kept touch. Even the touch of our fingertips was enough to convey to one another what our next steps were going to be. We knew each others moves well. I kept Adrian oriented.

We were having a wonderful time. The food and cocktails were among some of the best I had ever had. The chef was from Brazil and his signature dishes were a fusion between Portuguese and Japanese cuisine.

Adrian and I were out on the dance floor waiting for the next dance to start, when some guy stepped between us to take me out. Adrian stepped in between, grabbing me by the waist.

"Not tonight, buddy," Adrian said seriously. "The lady and I are having a special night."

I recognized the guy from our surveillance tapes at Luna Llena. It was Sam Sanz.

"I'll give the lady a special night, so get out of my way," Sanz pushed Adrian.

Adrian used the arm Sanz pushed him with to flip him forward onto the floor on his stomach with his arm directly behind him. Adrian held his arm with the right hand while pressing his left foot at Sanz's lower back. Tony and Frank were at Adrian's side immediately. Richard stayed back to observe the perimeter.

Three guys from the crowd came forward to Sanz's aide. Richard tapped one on the shoulder. He turned around to take a swing at Richard, who promptly used the same maneuver Adrian used. Now there were two on the floor. Tony swept the feet of the next guy from under him and pinned him to the floor by placing his foot on his chest. Frank walked towards the last guy with his fist in hand. The guy arrogantly lunged towards Frank. But that didn't stop Frank. Frank was quicker. He punched him in the throat, causing him to fall to the floor. Tony quickly filled Adrian in on the events that had unfolded.

It was quite a spectacle. The club security as well as Adrian's friend were now on the scene. Adrian's friend, the owner of the club, asked him what the trouble was. Adrian gave his explanation, which of course didn't matter. His friend had already made up his mind on how to handle the situation.

Adrian released Sanz. Sanz, who was obviously embarrassed, was not going to be outdone. He dusted off his suit and turned to me.

"Mrs. Zaragosa, this is not over. You think your security and husband are going to keep you safe. Your homes are not the fortress you think they are."

Adrian lunged at him saying, "Are your threatening my wife, asshole?" Instinctively, Adrian knew it was Sam Sanz.

Adrian's friend and the club security stepped in between the two men, avoiding another skirmish. Without another word, Sanz and his friends were ejected from the club.

"Shit, we can't have a peaceful moment," an exasperated Adrian blurted.

"What are the chances he would be here tonight?" Sarah asked.

Adrian gazed in my direction and we both spoke at the same time, "We were followed."

A worse thought occurred to me.

"Adrian, the children and my mother."

"Everyone, let's go," he ordered, grabbing my arm.

"Richard and I will beat you there," Sarah said as she and Richard jogged to her car, a fire-engine red Mustang.

Tony and Frank left in the car Adrian had rented for them, a black Escalade. Adrian and I drove off in my black Escalade. The fastest car was not going to win the race but the driver who knew the shortcuts from midtown to the East Bronx.

"Call the house, Adrian. Don't alarm Mom, but give her a heads up."

Adrian called the house, but there was no answer.

"Try her cell phone."

"There is no answer," Adrian informed me in a voice that betrayed his emotions.

"Try Earl," I suggested.

"No answer," he said, this time more worry in his voice.

Adrian and I didn't speak a word the rest of the way. He held on for dear life as I floored the gas pedal and mashed the brakes as necessary. I sped on the highway, bobbing and weaving in and out of lanes. I exited onto Randall Avenue making sharp rights and lefts until I reached the block our house was on. From the corner of our street, I hit the remote to open the front gate.

Adrian and I were the first to arrive. We raced hand in hand into the house.

"Mom," I yelled several times as Adrian and I raced to the top of the stairs.

"What is it?" she answered, wrapping a robe around her as she came out of a bedroom.

"Why didn't you pick up your phone?" I asked sternly.

"I have it charging."

"What about the house phone?"

"I didn't hear it."

"What about Earl's phone?"

"Millie, Earl had to go home. He didn't stay. What the hell is going on? Why are you barking at me?"

I didn't answer. Adrian and I, hand in hand, continued to the nursery where all three children were.

"Adrian, they are asleep," I informed him with a deep sigh of relief. I led him to them and placed his hand on Angelique. He touched her gently from head to toe. He repeated the same gestures with Adam and little Adrian.

He, too, let out a sigh of relief and we embraced each other. Richard and Sarah followed by Frank and Tony reached the top of the stairs. Mom was now frantic.

"Will someone tell me what the hell is going on?"

"Mrs. Angeles, we had reason to believe that you and the children might be in danger," Sarah offered.

"What?" she exclaimed in a hysterical voice.

"Mom, it's OK. It was just a suspicion. Thankfully, we were wrong. Go figure," I said, trying to bring her back to earth.

"You scared the shit out of me," she admonished.

"So what is wrong with Earl?" I tried to deflect.

"He has a painting he wanted to finish. He has a show soon."

"Great. Why don't we all go downstairs?" I suggested.

Everyone filed down the stairs into the foyer.

"Mr. Z," Tony called, "Frank and I will give the house a sweep to secure it, then we will wait in the car for you. We can watch the house from outside."

"Sure, I'll be with you shortly."

My heart sank for the second time this evening. The thought that my children and mother might be in danger and now the thought that our special evening was abruptly coming to an end was more than I could take. I slumped onto Adrian, burying my face in his chest and wrapping both arms around him. He gently put one arm around my shoulders.

"Hey guys," he addressed Sarah, Richard, Tony and Frank, "thanks for being there for us. Millie and I appreciate it immensely. Richard, Sarah, maybe we can get together tomorrow or the next day.

"Tony, Frank," he continued, turning to address them, "there is no need to secure the house. Millie and I will do that. I'll be out shortly."

They all left. Mom, Adrian and I were the only ones now in the foyer.

"Judy," he addressed Mom, "I'm sorry we frightened you. We over-reacted. If you don't mind, I would like a moment alone with Millie."

Adrian was good at dismissing people without offending.

"Sure, Adrian. I'm glad it was just that, an overreaction. Good night, both of you."

I was still holding onto Adrian with my face buried in his chest.

"This is not how I wanted this evening to end," he said, holding me tighter.

I was so overwhelmed with a mixture of emotions, I began to sob uncontrollably.

"Baby, baby," Adrian crooned in my ear, "everything is fine. The children are safe."

"I miss you," I said in a small almost inaudible voice.

"I'm here," he whispered. "Hey, can I interest you in something?"

"What?"

"Come, let's go into the family room."

I lead the way. He felt his way to the docking station where he had left his iPod. He put on one of the play-lists he had created. They were ballads in Spanish.

"Will you dance with me, Milagros?"

Adrian held out his arms. I silently walked into them. We danced slowly. His embrace is all I wanted. It was warm and inviting. I felt protected in his arms.

A beautiful song came on. Adrian sang along. It spoke of a broken heart. He palmed my face and leaned in for a passionate kiss. I responded, seeking his tongue with mine. We drank each other in hollowing our cheeks.

Adrian, please don't leave.

He rocked me in his arms to the tune of another love song. He leaned in again for another kiss. This time he tightened his grip around my waist, lifting me off my feet. He walked us a few paces to where the sofa was and gently lay me down. Adrian removed his suit jacket, tie and shirt. He removed his belt and undid the button and zipper to his trousers. I stopped my crying and began to enjoy the show. He then bent down, feeling for my skirt. With one hand he raised my skirt while the other felt for my panties. I was panting.

"Adrian, what are you doing?" I asked in a throaty voice.

"Courting you, baby. Courting you the only way I know how," he responded in a throaty voice as he removed the panties.

"Mrs. Z," he continued in the same throaty voice, his fingers finding their way to my sex, "you never disappoint. You're ready for me."

There would be no foreplay. He eased his massive erection inside of me. His thrusts were met by mine. We were both anxious. Without breaking the connection, he pulled his chest away to slip the top of my dress down below my breasts. He fondled my breasts, rolling the nipples between his fingertips, tugging at them with enough pressure to send a tingling to my insides down in that special area. I gasped at the sensation. Again, he lowered his chest on top of mine. The thrusts were more forceful against that sweet spot that he knew all too well. I felt that familiar contraction that would lead to a wave of convulsions.

"Adrian, you feel so good," I crooned. "I can't hold out."

"I'm right there, baby, go for it."

We reached our release simultaneously. We lay together in each others embrace until our hearts and breathing slowed. Adrian slowly withdrew and raised the top of my dress. We were kissing when I heard my mother descending the steps.

"Millie," she called, "where are you?"

Adrian stood to adjust his trousers. He held out a hand for me to hold onto as he lifted me to my feet. Mom walked in as he smoothed down my skirt. Adrian ignored her presence and embraced me, rocking us gently.

"Millie," she repeated, "your son is crying. He needs you."

"I hear him, Mom. I'm on my way."

"Good night," she said sternly and left.

"Well, that was awkward," Adrian said, amused. "Now your mother and Hilda are even catching us in compromising situations."

"I think Hilda handled it better. Adrian ..." I paused, not knowing whether to finish the statement.

"What is it, baby?"

"Will you stay tonight with me?" I asked timidly.

"Yes," he whispered in a husky voice. "Tonight and every night for the rest of our lives."

Chapter 20

The morning was hectic. Little Luna Llena now truly resembled big Luna Llena, bodyguards and all. I was frantic, cooking breakfast for everyone. My mother was feeling awkward about the previous night. She had been startled and then walked in on Adrian and me. Sure, we had finished, but that is exactly what made her feel awkward; the fact that she knew we had just finished being intimate. She had her overnight bag with her and refused to wait for coffee.

"I have to run, sweetie. I'm glad things have worked out between you and Adrian. Give him my love. I'll talk with you later."

"Mom, wait for Richard. I want him to escort you home."

"That is not necessary. Did you forget you and Adrian placed a bodyguard at Earl's house?"

"Yeah. He's at the house. I want you escorted."

"I don't know what is going on around here," she said conspiratorially, "but things were quiet before," and she didn't finish the statement.

"Mom, we overreacted. That's all. You still need an escort."

"No!" she barked, "I'm out of here. Talk to you later." She stormed out of the house. Adrian entered the kitchen as she left.

"What was that all about?" he asked with knitted eyebrows and pursed lips.

"I don't know. Mom was anxious to get home and refused to have one of the guys escort her."

"Do you think she was upset about last night?"

"She has a lot to be upset about, don't you think?" I noted with a chuckle.

"I guess. Mrs. Z," he said, rounding me, "we need to hire temporary help for this house. You can't do it all."

"I'll look into it after breakfast."

He placed my arms around his waist and held me with his. He leaned in for a chaste kiss on the lips and then he kissed my hair.

"I need to do some work this morning," he said softly, "but I would like to spend some time with you this afternoon to talk. I owe you an explanation. Will you be available?"

"Yes. After we have our lunch. I have some work to do this morning also."

Adrian busied himself in an office that had been set up for him on the first floor. I met with Tony, Frank and Richard in their office. I was proud of the work they had done the night before. Our training had paid off. I, however, was not happy with Ralph White. He should have given me a heads up on the movements of Sam Sanz. Instead, we were caught off guard.

"Hi, Millie," Ralph greeted on the phone.

"Hello, Ralph," I responded more formally. "I want to discuss last night with you."

"Last night?"

"Yes. Last night. Where was the tail you had on Sam Sanz?"

"They were watching him. Why do you ask?"

"You said 'they,' Ralph. There are more than one on Sanz?"

"That's right, Millie."

"Well, then where were they?"

"Millie," he said a little testy, "they were watching Sanz. The same thing they do every night since you contracted me."

"Ralph, I suggest you call them in and find out what the fuck they were doing last night, because they sure as hell weren't watching him. Instead, he was watching me, my husband and my family. My husband and I went out last night with some friends to a night club and guess who showed up to make trouble?"

"Millie, I'll get to the bottom of it immediately. I am stunned."

"Ralph, maybe you need to investigate if these guys have been compromised. Send me their photos and names. Please get back to me."

"Sure thing, Millie. Please accept my apologies."

"Get back to me please, Ralph."

I wasn't buying it. Ralph dropped the ball. He should at all times be aware of what his staff is doing or not doing. Just like I check up on our security staff, he should be doing the same. So, I decided to do some investigating myself.

Richard knocked on the open door to my office.

"Mrs. Z, may I have a word with you?"

"Sure, Richard. Why are you being so formal?" Richard had come to call me Millie. It was hard to maintain a professional relationship since he was dating my friend.

"We are not alone now. There are other people here, including Mr. Z. I don't think he would appreciate it and I don't think it is appropriate."

"OK, Richard, what can I do for you?"

"I had taken the NYPD test months ago while visiting Sarah. I scored at the top of the list. I have been offered a job and there is a class beginning in the New Year."

"Congratulations, Richard. I guess you will be leaving our employ."

"I know you will eventually be going back to Luna Llena and I want to stay here with Sarah. I asked her to marry me and she accepted. We plan to wed next summer."

I became teary eyed. I was happy for my friend Sarah and for Richard. But I felt sorry for myself. Richard had become a friend. I respected his professionalism and abilities and I enjoyed working with him. His quirky sense of humor, his loyalty and work ethics are what I liked most about him. I was going to miss him.

"When did you want to terminate?" I asked.

"When are you leaving New York?" he asked.

"Never mind that, Richard. When would you like to terminate," I repeated. "I'm sure you will want some down time."

"I would like to have Christmas week with Sarah."

"Great," I responded with a heavy heart. "When does the academy start?"

"It starts the second week in January."

"I'll consider the twenty-third of December your last day of work. But I hope we can see you and Sarah socially during the holidays."

"Sure thing. But you have to check with her. She is the boss of our calendar."

It was almost noon. After the children were feed, I prepared lunch for Adrian and me. I knocked on the door to Adrian's office and announced myself placing Angelique and Adam in their baby-proof area where they were free to roam. Little Adrian went into his playpen where he would be sure to take an afternoon nap. I returned to the kitchen to retrieve our lunch.

Adrian was in the baby-proof area. He had given Angelique and Adam their blankets and they were lying down while he rubbed their backs. They soon fell asleep.

"Good job, Mr. Z," I praised.

"Thank you. I missed them very much," he said sadly.

"Lunch is ready," I announced.

Adrian sat on the sofa in the sitting area of his office. I sat on my heels on the floor next to him. Our favorite guitar music played in the background.

"Mrs. Z, what have you prepared for lunch?"

"A wrap. A Reuben wrap with potato salad."

"I guess it's made with a flour tortilla."

"Yes. The dressing is different from the regular Reuben. I made it myself with some cream cheese, spicy mustard and horseradish. Do you like it?"

"It is delicious. I love the potato salad. The apple is a nice touch."

We ate and talked about the children and the house. Adrian was pleased with the layout. It was very similar to Luna Llena, albeit smaller. He was more comfortable now than before the renovations. We discussed security for the house. I informed him that it was just as secure as Luna Llena. Perhaps more so because the house and property were smaller. I felt terrible about the previous night's incident with Sanz. Sure, Ralph had dropped the ball, but so had I. I should have been watching Ralph's operation a lot more carefully. Instead, I had become complacent, I confessed to Adrian.

"Don't blame yourself, Millie," he said as he finished his wrap. He wiped his mouth with the cloth napkin and sat back on the sofa. He then continued, "You have had a lot on your plate. I haven't made life easy either."

I didn't respond. I felt we had reached the moment in time where Adrian was going to address some of our issues.

"Have you finished eating?" he asked.

"Yes."

"Please sit next to me."

"I should clear the dishes."

"That can wait. I will help later. But first we need to have a discussion."

I suddenly felt frightened. Last night, after the Sanz incident, had been perfect. We made love for the first time in a little over a month and we slept soundly in each others arms. In the morning we resumed our daily routine as if nothing had happened. Was I being foolish in thinking that we could resume our lives? Would this be the moment where I realized I would not receive the two things I needed that would enable me to continue forward with Adrian?

Adrian brushed the back of my hand against his lips and cheek. He had a pained expression on his face.

Why the pained look? Is this it? Is Adrian done with us?

"Thank you for last night. I know I said I would stay for the rest of our lives, but I was caught up in the moment."

My heart sank. He's leaving me. He let go of my hand, leaning forward to rest his forearms on his knees. He rubbed his hands together nervously. I had never seen this side of Adrian. He cleared his throat.

"Millie, you have issues and so do I. I will address yours first."

His eyebrows were knitted and lips pursed. He was struggling to find the words. I was trying to breathe. My chest felt like it was in a vise.

"My behavior our last night together at Luna Llena was inexcusable. I'm ashamed. You did not deserve that. I have thought of that night often since then. I wish it never happened but it did. All I can do is to ask for your forgiveness."

He didn't pause to wait for an answer but continued.

"I have never cheated on you. I can understand why you might think otherwise, but I never have and never will. Milagros, you are the only woman for me. I need you to believe that. I also need for you to have more faith in me." He gazed in my direction for a moment, then turned his gaze back to his hands.

"I was stupid," he continued, "to enter into that last real estate deal with Susan. But I have to confess, it is not the only real estate deal we are involved in. There are others. Many others."

"How many, Adrian?"

"Many."

"Why did you not tell me before?"

"I didn't think it was important. I was foolish. Of course it was important. You should have known. As my wife, it was your right. Millie," he said, still struggling for words, "I own another building on Chauncey Street. I occupy the penthouse. It was my first apartment. That is where I met Susan. When I bought the building where you and I stay now, she followed. I didn't know she kept both apartments until the night you and the children left me.

"We had an affair years ago. I'll spare you the details. When you came to Luna Llena, I visited many women. You know this. She was one of them. You know this also since you were very good at your job as director of security." That made him smile.

"Susan likes watching herself on videos. They are for her personal viewing. She asked my permission to tape us. I agreed. Another stupid mistake," Adrian said as he rubbed his eyes. "When I agreed to be in her videos, I had no hopes of ever being with you or having children. I didn't care about anything. I had nothing to lose.

"You thought she was blackmailing me and you erased the videos. I knew when she found out it would enrage her. It did. She thought I had done it. I told her I had because I was now a married man with children. I explained I could not risk those videos falling into the wrong hands. She was not amused. She threatened to tell you everything and, if she had to, make up lies. She figured you would believe her. Quite frankly, I was afraid you would, too." Again, he gazed momentarily in my direction. I felt ashamed.

"I moved back to the penthouse on Chauncey when you left. I couldn't bear being at Luna Llena or our penthouse without you and the children. She followed me to torment me for the loss of her trophy videos.

"Millie, I liquidated the real estate holdings that she and I had in common. Some real estate holdings included other investors that had to be consulted. It has been exhausting setting up meetings to execute all these sales. Some were complicated. I unloaded everything except for the last project. We have a contract covering the project that will expire early in the New Year. I will have to sell the buildings with the penthouses. I can't evict her and I know you want her out of our lives. I want her out also. That's where I am at with the real estate portion of this mess. As you can see, I am not completely out.

"Millie, as embarrassed as I am about those videos, I was more embarrassed that you saw them and that you felt the need to erase them. Once again, you felt you had to come to my rescue. I should be protecting you. I should be the one coming to your rescue. This is a big problem for me."

"Adrian, you came to my rescue in the incident with Pablo Santos. And again last night. Without any concern for your personal safety, you had Sanz on the floor faster than I could have ever reacted."

"Millie, you were going to meet Nussbaum without me after we agreed."

"I know, I'm sorry. We parted company in not too friendly terms. I didn't think you would care to come to New York."

"How could I not care? I love you. But I have a hard time not being able to protect you or my children."

"Adrian, I forgive you for that last night at Luna Llena. I believe everything you have told me. I do believe in you and I do trust you. I promise to be better at it too. As for protecting me and the children, you do very well. I can't help who I am, Adrian. I will always jump to your defense and that of our children. It is who I am and this you knew about me. You and I are who we are. There are some things we cannot change.

"As for the video, we all made youthful mistakes. It doesn't bother me. I knew you weren't a virgin." We both laughed. "I didn't watch them. I couldn't. I saw some of her other work with other men and figured it was more of the same. I don't care. Can you forgive me for erasing them?"

"I can forgive you. I probably would have done the same had the roles been reversed."

"Thank you for telling me everything. Adrian, I appreciate it. You know she is not going to leave us alone."

"I know."

"Can we think of a united way of dealing with this?"

"We can do that. Will you tell me everything you are up to?"

"I can do that."

We sat on the sofa in silence for a few minutes. I was the first to speak.

"Adrian, what now? Where do we go from here?"

He leaned back and put one arm around my shoulders.

"We move forward, baby. Together."

Adrian and I played with the children before returning to work. Ralph sent me an email with the information I requested regarding the two men who were supposed to be watching Sanz. Their photos proved they were not the men with Sanz at the club the night before. I checked their financial records. There was nothing out of the ordinary.

They would be too smart for that. Or maybe they are just as they appear, employees.

I turned my attention to Ralph. He had been highly recommended by my old friend Joe Pirelli before he sold his investigating firm to Ralph. Ralph's financial proved he made a nice living, but nothing extraordinary. There were no large deposits to his accounts. He had, however, recently purchased a house in the Hamptons on Long Island.

That is pricey real estate.

He also had recently purchased his and hers Rolex watches, a Porsche Panamera 4S and a pricey sixty-foot Bertram motor boat.

Ralph appears to be living above his means.

There were no emails or messages between Ralph and Sanz. Ralph was diligent in erasing emails and text messages. It is amazing how many people are secure in the knowledge that they can actually delete emails. Depending on the length of time, almost anything can be recovered. My search revealed Ralph and Nussbaum were now buddies. The odd thing is that Gardel was never mentioned. Ralph and Sam Sanz were being manipulated by Nussbaum. Sanz was the strong arm. Ralph only had to pull away the detail assigned to observe Sanz's every move.

That is the service I am paying for. But what role, if any, is Gardel playing in this drama?

"Mr. Z," I called as I wandered into Adrian's office. "May I have a word with you?" I cooed as I sat on his lap.

"Sure, baby," Adrian replied with the winning smile that made me melt inside. He cradled me in his arms, abandoning his computer and earphones. "What is on your mind?"

"You are on my mind."

"I need a break," he whispered in that throaty, sexy voice that ignited my desires. "How about we take this upstairs?"

"Sure," I responded, not wanting to move from his lap.

"Come, baby, let's go to the bedroom. Where are the children?"

"In their usual places," I panted, barely able to think.

"Grab one, I'll take two."

Angelique, Adam and little Adrian were peacefully napping in the nursery. Adrian and I were slowly returning to earth. My legs were tightly wrapped around him. Adrian's face was snug against my neck, his body relaxed on top of mine.

"Mrs. Z, you do not disappoint," he crooned as he eventually rolled onto his side. He coaxed my body close to him.

We took a short nap. When we awoke, we were facing each other. I kissed him chastely on the lips.

"Nap time is over," I proclaimed. "We need to get up and be responsible parents."

"If you insist," he yawned.

"Yes, I insist."

We showered and then bathed the children. Adrian was enjoying the task. He didn't mind the splashing and screeching that was part of the ritual. I, in turn, enjoyed watching him.

Chapter 21

I t was dark outside and the temperature had dipped into the upper thirties. I struggled with what to wear. Sweat pants were out of the question. Adrian did not like me in them and I did want to please him. I opted for a button-down denim dress with a pair of knitted lace stockings that Isabel had knitted for me the previous year. I couldn't believe she had time to knit, write, and handle Juan Carlos. Adrian wore flannel lounge pants with a sweatshirt. He found a scarf and wrapped that around his neck. My California boy was cold.

"Adrian," I called out to him as he finished dressing, "try these slippers I bought for you."

They were suede lined with woolly fleece.

"Wow, these are great. My feet are warm and comfortable. Thank you."

"You are welcome. I'm glad you like them."

"How about some food? I am in need of calories. My wife gave me quite a workout."

"Funny guy."

We went through our usual ritual of feeding the children first. Then I started our dinner. I sautéed red and yellow cherry tomatoes in a white wine garlic sauce. I added freshly grated parmesan cheese, shrimp and cooked linguini. Adrian made garlic bread on the Panini. We sat in the family room in front of the fireplace to eat. The iPod was playing "Turn Me On" by Norah Jones.

Once again there was peace between us. All was well in our universe. Well, at least for the present moment.

After dinner, Adrian and I took the children to their bedroom and tucked them in. They were sound asleep. Adrian helped clear the dinner dishes while I cleaned the kitchen.

"Adrian, would you like some coffee?" I asked.

"No, thank you. I am stuffed. I think I will indulge in an after-dinner drink. Would you like to join me?"

"No. I am stuffed also. Why don't you go to the family room and pour yourself that drink. I'll join you shortly."

"But I like helping," he protested.

"I know you do," I said, rounding him. I placed my arms around his neck, pulling him down to meet my lips. We shared a passionate kiss.

"Hmm, Mr. Z, you taste delicious."

"Why thank you, Mrs. Z. You're not bad yourself."

"Now, go to the family room," I ordered. "Have your drink, dim the lights and set the mood for us to relax."

"You are bossy. Do you know that?"

"So I've been told."

With that he left and I continued my chores. The last chore was to secure the back door. I took a moment to step outside. It was a moonless night and very cold. The view to the Long Island Sound was limited due to the darkness, but everything looked as it should.

Next, I checked on Tony and Frank. Ever since Adrian was abducted, Roger was reassigned to Luna Llena.

"Tony, Frank," I called to them, "how was dinner?"

"Excellent, Mrs. Z," they both chimed.

"Not like Hilda, I bet."

"Just as good, Mrs. Z," Tony offered.

"How are things going here?" I asked.

"Quiet," Frank responded.

"Mrs. Z, Frank is on duty tonight," Tony volunteered. "I'm heading out for a blind date with Sarah and Richard."

"Have fun, Tony. I'll see you both in the morning. I want to discuss the upcoming holidays and your schedules."

"Sure thing, Mrs. Z," Tony said.

"Yes, Mrs. Z, see you in the morning."

Now, off to my man.

Adrian was standing in front of the fireplace with the brandy decanter in one hand and a crystal brandy snifter in the other.

"Adrian, are you cold?" I asked as I approached him.

"A little. The warmth from the fireplace and the brandy are helping." He gazed in my direction and gave me that big smile that melted me.

"Is that your first drink?"

"Are you nagging me, woman?" he asked, still smiling.

"Yes, I am."

"Well, then now that we cleared that up no it is not my first. It is my second."

"Give me the decanter, Adrian. I'll return it to its place on the bar, if that is OK with you," I ordered more than asked.

"Sure, baby."

Adrian was leaning against the fireplace with the hand that was holding the brandy snifter. He held his free arm out waiting for my return. I walked into his waiting arm. He drew me close, planting a kiss on my hair and inhaling its scent.

"Oh, baby, you feel and smell good."

"You too," I replied, pressing my nose to his chest.

"I like this dress," he commented while feeling the fabric. "It is denim but the styling is feminine." He slipped his free hand to my rear, feeling the full skirt.

"I like the stockings," he continued. "Are those the ones Isabel knitted for you?"

"Yes, they are."

He leaned down to kiss me again. This time I looked up. Standing on my toes, I intercepted his lips. We exchanged a passionate kiss.

"Why don't you go run us a bath?"

"Will you be right up?"

"Yes, after I finish this drink."

Little Adrian began to cry.

"I'll run the bath after your son gets his milk."

"Lucky, baby," Adrian said laughing. "Let me know when the bath is ready. Don't undress. I want to undress you."

"Yes, Mr. Z."

I changed the baby and sat with him to nurse. Once he drifted to sleep, I returned him to the crib. I then turned my attention to the bath, but thought first to check the surveillance cameras.

Just like in Luna Llena, there were cameras only in the perimeter of the house and some areas on the inside of the house. I did defy Adrian. I had placed a camera in the family room, in the kitchen facing the door and in the room where Tony and Frank worked. The surveillance cameras in the family room and Tony and Frank's office were only visible to me. I arranged it that way so that they would not be able to see if Adrian and I were to become intimate in the family room, and I did not want them to think I was spying on them. But I did want to see what was going on in my house. Adrian and I fought a great deal about surveillance.

The perimeter checked out fine except that a light in the back yard had gone out. The latch to the kitchen door was hanging. I had personally secured that door. Frank was not in the office. In the family room, I observed Adrian was still standing in front of the fireplace, but with his back to it. He sipped his drink and I could see Frank was in the room with him. Adrian suddenly straightened his posture and tugged at his belt. That was his tell sign that he was on alert.

Something is not right.

I slipped off my shoes and quietly walked down the staircase. I could see Adrian.

"Where is Mrs. Z?" I heard Frank ask.

"She is upstairs," Adrian responded.

Then I heard another voice. One I had not heard before.

"Your wife is stupid, Adrian. The diamonds need to go back to where they belong."

"Nussbaum said Gardel would wait until after the holidays," Adrian informed the stranger.

"Gardel called him this morning with a change of heart. He wants it now."

"Nussbaum was told the diamonds are not here," Adrian again informed the intruder.

"Too bad for you if they are not here. Enough talking. Call for your wife. For your sake and that of your children, she better have the diamonds here."

Oh no, you didn't, asshole. You're threatening my family. You are a loose end that is about to be tied off.

"Frank," Adrian called out, "how much are you being paid?"

"Mr. Z, I had nothing to do with this. I noticed a light was out in the back yard, so I went to replace it. When this asshole hit me on the back of the head." Frank sounded stressed. "Mr. Z, angel should give him the diamonds because I do not have a firearm on me. He has a Glock 19 in his right hand." Frank was using code talk.

"Shut the fuck up!" shouted the intruder. "I said enough talking. Call your wife, pretty boy, or I'll blow Frank's head off."

Adrian did not have to call me. I made noise as if I were coming down the stairs.

"Henry!" I yelled running into the family room. I hit the light dimmer, turning off the lights. Adrian and Frank hit the floor. The stranger shot his gun in my direction missing me. I fell to my knees, aiming in his direction and squeezed two shots out of my Glock. I heard him drop to the floor. There was no way to know whether he was seeking shelter or whether I had injured him. The kitchen door opened and I heard it shut. Another sound came from the dining room.

I crawled towards Adrian. I felt for his body and inched my way to his ear.

"Adrian," I whispered, "stay down and crawl to the stairs. Go upstairs and get your firearm, then go to the children and guard them with your life. Quickly, please."

I could not see the expression on his face, but he squeezed my arm and did as he was told. There was a skirmish in the general direction of where Frank and the first intruder were. It was quick and fairly quiet. I could only hope that Frank was the victor. A bump causing a rattle of crystal and silver alerted me that someone was approaching from the dining room. Frank would have heard it also. He had the advantage there. Then there was a creek on the wood floor. Someone was slowly approaching from the kitchen. I could hear hands searching for a light switch. Adrian and I had done exercises like these many times. Now it was only a matter of time before the lights would go on again.

*Frank, I hope you **are** on our side and I hope you have the guy coming from the dining room.*

Just then the lights came on. Kitchen guy had me in his sights. Dining room guy immediately diverted his attention towards Frank. Both men hastily shot once. Frank and I returned the favor, dropping them in their tracks.

Without speaking a word, Frank and I stood, kicking the firearms away from our intruders. We assessed their conditions. The first intruder had been shot by me in the shoulder and knocked unconscious by Frank.

Kitchen guy and dining room guy were quite dead. We separated to secure the house. Frank went through the dining room and checked that area of the house. I went towards the kitchen and secured that area. I met Frank again in the family room.

"Frank," I finally spoke, "call the police and tie this guy up so that he can't surprise us later. I'm going upstairs to check on Mr. Z and the children."

I walked with caution to the second floor. All the bedroom doors were open. I decided to head for the nursery first. Again, I approached with extreme caution.

"Adrian," I whispered as I reached the doorway.

"Millie," Adrian responded immediately.

I proceeded past the threshold and found Adrian standing in the dark with his firearm at the ready.

"Baby," I whispered, "lower your firearm. Everything is under control."

He did as he was told. I turned on the lights to the nursery. Adrian didn't move or speak. His eyebrows were knitted and lips pursed. I inched my way to him and noticed that the cribs and Angelique's bed were empty. My heart skipped a beat. Where could they be? Did Adrian know they were missing? Now my head was pounding.

He is blind. Dear God, maybe he doesn't know that they are gone! Maybe he does and that is why he is not speaking.

"Adrian, baby, where are the children?"

"I hid them in our dressing room. They are on the floor behind our clothes, nicely tucked away."

I threw myself on his chest and he quickly embraced me. We both fell to our knees.

"You are such a good daddy," I sobbed.

Adrian held me tightly in his arms and let me cry. When he felt I was all cried out, he kissed my hair and whispered, "Millie, help me get our babies out of the closet."

I pulled away from Adrian and we both chuckled at the thought of the children in a closet.

"Let's go," I replied and we both stood and walked towards our bedroom.

Frank intercepted us in the hallway.

"Mrs. Z, the police are on their way."

"Thanks, Frank. We will be down shortly," I replied.

"Mrs. Z, Mr. Z," he continued, clearing his throat, "I want you both to know that I had nothing to do with those thugs downstairs and what transpired here tonight."

"I know," we responded in unison.

"I'm sorry. I feel like I failed you both tonight."

"No, you didn't, Frank," I responded. "You know as well as I that the best security is not one-hundred percent perfect. We can analyze what happened tomorrow. Right now I need you downstairs to keep an eye on that asshole and to let the police in."

"Do you want me to call Tony and get him back here?"

"No. No need to spoil his night."

Adrian led the way to where he had hidden the little ones. He knelt on the floor and pushed some clothing to the side. He retrieved Angelique, first placing her on the rug by my feet. She was still asleep in her night-gown. Next out was Adam. He too was asleep. Little Adrian was the last one out.

"I'll return Angelique to her bed."

"No. We will take them downstairs with us."

"Adrian, in a few minutes there is going to be a great deal of commotion downstairs and they will be wakened."

"I don't care. I want them with us."

I looked at him. Beyond the knitted eyebrows and pursed lips was a terrified man who came very close to losing his family. I didn't argue. We barely reached the family room when little Adrian woke up and started crying. Adam and Angelique followed. When the police arrived, Adrian had two crying children in his arms while I tried to quiet little Adrian with a nipple. For modesty's sake I threw a baby blanket over us.

It was complete mayhem with policemen, detectives, EMS personnel and the New York City medical examiner amid screaming babies. That is when Tony entered the house.

"What the fuck happened here?" he exclaimed.

"Who the fuck are you?" one of the detectives asked.

That started another wave of screaming babies and a pissing contest between grown men.

It was a long night. Finally, everyone was gone. Frank filled Tony in on the events of the evening. Adrian and I went upstairs to put the children to bed.

"Millie, I am exhausted. I am going to run that bath we were supposed to have hours ago. Could you go to the bar and bring the brandy and two glasses for us?"

"Sure thing. I'll meet you in the bath tub."

Adrian was already sitting in the tub when I returned. I served us each a drink and joined him. The water was hot and welcoming. Adrian sipped his drink and put his arms around me. I pressed my face against his chest, inhaling his scent.

"Adrian, about tonight," I started but he did not let me finish.

"I don't want to talk right now if you don't mind. I have had enough stimulation for one night. Let's just sit here and enjoy our hot bath, good brandy and good fortune." He kissed my hair, then continued, "I am grateful that we survived the night and that our children are safe. As your favorite literary character would say, after all, tomorrow is another day."

Chapter 22

The surveillance camera in the family room served to corroborate our version of the events the night before. The detective in charge informed us that none of our assailants had identifications on them. The one who did survive was refusing to cooperate. The detective further told us a Mr. Nussbaum was representing him.

No surprise there.

My own investigation revealed they gained access from the property of a neighbor, who had been out for the night. I knew Sam Sanz was involved. These weren't trained assassins. They were neighborhood thugs working for Sanz and Nussbaum. These two were beyond becoming loose ends.

Adrian had wanted to contact Nussbaum, but I managed to convince him not to.

"What would be the point?" I reasoned. "We don't have the diamonds. He is desperate for them."

"That is precisely why we should give them to him, Millie. He won't stop these attempts on our lives," he argued with knitted eyebrows and pursed lips.

"Adrian, he won't try the same thing twice."

"What do you think his next move would be?"

"I don't know, Adrian."

No. I don't know, but I have an idea.

"Baby, we can deal with him later. Let's get through the holidays. Don't let him spoil this for us," I pleaded.

Adrian reluctantly agreed to follow my lead on this one. But there was no doubt in my mind that my California boy couldn't wait to get back on his turf.

In the ensuing days I researched Frank and Tony. I needed to be one-hundred percent sure of their loyalty and whether or not they had been compromised by the enemy. I even followed up with a call to Sarah.

"Hi, Sarah," I greeted.

"Mill, how are you, Adrian and the babies?"

"We are just fine."

"I heard about your troubles the other night," she commented. "I'm sorry Richard and I had not been there for you, Millie. But most of all for taking Tony away for the night."

"Oh, Sarah, that's OK. Thankfully, everything turned out well. How was your evening? Tell me about this blind date of Tony's," I said conspiratorially.

She was more than happy to oblige and proceeded to give all the details of their evening and of Tony's blind date. The lady in question was a new co-worker of Sarah's. She was just as geeky as Sarah and in need of some fun, according to Sarah.

"Tell me, Sarah, how did you come about picking Tony over Frank? They are both young and good looking."

"I tossed a coin. Tony was heads, Frank was tails. Simple, but efficient," she snickered.

I swear she is beginning to sound and act more and more like Richard.

And just because my paranoia was on a rampage, I researched Sarah and Richard. To my delight and relief, they were squeaky clean.

Hilda and Hector, Daisy and Paula flew into New York together on the Gulfstream. I decided to invite some of my friends that I had not seen for some time for Christmas Eve. Mom, Hilda, Paula and Daisy helped me arrange a buffet table for all our guests. Adrian played his selection of Christmas music. He looked at ease, not claustrophobic as before. The renovation of the house was more to his liking. He had taken time to become familiar and commit to memory the layout, which was similar to that of Luna Llena and not difficult for him. The children were a big hit with everyone taking turns fussing over them.

Christmas Day we had a quiet dinner with our house guests. We were joined by Mom and Earl, Sarah and Richard.

I took advantage of the fact that this was Hilda and Hector's first trip to New York and convinced Adrian to join us on day trips into Manhattan to show them the sights. We took plenty of photographs. Finally, I had the photograph I wanted of Adrian, the children and me. It was an early evening shot in front of Rockefeller Center.

Hilda and Hector were in awe of the city. The famous New York City skyscrapers, Christmas decorations, city lights and the energy of her inhabitants made them giddy.

Daisy and Paula sometimes ventured out with us while on other occasions they went their own way. Daisy wanted to take Paula to some of her favorite places.

Little Luna Llena, my new name for the house I had grown up in, was filled with the warmth of family and friends, but mostly with the love Adrian and I were once again feeling. Our most recent troubles were now a distant memory.

"Millie," Adrian called out as he walked into our bedroom from the en-suite.

"Adrian," I responded, "I am in the dressing room."

"We should discuss a few things."

"Sure. What would you like to discuss?"

"Nussbaum, for one thing. Our trip to Baja California and Tahiti."

"I'm looking forward to our trips. But Nussbaum is another subject altogether."

"Shall we start with the trips then?"

"Sure, Adrian. What is on your mind?"

"I would like to spend some time with Tía Carmen and Hilda. But I can't be away too long from work."

"Oh," I responded, wondering what trip would be sacrificed.

"Do you mind if we postpone Tahiti for a few months?"

"I don't mind, Adrian," I lied, trying to hide my disappointment.

"I promise we will go with the children in the spring," he offered, holding me close to his body. I inhaled his heavenly scent.

"I'll look forward to it."

"That's my girl," he said as he leaned down to kiss my hair.

"Can we go to Baja California as soon as we get back home?" I asked.

"What's the hurry? Shouldn't we take care of Nussbaum first? Don't you think we should return immediately to New York?"

Mr. Multiple Questions is back.

"I need a vacation, Adrian. I'm stressed," I purred in his ear.

"I know, baby, but what about Nussbaum?" he purred back.

"He can wait. He can't get to us while we are on the move."

"Now, what are we going to do about Nussbaum?" he asked.

"Adrian, this has become somewhat complicated."

"Come, baby, let's sit," he said, taking me by the hand, leading the way to the sofa in the sitting area.

"What is going on?" he asked, placing one arm around my shoulders. His touch made me feel secure and loved.

"Adrian, I have been monitoring Nussbaum's communications," I said softly, bracing myself for his reaction. Adrian was adamant against hacking computers and it was a point of contention between us. His hold on my shoulders tightened, eyebrows knitted and lips pursed.

"Tell me, exactly what communications?"

"All communications."

"You hacked his computer?" he blurted incredulously. "You know this man has skills."

"I do. His equipment is well protected. However, not well enough. I was able to navigate through using my usual labyrinth of networks. Once in, I was not detected."

Adrian closed his eyes and leaned back, not loosening his grip on me.

"Millie, that is very dangerous."

"It was necessary."

"What have you discovered?"

Well, that went well.

"There has been no communication between Nussbaum and Gardel."

"Maybe they communicate with cell phones."

"Nussbaum hasn't communicated with Gardel at all," I repeated.

"I guess I don't want to know how you know that," he said, gazing in my direction with knitted eyebrows and pursed lips.

"No, no, you don't."

He removed his arm from around my shoulders and rubbed his eyes.

"What about Sanz?"

"I fired Ralph. He could not give me a satisfactory explanation of what happened the night we were at the night club."

"OK, Millie, I can see why you would do that, but who has been watching this guy Sanz?"

"I have."

"Millie, baby, please just tell me everything. I feel like I'm pulling teeth."

Here goes nothing.

"I had surveillance cameras placed outside his home and place of business. I also had a tracking device placed on his vehicle. His cell phone and land line are also being monitored."

"I guess I don't want to know how you managed that."

"No. No, you don't."

The air was getting a little thick and the temperature was rising although it was frigid outside.

"All right, let's move on." Again he rubbed his eyes. "So you don't believe Gardel is in on this."

"No. He is not in on this. In fact, neither is Sanz."

"Sanz is only interested in a vendetta against you."

"That is right. Adrian, the only question that goes unanswered is why Oscar Sanz shot Danny."

"It has to be the money laundering. Danny was involved in the money laundering." Now Adrian was getting agitated.

"We know his brother, Ed, was involved. I'm not convinced about Danny."

"Your loyalty sometimes blinds you," he spat out.

"What is eating you, Adrian? I am not blind. I am not convinced. That is all."

"OK. OK. Let's move on," he said, not wanting to argue the point. "What are we going to do with Nussbaum?"

"After our trip with Hilda to see Tía Carmen and return home, we can retrieve the diamonds, go to New York and give them to him," I lied.

I will not allow you to take part in what could turn out to be a very dangerous adventure. Our children will need at least one parent.

"A trip back here to New York," Adrian groaned.

"Yes. But it will be a quick one. I promise."

"Good."

"Adrian, baby, what is wrong? You seem a little testy tonight."

"I'm sorry. I don't mean to be. We have unfinished business and it is driving me crazy."

Wow, that is the first time Adrian has admitted to feeling stressed over anything.

"We will get through it," I offered.

"There is something else, Millie."

"What?"

"Susan."

"Oh."

"The contract I spoke to you about will be expiring soon after we return home from Baja. Things may get tense and or ugly."

"Adrian, what is really concerning you?"

"You, baby. You."

"I'll be fine, Adrian."

"I need you, Millie. I need you by my side. Steadfast and loyal."

"Then you have no concerns."

Chapter 23

O ur trip to Baja California on the Gulfstream was pleasant. Hilda and Hector were excited to get there. As usual, Tony and Frank accompanied us. They looked pleased with this assignment. I was excited to get away from all our troubles.

Two black stretch Escalades were waiting for us.

My man has a thing for these vehicles.

Hector drove one with Hilda and Frank. Tony drove the other with us in it. The ride to Tía Carmen's house from the airport was simply breathtaking. The late morning cerulean sky, the sun shining overhead and gentle warm breeze transported me to another world. A world free of troubles and violence.

The two Escalades pulled up a long driveway to a white Mediterranean styled two-story home.

Hmm. It reminds me of Luna Llena.

It was surrounded by palm trees and low-growing palmettos. The fan-shaped leaves swayed gently with the breeze.

A young woman, about my age, opened the front carved-wood double doors.

"Tía Hilda," she screeched, running to Hilda, embracing and kissing her. She then turned to Adrian. Wrapping her arms around his neck, she pulled him towards her and planted a kiss on his lips.

Well this isn't going to go well.

"Eva," Adrian greeted, pushing her away. "It has been a long time."

"Too long," she crooned.

Not only is this not going to go well, but now I am invisible.

"Eva," Hilda interrupted, looking mighty uncomfortable, "this is Milagros, Adrian's wife."

We just stared at each other, barely uttering a "hello."

Yeah, this isn't going to go well.

Adrian busied himself with the children. He lifted little Adrian out of his car seat and called for me.

"Millie, can you please help?"

"Sure," came my sour reply.

I placed little Adrian in the seat of the stroller. Next was Adam. He went into the front seat. Adrian smoothed Angelique's dress, kissed her and set her on the ground, taking her by the hand so that she could walk.

Eva had not stopped talking and laughing like a hyena. She was most annoying.

"Adrian," she screeched, "can I help?"

"No thanks," he answered quickly. "Milagros and I have it."

"And these are their children," Hilda chimed in nervously, "Angelique, Adam and little Adrian."

"Ha! They all start with an 'a,' just like you, Adrian," the hyena exclaimed, laughing.

Where have I heard that before? Oh yes, Hot-to-Trot in San Francisco. Gee, Adrian sure does attract dingbats. Their powers of observation are stunning.

"Adrian, I'll show you to your room, then you can go see Tía Carmen," she continued without missing a beat and laughing all the while. "She is out in the back yard resting."

"Eva," Adrian said calmly, "I know where my room is. You can show Tony and Frank to their rooms. We can all meet later in the back yard." Just like that my man dismissed her. He held Angelique with one hand and with the other he held me by the waist. I pushed the stroller and together we walked into the house.

Adrian stopped by the stairs and gazed in my direction.

"Millie, this will be a little tricky. Our bedroom is on the second floor and there is no elevator."

"I can carry little Adrian, you carry Adam and with our free hand we can help Angelique climb."

"OK," he replied, "do you think she can manage?"

"No, silly, we will have to lift her to each step. She will enjoy it. She is used to playing that game with us."

"Adrian," I said as we entered our bedroom.

"Yes."

"Are all you women dingbats? I know I'm not."

"Millie," he responded, knowing fully well what I meant, "I promise you there has never ever been anything between me and Eva. She is Hilda's niece. I don't know what she is doing here. She doesn't live here."

"Then why was she all over you? And that kiss on the lips. She is very familiar with you."

"We spent summers here as children. As teenagers, she had a crush on me, but I swear I never ever had any romantic entanglement with her. Never ever," he repeated.

"Fine. I believe you."

What else could I say?

The house was beautiful. I couldn't help wonder how Hilda's aunt could afford it. This was prime real estate. The back of the house overlooked a private beach and the Sea of Cortez. The patio was large with beautiful lawn furniture under huge blue-canvased umbrellas. There was a glass-topped dining table surrounded by chairs with blue-and-white-striped cushions. The table was set with matching placemats and napkins in blue and yellow. At the other end of the patio was an outdoor kitchen complete with stainless steel barbecue. To say it was stunning would be an understatement.

Adrian explained to me that Tía Carmen was Hilda's aunt. Tía Carmen had no children of her own, but she had practically raised Hilda and her sister and brother when their mother took ill and eventually died. Eva was Hilda's only niece from her sister. She grew up in Texas and still lived there. Hilda's sister also lived in Texas. Adrian informed me that Hilda and her sister did not speak to one another, but he did not know why. Her brother had many children and they all lived nearby.

"Adrian, I want to freshen up a bit. Why don't you take Angelique with you to meet Tía Carmen? Leave the boys with me."

"Can you manage by yourself?"

"Yes, I can."

"Don't be too long. Give me a kiss," he ordered.

I did as I was told and he left with his daughter. Adrian knew the layout of the house very well and I could tell he felt very comfortable. I was glad to be alone. I booted up my computer to check for messages and emails. Mr. Nussbaum had been quiet for the last few weeks. Adrian and I had ignored most of his emails, agreeing that we would stall him. The one conversation Adrian had with Nussbaum was not pleasant. He became aggressive and Adrian didn't like it, terminating the conversation with a few choice words.

Firing Ralph posed a new challenge in keeping tabs on Sam Sanz. I decided not to hire a replacement. Instead, I had put my own surveillance in place before leaving New York. Richard had agreed to do some freelance work for me whenever he could. That work was mainly checking up on Sanz.

I had two emails marked urgent. The first email was from Detective Doran informing me that an attorney by the name of Nussbaum had been successful in the early release of Tito Sanz. He wasn't quite sure of the release date, but it would be soon.

The next email was from Richard. Sam Sanz had purchased an old abandoned warehouse in a remote part of Brooklyn. Richard would try to get some surveillance equipment set up as soon as time allowed him to do so. The more troubling part of his email was information about Nussbaum. The talented attorney was able to convince a judge to sign off on the early release of Edgar Sanz.

Talent, my ass. It's more like the power of money.

Richard promised to double his efforts of surveillance on the Sanz brothers. I emailed him back, telling him that Tito had also been released from jail and that I could only assume he would head back to New York.

I powered off the computer and made the mental decision not to let this ruin our family vacation. I would alert Tony and Frank to be more vigilant, but I would keep this information from Adrian. There would be plenty of time after our vacation to tell him.

Hilda rushed to the boys and me, taking Adam into her arms.

"Millie," she said, "I could have helped you."

"Thank you, Hilda, but we were fine. I don't want to be a bother."

"You and these two little angels are no bother. Come," she said excited, "Tía Carmen wants to meet you."

Adrian was sitting on one side of Tía Carmen with his arm around her shoulders. Angelique was on her lap, taking in all her hugs and kisses. The hyena was on a chair next to Adrian. She was still talking and laughing. I'm not sure anyone was listening to her.

Hilda introduced me to her aunt and gestured for me to sit at her other side. Tía Carmen looked frail and Angelique was proving to be a handful. Hilda asked Adrian to take Angelique. Tía Carmen promptly turned to me and asked if she could hold little Adrian. She held him for

THE BLACK CALLA LILY

a short time, then handed him back to me so that she could fuss over Adam who was standing, holding on to her legs. Hilda, her aunt and Adrian were in heaven. My man was totally relaxed, hugging Tía Carmen and making her laugh with jokes and recounting stories of his childhood visits. It seemed my husband was a handful in his youth.

The hyena was still talking and laughing. It was amazing that no one was really paying attention, but that didn't stop her. Soon I had managed to tune her out also.

Dinner was held out on the patio. Hilda's brother, Marco and his wife Maria came to dinner. Two of their children with their spouses and children also joined us. They were delightful people. The food was excellent, but the family atmosphere was the crowning touch. The stories, the laughter, the shared memories gave me new insight to another part of Adrian's childhood. I was happy for him. Maybe he didn't have the mother he wished for, but he had this beautiful and loving adopted family.

Shortly after dinner Tía Carmen retired to her room. Hilda's brother and wife were soon saying their goodbyes. Their children stayed on. Miguel, their son, engaged me in conversation and was delighted to learn that I knew how to scuba dive.

"You know, Millie," he said conspiratorially, "I own a scuba shop in town. Tomorrow I have a party of eight going out with two dive masters. Would you like to go?"

"Oh, thank you, but no. I appreciate the invitation."

"Why not?" he insisted. "You are on holiday. Adrian, tell her she can go."

OK, now you're becoming obnoxious. I don't need my husband's permission.

Adrian looked uncomfortable, but he calmly placed an arm around my chair and said, "Miguel, my wife doesn't need my permission." Then he gazed in my direction.

"Millie, it has been a while since you have been scuba diving. You need some down time. Why don't you consider the invitation?"

"Yes, Millie," Miguel shouted, "you need some down time. Come tomorrow. I insist. I will send a car for you at seven in the morning."

"I just flew today. It wouldn't be safe for me to dive so soon," I protested.

"Nonsense," Adrian volunteered. "It was a short flight. There is no danger."

What the fuck? Is he trying to get rid of me?

"It's settled then," Miguel shouted out again. This man was very robust in his speech.

"Fine," I finally gave in.

"Adrian, what the hell is wrong with you," I complained once we were alone in our bedroom.

"What do you mean and keep your voice down. We are not home," he warned. "We don't have a wing of the house to ourselves. Hector and Hilda are in the next room. Eva is at our other side. Tía Carmen is across the hall. Not to mention Frank and Tony who are also across the hall."

"Why did you insist I go scuba diving? I don't want to go. I want to be with you and the children."

"Baby," he crooned, turning in my direction and stretching out his arms for me. I walked into his waiting arms.

"Baby, I know you," he whispered in my ear. "You like water sports. You deserve to have some fun. It has been a long time for you."

"But, Adrian," I protested, "I don't want to go. I want to be with you and the children."

"You are always with us," he whispered in my ear, holding me tighter in his embrace. "Angelique is almost three. You have been pregnant every year and giving birth. You have been busy for the last four years battling with me, taking care of me and our ever growing family." He lifted my chin and leaned in for a chaste kiss. Then he continued, "These opportunities don't come around too often."

He leaned in again for another kiss.

"Baby, please go and have fun. Miguel is a riot. The children and I will have fun on the beach. Please go."

"OK."

"That's my girl," he crooned. "Now, may I have my way with you?"

Next morning at precisely seven, a jeep was waiting to take me to the marina. One of Miguel's sons was the captain of the boat. It was a nice dive boat. There was plenty of room for divers and all the diving equipment. There was a center console and the cockpit was equipped with sonar. Miguel Jr. was accompanied by two dive masters. They were diligent in their duties, taking attendance, doing a head count and delivering the dive plan. They advised us on the weather conditions and the currents. They stressed the currents. Since everyone on board was a certified advanced diver, we would be doing challenging dives. I suddenly became excited. Now I was looking forward to this outing. I quickly forgot my protest of the night before.

Counting me, there were nine divers on board. Three married couples, two single men and me. The first dive was spectacular. I had been diving many places but this was beautiful. The reefs were alive and filled with all sorts of reef fish. It wasn't a deep dive so I stayed down for fifty minutes. Although I had not been diving in a while, I came up with plenty of air to spare.

The captain set out lunch for us. On the center console were platters of sandwiches and fruit, two different salads, crackers with cheese and plenty of sodas and water. We were all laughing and talking about our dive experience. The two single men engaged me in conversation. They were friends of Miguel Jr. Both men worked and lived in the area. As it turned out they were both doctors and this was their day off. I told them as little about myself as I could, volunteering only that I was married with three children.

"Your husband is crazy to let such a beauty out of his sight," Jose commented, eyeing me intensely. Both men were very good looking, but not as good looking as my man.

"It's hard to believe that you are the mother of three with such a fine figure," Ricardo chimed in, eyeing me from top to bottom.

These assholes have got to be kidding.

"Well," I said slowly, eyeing them both from top to bottom. "My husband is not crazy. He is very sane and very secure in our relationship. And you can believe that I have three of the most adorable children in the world."

Not enjoying their company at all, I excused myself. I walked to Miguel Jr. as he started the engine to travel to the next dive spot.

"Millie," he said animated, "you will enjoy this next dive. It is a deeper dive and you will be sure to see some big animals. Unfortunately, it is too early in the season to see the shark whale, but there are plenty of other marine life to see."

"I'm looking forward to it. Your father was very kind in lending me all this equipment."

"It was his pleasure. He wants to make sure you have a good time. The whole family loves Adrian. My father and Adrian are like cousins. Anyway, that is how we feel about him."

Miguel Jr. had an accent, but he spoke English well.

"Adrian loves it here. He feels very much at home," I contributed.

"Hilda use to bring him here when he was just a boy. He and my father and uncles used to play together. My father says they would look after him like he was their little brother."

"I can't imagine Adrian as a young boy."

"No?" he asked, looking at me. "My father says your boys look just like Adrian. So, if you look at your boys you can see Adrian as a young boy."

We both laughed at the thought of Adrian as a young child. Miguel Jr. was right. I could imagine Adrian as a young child. But when it came to our children, not only did the boys look like him, but so did Angelique.

The second dive was everything Miguel Jr. had said. The visibility was about eighty feet, if not more. We saw sea lions at a distance and a couple of hammerhead sharks. I stayed close to the dive masters,

avoiding the two doctors. I did not like them and did not feel comfortable around them.

We were back at the dive shop at three. I took my gear to the
back of the shop. There was a cement tub filled with water out on
the yard. This was used for rinsing all equipment. I was thankful that
the ladies of the group joined me. The men stayed inside waiting
their turn. There were two outdoor showers. The three ladies and I
took turns rinsing the salt water off. I dressed into the pareo I had
bought in Tahiti and quickly went inside to thank Miguel Sr. and Jr.
for a wonderful time.

"You are most welcome, Millie," Sr. said, kissing me on the cheek.
"You are welcome to come back anytime."

"Thank you, Miguel."

"The jeep is waiting to take you back."

"Thank you, again, Miguel. You are much too kind."

"We will see you later."

"Oh," I looked at him not knowing what he meant.

"I invited everyone to my house this evening. Maria is roasting a
whole pig in the yard. Adrian and Hilda know," he assured me.

"All right then, we shall see you later." I bid goodbye to my fellow
divers and left.

Adrian and the children were in our bedroom. He had bathed them
and was putting them down for a nap.

"Hey, baby," I greeted.

"Hey, baby," he greeted back, standing with outstretched arms.

I walked into his arms for a hug and a much needed kiss.

"How was your dive trip?" he asked, inhaling the scent of my hair.

"It was wonderful. I can tell you later. How was your day?"

"Great. The children and I went to the beach. We were there all day.
I bathed them and you know how they are after a day of sun, fresh air
and salt water. They are ready for a nap."

"I could use a nap." I laughed.

"Me, too," he said, holding me tighter. "How about a shower together, some sex and then a nap?"

I looked up at my husband. He was sporting that half-cocked smile that melted my insides. I pressed my face against his chest to inhale him.

"I would like that very much."

The nap did everyone a lot of good. The children were all in a good mood and looking beautiful. Adrian and I were well rested and sated. He looked gorgeous in tan slacks and a light-blue linen shirt with the top buttons open, showing the slightest hint of his silky black chest hairs with sleeves rolled up exposing his Braille watch on one wrist and his platinum cuff bracelet on the other. I wore a long, white, cotton halter dress that was perfect for the warm evening with tan espadrilles. I wore my hair high up in a bun and my matching platinum cuff bracelet.

"Mrs. Z," Adrian called, "are you ready?"

"Yes."

"Let me see you," he said, stretching out his arms.

This was our routine. He always asked to touch me so that he could visualize what I was wearing. It never failed by the time he reached my shoulders, I was already hot for him. His touch did that to me. His hot breath on me did that to me.

I walked towards him, standing close. He started by touching my hair.

"A bun," he said smiling.

He then proceeded to touch my earlobes.

"Ah, black pearl earrings," he said smiling. His long slender fingers slid softly down my neck.

"Halter top," he said as his hands rounded my shoulders, gently caressing my sun-tanned skin.

He touched my breast lightly but did not linger. He ended by resting his hands on my hips. He was now sporting that big broad smile that melted me.

"You are wearing the long, white cotton dress I like."

"Yes," I answered in a low throaty voice.

"Mrs. Z," he said, gazing in my direction, "are you getting hot for me?"

"Yes. Yes, I am."

"Well, baby, you are going to have to wait." He leaned down seeking my mouth and I complied. We kissed deep and passionately.

"But," he continued, "I promise to take care of you when we get back."

Adrian, the children and I rode in one of the Escalades with Tony driving and Frank riding shotgun. Hilda, Tía Carmen, and Eva rode in the other Escalade with Hector driving.

The SUVs made their way down the driveway to the road alongside the shore. The waves rolled gently towards the shoreline, reducing themselves to a white foam. The purple-orange glow of the disappearing sun hung at a distance in the horizon, giving way to a clear-blue night sky.

We veered off the road onto another road headed inland. The vehicles made another turn onto another road. We traveled a short distance before turning onto a street where houses were now visible. Finally, the cars stopped in front of a nicely kept yard. Beyond the yard was a Mediterranean styled home much like Tía Carmen's, only this one was painted yellow and smaller. Miguel Jr. appeared from the side of the house.

"Welcome, welcome," he greeted as boisterously as his father and with the same wide smile. "Come, everyone is waiting."

He led us to the back yard. There was a long table dressed in a fine lace tablecloth, dishes beautifully decorated in hues of blue and yellow, blue glassware and earthen covered pots. A wooden pergola stretched above the table. It was adorned with white tulle, ivy garlands and tiny white lights that twinkled.

Miguel's family flocked to greet us. Miguel Sr. shouted a heartfelt greeting from a fire pit in the distance where he was basting a pig that was cooking over the fire.

The men were drawn to Adrian like moths to light. He had the same effect on women. They all announced themselves to him and then proceeded to hug him. He knew them all and was delighted to be among them. They were all related to Miguel Jr. and Sr. and to Hilda.

"Adrian," Miguel Jr. chirped, "I want you to meet two friends of mine."

That is when I saw them. Ricardo and Jose. Thankfully, Hilda whisked the children and me away to meet the other family members. During dinner Adrian and I sat close to Miguel Jr., who was seated at the head of the table. Ricardo and Jose were across from us at the opposite end. Their stares at Adrian and me made me very uncomfortable. Adrian and Miguel dominated the conversation at our end of the table. I was grateful for the great food, lively conversation and for our children who provided a temporary distraction.

It didn't take long after dinner when Miguel and his father brought out the guitars. They gave one to Adrian, who was more than too happy to comply. The tequila in him was working. My husband was very entertaining when inebriated.

They played well together. I loved my husband. He was always relaxed when performing in front of family and friends. That was a talent I did not possess. They coaxed Adrian into singing the majority of the songs. Tía Carmen was outwardly pleased to listen to the men play and to listen to Adrian sing in Spanish. She sat next to him, applauding and kissing him at the end of each song. The entertainment ended with the serving of dessert.

"Millie," Hilda called as she approached me, "Tía Carmen is very tired. Hector is going to drive us back to the house."

I saw an opportunity to escape.

"Hilda, I want to leave also. The children have fallen asleep and I am tired. Let me get Adrian so we can all leave together." She took little Adrian in her arms while I went to get Adrian.

"Adrian," I said, interrupting his conversation with Miguel Jr., Ricardo and Jose, "please excuse me, but Tía Carmen is very tired and wants to leave. The children have fallen asleep. Baby, I think we too should leave."

"Sure, baby," he replied, turning to face me, "you must be tired also."

"I am. Please let's go."

It didn't matter how much Adrian had to drink, or how much fun he was having; his family came first. He was sensitive to our needs. We started to say our goodbyes when Ricardo grabbed Adrian by the arm. Adrian and I immediately stiffened. If my husband had been inebriated, he was not now.

"Adrian," Ricardo blurted out, "I know your lovely wife likes to golf and I would like to host her at the premier golf course in all of Cabo San Lucas. That is, of course, with your permission."

"My wife doesn't need my permission," Adrian replied as his neck slowly reddened. "Millie, would you like to golf?"

"No, Adrian, I would not. Thank you," I said addressing Ricardo, "for the invitation, but we have plans."

"It is an open invitation. I can work around your schedule."

"A premier golf course would require prior arrangements," I reasoned.

"I own it. Trust me, we can go anytime," he replied quickly. "Surely you can get away for a few hours tomorrow morning."

"Go ahead, Millie," Adrian said, putting his arm around my shoulder and kissing my hair. "You like the game. The children and I can entertain ourselves until you return."

I knew Adrian meant well. He wanted me to have fun and he had no idea that these two men made me feel uncomfortable. Tony and Frank were now at our side.

"Sure," I said to Ricardo. "When is tee time?"

"Let's make it for eleven in the morning. I will send my car for you."

"That will not be necessary," I quickly replied. "Give me the information and I will drive myself."

"Nonsense," Adrian blurted out. "Frank or Tony can drive you."

"Yes, Adrian, of course they can," I agreed.

Ricardo looked like he swallowed a lemon. Bodyguards were not part of his plan.

"Then it is settled," he finally said. "Here is my card with my cell number on it."

"Thanks," I said, less than enthusiastic.

"Mr. Z," Frank interjected, "Hilda and Hector are out front with the children. We are all ready to go."

Adrian said his final goodbye to Miguel Jr. and Miguel Sr. and we left.

I was conflicted on whether to tell Adrian how these two men made me feel. It's not like there was one thing I could point out. I was too tired to get into this conversation and decided not to say anything.

Chapter 24

Hilda's knock on the bedroom door woke me. "Millie, it's ten in the morning. You will be late for your golf appointment."

Shit! I slept late. Damn Adrian for keeping me up.

"I'll be quick. Thanks, Hilda. By the way, where are Adrian and the children?"

"Adrian took the children to the beach earlier. Eva helped him."

Oh, Eva. Of course she did.

"Hilda, is everything all right?" I asked. "You look worried."

"I'm fine, Millie. Thanks for asking. Tía Carmen has me worried."

"She looked fine last night," I commented.

"I think last night was too much for her. She didn't get up as usual this morning," Hilda said softly. "She said she was tired. I took her breakfast to the bedroom, but she hardly touched it."

"Should we get a doctor to see her?" I asked.

"No. That would make her angry. I don't want to upset her. Besides," she whispered conspiratorially, "I asked her if she was feeling something other than tired, you know, like pain, and she said no. What else can I do?"

"Well, Hilda, maybe she is just tired. Let's give her a couple of hours and see how she does. If she doesn't improve, we should call a doctor," I advised.

"I agree, Millie. Now hurry, you are going to be late."

I showered and dressed in a red bikini with a long, flowing, red cotton skirt and red sandals. No shirt. With camera in hand, I headed for the kitchen to grab a quick cup of coffee.

"Millie, is that what you are wearing to the golf club?" Hilda asked, trying to disguise the horrified look on her face as she entered the kitchen.

"No, Hilda," I replied laughing. "This is what I am wearing to spend the day with my husband and children. See you later."

I ran out of the house, not giving her an opportunity to interrogate me.

The beach was beyond the back yard. I could see Adrian sitting on a blanket under the shade of a palm tree with little Adrian on his lap, while Angelique and Adam played in the sand next to him. I could see him constantly touching them, probably to make sure they were where they were supposed to be. I spotted someone swimming in the deep, but I couldn't make out who it was. However, I could guess.

"Hi, baby," I announced myself as I approached Adrian.

"Millie," he replied with a surprised look on his face. "What happened to your golf date? What are you doing here? Are you OK?"

Mr. Multiple Questions is never far away.

"I sent my regrets to Ricardo via text message. I would rather be on the beach with you and the children."

"Aw," he exclaimed, stretching his arms out for me.

I sat down next to him and we embraced. Adrian leaned into me for a kiss. I responded by placing my hand behind his neck, pulling him closer, giving him a full open-mouthed kiss. Our cheeks hollowed as we drank each other in, tongues swirling around. I reveled in the sweet taste of my husband.

"Mrs. Z," Adrian sighed as he pulled away, "didn't you get enough last night?"

"I can never get enough of you," I purred, pulling him towards me again for another passionate kiss.

Adrian held on to his son with one hand and with his free hand cupped my breast, feeling and tugging gently. His hand then slid down my waist. He felt the skirt from my waist down to my thighs, stopping at the knee. He pulled up the skirt until he could feel skin. Slowly his hand crept up the side of my thigh until he reached the bikini bottom. His fingers curled around the skimpy material at my hip and tugged.

"Ah," he exhaled once again, pulling away. "You have on a bikini," he said approvingly. "Which one is it?"

"The red one you bought for me in Tahiti."

"I like it. We had a lot of fun with that bathing suit," he said laughing.

"Yes, we did."

"We could have some more fun, you know," he crooned.

"Adrian," I said as I saw the person swimming coming closer, "did I interrupt something?"

"No, baby. Why do you ask?"

"Because Eva has finished her swim and is coming towards us."

"Eva swimming?" he asked with eyebrows knitted and lips pursed.

"Yes. Eva swimming," I repeated.

"I thought she had left. She helped me with the children and then left."

"Apparently, she did not leave."

"Hi, there," she greeted. "Millie, I thought you went to golf."

"I sent my regrets. I'd rather be here with my husband," I replied, stroking Adrian's back, "and my children."

"I see," she said sourly. "I'll see you both back at the house."

"Eva, can you do us a favor before you leave?" I asked.

"Sure, what is it?" she asked, knitting her eyebrows together.

"Please, can you take a picture of us," I asked, handing her the camera. "Count to three so Adrian will know you are about to snap the picture."

I posed Angelique and Adam on the sand in front of us. Little Adrian sat on his father's lap. Adrian wrapped his arm around my shoulders. Eva counted one, two and just as she said three, Adrian buried his face in that tender spot between my neck and shoulder.

I will treasure that photo forever.

"Adrian, behave," I admonished. "Sorry, Eva. Can we do this again?"

"Sure."

This time Adrian behaved and Eva was able to snap our photo. She handed the camera back to me and without a word left.

"Millie?" Adrian muttered, gazing at me with a puzzled look on his face.

"She is headed back to the house," I answered the question he hadn't asked.

"So, are we alone?"

"Yes."

"Good," he said, burying his face in my cleavage, kissing and nipping my breasts.

"As inviting as that is, Mr. Z," I said, laughing and pushing him away, "we do have our children to look after. Let's play with them in the water."

"All right, Mrs. Z, but you owe me."

We spent the rest of the day sitting in the shallow water playing with our little ones. I extended my arm and snapped more photos of the five of us and of Adrian with the children.

Our family vacation proved to be relaxing, almost magical. We left the house only a few times to do some sightseeing, but we spent the majority of our time at the house or on the beach. Adrian logged on to his computer briefly in the mornings to catch up with his emails and his office. He continued to keep his smart phone in silent mode. I checked my emails, but my focus was mostly on our troubles back home. I kept an eye on Mr. Nussbaum and the Sanz brothers. Nussbaum had left a few nasty messages for me and for Adrian. He was not a happy camper when he learned that we would not be going back to New York until the spring. Now I was just fucking with him.

"Why don't we just give him what he wants," Adrian asked exasperated one day. "This man is dangerous."

"I am not convinced that giving him the diamonds will put an end to our relationship."

"He has made it abundantly clear he wants those diamonds. What else could he possibly want?"

"Adrian, let me remind you that the diamonds he wants do not nor have they ever belonged to him."

"You don't want them, do you?"

"I don't want them."

"Then let him have them and maybe then we can have some peace," he reasoned.

"I wish it were that simple."

"Baby, tell me what is on your mind," he said, gazing in my direction.

"As I said before, those diamonds are not his. He wants something that is not his and he will go to any lengths to get them. We know this."

"OK, we know this, so why not give them to him?" Adrian retorted with frustration.

"After he has them, what will stop him from coming after us for something else? I don't want him to consider us an easy mark."

"You mean target us for money?" he asked.

"That is right, Adrian. He knows who you are. I am sure he has done extensive research on you."

"I have people come to me all the time with schemes or stories trying to get money. He wouldn't be the first nor will he be the last."

"True. But I doubt the others have been as ruthless as this man. Don't forget he either murdered or had Ed murdered. Either way he will stop at nothing."

"What do you intend to do with him," Adrian asked, gazing in my direction with knitted eyebrows and pursed lips.

"I don't know. I am hoping that time will help to bring clarity to this situation."

"Millie, I hope you know what you are doing. Personally, I say give him the damned diamonds and let's be done with him."

Tía Carmen joined everyone for dinner and seemed to be doing better. She enjoyed listening to Adrian, who after dinner entertained everyone with his singing and guitar playing. She was the first to retire with Hilda and Hector next. Eva, Adrian, the children and I held out a little longer out on the patio. It was a warm evening with a light breeze.

Adrian served us drinks and for the first time since we arrived, Eva spoke to both Adrian and me. The nervous hyena laugh was gone. She spoke of her life back in Texas and her career. She played with Angelique and Adam and engaged us in conversation about our life back in Luna Llena. She also asked me questions about my days in the New York Police Department. Perhaps seeing us together on the beach as a family helped her to realize that she was no longer a teenager with a teenager's crush.

Little Adrian had fallen asleep and the other two had started to nod out.

"Adrian," I said, changing the conversation, "little Adrian fell asleep. Angelique and Adam are on their way. I'm going to take the baby to the bedroom and I'll return for the other two."

"I will help you," he volunteered. "Eva, I hate to end the evening, but it's time for us to put the little ones to bed and hit the sack ourselves."

"I'll help carry one upstairs," she offered.

Adrian and I had the bedtime ritual down to a science. We quickly changed each child and put each to bed. Adrian showered as I tidied the bedroom. Then it was my turn to shower. I wondered why our bedroom was referred to as 'Adrian's bedroom' by everyone in the house. It also was the only bedroom with its own en-suite.

Adrian had turned off the lights to the bedroom. The only light came from one candle. He was busy trying to maneuver the mattress onto the floor.

"Adrian," I said, announcing myself as I entered the bedroom. Adrian was naked and struggling with the mattress.

"What are you doing?"

"I'm putting the mattress on the floor," he said as a matter of fact.

"Why?" I whispered.

"This way there won't be any noise," he replied smiling. "Come baby, give me a hand."

"Um. Mr. Z, is there something on your mind?"

"Yes, yes, there is, Mrs. Z. I want you tonight." As we placed the mattress on the floor, he continued, "I'm only sorry we don't have any toys here and I didn't think of bringing any with us."

"You're getting slow in your old age, Mr. Z."

"Old am I," he said as he threw me onto the mattress. I let out a scream.

"Shh." Adrian laughed as he fell to my side. "You'll wake the children."

Adrian used his hand to search for my face. He rolled on top of me, straddling my sides with his legs holding me tightly in place. His arms rested by my shoulders as his hands cradled my head. He leaned in and we kissed passionately savoring each other. I ran my fingertips lightly up and down his back. I tried to touch his chest, but he denied me access, pressing closer. I then tried to move lower down his torso to the front, but access there too was denied.

Adrian pulled away from our kiss to slowly kiss and nip my jawline on his way to my neck and that tender spot between the neck and shoulder. My chest started to heave from the pleasure of his touch. I wanted more. I wanted to return the favor. I needed to kiss him and taste his body with my mouth and tongue, but I couldn't move. He was holding my head firmly.

"Baby," I purred, "I want to touch you."

"No," he crooned in my ear as he tugged on my earlobe with his lips.

"Baby, please," I begged, "I want to touch you. I want to taste all of you." I could feel his hardened erection pressed against me, making me want him more.

"You broke a rule tonight."

Ah! So my man wants to play.

"What rule?" I asked coyly.

"You know to come to bed naked," he whispered in my ear again, tugging at the ear lobe. He slid to the neck, nipping and sucking the skin, causing a tingling sensation throughout my body. He then continued, "I should be pressed against your naked body, not this damn nightgown."

I wanted him. I was ready. My heart was pounding against my chest and I could feel my entire body throbbing in desire for him. I didn't much feel like playing his game.

I need to speed this up and change his game plan.

"It is pretty, baby. I thought you might enjoy seeing it," I purred again. He stilled for a moment, then lifted his head above mine. I could feel his delicious hot breath on my face.

"I thought you might be in need of a spanking for the transgression, but now I understand you were thinking of me."

"Yes, I was. I know you love seeing with your hands what I'm wearing," again purring in a throaty voice, "and I enjoy it when you remove my clothes."

He gazed for a moment in the direction of my face and I could see his half-cocked smile.

"Well then, let's see," he said, loosening his grip on my head and legs.

Adrian slid his long slender fingers down my throat and across the décolletage of my nightgown, fingering the exposed part of my breasts. He didn't linger long, moving to my shoulder.

"Spaghetti straps," he commented in a low throaty voice. "What color?"

"White," I replied in an equally throaty voice.

His hand continued down my chest, stopping over one breast, then next cupping and squeezing each. He bent down to place a breast in his mouth. He sucked on it through the gauzy material, causing it to cling to my breast. He then repeated it with the other breast. My chest started to heave once more. I could feel a low throbbing throughout my body. I was ready for him.

"The material is a cotton gauze."

"Yes," I whispered, squirming under him, begging for more.

"I bet your body is visible through it."

"Yes, baby, it is."

He licked his bottom lip and smiled. His hand went down to my belly and stopped.

"It has lace. Is it see-though?" he asked as his hand swiftly moved to between my legs.

"Yes, it is, baby," I purred from the sensual pleasure he was giving me.

He cupped my sex through the material, squeezing and causing me to gasp with delight at his touch.

"You don't have on any underwear," he stated more than asked.

"That's right. None."

"Ah," he sighed as he sat up, pulling up the nightgown to my waist. "You were thinking of me."

I sat up and kissed his neck, then snaked my way down to his nipple. I took one in my mouth while my hand caressed the other. He groaned with pleasure.

Adrian slipped two fingers inside me, causing me to let out another gasp of pleasure. I straightened so he could easily remove my nightgown. Fully naked, I put my arms around his neck, planting an open-mouthed kiss on his lips. I wanted to drink him in. All of him. Adrian continued thrusting his fingers in and out while his thumb stroked my clitoris.

"Please, Adrian," I begged, "I need you now."

"No, baby, not yet." He wrapped his free arm around my waist to hold me in place. "Stay as you are," he ordered, "I'm going to make you come." He picked up the pace and, tightening his grip around my waist, he commanded, "Come for me, baby. Let me feel your pleasure."

My heart was pounding against my chest faster. My whole body was throbbing and then the familiar wave of convulsions took over. Adrian didn't let up, continuing his assault with his hand.

"Ah!" I let out as my body bowed forward to still his hand with both of mine. "Stop!" I ordered.

Adrian laughed as I slumped back onto the mattress. I tried closing my legs, but he stopped me with his hand and legs.

Kneeling in between my legs, he crouched over me so I could feel his hot breath on my face.

"Baby, don't you want me inside of you?"

"Yes, Adrian, I do," I whispered. Throwing my arms around his neck, I pulled him towards me for a passionate kiss. We drank each other in hollowing our cheeks and savoring each other with our tongues. Adrian pulled away.

"I've never met a woman like you. I've never had a woman like you," he whispered in a throaty voice. "One who enjoys everything that I enjoy." Those few words from his lips got my blood pumping again. We kissed fervently. I wanted more of him. I needed more. Adrian broke away. This time he slipped an arm around my waist and lifted me onto his lap. Sweat covered both our bodies. Our bodies glistened in the dim light of the candle.

Adrian felt between my legs to determine if I was ready for him. I was. I was already throbbing in anticipation of feeling him inside of me. He lifted me so I could ease myself onto his massive erection.

"Um," I groaned with pleasure. My hips gyrated on top of him. Adrian's arms were wrapped around me. He held me tight, meeting my gyrating with forceful thrusts. My already swollen insides tightened around his erection. I could feel him against that one sweet spot. The throbbing was becoming more intense. That familiar convulsing was not far behind.

"Oh, Adrian," I cried, "I can't hold out."

He lowered his arms, placing his hands on my rear, pulling me in to meet his thrusts. Adrian sensed I was close to a climax.

"Go for it, baby. Let me feel you," he crooned and then gave my rear a light slap. "Come for me," he ordered. And I did just that. The throbs turned into convulsions, forcing my body to bow forward. I leaned on Adrian completely exhausted. He wrapped his arms around me, tilting me backwards and gently lay us both back on the mattress. He continued thrusting in and out, seeking his own relief. I soon felt his release. We embraced until the beating of our hearts returned to normal.

"Adrian, I want to ask you for something," I said, kissing his hair and face.

"Anything, baby, anything. Name it and it's yours."

Adrian curled to my side, his arms still embracing me. I wrapped my legs around his and together we formed a human pretzel. We held that position as we surrendered to sleep. The question forgotten.

Chapter 25

A knock at the door startled me. I started to move, but Adrian held me in place. He buried his face in my neck. I relaxed and followed his lead to ignore the knock.

The knock came again but this time accompanied with a voice.

"Adrian," came the whisper of Hilda from the other side of the door. Again she knocked, "Adrian."

"Adrian," I whispered in his ear. "Go see what Hilda wants."

"No. She will go away."

"Adrian, please go see what she wants. She never knocks on our door."

"That's not true," he argued. "She's been known to knock."

"Not in the middle of the night," I argued back.

"Adrian." Hilda repeated knocking on the door more frantically.

"Coming," he finally answered. "Didn't we have a towel somewhere here?"

I handed him the towel. He crept to the end of the mattress kissing my body on his way down. I watched him as he stood and wrapped the towel around his waist.

Honestly, he could have put on a robe except he doesn't have one.

"Hilda," he said, trying to open the door, which was being obstructed by the mattress on the floor. He stepped out onto the hallway through a narrow opening. "What is the matter, Hilda?"

"What's wrong with the door?" she asked.

"Nothing is wrong with the door," he answered a bit agitated. "Millie and I put the mattress on the floor."

"Isn't the bed comfortable for you?" she asked with great concern. She was always concerned for his comfort.

"Yes, Vieja, the bed is just fine. If you must know we didn't want to make too much noise."

That's just like my man to put it all out there.

I could hear Hilda chuckle. Adrian was not amused.

"Well, Vieja, what is the matter," he repeated.

"It's Tía Carmen, Adrian. She doesn't look well and she is non-responsive when I speak to her. Eva also tried to wake her."

"Yes, Adrian, I tried to wake her but nothing. And her breathing seems labored," Eva offered.

"Eva, I'm sorry I didn't know you were here."

I could hear Hilda and Eva apologizing for not making him aware of Eva's presence.

"Eva, please call for the doctor or an ambulance," Adrian ordered.

"Yes, Adrian." I heard Eva walk back to her bedroom.

"Hilda, I'm going to get dressed. I'll meet you in Tía Carmen's room."

"Thank you, Adrian."

He kissed her and returned to the bedroom.

"What's wrong?" I asked as I stood up on the mattress.

"Tía Carmen isn't doing well. I'm going to take a quick shower, dress and join Hilda in Tía Carmen's room. Eva is calling for the doctor and the ambulance. God only knows how long that will take."

"Adrian, help me put the mattress back."

Together we placed the mattress where it belonged and I made the bed with fresh linen. Adrian went to the nightstand where the candle was burning. He blew it out, then licked his fingers pressing them to the wick, making sure the flame was extinguished.

"Now you've left me in the dark," I complained.

"I'm always in the dark."

"Funny guy."

"Baby, you want to take a quick shower with me?"

"No. It wouldn't be quick. You go first. Hilda needs you."

"Can you take out some clothes for me?"

"Sure. What would you like to wear?"

"Whatever you pick will be fine. You know me."

"Yes, I know you. Slacks, shirt and shoes."

Adrian laughed as he walked towards the bathroom. I picked beige slacks, blue linen shirt and brown shoes. This was as casual as Adrian dressed.

I had barely finished dressing when Adrian entered our bedroom.

"Hi, baby, how is it going?" I asked.

"Millie, Tía Carmen is gone."

We hugged and he sobbed silently on my shoulder. I had come to understand that besides his father's family, Hilda's family was like his own. This is where he spent summers and vacations with Hilda and sometimes his father. This was his second home. I held Adrian tightly for a few minutes until he finally composed himself. He straightened and cleared his throat.

"Millie, Hilda is inconsolable. She won't leave Tía Carmen's side. She is on the bed crying. She won't listen to me." Tears streamed down his face again.

"Oh, baby, let her cry. You both need to let it out. I have the baby monitor in my hand," I informed him. "We can go and be with Hilda. It's what we must do."

Adrian, Hilda and Eva planned a beautiful funeral. Family came from everywhere. There were neighbors and friends present. The vigil was held at the house as per Hilda's request. The flowers barely fit inside the house. Adrian arranged for most of the flowers to be delivered to Tía Carmen's church. They served to adorn the funeral mass and services on Sunday. The priest was most appreciative.

I kept the children away from the vigil part, but they were present for the church service and the burial. They were generally well behaved. Angelique, who usually favored being on her father's lap, insisted on being with Hilda. I tried to liberate Hilda, but she wouldn't hear of it. Hilda held on tight to Angelique. Somehow she found comfort holding on to her "little girl."

Adrian arranged a brunch for all the attendees of the funeral at a local restaurant by the water. The food was absolutely delicious. At the appropriate time, Adrian stood and addressed the guests to thank them for standing with the family in the saddest of occasions. He then started telling stories about Tía Carmen and how she would intercede on his behalf when he misbehaved and Hilda wanted to reprimand him. Everyone present laughed at his stories, including Hilda who was still holding Angelique. Other family members stood with Adrian to recount their stories and more laughter ensued. Eva also shared her experiences, which were similar to Adrian's.

Soon the circulated drinks and tequila had the desired effect on lifting everyone's spirits. Hilda seemed to take comfort in listening to Adrian and the others. And through it all, Hector did not leave her side for a moment. What impressed me most about Hector is that he did not allow himself to indulge in the drinking. He kept a keen eye on Hilda, Adrian and his surroundings. He reminded me of Richard, Tony and Frank. He took the security of the family seriously. After all, it was his family too.

The time had come to say goodbye. We headed back to the house and not a minute too soon. Little Adrian was becoming irritable. He was in need of his afternoon bottle, a diaper change and a nap.

"Adrian," I said as we entered the house, "can you watch Angelique and Adam. Little Adrian is irritable and it is only a matter of time before he starts wailing."

"Sure, baby," he said, kissing my hair.

I changed young mister Adrian and gave him his bottle. Cradling him in one arm, I opened the doors to the terrace. The view of the sea was spectacular. I wondered what would happen to the property now that Tía Carmen was gone.

The fresh air was getting to my little one. His blue eyes were giving way to sleep. I stared at him, counting my blessings for the children and for a wonderful husband. I offered a silent prayer of thanks. Little Adrian must have sensed the peace surrounding us because he finally drifted off to sleep.

I changed my clothing into a more comfortable dress and flat shoes. I carried the baby downstairs to join the others. As I approached the kitchen, I could hear Hilda, Hector and Adrian talking.

"Adrian," I heard Hilda say, "what does this mean? How will Millie react to this?"

"Not well," he replied.

"What should we do?" Hector asked.

"Follow Millie's lead."

"Adrian," I said announcing myself, "little Adrian fell asleep. I'm putting him in the crib down here."

"Oh, good."

"What's going on?" I asked, looking at the three of them.

"Baby, come here," he said, stretching out his arms.

I walked into his embrace sensing trouble.

"Adrian, what is going on?" I repeated.

"Flowers were just delivered."

"Oh, do I have to go chasing after someone?" I joked. Nobody laughed.

"Adrian," I said, pulling out of his embrace, "for the last time, what is going on?"

"The flowers are in the dining room," he offered.

I walked into the dining room and there they were. A huge bouquet of white calla lilies with a back one in the center. There was a card attached. The envelope had my name on it. I opened it. It read, "With deepest sympathy from New York with love. Millie, hurry back before I send someone for you." My heart sank. I knew the security of the house had not been compromised. I had checked the video feeds myself. I went to see Frank and Tony. Tony had accompanied us while Frank watched the premises.

"Frank, Tony," I announced myself. They both stood. "Have you seen the flowers?"

"Yes, Mrs. Z," Frank responded. "A legitimate delivery truck brought them. I checked it out myself. I took the driver's name and called the florist who verified that he worked there. I also asked him who sent the flowers."

Wow! Frank was really on top of things.

"What did you find out?" I asked.

"They were ordered from New York. A Mr. Nussbaum sent them."

Son of a bitch! I guess a good researcher would be able to track us.

"Thanks, Frank. That was good work."

"Thank you, Mrs. Z."

"What now, Mrs. Z?" Tony asked.

"We move out. Ready yourselves."

I composed myself and went back to the kitchen, announcing myself as I entered.

"Millie, are you all right?" Hilda asked.

"Yes, Hilda, I am fine. But we need to make arrangements to leave immediately."

"I can't leave," Hilda protested. "I need to properly close the house. I need to go through my aunt's things."

"I can't leave you here," Adrian interjected.

"Adrian, the house, my aunt's things. I have things to do before I leave."

"You listen to me, Vieja," Adrian spoke to her forcefully, "if we leave, you leave. We will close up the house together. Millie has the house under surveillance. Nothing is going to happen. Even if something did happen, so what? It's only a house. You are more important," he reasoned.

"Millie, how soon are we leaving?" Hilda asked. She knew better than to argue with Adrian.

"As soon as Adrian can ready our flight home."

"Consider it done," Adrian blurted.

Chapter 26

The trip home was uneventful. Just the way I liked things. Eva flew to California with us and the Gulfstream would take her onto Texas. The return to Luna Llena was bittersweet for me. I knew it was a matter of time before I would have to face Nussbaum again.

Adrian and I were in each others arms in our own bed in our own bedroom. I buried my face in his chest, inhaling his scent.

"Are you OK?" he asked.

"I am more than OK. I'm elated to be home."

"Um, me too," he crooned. "Have you thought about Nussbaum and what to do with him?"

"Not tonight, Adrian, please. Let me enjoy the peace."

"I'm sorry," he said, kissing my hair. "Will you come tomorrow with me to the office in San Francisco?"

"Yes. Is there something in particular you need me to do?"

"Yes and no. You can help with a few contracts. Millie," he said, rolling me on my back, "I hate to disturb your peace, but I need to discuss something with you. I meant to mention it while we were in Baja, but then Tía Carmen passed and my attention was diverted."

"What is it, Adrian?"

"The day after tomorrow I have a meeting with Susan. The contract expires and I need to bring this chapter of my life to a conclusion. I don't want you there, but I can use your help tomorrow preparing for the meeting." He paused and then continued, "I need to know that you're going to be OK during this process. You have a lot on your mind right now."

"Baby," I said, caressing his face, "I am going to be just fine. I will help you in whatever you need. I want to take the children with me. Can we stay in the penthouse tomorrow night?"

He knitted his eyebrows and pursed his lips at my request.

"Why do you want to stay there?"

"I want to go shopping for a few things. Maybe I can meet Daisy for lunch, if she is available."

"Sure, we can stay."

My bliss came to an abrupt end. A funeral, Nussbaum, Hot-to-Trot, and I knew the Sanz brothers were not far behind.

On our way to the office, I couldn't help but take pride in my family. The children looked beautiful. My husband was hot. And I looked amazing, if I did say so myself. I wore a red sleeveless shift and because it was still chilly out, I wore a red swing jacket over my dress. Adrian made it a point to 'see' me with his hands. He approved of my attire.

"Mrs. Z, you look, as usual, beautiful. The firearm at your side goes well with your outfit," he joked.

I laughed and wrapped my arms around his waist to place his firearm in the waistband of his trousers where I could get to it if the need should arise.

We arrived at the office at precisely nine. Adrian's staff was already at work. However, I was surprised to see Paula.

"Adrian, Millie, how are you?" she greeted, hugging us both and then the children. "I was sorry to hear about your aunt's passing."

"Thanks, Paula. You're here early," Adrian replied.

"I needed some material for a meeting I have tomorrow in Hong Kong. Adrian, you do remember I emailed you about our new customer?" she asked more than stated.

"Yes. Yes, I do remember. I may have to ask you to slow down," he added with a laugh, then continued, "I don't know that production can keep up with you."

"In the business world we call that a happy problem," she cheerfully offered.

"Yes, we do," Adrian agreed.

"Well, I hate to leave you two, but I have a flight to catch."

"Paula," I interjected, "is Daisy busy this week? Do you know?"

"She is in Los Angeles this week. She won't be back until Friday. Did you want something?"

"No. I thought if she was around we might have lunch together tomorrow. Have a good flight, Paula."

Adrian and I settled the children in their baby-proof area. His secretary announced the arrival of his first appointment.

"Give me a moment," he said turning to me. "Millie, I totally forgot I had an appointment with Sharon. I promise not to take long."

"That's fine, Adrian. I have my own work to do."

Sharon was his personal shopper. She kept records of everything he owned. She always came equipped with samples of materials for clothing and suggestions, but mostly it was Adrian who gave her a list of the things he needed or wanted. I had offered to take care of some of those things for him, but he wouldn't hear of it. He reasoned my time was too valuable and occupied to take on this added chore. That suited me just fine. Shopping was not an interest of mine. He had suggested that

THE BLACK CALLA LILY

Sharon shop for the children and me, but I had declined. Not because I liked shopping, but because I was not used to having someone so intimately involved in my closet.

I busied myself in my office, going through the routine of checking our security on the premises. Tony and Frank were in their office checking the video feeds for the penthouse and Luna Llena. I had also given them the responsibility to check the surveillance cameras I had on Nussbaum and Sanz. I, too, checked the feeds. It wasn't because I didn't trust them, but our security was ultimately my responsibility.

Nussbaum had left another nasty message for me. Again he threatened to send someone to retrieve his package. He stopped mentioning Gardel. He was now clearly calling it his package.

The Sanz brothers were now together and busy with their operations. The only interesting development was the arrival of their two sisters. My surveillance revealed they were now involved in the family business full time. This was potentially a new complication. I couldn't understand how two married women with husbands and families could just pick up and leave their homes to join their idiot brothers in an illegal business. So I did some research.

The information I was fed by Ralph White, my last investigator, had been fabricated. They both had been serving time in a prison in upstate New York for drug possession with the intent to sell and for assault. This family was full of gems.

I was stumped on how to deal with Nussbaum. Sanz was an easier target, but getting Adrian's approval was not going to be easy. I had to figure a way of convincing him that my solution was the only solution. Nussbaum, the Sanz brothers and the two sisters had to be neutralized.

"Millie," Adrian called on the office intercom, "I'm ready if you are."

I went to his office. Sharon was packing her samples and notes.

"Mrs. Z," she blurted enthusiastically, "perhaps someday we can get together to go over your needs and the needs of the children. I have some great ideas for all of you."

"Mrs. Z is free tomorrow," Adrian volunteered.

"Wonderful," she screeched. "It's settled then. I can meet you here at two in the afternoon."

"I don't know," I protested.

"Baby, it will be fun. I insist you let Sharon shop for you."

"Fine," I agreed reluctantly.

"You know, Adrian," I finally said after Sharon left, "I feel like I've been blindsided. You know I don't want a personal shopper."

"I know, Millie, but trust me, it will make life easier and you couldn't have a better person than Sharon."

That was true. She was excellent at her job. Her eye for detail was impeccable.

Adrian and I worked together the rest of the morning going over contracts for his various businesses. He handed me another file. It was the file for his business meeting with Hot-to-Trot tomorrow.

"We can break for lunch and take this up later," he suggested.

Adrian and I gathered the children and sat in the sitting area of his office. We fed the children first. I took charge of Angelique and Adam while Adrian held little Adrian in his lap to feed him. It was amazing to watch. When the baby fidgeted, Adrian would kiss him and make faces at him to get his attention. Then Adrian would feel for his mouth and shove the spoonful of food in.

"How am I doing?" he asked.

"You are doing great."

"I worry that I'll make a mess and not feed him enough."

"Adrian, you are doing great. You have this feeding of the children down to a science. So what if it gets messy. That's what being a parent is, isn't it?"

We finished with the children and ate our lunch, making small talk. I decided to ask him a question.

"Adrian, what is going to happen to Tía Carmen's house?"

"Nothing," he responded, "it wasn't her house. The house belongs to Hilda."

"Oh, I had no idea."

"Millie, my father purchased that home for her when I was a child. Hilda had Tía Carmen live there to help her out."

"Your father was a generous man."

"My father was in love," Adrian said, smiling and gazing in my direction. Then he continued, "He didn't fool anyone. Hilda's family knew of their relationship. That is why Eva's mother, that is Hilda's sister, didn't speak to Hilda and still doesn't. She didn't approve."

"What about you, Adrian? Did you know? And how did Hector figure in all this?"

"I love Hilda. She was my mother. She did everything for me. My father hired Hector sometime after. I think he came to know that Hector was sweet on Hilda. That is when I started to travel alone with Hilda. He never accompanied us again. And at home he kept his distance.

"I told you once before my father was a foolish man. He denied himself happiness all because he refused to divorce my mother. But he was a gentleman to Hilda. He was not going to stand in the way of her happiness."

"Do you think she was happy giving up your father for Hector?"

"Yes, I do. Hector is a lot of fun. A bit of a rascal. Women like that, Millie. Don't they?" he asked rhetorically.

"Yes, baby, we do love those bad boys." We laughed and sat on the floor to play a little with the children.

"Miss, you can't go in there," I heard Adrian's receptionist and secretary yell in unison.

Hot-to-Trot was at the threshold of the office with the secretary and receptionist in tow.

"Adrian," she screeched, "I demand to speak with you."

I was stunned. My first inclination was to reach for my firearm, but I restrained myself. My second inclination was to jump up and bitch slap her, but again I restrained myself. Adrian sat the children on the floor next to me and stood, but not before he reached to caress my face and kiss me chastely on the lips. The crimson in his neck was slowly creeping to his face.

"It's all right," he addressed his staff. They protested but he assured them it was fine. They announced their departure and he waited a few seconds before speaking. Hot-to-Trot had her eyes fixed on the children and me. It was obvious she had not expected to see us.

"Susan, have a seat," Adrian offered.

"Adrian, I don't appreciate your ignoring my calls," she screeched again.

"Lower your voice," he ordered. "You are scaring my children. And you are interrupting my family time."

"How dare you ignore me," she countered in a slightly lower voice.

"I haven't ignored you."

"Yes, you have. I requested a meeting with you today."

"I didn't see the need for a meeting since we are meeting tomorrow and I communicated that to you."

"I wanted to speak to you before the meeting."

"What about, Susan?" he barked, making her jump.

"I wanted to speak to you about the meeting tomorrow."

"Please be more specific."

"I'd like to postpone the meeting."

"No. That will not be possible."

"Why not?" she demanded. "What's the big deal? It's only an agreement between you and me."

Now that is irritating. 'You and me,' bitch, are you crazy?

I turned my back on them and busied myself with the children. They were a lot more fun.

"Susan," Adrian said as he sat down at his desk, "have a seat."

He waited for her to sit before continuing. I stayed where I was, playing with the children and trying to center myself. He asked for my loyalty and faith. And that is what he was going to get.

THE BLACK CALLA LILY

"Susan," he calmly said, "tomorrow the agreement between you and Zaragosa and Company expires. We must meet."

"I am not ready to meet with you," she argued. "You can agree to postpone until a later date."

"I do not wish to postpone the meeting and it is not in your best interest to postpone."

"Really, Adrian? Not in my best interest. Who the fuck are you kidding?"

"Watch your language," he warned. "My children and wife are present."

"Adrian, this is a simple agreement between you and me. You can agree to postpone without any consequence to me."

"The agreement is between you and Zaragosa and Company," he repeated.

"What the hell is that supposed to mean?" she asked angrily.

"Millie," he called out.

"Yes, Adrian," I answered.

"Could you join us for a minute?"

"Of course."

I sat in the chair closest to Adrian. He waited for me to get comfortable before continuing.

"Susan, you know my wife, Milagros."

"Yes," she replied with a confused look on her face. "What does she have to do with this?"

"Everything," Adrian replied quickly. "Milagros is Zaragosa and Company."

The shocked look on her face was priceless.

"But you are the one who signed the agreement," she asked after the shock passed.

"Either one of us can sign an agreement," Adrian replied in his matter-of-fact tone.

What is Adrian up to? Sure, I'm his partner, but I don't know the first thing about any of his business enterprises.

Susan looked at me with disdain. The thought of having to deal with me was beneath her. And so she went for the kill.

"What do you know of this business arrangement?" she asked arrogantly.

Think woman! What the hell has Adrian thrown you into? Is this a test?

Engaging my mouth before thinking was how I usually rolled, so I decided to go with it.

"Susan," I said casually with a calm that miraculously took hold of me, "I know enough. Adrian entered into this agreement as a friend to help another friend."

"I need more time," she said, eyeing me carefully as to assess me.

"Susan," I said, this time with more confidence, "you are an attorney. You are fully aware of the terms of the agreement you signed."

I hoped she did. That would have made one of us aware of the terms, since I had not had an opportunity to read it.

"I am not ready," she repeated.

"Susan," I repeated her name to gain more confidence, "You knew this day would come. You have had ample time to ready yourself for this meeting."

"I need more time," she repeated more humbly. "Why can't you and Adrian give it to me?"

All right, that's what I'm talking about. Ms. Hot-to-Trot is not so confident now. But what does Adrian expect of me?

"Susan," again I repeated her name just because it seemed to disarm her at this point, "Zaragosa and Company is heavily weighted in the real estate market. This is not a good position for our portfolio, but I am sure Adrian must have said this to you at some point."

"Yes, he did," she said cautiously, still trying to figure out the game plan, "but what do you know about portfolios?"

Oh no, bitch! You did not go there. Hello. Here we go. Time to have some fun.

"Susan, dear heart, I know enough. The revelation that you are not ready for tomorrow's meeting is disappointing. I expected better from you."

Oh yeah, Millie, babe, you are on a roll! Go for it, girl!

"You are aware of the terms of our agreement." I stressed the 'our' so that she made no mistake that Adrian and I were a team and she was the interloper. "We will be at the meeting tomorrow at ten in the morning. We intend on moving forward and expect you to be there. If you do not show up, we will exercise our rights under the agreement."

Through my peripheral vision I could see a slight grin on Adrian's lips.

"Certainly you can extend me some more time?" she argued.

"No, we cannot," I answered. "Quite frankly, I have a dim view of your not being ready for this meeting. It leads me to believe that you are abusing the friendship."

"I am not abusing the friendship," she replied. Then unexpectedly her body language changed. She leaned back in the chair and crossed her legs like someone who had the upper hand in a situation.

"Adrian and I have been more than friends. You might say friends with benefits."

"That was a very long time ago, Susan," I reminded her.

"Maybe so. But I have my trophies. I could make those trophies public."

"Susan, dear heart," I said in a condescending tone. "That is not a card you hold," I reminded her again.

"Yes, but I still have other trophies. Tucked away where he couldn't get to them."

Through my peripheral vision I could see Adrian's neck redden.

"No, you don't," I stated with the authority of one who knows. "You don't have jack shit. I took care of all your stashes."

"So it was you and not him," she screeched. "I do have other trophies."

OK, bitch, I own your ass now.

"No, you don't, Susan," I said, crossing my legs and leaning back on my chair. I should know. I ransacked both apartments, cloud account, and the deep web. "But let me say this one thing to you. And I want you to listen carefully," I warned.

"You will be at that meeting tomorrow. If not, you are well aware of the consequences. If you doubt me, my resolve, my abilities, you will be greatly mistaken. Just for you edification, I have my own trophies of you with your boss. His wife is not a woman to be trifled with. She has her own power base not to mention that of her family. You will find yourself out in the cold, jobless and with a ruined reputation. Lady, do not fuck with me."

Her jaw dropped and she was speechless. Adrian, of course, could not appreciate this but her silence spoke volumes.

"Susan," he interjected, "we shall meet tomorrow as arranged. Please leave, you have a lot of work to do and Milagros and I have to get back to our children." And that is how she was dismissed by Mr. Z. He stood up and extended his hand for mine, which I promptly accepted. Together we walked to the baby-proof area, removed our shoes and climbed over the little fence to join our babies.

Now, that's what I call a power couple!

I collected little Adrian from his playpen and joined Adrian, Angelique and Adam on the floor. We commenced our gentle jostling and wrestling.

Yes, indeed, that is how this family rolls.

When I was sure Hot-to-Trot had left the offices, I spoke to Adrian.

"Adrian, she has left. What was that all about? Once again I feel that I was blind sighted."

Angelique and Adam were all over him. He gently sat them down, rubbed their backs and kissed them all over their faces before turning to me. They responded immediately to his gesture and calmed down.

"Come here, baby," he said, stretching his arms.

I inched closer to him. He cradled me in his arms.

"Millie, you are what I would call a fierce warrior. That is the side of you that I am most familiar with. And I am appreciative of that side of you."

He cradled me in his arms, kissing my hair.

"You are intelligent," he continued, "analytical and quick on your feet. But those are traits I have observed in more physical circumstances."

"Adrian," I blurted, feeling a heaviness in my heart, not knowing where he was headed, "you knew these things about me before we were married. You knew them before we were involved."

"I did, baby," he said, kissing me all over the face. "I love you for it, don't get me wrong. Millie, Susan presented a situation I could not pass up. I needed to know how you would employ those talents of yours in a business setting."

"Why, Adrian? Why is that so important? You know I have no interest in business. Why, Adrian?" I asked with all the anguish that was now consuming my heart, my very being. Where was this leading? Why was he testing me?

"Because it is important to me. Millie, I need to know that you can take over our operations if something should happen to me. I need to know you can take care of the businesses that are important to me. I needed to know you can preserve all that I have worked hard to grow for our children and their children. I need to know that our businesses are more important to you than your dislike of business and persons you may have to deal with."

The intensity in his eyes and words were more than I could bear. He held me tighter and closer. His eyebrows were knitted and lips pursed.

That was the test. Did I pass?

"Well, Adrian, what is the verdict?" I asked nervously.

"Mrs. Z, you never disappoint." He leaned down for a full open-mouthed kiss.

Tricia knocked on the door.

"Mr. Z," she said, trying not to look in our direction, "Mr. Freeman is on the phone about your meeting tomorrow."

Adrian left us to answer the telephone.

"Hello, Nathan," Adrian greeted. "Oh, I see. She called." There was a brief pause before Adrian continued. "Nathan, please let Susan know that we are moving ahead with our meeting tomorrow. If she does not show up, she will forfeit her shares of the project to Zaragosa and Company. So I suggest you have the title people present because by three in the afternoon, I will have a buyer. Do you understand? Good. Until tomorrow." He hung up.

"Adrian," I called from the bathroom, "I can't attend the meeting this morning."

"Why not?" he asked, knitting his eyebrows and pursing his lips.

"We don't have someone to look after the children," I reminded him.

"Oh, that is not a problem," he casually stated. "We can bring them with us."

"Is that allowed?" I asked.

"Baby," he looked at me with his half-cocked smile, "who is going to object?"

No one would dare object. After all, these were the children of Adrian Zaragosa.

The meeting went as hoped. Susan showed up with her new investor. He was an older man with some very deep pockets. Zaragosa and Co. made a nice profit for its investment, but more importantly my husband was extricated from Susan and her project.

We headed home to Luna Llena after the meeting. Adrian, the children and I spent the next few days enjoying our surroundings. The weather was warmer in the afternoons, allowing for family picnics in the great lawn by the winery surrounded by lavender. We were back to our daily routines. I didn't realize how much I had missed them. Luna Llena was without a doubt not only my home, but also my favorite place on earth.

Chapter 27

We had finished having our breakfast out on the patio when little Adrian began to cry. I held him in my arms to comfort him and noticed that he felt warm to the touch.

"Adrian, I think the baby is running a temperature."

"I'll call the pediatrician," he said as he picked up his smart phone.

Not only did little Adrian have fever, but so did Angelique and Adam. The doctor assured us they would be fine in a few days as long as they were kept still as best as possible and given the medications he prescribed.

Adrian and I cut our workday short to concentrate on the children. We kept them comfortable and they slept most of the day. We were not accustomed to having sick babies. Visits to the pediatrician were mostly routine. This was the first time they required medication. Adrian and I kept them close under watchful eyes.

Hilda teased us for being overly cautious. "Children catch colds all the time," she offered. "There is no need to lock yourselves in your bedroom with them."

Well, maybe she is right about the bedroom. Maybe we are overreacting.

"Never mind," Adrian argued, "they need to rest and not catch any other germs. We need to protect them."

"Have it your way," she conceded. "I will be in the kitchen if you need me."

My own mother laughed and teased me when I spoke to her in the afternoon. Naturally, she was concerned for the children, but based on the facts I presented her, she determined the same as the doctor.

"This is your first experience with a sick child," she reasoned. "You and Adrian have been very lucky. Your children are very hearty. God bless them." Then she tactfully changed the subject. It worked. I began to relax. Of course, she, Hilda and the doctor were right.

The following day breakfast was in the sitting room of our suite. Although the fever had subsided, they were now displaying sniffles and coughs. Adrian called their pediatrician who insisted that the children would be much better in a few days. He told Adrian to continue their medications until they were finished.

"There's nothing else to do, Millie," he informed me with exasperation in his voice. "I sure hope this doctor knows what he's talking about."

"I'm sure he does. We need to be patient," I offered. "Adrian, why don't you look at your emails while I change little Adrian. Angelique and Adam are fine."

"OK, I can do that. I'll use my laptop so I don't have to leave the suite."

That's not exactly what I had in mind, but it'll do.

The house land-line rang and as usual Adrian and I ignored it. We answered our smart phones and the business land-line. The house land-line was answered by either Hilda, Tony or Frank. The phone rang for the fifth time and no one picked it up.

"Why doesn't someone pick up that damn phone?" Adrian blurted in frustration as he stood to answer it.

"Hello," he answered rather forcefully. "Oh no, sure, of course," he replied to whoever was on the other end.

"Millie," he called. "Please come here."

"Just one minute," I replied. I finished changing little Adrian. He looked adorable. I hugged him close to my chest, smothering his little face with kisses.

"Millie, please," Adrian pleaded.

I handed the baby over to Adrian to hold and took the telephone from him.

"Hello," I greeted.

"Hi, Millie, it's Earl," came the baritone voice. "Sorry to call so early."

"Don't be silly, Earl. You know this household is up early. How are you and Mom?"

"Millie, that is why I am calling," his voice quivered, "your mother is in the hospital. She had a heart attack."

My legs weakened, causing me to lean on Adrian. He held the baby and me like the rock that he was.

"When, Earl? When did she have this attack?"

"A few days ago," again his voice quivered.

"A few days ago!" I asked incredulously. "Now you call me?"

"She didn't want you to know. I think you need to come to New York."

"Sure, Earl. I need to discuss a few things with Adrian first. I'll call you back in a few minutes."

"No, I'm not home. I can call you back in twenty minutes," and he hung up.

"Millie, what is wrong?" Adrian asked.

"Earl says Mom had a heart attack."

"Oh no, Millie. I don't know how we can travel with the children as sick as they are."

"No, the children cannot travel," I agreed. "But I must travel to my mother."

Adrian placed little Adrian in his crib and returned to where he had left me standing. He wrapped his arms tightly around me.

"Baby, I don't want you to go. Every time I say I will never let you out of my sight, something happens that we are separated."

"Stop saying *never*," I barked.

He loosened his hold on me and gazed down with a look of surprise and hurt on his face.

"Oh, Adrian, please forgive me. I didn't mean to bark at you." I buried my face in his chest and continued, "I don't want to leave you. I don't want to leave my children. I don't want to leave my home. But my mother needs me."

I broke down and sobbed. He tightened his hold on me and lowered his head to kiss my hair.

"Baby, please don't cry. Of course, you need to go to your mother. I'm a selfish man. Please forgive me," he whispered. "Don't cry. Baby, please don't cry. The children will be fine with me. I'll take care of them."

"Thank you, Adrian. What would I do without you?"

"You need not worry about that. Go get ready. I will call to have the Gulfstream ready. When Earl calls back, I'll give him the information on your flight. I'll let Hilda know also. Who will you take with you? Tony or Frank?" My man was in control of the situation.

"Neither. You need them here. I can reach out to Richard."

"I thought Richard was at the academy with the NYPD," Adrian noted.

"I understood from Sarah that his class had been delayed," I lied.

"All right then. I'll have a limo pick you up and take you to the house."

"Thank you, Adrian. You are wonderful."

"You'll do well to remember that," he teased, kissing me.

I packed a small weekender bag with my makeup, a pair of flat shoes and plenty of ammo for my firearms.

"Millie," Adrian called out.

"I'm in the dressing room."

"Earl just called. I told him your flight will leave in an hour. There are strong head winds," he advised, "so you should be in New York in four hours."

My man is so efficient.

"Thank you, Adrian. I appreciate your taking care of all this for me."

"It is my pleasure, Mrs. Z," he crooned as he hugged me.

He felt the one piece of luggage I had packed.

"Holy shit, Millie!" he exclaimed. "What the hell did you pack?"

"I have clothes in New York. All I need is my makeup and some ammo."

"Some ammo? You have enough to wage war."

"Don't be silly. We have plenty here at Luna Llena, but not in New York. I can store these in the safe at the house," I explained.

He felt my attire, a knee-length black pencil skirt with a crisp white blouse and matching blazer with stiletto heels. He approved. He rested his hand on my side where I carried my Glock 19 firearm. He gazed down at me and smiled.

"Will you allow me to see under your skirt?" he asked.

My man knows me well.

"Sure, baby. Go right ahead." I gave him my permission. It was all part of the game.

He slipped his hand under my skirt and in between my legs.

"Millie, you are wearing your garter holster with the Beretta 3032 Tom Cat," he said in disbelief. "Are you expecting trouble?"

"No, silly," I lied. "I haven't worn it in some time. I thought to try it on and maybe practice shooting it while in New York."

"Do you think you'll have time for that with your mother sick?" he asked incredulously.

"Maybe it's just wishful thinking. But I'll take it just the same. I can keep it under my pillow and dream of you."

"I don't know how to take that, but hurry. Frank is outside with the Escalade, waiting for you."

I had not lied to Adrian since our reconciliation and I was feeling guilty, but there was no way I could expose him and our children to the firestorm that was headed my way.

The children were in the sitting room. Angelique and Adam were entertained on the carpeted floor, playing with their stuffed animals. Hilda was sitting with little Adrian on her lap. I walked to Angelique. I held her in my arms, inhaling her sweet scent and kissing her soft cheeks. I sat her down and picked up Adam. He giggled, digging his head into my shoulder. I rubbed his back, inhaled his scent and kissed his beautiful little head. The tears started to stream down my cheeks. I sat him on the floor where he had been. Next was little Adrian. Hilda handed him over without looking at me. Her eyes were filled with tears.

Adrian sensed the drama that had unfolded. He turned away from us and headed to the door.

"Come, Millie. Frank is waiting." He didn't wait for my response and left to wait for me on the other side of the door.

We walked hand in hand to the lift. Adrian placed the overnight bag on the floor and rang for the main floor. As the doors closed, he suddenly took hold of my waist, pulling me close. He leaned down for a kiss. I met him with an open mouth. We kissed passionately, drinking each other in. I could taste the saltiness of the tears streaming down both our faces. As the lift slowed to a stop, Adrian pulled away. He removed a handkerchief from his back pocket to wipe both our tears.

"Come, baby," he said in a small voice.

We rode to the airport in silence. I lay across Adrian's chest where he cradled me tightly. I tried not to cry, swallowing hard.

Adrian and Frank walked me to the stairs of the aircraft.

"Call me as soon as you land," Adrian ordered. Then he did something he had not done in a long time. He searched for my wrist, touching the bracelet that served as a wedding ring. I in turn touched his. We kissed one last time and I ran up the stairs without looking back.

Just as Adrian predicted, the tail winds helped our speed and we landed at LaGuardia four hours later. The co-pilot carried my overnight bag down the stairs of the aircraft.

"Mrs. Z, this bag is heavy," he commented.

"We ladies need our things." He laughed and bid me goodbye. I spotted the limo and a driver, not Adrian's usual driver. He was sitting in the car talking on his phone.

I seized the opportunity to call Adrian before the driver came to greet me. The phone barely finished the first ring when Adrian answered.

"Hi, baby, did you just get in? How was the flight? Did you eat something?"

Mr. Multiple Questions was back.

"Hi, Adrian," I greeted. "We landed a few minutes ago. The limo is waiting. The flight was uneventful, the way I like it. And yes, I had a salad on board."

"That's my girl." Adrian sounded relieved.

"How are the children doing?" I asked.

"Better. They ate all their food at lunchtime and I put them down for a nap. I think I will join them when I get off the phone with you."

"That is a good idea, baby. Get some rest. I know you must have been worrying."

"I worried only a little," he teased.

"Well, get some rest," I repeated. "I'll call you later tonight. I love you."

"I love you too. Bye."

The driver finally came to meet me. He introduced himself as Joe and took my bag, placing it in the trunk. I could have asked about our regular driver, but what would have been the point?

Joe opened the door so I could get in. The privacy window was up. I sat back and breathed in deeply trying to center myself. I needed to put Adrian and my sweet children out of my mind. I would need all my wits about me.

Joe the driver missed the exit for the eastbound Grand Central Parkway heading towards the Whitestone Bridge for the Bronx. Instead, he took the westbound side. He looked in the rear view mirror and our eyes met. He smiled, then turned his gaze back to the road. I settled into my seat to watch where he was going. I didn't protest. What was the point? I knew where he was taking me.

It was early evening. The sky was clear and I could feel the familiar electricity of the city. People were bustling about, fighting traffic, waiting for buses that were running late, or running up the stairs of the "El" train. This was rush hour. Unlike most city dwellers, I actually enjoyed rush hour. I enjoyed observing life. I tried to imagine what their lives were like. Was there a spouse or life partner waiting somewhere? Did they have children? Were they going home or to a bar to meet up with friends? The good people of my New York always rushing. Oh, how I've missed you. Is this where it ends?

Thirty minutes later the limo rolled onto a street in a deserted and remote part of Brooklyn. The street was in desperate need of paving. The potholes rocked the vehicle. We approached a two-story warehouse that looked abandoned. Joe drove to the back of the building where the docking bays for trucks were located. The bay doors were drawn shut and there were no trucks in sight. At the far end of the building was a dump truck with garbage spilling over the sides. It was positioned close to the building. There were two SUVs parked by the side entrance. That is where Joe parked the limo.

He opened the door for me. I stepped out.

"This way, Mrs. Z," he said, his smile showing a gold tooth.

What is it with these guys and gold teeth?

"You know, Joe, you don't have to do this," I offered.

"Oh, but I do."

"Of course, you do," I agreed.

I hope Adrian took that nap.

"After you," he gestured towards the entrance.

"Why don't you lead the way?"

"I don't think so. Ladies first."

"But I don't know where I am going," I said, trying to buy some time to think.

"I can always carry you. I think I would enjoy that," he said, smiling again.

"That won't be necessary." I walked towards the entrance. The lights were dim. I could hear voices in the distance. There was talking and laughter. I could hear music also.

"Keep going straight through those swinging double doors across the room," Joe ordered.

I could see a single fluorescent light swinging beyond the double doors. No doubt that was where my captors were waiting for me. I walked slowly like a sentenced man on death row taking his final steps. I reached the double doors and placed my hand on one of them. I caught a glimpse of my bracelet and thoughts of my beautiful children and husband came back.

They are all napping. Forget them. Think.

I pushed the bracelet back on my forearm under my jacket so that it could not be seen. I took a deep breath and walked in. Just then I felt the vibration of my smart phone. Ignoring it I prayed it wasn't Adrian calling.

The talking and laughter came to an abrupt halt. Someone turned off the music. There in the middle of the room stood Sam Sanz. There were two women sitting on an old raggedy looking sofa. There was another man sitting in an equally raggedy looking chair adjacent to the sofa. Another man stood near an old reel-to-reel player that was connected to two huge retro speakers. I recognized Tito and Edgar.

There was a glass cocktail table between them. There was some cocaine on the table. There were loads of weed along with paraphernalia used for smoking. A lit candle in the center of the table provided fire for lighting joints. A few bottles of rum and glasses were scattered around the table.

Further back from where they were sitting were long tables with bricks of what I could only assume was cocaine.

"Well, look who is here. If it isn't the elusive Millie Angeles Zaragosa."

Joe the driver pushed me towards Sanz. I stumbled forward but Sanz caught me. He held me by the shoulders and then slowly slid his hands down my side until he reached my firearm.

"Joe, you idiot, didn't you search her? Look what she is carrying." He pulled out the Glock and showed it to him. "You're lucky she didn't use this on you."

"Sorry, man. Who would think such a delicate flower would be packing," Joe said in his own defense.

"Millie, let me introduce you. You met Joe. These are my two sisters, Tiny and Minnie."

How cute. Tiny and Minnie. There is nothing Tiny or Minnie about them. They look like two bulldozers.

"And you know my brothers, Edgar and Tito."

Fuck me! This family was built like refrigerators. Fighting my way out may not be an option. The Beretta may not be enough firepower.

"Everyone, this is Millie. The woman who killed our younger brother and caused the death of our second youngest brother. I also believe she had you two jailed.

"What do you have to say for yourself?" he asked, turning to face me.

The others had stopped smiling and laughing. The mention of their dead brothers seemed to sour their moods.

"Well," I started, "your dead brothers got what their hand called for."

Sanz smacked his back hand across my mouth, knocking me backwards into Joe. Blood started to trickle down from the corner of my mouth. I wiped it with the back of my hand and continued.

"Jail for you two assholes was a gift for your mother."

"Our mother is dead, bitch. And tonight you will get what your hand calls for. You will join my brothers in the hereafter, but not before we have a taste of that pussy your husband has been enjoying."

"Yeah, yeah," I spat out. "Tell me something, dip shit." Before I could finish, he gave me the back of his hand again. More blood trickled down.

"As I was saying," I continued as I wiped my lip, "why did your brother kill my partner Danny?"

"Why should I answer any questions?" he blurted.

"Because I would like to know before I meet my maker. Surely, you can tell me. What does it matter now?"

"True, it doesn't matter now. Who am I to deny a dying woman a last request as it were?" He laughed.

"Well, bitch, it's like this, my little brother was asked to bring Danny to Nussbaum. Instead they got into an argument and one thing led to another. Danny's death was unintentional."

"What business did Danny and Nussbaum have?"

"That I do not know."

"What about his brother, Ed. Why kill him and who killed him?"

"You sure asking a lot of questions," he complained.

"I'd like to know. Don't send me to the hereafter with unanswered questions."

"All right. Ed was a real prick. No one liked him. That is no one except Nussbaum. They were into a relationship."

I didn't see that coming.

"You mean to tell me that Ed was gay?" I asked. How could I not know?

"Nussbaum is gay. Ed is bi. He goes either way. And he was pretty nasty to Nussbaum at times. We were having a party one night and they began to argue."

"What were they arguing about?" I interrupted.

"Ed was flirting with one of our girls and Nussbaum didn't appreciate it. Anyway, one thing led to another. Nussbaum became enraged and shot him!" he exclaimed as if he were reliving the incident.

"One last question. What is your interest in the business between me and Nussbaum?"

"I have no interest. I don't care what your business is with him. It must be huge because he wants you bad. He asked that I get you here and I have done that. There's only one thing," he paused, looking me over, "he expects to see you tomorrow, but that is not going to happen. You won't be around tomorrow."

"Don't you worry that he'll get pissed at you? If I'm dead, he can't get what he wants."

"I have my own plans for Nussbaum. He has outlived his usefulness. That motherfucker could have had my brothers released from jail a whole lot sooner."

"Why not ransom me? My husband would pay," I suggested. I needed to know the whole game plan.

"Oh, your husband will pay. Believe me. I'm taking a little trip to California with some of my boys to pay a visit to your husband and children. That's enough talking," he turned to Joe. "Take her upstairs. You know what to do."

"Sanz," I blurted, "Where is Earl?"

"You'll see. Now, Joe," he barked.

Joe grabbed my arm and led me past the closed bay doors to a stairwell at the opposite end of the building. I noticed a small kitchen equipped with a table, chairs, refrigerator and gas stove. An espresso pot sat on one of the burners.

We climbed the stairs in silence until we reached the first landing.

"Joe, do you ever wonder why they designed stairs this way? You know with a landing. Why not just make them go straight up?"

"No, I don't wonder. Now shut up and be quiet."

"That's redundant."

"What do you mean redundant?"

"Shut up and be quiet."

"No, I mean what is redundant?"

"Never mind."

A rocket scientist.

We reached the second floor. Joe opened the door and shoved me into another huge open room. The lights were dim, but I could see Earl slumped on a chair tied up. I ran to him and knelt at his feet.

"Earl, Earl," I said, shaking his arms.

He lifted his head. He had suffered a terrible beating. One eye was swollen shut and he could barely see out of the other eye. His nose and lips were bloodied. I could tell the old guy fought back. His knuckles were also swollen and bloodied.

"Get up!" Joe shouted. "Sit on that empty chair next to him. You can chit-chat later."

I sat on the chair next to Earl and Joe proceeded to tie one hand to the armrest with a zip tie.

"You know, Joe," I said, distracting him. "You don't have to do this."

I made a fist and turned my wrist, taking advantage that he was looking at me instead of what he was doing.

"We had this conversation already," he said, looking at me while tightening the zip tie.

I quickly relaxed my fist and flattened my wrist on the armrest. He moved on to the other hand.

"My husband would show his gratitude if you helped me out of this jam." Again he turned to me and I repeated the fist and wrist action.

"I'm not interested. We're going to get your husband's money anyway." He looked at me, smiled and tightened the zip tie.

"Why don't you let him go?" I asked, nodding towards Earl. "He has nothing to do with this business."

"Nah, he's seen too much. You and he are going out together. Oh, and by the way, so is your mom. She'd be here except we couldn't find her. There will be time after tonight." He finished tying my ankles to each chair leg.

"I'm giving you one last chance, Joe. I can take care of you when I leave here."

"Leave here? Look at you." He laughed. "No one is leaving here tonight."

"I believe you're right, Joe," I agreed.

Trust me, rocket scientist. If Earl and I don't leave, neither will you or your friends downstairs.

"I'm going to join the party downstairs. We will be back soon to party with you." And he left. I made sure he was gone before speaking.

"Hey, Earl, are you OK?"

He shook his head no.

"Dude, I hate to tell you this, but you look all fucked up."

He lowered his and started sobbing. My heart hurt to see him like this. I couldn't help feel responsible.

"No, no, Earl. Don't do that. Your nose is bloodied and you won't be able to breathe."

"Millie, I'm so sorry for getting you into this mess."

"You have nothing to be sorry for. I'm the one who is sorry. You're in this mess because of your association with me. This is all on me."

"Millie, they threatened to find and kill your mother if I didn't co-operate. I knew you could take care of yourself. But your mother is not like you."

"Earl, you chose wisely."

"I don't know, Millie. They are still going for her. You heard him. They are going to kill the whole family."

"That's what he thinks. Do you think you can walk?" He laughed.

"Millie, I don't know. Maybe if I weren't tied up."

"Can you move your toes?"

"Yes."

"Then you should be able to walk a short distance."

"Short distance? Did you climb the same stairs I did?"

"Well, I can't carry you, so you don't have much of a choice. You can't stay here," I argued.

"How do you propose we get out when we are both tied?"

I slipped my hands out of the zip ties and clapped them so that Earl could see and hear that I was free.

"How the hell did you do that?" he asked incredulously.

"Trickery, Earl, trickery."

"How are you going to get your legs loose? These zip ties are impossible to break."

"I could slam the chair against the floor to break it up."

"You can do that?" again he asked incredulously.

"No, Earl, I can't. But I can take my free hand and go into my padded bra and retrieve a knife I hide there." He laughed some more.

"Does your husband know you hide knives in your bra?"

"Yes, he does. You should see what else I hide in there."

"Millie, you are something." He laughed, grimacing from the pain.

I cut the ties, freeing my legs. I then cut the ties around Earl's hands and legs.

"C'mon, old man."

"Who you calling old? Are you going to call for the police?"

"No. There is no time. Earl, I need your help. Follow me."

I led the way to the windows. There were long built-in storage cabinets lined along all the windows. The windows were old and over-sized.

"What do you need, Millie?"

"Help me to open one of these windows."

I looked and found the one window that was directly above the garbage dumpster outside.

"This window, Earl."

"I'll have to stand on these cabinets," he observed.

"I'll climb up first so I can help you."

"Are you absolutely sure you need to do this?"

"Yes. Hurry, Earl, before they come for me."

"OK, OK."

I took off my shoes and placed one in each pocket of Earl's jacket.

"Take good care of them, Earl. They are very expensive."

Earl helped unlatch the security on the window and together we opened the window to the maximum.

"Now what, Millie."

"You see that garbage dumpster?"

"Yeah."

"I want you to hide in there. I also want you to cover yourself as best as possible with the garbage bags and stay there until I come to get you."

"Why, Millie? Why hide there? Why cover myself with garbage bags?"

Maybe it's me who brings out the multiple questions in men.

"The dumpster is made of steel. The garbage bags will protect you from falling debris."

"Oh," he said, trying to understand. "But, Millie, I don't think I can climb up into it. It's kind of high for me."

"Are you sure? Take a better look."

He placed his hands on his thighs and leaned out slightly to take a better look from his one functioning eye.

"I don't know," he didn't finish because I placed my bare foot against his rear and shoved him out the window. He yelled all the way down. Luckily, the music on the first floor drowned him out.

I crept down the stairs. The party was in full swing. They were indulging in smoking weed and consuming large amounts of rum.

With all this shit in their bodies, who do they think they're going to fuck? They're lucky if they can find their dicks.

There were now two additional candles lit on the cocktail table. Suddenly, I remembered the kitchen. I crawled there undetected. I moved the stove to one side, dislodging the gas connection. Immediately, I could smell the gas in the air. At the far side of the warehouse there were barrels of acetone and ether. I crawled to where they were and opened the lids to some of the barrels with acetone. Next I opened the valve to one of the ether cylinders. This would be my finest work.

Maybe a little overkill, but what the heck.

I walked towards the nearby double-swinging doors and stopped. My Glock. I could not leave any evidence of my having been there. I ran to where my abductors were sitting and snatched the firearm from the cocktail table. They were too stunned and stoned to react quickly. I ran like the devil himself was chasing me.

And I almost made it. The explosion lifted me into the air, propelling me through the double-swinging doors.

Chapter 28

I *can't move. I am surrounded in black darkness. Not a sound anywhere. Where am I?*

I tried to move but I couldn't. Maybe I was dead.

Poor Adrian. He is going to miss me. And my children. Poor things, growing up without their mother. Maybe Adrian will re-marry.

Was I in a holding stage awaiting my fate? Was this the Ante-Inferno where souls who couldn't commit to good or evil were doomed to spend their days while hornets sting and worms lap up their blood?

Dante Alighieri. Is he here? Will he lead me to heaven? Did my father send him?

Heaven or Hell? What was it going to be? I can smell smoldering and feel heat.

Oh no, not Hell!

The smell was mixed with something else. Chemicals.

Shit, this isn't Hell or Heaven.

I'm buried alive under debris from the building. How long had I been unconscious? I remembered the explosion. Why weren't there sirens blaring? Where were the police and firemen?

Only in New York.

Suddenly, I heard tires screeching and then the car came to a halt. Doors slammed.

"Hurry, look for her. I smell fire. What the hell is going on? Somebody talk to me."

Adrian! My darling, frantic hero. How could this be? You're in California with our babies. It's true. I am dead. This is an outer body experience or wishful thinking.

"Mr. Z, this building has been leveled. The fire you smell is now smoldering," I heard Frank say. "Mr. Z, I don't see how anyone could have survived this disaster."

"Oh God, oh God!" came the anguished voice of my love. "I can't believe it! Search for her, damn it. Search! The signal from her bracelet is coming from this area here. Her smart phone too. Search, damn it!"

"Frank, come here," Richard called.

Richard! My friend. I am in Heaven.

"Mr. Z is right. The signal is strong right here. I can see a solid piece of something gray under this pile of bricks and wood. Just don't step on top there. We don't want to crush her."

"No, no. Don't crush her," my man pleaded. "Richard, tell me what I can do to help."

"Mr. Z, kneel where you are. Reach forward and remove the bricks and wood pieces you find. Frank and I will do the same from different points."

That Richard is a smart guy. I knew he was a gem. And what can I say about that man of mine? Hey, maybe I'm not dead.

I heard them work fervently in silence. They tossed brick, wood and God knows what else. My face and limbs were squeezed to the ground. I tried to move but I couldn't. I cleared my throat and heard a noise come out. I cleared it again.

"Adrian," I uttered in a small voice. "Adrian." The sound of his name comforted me.

"Shh, listen," Adrian ordered.

He heard me!

"Adrian," I repeated in the same small voice. "Adrian."

"She's alive! I told you she was alive! Quick, keep digging her out."

"Look," Richard blurted, "it's a gray door. This we can lift. Mr. Z, you grab your end. Frank, grab the side and I have the other end," Richard barked. "Good. OK, on the count of three, let's lift it and walk it to the side away from this area. Ready. One, two, three and lift!"

I felt relief as the weight came off me. Although the door had me pinned, because of how it fell on debris around me, it also prevented me from being crushed.

"There she is, Mr. Z," Richard yelled.

Adrian knelt down where he had been and gently searched with his hands. "Baby, speak to me."

"Adrian," I said in the same small voice.

He touched my hand and immediately felt the bracelet. He inched closer, running his hands up along my arms to the shoulders, to my head.

"Oh, Millie, baby," he cried. "Baby, talk to me."

"Adrian, I love you."

"I love you, baby."

"Mrs. Z," Richard spoke, "Can you move your arms?"

I moved my fingers first and then my arms.

"That's fine, Ms. Z. Now, can you move your feet?"

I moved my toes first. Next I flexed my ankles.

"Does anything hurt?" Richard asked.

"Not yet," I whispered.

"We should call for an ambulance," he announced.

"No," I answered more forcefully. "Try to lift me."

"Millie, Richard is right. We don't know how serious your injuries are," Adrian protested.

"Adrian, please lift me," I pleaded.

"Millie, listen to reason," Adrian snapped.

"Mr. Z," Richard interrupted, "we can lift her onto her knees. If she screams or passes out, we can call the ambulance then."

"All right, all right!" Adrian acquiesced. "Richard, take her by the other arm.

"Gently," he ordered.

They brought me to a kneeling position. I took a deep breath. I didn't scream nor did I pass out. I did, however, lean on Adrian. The warmth of his body was comforting. His embrace instantly made feel better.

"Adrian, what can I say? You are my angel. My hero. Thank you. Richard, Frank, thank you. Thank you. I can't say it enough." I swallowed hard, trying not to cry.

"Baby, are you OK?" Adrian asked as he ran his hands up and down my limbs, squeezing, searching for cuts, bruises, fractures and who knows what.

"Yeah, I am OK," I said, looking down at myself. "Oh, shit! Earl!"

"What about Earl? Do you know where he is?" Adrian asked.

"Yes! Richard, Frank, please go to that dumpster at the far end of what once was a building and help him out."

They ran immediately to fetch him.

"What is he doing in a dumpster?"

"I asked him to hide in there for his protection."

"Oh. Let's try to stand you. We have to hurry. The aircraft is waiting for us."

I was able to stand and walk without assistance, but I held onto Adrian.

"Adrian," I said softly, looking up at him, "I can't leave just yet."

"Why not?" he barked. "Your mother is fine. There is nothing wrong with her. I need to get you back home."

"And I want to be back home. There is no other place on earth I would rather be but at Luna Llena with you and my babies. But I need to end this tonight."

"From what I've heard, smelled and felt, it seems you pretty much ended things here. I can't wait to hear this story."

"There is still one loose end. Nussbaum. I need to make a delivery."

"Fine. The guys and I will go with you and then we'll go home."

"I'd rather you didn't go," I squeaked out.

"You are fucking incredible. Milagros, I just flew three-thousand miles on an aircraft that is not mine, dug you up from what I understand was debris from an explosion and you want to go off on another mission without me. I am not letting you go. Period." My man was red in the face with knitted eyebrows and pursed lips.

"You and the guys can drive me, but I go see him alone."

"No! We will drive you and we will all go together."

"You and the guys can drive me and let Richard come with me."

"Why don't you want me there?" He looked hurt.

"I don't want any witnesses," I whispered. "Adrian, I need to take care of this. My way."

Richard and Frank were assisting Earl to walk.

"Hey, Millie," Earl shouted. "I thought you would never come for me."

"How long have we been here?" I asked him.

"I don't know. Four, maybe five hours, I guess. I don't know if I fell asleep or passed out from the explosion."

Everyone laughed, including Adrian. The guys helped Earl into the Escalade. Frank took my bag out of the limo and put it in our vehicle while Richard searched where I had been for my firearm. We were finally ready to go.

"Richard, Mrs. Z has an address to give you," Adrian offered as he gazed down at me and wrapped both arms around me, pulling me closer.

"We are going to the hospital?" Earl questioned.

"Yes, Earl, we are but not this minute. Millie needs to make one more stop," Adrian informed him.

"Oh, well, I trust Millie. She is something," he half said to himself.

"Richard," I warned, "don't park in front. Park on the side street facing the avenue."

He did as I asked.

"Richard, will you accompany Mrs. Z?" Adrian asked.

"Sure thing, Mr. Z," Richard responded enthusiastically.

"Thank you," I whispered in his ear and gave him a kiss.

"Come back to me, Millie."

"I will. Promise."

Richard and I gained access to the house through a side entrance. All the lights were out except for one room on the second floor. I didn't bother removing my firearm from its holster and for some reason neither did Richard.

Nussbaum was sitting at his desk with his back towards us and his feet up. He was listening to some jazz from the stereo. His laptop was closed. It seemed Mr. Nussbaum liked the drugs also. There were lines of cocaine and a cut straw on top of his desk along with a half-empty bottle of vodka. He was not moving.

"Hey, Moronicus Maximus," I yelled.

He didn't move. I looked at Richard and we both shrugged our shoulders.

"Come on, moron, wake up," I said more forcefully. "I heard you were looking for me."

There was no movement. I walked around his desk and was surprised at what I saw. Richard followed me and jumped back at the sight. Nussbaum's throat had been slit from one end to the other. He had been dead for hours.

"Richard, go through the draws in those cabinets and I'll search the ones on this side. We are looking for ledgers. Any ledgers where he might have kept records."

Richard went to work immediately. I found nothing.

"I have something of interest here," Richard announced. "This is a document purchasing a home through a bank-approved short sale. It's

Danny's house." He paused to look at me. "There is another document, which appears to be a private agreement between Nussbaum and Danny whereby Nussbaum agreed to sell the property back to him at the short-sale price."

"Danny's house must have been worth less than the money he owed to the bank. So they did have a business relationship. Keep looking."

I turned on his computer to search his files. There was nothing. A few years had passed since Danny's murder and Ed's. So it was reasonable to think that those files would have been moved. I spotted an external drive sitting on a shelf in the credenza behind Nussbaum. Using his computer I searched all the files and bingo! I found the ledgers. He paid Danny and Ed ten-thousand apiece in cash every month for their money-laundering services. The money was ultimately funneled to a variety of businesses.

So it was true. Danny was buying diamonds to hide his money. Upon his death, Ed felt entitled to the diamonds. Upon Ed's death, Nussbaum then felt entitled.

"Let's go, Richard. We are done here."

"Are you going to call your detective friend and tell him what you know?"

"No. Nussbaum will start stinking up the joint soon enough. They will find him and put together all the pieces. Let's go home."

We drove Earl to the hospital and he was seen immediately. Adrian had called ahead to arrange a private suite and discretion in this matter. I had refused medical attention. Adrian was much too tired to argue with me. All he wanted was to board the Gulfstream and whisk me away back home.

Richard picked up my mother to take her to the hospital to see Earl. He did not give her information other than Earl was in the hospital.

Frank, Adrian and I sat in the waiting area while the medical staff took care of Earl. Frank started to laugh to himself.

"You know, Frank," I said, "only crazy people laugh to themselves."

He laughed some more and then cleared his throat.

"Sorry. I was just thinking about Luna Llena."

That caught Adrian's attention. He was sitting with his legs far apart, leaning forward and resting his forearms on his thighs. He gazed in Frank's direction with knitted eyebrows and pursed lips.

"What about Luna Llena?" I asked.

"Well, Mrs. Z," he started, "shortly after you called, saying that you had arrived, Mr. Z announced he was going to take a nap in the sitting room with the children." Frank laughed some more.

"I was doing my security check around the house when I decided to check in on them. Sure enough, he was lying down on the floor with them, but he was not asleep."

Adrian straightened in his chair, leaned back and put one arm around my chair.

"Frank, I'm sure somewhere there is a point to this story. And I fail to see what is so funny," Adrian barked. Frank laughed some more.

"Let him finish, Adrian," I said, running my hand on his thigh to soothe him.

"I announced myself as I always do and asked if you had called. Mr. Z said, 'She called about thirty minutes ago,' and he stood up rather suddenly. He went for his smart phone, saying that you were probably at the house already. He called the house and there was no answer. And he looked up to the ceiling, making that face of his. You know, eyebrows together and lips bunched up." Frank laughed some more.

"Then he said, 'That's weird. I'll call her smart phone.' And he did just that. But when you didn't answer, he lost it." Frank laughed some more.

"What do you mean, he lost it?" I asked.

"Yeah, Frank, what do you mean?" Adrian was getting irritated I think because Frank was laughing at his expense. This behavior was unusual for Frank. No one laughed at Adrian's expense. But I suspected he was trying to bring some levity to the situation.

"He raised his voice saying, 'Why isn't she answering her phone? She knows the rules about the phone.' And then he pulled out his ear buds and started tracking the signal on your bracelet. When he discovered that you were nowhere near the Bronx but in some obscure part of Brooklyn by the water, he lost it again." Frank laughed heartier this time. I joined in the laughter. I could picture Adrian, crimsoned neck and all.

Frank stood up to re-enact the following scene.

"Mrs. Z, he took his smart phone, swung his arms back in a motion to throw the phone and yelled at the top of his lungs, 'Motherfucker!'"

"What happened next?" I asked excitedly.

Adrian was still not amused.

"I took a hold of his wrist to prevent him from throwing it. With rage on his face, he turned in my direction, but before he could react I said, 'You're going to need your phone, Mr. Z.' Just then the phone rang.

"It was your mother," he exclaimed, laughing some more. "The conversation went something like this, 'Hello, Judy, how are you, what do you mean you're fine, what do you mean you want to speak to Millie, how the hell should I know where Earl is, what do you mean he's been missing for hours, where the hell are you Judy, what the fuck do you mean you're in Earl's house? Judy, Judy, Judy, I have to hang up.' And he hung up."

I was hysterical, watching him imitate Adrian's voice and facial expressions. He had his body language perfectly. His free hand tugging on his belt, then slipping into his pocket and then back to tugging his belt.

"Adrian, Frank can imitate you very well," I said as I described what Frank had been doing. Adrian drew one arm across his eyes as if to erase the images from his brain. There was a trace of a smile.

"Frank, what happened next?" I egged him on.

"Hilda walked in to ask about you. Mr. Z lost it again!" Frank and I were hysterical with laughter. Adrian was now laughing, too, with his arm still across his eyes.

"He yelled at Hilda, 'How the fuck should I know how my wife is? She's disappeared from the face of the earth.'"

"You do exaggerate, Adrian," I blurted.

"Mr. Z said, still yelling, 'My wife is missing, Earl is missing, no one is where they're supposed to be.' Hilda said, 'Adrian, what are you talking about?' Again he yells at her, 'My wife is fucking missing, woman, didn't you hear me?' Poor Hilda winced as she asked him, 'Adrian, what are you going to do?'

"Mr. Z turned to me and said, 'Frank, you and I are going to New York immediately.'" Frank couldn't contain himself and commenced laughing uncontrollably.

"Frank, please tell me what happened next," I pleaded.

"I looked at him and said, 'Mr. Z, the Gulfstream is in New York. It will take possibly five hours, possibly six, for it to return here. The head winds are strong.' Again Mr. Z went to throw his phone but thought better of it. Instead, he yelled, 'Motherfucker!' He then ordered Hilda to pack a bag for herself, the children and him.

"Hilda winced again saying, 'But, Adrian, the children are not well and where are we going?' Mr. Z yelled again, 'Stop asking so many questions. The children will be fine. Pack their medicines. You will have to give it to them. I want you, the children, Hector, Tony and Roger at the penthouse. You will be safe there. Frank and I are going to New York. I now have to pay to charter a fucking flight because my fucking aircraft is in fucking New York. Frank, what are you still doing here? Go pack and get the Escalade. And tell Roger to get the other Escalade. And I want everyone ready in thirty minutes or I'm leaving without you. Motherfucker! I can't fucking believe this.'" Frank took a moment to compose himself and breathe.

"Mr. Z, it sounds like you cursed up a storm and in front of the children," I said, turning to Adrian. "I thought we were going to watch our language?"

"You heard Frank, I lost it. I didn't know where you were. I didn't know what to think. I just knew I had to find you. I knew you were in trouble."

"Oh, Adrian." I hugged him, burying my face in his neck.

The elevator door opened. My mother and Richard had arrived. My mother saw me and walked directly towards us.

"Millie," she greeted as she took a long hard look at me. "What happened to you? My baby." She hugged me tighter than I could bear.

"Ouch, Mom," I cried.

"Sorry, Millie. What happened?" she repeated but did not wait for an answer before continuing, "You look like hell. Your lips are swollen and bloodied. Your hands are bloodied. Your clothes are filthy. You are a complete mess."

"Thanks, Mom."

"Adrian," she called out to him, "You look no better. Your hair is a mess, your shirt is bloodied and filthy. I have never seen you like this."

"Hello, Judy, it's nice to see you," Adrian said sarcastically.

She ignored his remark and continued, "Millie, what happened and where is Earl?"

"Judy, it's a long story. Earl will fill you in. Now that you are here, I'm going to take my wife home to Luna Llena where I can take care of her."

My mother looked at all of us and decided she could wait for the details. She threw her arms around Adrian's neck, saying, "You do that, Adrian. Take her home. I know you will take good care of her."

"I'm going to say goodbye to Earl, Mother," I said. "I'll let you know if the doctors are done with him."

Earl was alone when I entered his room. They had attended to all his injuries and the staff had cleaned him up nicely. I was glad Mom wouldn't see him in his original state.

"How do you feel, Earl?"

"I've been better. How about yourself? Did the doctors see you?"

"No. I'll be fine."

"It was nice of Adrian to arrange all this for me."

"Yeah, he's a keeper. Earl, I want to say goodbye. Adrian wants to leave immediately for Luna Llena."

THE BLACK CALLA LILY

"Why is that man of yours always in such a hurry?"

"I don't know. I think he's afraid the authorities are going to come for me and lock me up," I joked. We laughed and I hugged and kissed him amid both our cries of pain.

"All right, old man, take good care of yourself and stay out of trouble."

"Who you calling old man?"

We stopped at little Luna Llena for a bath and a change of clothes. Adrian and I showered together. He took great care not to cause me pain while lathering my body. He tenderly washed and dried my hair. He prepared an ice bag for my lip and we were off to meet the Gulfstream.

It was late and I hadn't eaten in almost twenty-four hours. The flight attendant fixed everyone dinner. Frank stretched out in the lounge area and almost immediately fell asleep. Adrian and I went to the back bedroom. We crawled onto the mattress with our clothes on.

"Oh, Adrian," I purred, snuggling to his chest, "you came to my rescue."

"Always, baby, always," he said softly while wrapping his arms around me.

Thank you for reading "The Black Calla Lily." I hope the love between Millie and Adrian, as well as the love they have for their family and friends has found a home in your hearts. If their adventures, sorrows and moments of levity moved you, then I have done my job.

Millie and Adrian have completed their journey. Or have they?

Turn the page for the beginning of another adventure.

DEEP WEB

of

DECEPTION

BY

ISABEL PIETRI

Chapter 1

I was glad to be back home. Twenty-four hours ago I wasn't sure if I would ever see my children, my husband and my home again. I was filled with gratitude and thanked God for my return. I had time to take stock of some of my actions and promised to change.

I spent the next few days playing with and taking care of my children. Frank and Tony did the security checks without me. Hector and Roger assisted them. For now all I wanted to do was to be a wife and a mother.

"Millie," Adrian announced himself as he entered the nursery.

"I'm by the crib with little Adrian," I replied.

He walked towards the crib and using his hands searched for me.

"What are you doing?" he asked embracing me from behind.

"I was changing little Adrian. He is ready for a nap."

"Um, he is a good baby," Adrian said lovingly. "Millie I remembered something."

"Oh, what did you remember?"

"When we were in Baja California you said you wanted to ask something of me, but you never did. What was it?"

I turned towards him and buried my face is his chest. His scent was heavenly. The top two buttons of his shirt were open exposing his silky black chest hairs. I kissed him there and held him tight. He kissed my hair tightening his embrace.

"Come on baby. Tell me. What is it you wanted from me?"

"Adrian, given my recent history I don't know that I should ask."

"Millie please, you need to forget that nasty business. You are free from those scoundrels. So, tell me. What is it you want from me?"

I looked up at him and rested my chin on his chest.

"I would love to have another baby," I whispered shyly.

He leaned down to kiss me.

"Millie Angeles Zaragosa, sometimes I barely recognize you. You were the woman who did not want to marry, the woman who didn't want to have children and look at you now. These past few days you have been the perfect wife and mother. And now you want a baby. I don't know what to say."

"Wouldn't you like to have another child?"

"I was happy with three, but four seems like a good number. Yes baby, I would want another child. We can try." He leaned down again this time for a passionate kiss.

His smart phone rang. It was Frank.

"Mr. Z there is a gentleman at the gate wishing to speak to you and Mrs. Z. He says he is from the NSA."

"NSA? If he shows you the proper credentials show him to my study. We will be there shortly."

"What's going on Adrian? NSA?"

"I don't know. Frank says there is a man from the NSA at the gate. Let's go find out what he wants."

We gathered our children and hand in hand we walked down the stairs and into Adrian's office.

Frank announced a Mr. Ross Blake from the NSA Counter Intelligence unit.

Adrian sat at his desk and invited Mr. Blake to sit on one of the chairs across from him. I sat to the left of Adrian.

"Well, Mr. Blake, what can I do for you?" Adrian asked. His long legs were stretched out under the desk one ankle crossed over the other. One hand was placed pensively to his temple while the other stroked the cherry wood.

"Mr. Zaragosa, I am sorry for the misunderstanding but I came here to speak with your wife," Mr. Blake replied eyeing me with a smirk on his face.

Here we go.

"Oh, I see," Adrian said gazing in my direction.

I get the feeling I'm going to need an attorney.

"Mr. Blake, my husband and I have no secrets. Whatever you need to say to me or discuss with me will be done in the presence of my husband."

"Very well," he replied looking uncomfortable.

Hmm. Looks like Mr. Blake is changing tactics.

"Mrs. Zaragosa, the NSA is working on a project that requires talents that you possess."

"I am flattered Mr. Blake, but I no longer work. Today I am a housewife and mother. I no longer possess those talents of which you speak."

Adrian had not moved and inch. His brows were knitted and lips pursed. He was listening intently.

"I am here to ask you to fly back with me to Ft. Meade today."

Adrian exhaled loudly uncrossing his legs and placing both hands on the arm rest of his chair.

"Mr. Blake," I said quickly, "I am terribly sorry you went to all the trouble to travel here. I am not going with you to Ft. Meade. I am a housewife and mother of three small children."

"I'm not asking," he advised flaring his nose at me.

This is taking a nasty turn.

"Listen here Blake," Adrian blurted, "Don't speak to my wife in that tone and you don't give orders to her."

"Mr. Zaragosa, I came here to take her back East with me."

I zoned out for a few seconds. The mention of flying back to the East Coast after my last adventure made my head pound. I came so close to losing everything. My husband, my children, my home and my life. The memories terrified me.

"You are not taking her anywhere," Adrian replied calmly but the blood in his neck was creeping to his face.

"We want her to do work for us and I am afraid that this is not up for debate."

"Mr. Blake, you need to leave. And you will leave alone."

"I certainly didn't expect this reaction," Mr. Blake offered not moving. "Mr. Zaragosa it is in your wife's best interest to accompany me and do as she is told."

He didn't quite finish speaking that Adrian sat forward in his chair glaring in Mr. Blake's direction.

"Get the fuck out of my house. Who the fuck do you think you are? You don't give orders around here and much less to my wife."

"I'll tell you who I am," Blake challenged. "I am the man that is going to take your wife to Ft. Meade or she will be prosecuted for hacking computers. Your wife is guilty of gaining unauthorized access to computers for the purpose of retrieving information, intercepting and changing resources."

"I have never done any such thing," I defended. "You have no proof of what you are saying."

"I have plenty of proof. You have been on our radar for quite some time. It's only now that we require your services."

"I told you to get the hell out of my house," Adrian blurted pushing his chair back and standing.

Blake also stood.

"You can easily buy her out of a Class B misdemeanor but, assuming your family and business can survive the bad press, I doubt you can save her from a Class B felony which can carry up to twenty years in jail. That is what 'cracking' will get her. Cracking," he continued, "is unauthorized access to computers for malevolent purposes such as introducing viruses and rendering computers useless."

"You have no proof," I reiterated.

"Sweetheart, I have all the proof I need. The icing on the cake will be what is in your computer."

"That's it mother fucker. Get out of my house," Adrian yelled walking in his direction.

"Mr. Z," Frank announced running into the office. "Is everything alright?"

"No Frank. Show this scum bag out."

"With pleasure Mr. Z." Roger and Tony were now behind Frank.

"I'll leave," Blake volunteered. He threw his business card on Adrian's desk. "But I will be back with a search warrant for the house and your office in San Francisco. I hope you're ready to do battle with the Federal Government."

Millie and Adrian Trilogy

LOVE in the DARK
Book One
http://www.amazon.com/Love-Dark-Milagros-Adrian-Volume/
dp/0615774253
Kindle: http://www.amazon.com/dp/B00GQKHDMQ

Follow Isabel Pietri on:

Facebook
https://www.facebook.com/MillieandAdrianTrilogy

Twitter
https://twitter.com/sheba915

Blog
http://isabelpietri.wordpress.com

www.ingramcontent.com/pod-product-compliance
Lightning Source LLC
Chambersburg PA
CBHW061306170626
46817CB00001B/69